Available in April 2010
from Mills & Boon® Intrigue

BACKSTREET HERO

"You're not sleeping in that bedroom with the balcony."

Lilith stared at Tony. He saw her delicate jaw set and knew he was going to have a fight on his hands. And he wasn't in the mood. So instead of trying to persuade her with convincing arguments, he cut straight to the one he figured would win the quickest.

"You have two options," he said evenly. "First, you sleep in the guest room without the balcony."

She arched a brow at him. "Or?"

"Or you sleep in your bedroom, in your bed... with me."

BECOMING A CAVANAUGH

Kyle knew he should disengage himself from her.

Knew that he should say something about being her superior on this case and that they had a professional relationship to maintain. They were co-workers and these kinds of things – even if it was only a one-time thing – rarely, if ever, worked out. He wasn't in the market for a relationship and a one-night stand with a fellow detective just wasn't a good idea.

But for the life of him, he couldn't voice a single protest, couldn't put a single thought into words. He was only aware of the overwhelming desire that beat like the wings of a hummingbird within him. A desire that was growing by the second.

He wanted her.

All the characters in this book have no existence outside the imagination of
the author, and have no relation whatsoever to anyone bearing the same name
or names. They are not even distantly inspired by any individual known or
unknown to the author, and all the incidents are pure invention.

First published in Great Britain 2010
Harlequin Mills & Boon Limited,
Eton House, 18-24 Paradise Road, Richmond, Surrey TW9 1SR

Backstreet Hero © Janice Davis Smith 2008
Becoming a Cavanaugh © Marie Rydzynski-Ferrarella 2009

ISBN: 978 0 263 88215 5

46-0410

Harlequin Mills & Boon policy is to use papers that are natural, renewable
and recyclable products and made from wood grown in sustainable forests.
The logging and manufacturing processes conform to the legal environmental
regulations of the country of origin.

Printed and bound in Spain
by Litografia Rosés S.A., Barcelona

BACKSTREET HERO
BY
JUSTINE DAVIS

BECOMING A
CAVANAUGH
BY
MARIE FERRARELLA

BACKSTREET HERO

BY
JUSTINE DAVIS

Justine Davis lives on Puget Sound in Washington. Her interests outside of writing are sailing, doing needlework, horseback riding and driving her restored 1967 Corvette roadster – with the top down, of course.

Justine says that years ago, during her career in law enforcement, a young man she worked with encouraged her to try for a promotion to a position that was at the time occupied only by men. "I succeeded, became wrapped up in my new job, and that man moved away, never, I thought, to be heard from again. Ten years later he appeared out of the woods of Washington state, saying he'd never forgotten me and would I please marry him. With that history, how could I write anything but romance?"

Chapter 1

It was, Lilith Mercer thought as she rubbed at her shoulder, her own fault. She hadn't been paying attention, and had walked right into some kid's practical joke. And had landed ungracefully on her backside.

"Are you sure you're all right?"

She smiled at her concerned neighbor. "Except for my bruised dignity, I'm fine."

"That was horrible," Mrs. Tilly said. She'd come rushing out at the no doubt embarrassingly loud thud Lilith had made hitting the landing outside her front door. "You could have fallen all the way down those stairs."

That fact hadn't escaped Lilith. If she hadn't managed to grab the stairway banister, the tumble down the concrete steps would have been ugly. Exiting her second-floor condo in a Monday morning rush with her hands full as usual, her mind already on the busy day ahead—also as usual—she hadn't seen the thin, silver wire strung tight across the top of the stairs.

"Lucky my reflexes are okay," she said, although to herself she was wondering just how sore the shoulder she'd wrenched in the process was going to be in a couple of days.

"It has to be that Wells boy," Mrs. Tilly said. "He's going to be the death of us all. The other day I saw him with a barbecue lighter, trying to start a fire on their patio."

Personally, Lilith found the apparent booby trap clearly intended to cause injury—if not worse—a bit more unsettling than a young boy's typical fascination with flames, but in Southern California, a state with a deadly yearly fire season, nothing to do with fire was taken lightly.

"It's a good thing you're a youngster and can bounce," Mrs. Tilly said grimly.

Lilith thought that at forty-four, she'd officially left being a youngster behind some time ago, but she supposed to her seventy-five-year-old neighbor that was a relative thing. And the implication was painfully true; had the older woman been the one to discover that wire the hard way, the results could have been horribly different.

"Someone needs to talk to Callie again," the woman said sternly.

The implication that, as usual, that someone should be her didn't escape Lilith. Martha Tilly hated confrontation and had decided—deservedly so, Lilith thought—that at her age avoiding it was her right. She didn't really mind; Mrs. Tilly was nothing if not blunt, sometimes to the point of rudeness, and Lilith wasn't sure that was the right approach with their down-stairs neighbor. Especially just now.

"She has her hands full being a single mom with two kids, one of them a toddler," Lilith said. "I hate to pile more on her."

She also suspected, although she'd never spoken of it, that Callie had escaped the hands of an abusive husband, which put Lilith soundly on her side for more reasons than Mrs. Tilly knew.

"But that boy's getting out of hand," Mrs. Tilly said. "Why, you could have been killed!"

"I'll speak to her," Lilith promised, knowing that if she did, at least it wouldn't be a formal confrontation that would put the harried young woman on the defensive.

Reassured, Mrs. Tilly at last let her continue on her way, although not without a promise to give young Billy Wells a piece of her mind if she saw him.

As she got into her car, Lilith felt a little tug in her shoulder, and, she noted ruefully, a spot on her backside that she was sure would be sore by tomorrow. She might well spend tomorrow working on her feet, she thought.

By the time she got to her office in the Research and Development division of Redstone Inc., she'd almost forgotten the incident. The huge task that still lay before her took her full concentration, and her determination to fix this situation for Josh Redstone demanded she give it just that. That Josh of all people, the most generous and loyal man she'd ever known, had been the victim of industrial spying rankled her beyond belief. She would find every last detail of what had happened and salvage everything that could be salvaged, no matter how long it took.

She sat down at her desk—a U-shaped arrangement that was more functional than decorative—and booted up her computer, still feeling the surge of energy that hit her every day when she arrived at Redstone Headquarters. She had a very proprietary feeling about Redstone, and about its brilliant founder, Joshua Redstone. She'd known him for better than twenty-five years now, and he had soared past even her own stellar predictions for his future.

As an eighteen-year-old teacher's aide, she hadn't been fooled by the languid drawl; even at fifteen the intelligence in those gray eyes had fairly snapped at her. She'd guessed early on that the air some mistook for laziness was merely boredom with a curriculum that didn't challenge him, and she'd taken it upon herself to provide that challenge, guiding him toward more advanced work that he could undertake on his own.

And eventually, toward getting his G.E.D. and getting out before his seventeenth birthday; he was already so far beyond high school she didn't think he'd survive two more years, and was only where he was because his small family—himself, his father and his older brother—had moved around a lot.

At first he'd been suspicious—neither did that drawl mean he was a fool, as many had learned along the way, to their detriment—but she'd kept on, until he rose to the bait. She'd had the feeling he'd known exactly what she was doing, but had let her lead him. And then, after he'd easily passed the G.E.D. tests and she'd told him exactly how far she thought he could go, he'd made her a promise. She'd been the first person other than his brother to really believe in him, he'd said. Someday he'd repay her.

He certainly had.

"What's wrong, Lilith?"

Only when she heard the voice of her assistant, Liana Kiley, did she realize she'd been rubbing her shoulder again. She looked up at the young woman and ruefully explained.

"A wire?" Liana stared at her, eyes wide. "You could have been seriously hurt. Or worse."

"So my neighbor informed me," Lilith said. "But the only damage was a scrape on my briefcase, and sore spots in my shoulder and…landing zone."

That got her a smile, but Liana's concern didn't abate. It was one of the first traits Lilith had noticed about the bright, lovely redhead; she had a large capacity for compassion, a trait that made her an excellent fit for Redstone.

It had also netted Liana the man in her life, new Redstone Security team member Logan Beck. Liana's concern for the ex-cop who had once saved her life had not only gotten him out of a morass of injustice, it had opened up a new life for both of them, together.

"And it was only last Thursday that truck nearly hit you. You could have been killed."

Lilith smiled to reassure Liana. "Let's hope it's not going to be a string of bad luck."

Liana frowned. Lilith knew that look. Liana had worn it often enough in her first days here, when Logan had been struggling against false accusations of being a crooked cop.

But they'd come through it and become yet another of the growing list of couples brought together under the Redstone banner. Lilith found it amusing as well as bemusing that so many soul mates had found each other through Redstone. She'd teased Josh once about his heretofore unknown matchmaking talent, but she actually tended to believe longtime Redstone pilot Tess Machado's more pragmatic explanation—when you brought smart, talented people with the same principles and standards together, as Redstone did, it was only to be expected.

"Let's get going," she said briskly, knowing Liana would accept that as a diversion; even now she was still feeling a bit guilty that her first days on the job had been taken up completely by her quest for justice for Logan. Even though Lilith had assured her she'd more than made up for it in the months since, the young woman she'd come to genuinely like would never take Redstone for granted, not after what they'd done for her and Logan.

About an hour later, Lilith had just hung up from a conversation with Redstone's resident genius inventor, Ian Gamble, the man whose work had been the target of the industrial spying that had blown up into the scandal that had destroyed the JetCal Corporation and sent both their CEO and Redstone R&D head Stan Chilton to prison, when Josh himself appeared in her doorway.

While it was a tradition for Redstone's leader to make a tour of his headquarters any day he was present, he usually came by earlier in the day. It was common knowledge to all Redstone people that this was their chance to ask him anything, as Liana had learned; a casual mention had resulted in the mobilization of Redstone's much vaunted private security team and the vindication of Logan Beck.

"Running late?" Lilith said with a smile.

Josh didn't smile back. His gray eyes fastened on her intently as he came into the office. And he didn't stroll, in that loose-limbed, lanky way he had, he strode in like the head of a multinational conglomerate that he was.

Instinctively responding to the difference, Lilith stood, wondering with some trepidation what was wrong. "Josh?"

He just stood there for a moment, looking her up and down. She knew better than to think he disapproved of her casual attire; jeans and the red knit shirt with the Redstone logo were the unofficial uniform for many of Redstone's people, and she'd been glad she'd had the tough denim on when she'd hit the concrete this morning.

The moment the thought came into her mind, her puzzlement vanished and Josh's demeanor and actions made sense.

"Liana, I presume?" she said ruefully; she should have known the girl wouldn't keep this to herself.

"Logan."

"I'm fine, Josh."

He looked her up and down once more. She held up her arms to display she was unhurt. "See? Nothing broken, snapped or otherwise seriously impaired."

He didn't look convinced.

"Repeat after me," she said, in her best teacher's voice, "'You look fine, Lilith.'"

At last he eased up. "You look…elegant, as usual, even in blue jeans, Lilith."

She laughed. This was old ground between old friends as

well; he teased her about what he called her refined air and elegant grace, so opposite of his own down-home, laid-back demeanor. Hers, he had once said, masked a steely spine, boundless energy and whip-smart intelligence. She had simply looked at him, and in a deadly accurate imitation of his own lazy drawl, had said, "Back at you."

"You know," he said now, with a casualness that warned her he was anything but, "I don't believe in coincidences. Not when it comes to danger to my people."

Lilith's brows rose. "Danger?"

"Two narrow escapes in a week?"

She chuckled. "That sounds so dramatic. I nearly had a traffic accident. And this morning I ran afoul of a child's prank."

"Maybe."

"Coincidence, Josh."

"You know what Draven says about coincidence."

"Draven," she said, "is a born cynic." Then remembering how the Redstone Security chief had mellowed since his marriage to Grace O'Conner, she added, "At least, he was when he always used to say that."

"And now he's more protective than ever. So when I tell him about this, he's going to take appropriate action."

"Tell him? Why on earth?"

"Because I don't believe in coincidence, either. Not when one of my brightest and best has uncharacteristic 'accidents.'"

"Thank you for the compliment, but really—"

Josh stopped her with an upheld hand. "No compliment, just truth. As is the fact that you're going to have to tolerate a little attention for a while, until I'm sure this doesn't mean anything."

"Mean anything? You mean like someone's intentionally trying to hurt me?"

She started to laugh even before she finished the words, but when Josh simply looked at her, his jaw set, realization struck and her laughter faded away.

"Yes," he finally said, his voice echoing with grim acknowledgment of what they both knew but she had managed to put out of her mind.

There indeed was someone who could be trying to hurt her. Or even kill her.

Because he'd tried it before.

Chapter 2

Tony Alvera didn't stop to knock on his boss's door, any more than he had bothered to park his racy blue coupe in an allotted slot; he was in too much of a hurry. He knew he'd committed a breach of decorum when he realized John Draven was with someone in his small, efficiently organized office, but there were times when he reverted to his younger days of not caring about such things, and this was one of them.

"Sorry," he said perfunctorily, nodding at the woman in the office.

Because he wasn't really sorry, there wasn't much sincerity in the apology, and Draven lifted a brow at him. Since it was the one already slightly twisted by the scar that slashed down the left side of his face, the look was even more intimidating.

But Tony Alvera wasn't a man who was easily intimidated.

"I need to talk to you," he said.

"Taylor Hill," Draven said mildly, "meet Tony Alvera. Pay

attention, you may have to work with him someday. I hear it's an adventure."

Tony had heard that Draven was bringing in someone new, to fill in now that Samantha Gamble, married to Redstone's resident genius, Ian Gamble, was visibly pregnant. Sam might grumble about being tied to a desk, but her work instincts were trumped by newfound maternal ones, and she'd ruefully agreed that going into the field on assignments that could turn risky was not in her best interest just now.

For a moment Tony thought of Ian, that brilliant, creative mind that had put Redstone on the map in so many new fields that not even Josh could keep track of them all. As had most at Redstone, Tony had marveled from the beginning at the unlikelihood of Ian and Sam's relationship—the man some teasingly called the absentminded professor and the stunning, leggy blonde.

He'd been even more bemused by the easy way Ian seemed to accept the differences between them, accept Sam's sometimes dangerous job and the fact that she was one of the best at it. He often joked he was the brains while his wife was the brawn with brains. Tony wasn't sure he could so blithely accept his woman working in a traditionally masculine role.

At the same time, he utterly and totally respected Samantha Gamble and her skills and would gladly have her at his back in any tough situation. The conflict niggled at him, but he didn't dwell on it much, preferring to see it as a hangover from days past that he tried not to think about. When he did think about them, it was usually with a rueful jab at himself and the street gang culture of machismo he'd grown up in.

The woman in the office was standing now, studying him less than subtly as she held out a hand. He took it—her grip was solid but not overly so—and automatically assessed her in turn, a habit ingrained in him during his years with Redstone Security.

Taylor Hill was an ordinary-looking woman, with straight, medium brown hair pulled back rather severely at the nape of her neck. She was average height and build, her features regular but not striking. She was neither unattractive nor beautiful, but fell in the unremarkable category.

The perfect person for security work, Tony thought. She could probably blend in anywhere.

"Nice to meet you," she said politely, and his opinion suddenly changed. That low, husky voice would stand out in any man's mind. And make him wonder, if she sounded like that now, what she might sound like in more intimate circumstances.

But he had no time for speculating about other women at the moment.

"You, too," he replied, aware it was a disconnected nicety but unable to help it.

"I was about to send Taylor off on her first assignment," Draven said in a casually chatty manner completely unlike him. "Nothing like starting out doing a favor for Josh himself."

That snapped Tony to attention. Was there something else going on at Redstone besides what he'd come here about? "Josh has a problem?"

"One of his people has a problem, so yes, you could say that."

Tony felt the adrenaline spurt ebb a little. He looked his boss in the eye, a task more easily said than done to almost anyone who had to deal with the steely, tough John Draven.

"Lilith," he said.

Draven's brow rose again. "You know?"

"Beck," he said briefly, knowing that would explain; Logan Beck, the newest—well, now apparently second newest—member of the security team, was engaged to Liana Kiley, Lilith Mercer's assistant.

He was also Tony's partner in situations that required a two-man team; they'd worked well together on Logan's case, and although he generally preferred to work alone—as did Logan—Tony was now amenable to the pairing when necessary.

"I'll handle it," Tony said.

Draven lifted a brow. "What?"

"This one's mine." At Draven's expression, Tony turned back to Taylor, who was watching this exchange curiously. "Would you excuse us for a minute, please?"

The woman's glance flicked to Draven, who, after a split second, gave her a barely perceptible nod. She didn't miss the signal and left without a word.

"She's going to be good," Draven said when Tony didn't speak right away.

"Yeah," Tony muttered.

He began to pace the small room. Now that he was here and had his boss's attention, he had no idea what to say. He should, he realized, have thought about this a little more before he'd burst in.

He should have thought about it a little more, period, he thought. Had he learned nothing from Lisa? Had he forgotten standing in the morgue, looking down at her lifeless body, knowing she was there because of him?

I'm trying to stop something like that from happening again, he told himself as Draven continued to speak of the woman who had just left.

"She did some good work at Redstone in Toronto. She was ready to move up."

"Yeah."

Silence seemed to echo in the room while Tony continued to pace and tried to figure out what to say.

"You got back last night?"

"Yeah."

He left it at that. The Hawk IV that had picked him up in Caracas had actually touched down a little after 1:00 a.m., so technically this morning, but he knew Draven already knew that. And he'd already filed his report in flight, so he knew Draven knew the final result of his investigation into the local kickback problem as well.

"You know," Draven said at last, "I'm told I talk more than I used to these days, but I'm in no way comfortable carrying on a whole conversation myself. What do you want, Alvera?"

Tony stopped mid-stride and spun around to face his boss. "I want this job." There, he thought. It was out.

"What job?"

"The one you were going to give her," he said, jerking a thumb toward the door where Taylor had exited.

Draven frowned. "I don't think this is anything that requires your…unique skills, Tony."

"Nothing does, at the moment."

Not really his decision to make, but he knew it was true. Lucky for him, Draven was in a flexible mood this morning.

"There may not even be a real problem," his boss said. "It could just be a fluke, coincidence. Accidents and pranks do happen."

Not to Lilith, Tony thought.

"It's probably nothing, but Josh wants to be sure," Draven said. "You know how he is about his people."

"Yes. I do."

No one knew better than he did about Josh Redstone. Tony doubted there was another man on the planet who would have done what Josh did after an angry, scared, knife-wielding gang-banger had tried to mug him outside an L.A. hotel. Tony hadn't even realized he was trying to rob the wunderkind whose Redstone Aviation was beginning to soar, had seen only a man headed toward a limo, which to him had meant money and made the man a target.

He hadn't expected that the man would fight back, and well enough to have his sixteen-year-old ass on the pavement in less than ten seconds.

And he never would have dreamed that that man, not even ten years older than he himself, would see something in that angry kid, something that, instead of calling the cops as he should have, made him give Tony the chance of a lifetime. The chance at a life.

A life he would always owe to Josh Redstone.

"This is probably nothing a couple of days of simple investigation can't close," Draven said, looking at him with growing curiosity, the last thing Tony wanted.

"Then I won't be tied up long," he said, more sharply than he liked.

Draven's mouth quirked slightly. "You really want this?"

"I want this. Sir," he added, not caring that it was so obviously an afterthought tacked on to ameliorate the gruffness of his prior words.

Draven's brows lowered even farther. "You don't look—or sound—too sure about that."

Leave it to Draven to see past the surface, because truth be told, he wasn't. In fact, he was reasonably sure he would regret it; it was only the extent of that regret he wasn't sure of right now. But that didn't seem to make any difference.

"I mean it," he insisted.

Draven studied Tony for a long, silent moment. Tony set his jaw and waited, knowing Draven wasn't a man to be pushed.

"Why?" Draven finally asked.

Tony had prepared for that question, at least. "You know I worked with her a lot, during Beck's case. We…got along. I'd like to help, and I'm free, with nothing on the horizon that would require me more than anyone else on the team."

Draven listened, looking thoughtful. If he noticed that this prosaic explanation was at odds with the inner tension Tony was feeling—and Tony had little doubt Draven would sense that, there was very little that escaped him—he didn't comment on the fact.

Just when Tony thought he'd blown it, and that Draven, with that preternatural instinct of his, had somehow guessed the secret Tony Alvera kept hidden from everyone, his boss slowly nodded.

"All right. But if something in your area comes up—"

"I understand," Tony said, barely aware of interrupting the

legendary head of Redstone Security, something few dared to do. Or had the chance to do; as he'd said, Draven wasn't known for talking a lot.

The size of the relief that flooded Tony at actually getting the assignment set off alarms clanging in the back of his head, but he was too thankful to pay them much heed.

A few minutes later he was back outside the airport hangar that served as operations for Redstone Security. They had always been housed off-site, keeping a low profile away from headquarters for the most part, a strategy that paid off on those rare occasions when a Redstone operative needed to go unrecognized. Plus, the airport location made quick response times easier, when some far-flung part of the Redstone empire needed their attention.

So you've got the job, he thought as he got into his car. Now what?

He had no answer. He told himself he should simply proceed as if this were any other job. Redstone Security had a reputation for efficiency, speed and success; all he had to do was live up to that. All he had to do was keep Lilith Mercer safe. No problem.

Never mind that he'd just volunteered to walk into a personal minefield.

He was so going to regret this. But he had to do it. He couldn't let anyone else take the job. Not this job. Because nobody else had a bigger stake in this than he did. Nobody else in Redstone Security was in his unique position.

Hell, nobody else would believe he was *in* this position.

Nobody would ever believe that onetime L.A. gang member, repeat juvenile offender, street-tough, tattooed Tony Alvera had been half in love with the elegant, classy, refined, beautiful and near-perfect Lilith Mercer since the first time he'd laid eyes on her.

No, no problem at all.

Chapter 3

Lilith felt absurd, but it was clear to her that Josh wasn't going to back down. And when Josh Redstone was set on something, it would take more than a mere protest to shift him. Besides, with what she owed him, she would tolerate a lot worse than having someone from security hanging around to placate his fears, however unfounded they might be.

Might, she thought, being the operative word.

Because once she'd read the thoughts in Josh's steady gray eyes, she'd realized she couldn't say with one hundred percent certainty that there was no one who would want to hurt her.

"Are you angry with me?"

The quiet question from her office doorway interrupted Lilith's unsettling thoughts. She looked up, into Liana Kiley's troubled blue eyes.

"No," she said to the young woman who had rapidly become indispensable to her in the task of finding and assessing the damage done by Stan Chilton, and had in the process become a friend as well. "I'm not angry. It's all right, Liana."

"I couldn't help worrying, and Logan agreed. I know the people who did this—" the redhead made a general gesture toward the research lab "—are in jail, but still…"

Lilith masked her start of surprise. That possibility hadn't occurred to her. She'd assumed, as had Josh, that if there was indeed some nefarious plot to harm her, only one person could be behind it. Of course, Liana didn't know about that person. No one did, except Josh, and at his request, security chief John Draven.

If she had to accept that something was really happening, she wished she could believe it was something as sanitary as fallout from the industrial spying case. That would be preferable to the alternative. But the alternative, unhappily, made a lot more sense.

"Thank you for being worried," Lilith said. "Although I don't think it's necessary."

"Logan thought it was better to be sure. You're not upset that he said something to Josh?"

"I wish he would have talked to me first, I could have eased his mind—and yours—but I try not to get angry with people who care enough to worry about me."

Liana smiled in obvious relief. "What's Josh going to do?"

"Pester me, no doubt," Lilith said, with fond annoyance. "Or rather, some unlucky person from security who no doubt has much more important things to do than find a plot where there is none will get that job."

"A bodyguard?"

Lilith laughed. "Oh, please. That's the last thing I need."

"They do that, though, don't they? Security, I mean? Because Logan would be happy to—"

She stopped when Lilith held up a hand. "I do *not* need a bodyguard."

A sudden image flashed through her mind, of the aftermath

of the last time a Redstone Security agent had taken on body-guard duties. In her mind she saw Ian Gamble, dressed in a sleek tuxedo that erased any memory of his usual, casually untidy self, just as his intense expression as he waited for his beautiful bride had erased the memory of his usual, endearingly distracted self.

Ian Gamble, genius inventor, who had fallen in love and married Samantha Beckett, top-notch Redstone Security agent.

His bodyguard.

Yet another in the ongoing string of Redstone weddings.

She shook off the image briskly. "I'm sure he'll simply have someone look into both incidents, discover they were indeed unfortunate accidents and we will all go on about our business. Which is," she added, "what I intend to do now."

"Not just yet."

The deep voice from the doorway spun Liana around and made Lilith's nerves jump. Liana greeted the man standing there with a happy exclamation. "Tony! When did you get back?"

Lilith just tried to remember how to breathe.

"Hello, my lovely Liana. This morning," Tony said.

"Have you seen Logan?"

"Your knight in shining armor with the luck of a thousand men to end up with you? No, but I spoke to him, also this morning."

Liana laughed. "You're incorrigible. But that's what I love about you."

Lilith smiled to herself a little wistfully; the teasing repartee was so carefree. Tony Alvera was an incurable flirt, and Liana obviously knew it. Although even if he had been serious, it wouldn't have made any difference; the girl was head over heels in love with her ex-cop.

Lilith wondered if Tony Alvera was ever serious when it came to women. She was reasonably sure, from what she'd observed during his work on Logan's case, that he would never poach on another man's territory. Or perhaps that only applied to men he respected, as she knew he did Logan Beck. In any case, Liana was as safe from his predatory charms as if she'd been his sister. That, Lilith was certain of.

"But alas," Tony was saying with mock drama, "as always, I am too late to win the fair lady."

Lilith at last found her voice, and her poise.

"Children, children," she said in mock severity, "take the bantering outside, please. I have work to do."

Liana laughed, patted Tony's arm in a way that put her previous words clearly into that sisterly category and went back to her own office.

Tony Alvera didn't move. And at Lilith's teasing words or tone, something had flickered in his eyes that had caught her attention. Something that reminded her that for all his easy, practiced charm, this was a dangerous man.

Something you shouldn't forget, she told herself, although she wasn't sure why it seemed so important at this moment; since they were both Redstone, he would never be dangerous to her.

For a long moment he stood there, just looking at her. He wasn't a huge man, just under six feet she guessed, but he somehow managed to fill the room anyway. It must be the combination of obvious strength, the striking looks, dark eyes coupled with golden skin and the rather rakish patch of beard below the middle of his lower lip, and the edginess he radiated at almost every moment.

The evidence that the edginess was for real was clear in the barely noticeable patches of slightly lighter skin on his neck and hands, where she knew gang tattoos had once been.

When she'd first met him, when he'd been assigned to help Liana and Logan, she'd found him disconcerting, to say the least. When she'd learned his story, from Josh himself, she'd found him admirable.

Right now, standing solidly in her office staring at her a little too intently—and for some reason apparently not willing to leave as Liana had—he was nothing less than unsettling.

And suddenly the obvious answer hit her.

"Not you," she said, nearly groaning it.

His face changed. The transfixing look vanished, replaced by the practiced charm she'd seen him use so effectively before. Not the teasingly flirtatious manner he'd had with Liana; that had been oddly innocent and sincere. This was the demeanor he used to beguile people, mostly women, she was certain, into giving him what he wanted.

Whatever that might be.

That was something that hit a chord deep within her, and not in a good way.

"Sorry, Mrs. Mercer. Luck of the draw."

She was hideously aware that she'd uttered her gut reaction aloud. And since she wasn't even sure what had prompted that reaction, she didn't know quite how to explain it to herself, let alone to the man she'd just unintentionally insulted.

But manners dictated she say something, so she opted for simplicity. And truth, which was never an optional choice for her, not anymore. "I'm sorry. I'm just not sold on this whole idea, and it seems absurd to pull you, of all people, in on such a silly little thing."

And that was all true, she told herself. It just wasn't all of the truth. There had been something much more deeply rooted in that involuntary response to his presence. It wasn't that he wasn't efficient and effective—he wouldn't have lasted in Redstone Security if he wasn't And she had admired how he'd handled Logan's case, including how he'd dealt with the stubborn, reluctant ex-cop. But that contact had been intermittent. She couldn't imagine having to deal with his intense presence all the time.

His expression changed again, but only slightly. After a moment he nodded, as if in acceptance of her explanation. But the original, riveting stare didn't return, and somehow that un-settled her even more. Why, she didn't know. She was usually unruffled and ever calm; it was the trait most commented on by anyone who knew her. But now—

"We need to talk about what's happened. Who might want you hurt. I'll try not to disrupt your life too much. But this is on Josh's orders, and you know what that means."

"I know it means anyone at Redstone would walk through fire if he asked, yes."

"Even if he didn't ask," Tony said. "Because he wouldn't."

"He wouldn't have to," Lilith said, thinking of her own debt to the man who had built this empire.

"No," Tony agreed.

This, at least, they had in common, she thought. They would both do anything for Josh Redstone. She knew why Tony would; his story was legend at Redstone, along with Draven's and Ian's and many others.

And it suddenly hit her that she was going to have to tell him her own story. And that made her feel faintly nauseated.

If only Samantha wasn't pregnant. She could have told her, much more easily. She doubted the tough, beautiful blonde could have related—she doubted Samantha Gamble had ever been truly afraid in her life—but she would have understood.

The moment the thought formed she was appalled at herself; Samantha and Ian were delighted, if bemused, at their impend-ing parenthood, and to wish that away, even for a split second, for her own benefit made Lilith ashamed of herself.

It was time to get a grip.

"Close the door, would you, please? The fewer people who know about this, the happier I'll be."

Tony complied without a word. Lilith walked back to her desk and sat down. Normally she would have taken the second chair in front of her desk, but she needed the bulwark.

Because she had just shut herself into a small room with the one person at Redstone who made her unbearably nervous.

It was going to be a very long morning.

Chapter 4

Just when did you become a masochist?

As he sat in the chair opposite her desk, relieved now that he'd seen for himself that she indeed seemed uninjured, he was very aware that she'd chosen to take her desk chair for the feeling of power or security it gave her, and the benefit of the desk between them. He also knew the answer to his own question. The moment he'd realized Josh was convinced Lilith could really be in some kind of danger, he'd had no choice. Even knowing he was going to regret it.

He already did.

The moment he'd walked in and seen her, all the truths he'd lived with since he'd first met her had risen up to swamp him anew. Lilith Mercer was everything he was not: elegant, refined, classy, cultured. He knew, thanks to the world Josh had opened to him, that he could put on the appearance of all those things. But he also knew that in him they were only skin deep. In Lilith, they went clear to the bone.

And he hadn't missed her reaction when she'd seen him; she didn't want him around. It puzzled him for a moment; they had gotten along well enough during his work on Logan's case, when she had asked him to keep her posted for Liana's sake.

But this was different, he supposed. This was her own situation, and because of that the contact would be much closer. He probably seemed like some kind of alien being to her, and he couldn't blame her. He knew who and what he was, and all the polish he'd acquired since his days on the street couldn't change that. His world and hers couldn't be further apart.

That hadn't stopped him from falling like a fool the moment he'd first seen her at the Redstone Christmas party, after Josh had called her in to clean up Stan Chilton's mess. He knew the image of her in that striking red dress would be with him until he died. Somehow the red had startled him; she seemed so reserved, but someone—he couldn't remember who, just as he couldn't remember much of what had happened that night after he'd seen her—had told him it was her favorite color and she wore it often.

He could see why; today she had on the Redstone logo shirt in a more muted shade, and it still set off her hair like golden fire.

He stared at her, all the warnings he'd given himself on the way over lost in some kind of hot haze. If there was anything more absurd or impossible in his life than such a reaction to her, of all women, he couldn't think of what it was. Not only was she all those things he wasn't, but she was a Redstone department head and one of Josh's oldest friends. That she was likely a bit older than he was didn't bother him, but all the rest did. He owed his very life to Josh, and he would never forget that.

And if that doesn't work, he told himself in an effort to clear the fog, *just remember the last time you felt anything like this for a woman.*

That memory—the image of a lovely, lifeless body lying on a cold metal table—managed what nothing else had. The last time he'd let himself truly feel something for a woman, it had gotten her murdered.

Back in control now, his rioting senses jammed back into the cage where they belonged, he repeated his promise. "I know this is a nuisance for you. I'll try to keep out of your way."

"I am sorry," she said, and she sounded more genuine this time. "I didn't mean to react that way. But this is a bit…below your talents."

"Some of them," he said, quashing the thought of other talents he'd like to exercise with her, shoving that cage door shut. "But I'm here, free at the moment, and we're not…strangers."

"No," she agreed. "And you know I was very impressed with what you did on Logan's case. I know he was… difficult, at that point in his life."

Tony chuckled, feeling a bit easier now. And pleased with her praise, he admitted ruefully. "Difficult? Yes, like a croc with a toothache is difficult."

When she laughed in turn, he felt an odd sense of gratification that his rather lame joke had done it. He shoved a little harder on that cage door.

"I just don't think this is anything serious. I'm not sure it's anything at all."

"Then it should be quick," he said smoothly, determined now to approach the job as if it were any other in-house assignment. "I'll need to see where that wire was rigged. And talk to the kid your neighbor suspects. But for now, why don't you tell me why Josh is convinced that you're in continuing danger?"

She looked puzzled. "He didn't tell you? Didn't Draven?"

"I wanted you to tell me. One less filter to go through."

She lifted one shoulder, somehow making even that half shrug seem elegant. "He has some idea my near-accident last week and what happened this morning are connected, I presume." She met his gaze then. "He did tell you that much? What happened?"

Tony nodded. "He said you weren't hurt. Is that true, or were you trying to keep him from worrying?"

"If I was, I obviously didn't succeed," she said, her dry tone making him smile in spite of himself.

"Josh is a hard sell when it comes to the welfare of his people."

"How well I know," she agreed, at last giving him that smile that could warm a room, the smile that encompassed everything, that drew him to her so impossibly; warmth, charm, grace and the generous spirit that had quickly made her one of the most loved Redstone people. That the smile wasn't really for him, but rather for the absent Josh, didn't lessen the impact.

"I'm fine," she said in answer to his original question. "No serious damage except to my pride and my derriere."

And a fine one it is.

The thought formed before he could stop it. Although she generally dressed fairly conservatively, her fire and flair coming in the frequent splashes of her favorite red, when she wore jeans as she did today, there was no disguising the fineness he'd just thought about.

Hell, he thought about it every time he saw her, and that alone made him aware of how out of line he was. He couldn't imagine any other man at Redstone having raunchy, lustful thoughts about Lilith Mercer. Longing, aching, desire, yes, but not the kind of urgent, desperate craving she made him feel.

That everyone at Redstone seemed to think he had a harem of women at his beck and call only made the irony bite deeper. He couldn't deny that there were women. And although he'd long ago quit trying to analyze why the combination of his looks and demeanor had a rather astonishing effect on some, he couldn't deny the fact, either.

Nor could he deny that he did, on occasion, use that fact. The only thing he tried to deny, to himself, was how meaningless it all was. What had once seemed like a dream come true, had become…he wasn't sure what. While if necessary he still turned on the charm to get what he needed, be it information or entrée to somewhere he normally couldn't get into, the instances where he pursued the connection to the inevitable destination— a willing woman's bed—had become few and far between.

He wasn't sure exactly why. He just didn't seem to have the energy or the desire to continue the facade anymore. He'd wondered if something was wrong with him, if he'd somehow lost the ability to feel any real desire.

Then he'd met Lilith Mercer. And the ferocious kick in the gut and points south had disabused him of that idea forever.

And forever was about how long he'd have to wait for the likes of Lilith Mercer to have a corresponding response to the likes of him.

He gave a final, hard shove to thoughts and urges that had no place here, and this time he locked the damned cage door.

"Tell me," he said, sounding gruffer than he'd intended. Keeping a leash on his unruly thoughts was proving harder than he'd expected.

Lilith sighed. Lowered her gaze to her hands. That alone had him sitting up straighter; of the myriad things he'd noticed about her since he'd met her, one was that she never avoided, never shrank from any difficult situation. As Josh said, she met it head-on and always gave it her best shot.

And her best shot, Josh had added, was very good indeed.

But she was avoiding looking at him now. He knew better than to think it was anything to do with him. It was something to do with this situation, and his gut was telling him that maybe Josh was right. Maybe there was more to this than just a couple of accidents.

His gut wasn't liking that idea. At all.

And she still wasn't talking.

"Stan Chilton's in jail," he said, managing a calmer tone this time. "And so is Joe Santerelli, from JetCal. Not to mention the fact that all you've done is come in to clean up the mess they caused. You didn't have anything to do with putting them there."

She still didn't look at him. But she answered. "I put together a lot of the data evidence that helped put them away."

She'd said it, but Tony sensed she didn't truly believe it. "True enough," he said, and waited.

"But if they wanted revenge, wouldn't they go after Draven? Or Sam and Ian?"

"Didn't work out so well for them last time, going up against those two."

At the mention of the unlikeliest couple at Redstone a trace of a smile curved her mouth.

That luscious mouth he couldn't keep his eyes off.

¡Maldita sea!

He knew when he resorted to his native Spanish that he was in trouble. And damning everything at large seemed to require that.

"You don't think it has anything to do with the spying case, do you?"

The smile faded. He regretted that, but this was more important.

"No," she said, in a tone of voice he could never have imagined coming from her. Weary, hurt, broken…he wasn't sure what it was, only that he didn't like it. Not from her.

"Then what? Or should I ask, who?"

Finally, she looked at him. Her usually bright blue eyes were shadowed now. Haunted, in a way he'd seen only in people in trouble, or in people from his days on the streets.

"Lilith," he said softly, aware but unable to stop himself from removing the safe barrier of formality of last name only.

"Daniel Huntington." She took a deep breath. "My ex-husband."

He blinked. He'd known she'd been married, but also that it

had ended before she'd come to Redstone. Long enough ago that it hadn't concerned him. Realizing he'd been glad to learn that had been his first clue that he was slipping into dangerous territory.

His brow furrowed. "I thought… Then why 'Mrs.' Mercer if it's your maiden name?"

"I dropped his name. People assumed the Mrs. because they knew I'd been married, and it was just…easier."

And kept men away? he wondered. Not that it would keep some away, but the some it wouldn't deter would be the kind she wouldn't be interested in anyway. He knew that much already.

"What about him?" he asked.

"Josh suspects that if these things are more than accidents…he might be behind it."

"Why would he think that?"

"Past history. But it's as impossible that it's him as it is that it's Stan Chilton or Santerelli."

He could see that she didn't want to get into it, so although he knew they'd have to talk about it eventually, he changed tacks. "Where is he? Local?"

"That depends," she said, finally giving him the level look that was her norm, "on whether you consider Chino local."

He shrugged off the first thought that hit him; half the kids he'd grown up with were in Chino. At the California Institute for Men. But there was no way…

His thoughts faded as the way she was looking at him slowly registered.

"Yes," she said, that weariness he'd heard before echoing in her voice again.

"He's…in prison?"

"Has been for nearly two years."

He was beyond puzzled. The only thing he could think of was that the man had committed some white-collar crime.

"He's on the Level I side? Minimum security?" he asked, although he didn't understand why the man wasn't in some

country club kind of place instead of a hard-core lockup like
Chino. Guys from *his* world went to Chino. Not hers.

"No. Medium security."

Belatedly it hit him. If Josh suspected her ex might be behind
what had been happening to her, then he must have a reason.

"What is he in for?"

She held his gaze with that nerve that had only wavered for
a moment. "He tried to kill me."

Chapter 5

She'd seen that look before. The shock, the incredulity. It was nothing new to her, that kind of skepticism.

So why did it hurt, when she'd thought herself inured to it long ago? Had she simply gotten unused to thinking about it? Or was it more complicated—was it that it was this man doubting her that made it sting?

She gave herself a mental shake. She'd left all the doubts behind, and she was not going back. She stood up abruptly. "If you don't believe me, then you surely can't believe there's any need for this. Tell Josh so, and we'll both get back to business."

He was on his feet before she could take a step. "I never said I didn't believe you."

"You didn't have to, Mr. Alvera." She saw him wince slightly at the formal appellation, but didn't stop. "I've seen that expression too many times to mistake it."

"What you saw was…shock. Amazement. Astonishment. But not disbelief. You wouldn't lie."

That flat, bald assessment mollified her somewhat. But the way he was looking at her still made her uneasy. She studied him. Tried to separate the tough and efficient agent she knew he was from the darkly handsome, rakish appearance. Tried to think only of his dedication to Josh and to Redstone, and not how the dimple that carved his right cheek when he smiled took him from dangerous to charming in a split second.

"This isn't just going to go away, is it?"

He shook his head. "Nor am I. So we might as well get started."

She was, she thought tiredly, going to have to explain. She sank back into her desk chair, wishing herself anywhere else, confronting any other onerous task.

And when did wishing ever help you out of a bad situation? she asked herself.

"Never," she muttered.

"What?"

She grimaced; she hadn't meant to say it aloud. "Just reminding myself that wishing is for children."

He sat back down himself, and was silent for a moment before he said softly, "Yes, it is. And the day you outgrow wishing is a sad one that comes too early for too many."

Something about his tone enabled her to get it out, what she never talked about. "You want the condensed version?"

"For now," he said, and the implication that there would be more later was nearly as unsettling as his presence.

She braced herself, then began. "Daniel Huntington. Pillar of the community. Wealthy family. Perfect manners. Charming. Polished. Urbane. Blue blood. Only one little glitch in his perfection."

If the staccato presentation registered with him, he didn't show it. His expression never changed when he said, "Which was?"

"He beat his wife."

The emotionless mask vanished for only an instant, but Lilith didn't miss the suddenly feral look that flashed in his eyes.

"The perfect cover," he muttered.

Startled at his quick understanding, she nodded. "Exactly. His stature in the community, his background, his Ivy League upbringing, it all made it nearly impossible for anyone to believe."

Something changed again in his expression. "If it was anyone but you telling me…"

She didn't miss the implication of what he was saying, recognized a second assertion that he'd never not believed her, specifically.

After a moment, he went on. "I didn't think things like that existed in…your world."

A wry sort of amusement quirked one corner of her mouth upward. She perhaps could forgive him more than most; the world he'd grown up in was so radically different, hers must seem like some perfect dream. It spurred her to more explanation than she'd given to anyone in a very long time. "I was as…surprised as you. I never would have believed it if I hadn't lived it. It took me a long time to realize that in Daniel's case, he could only have become what he was in his world."

"But it was your world, too."

"Yes. But I had parents and grandparents who had worked incredibly hard to get where they were. Daniel's family was a few generations down from the workers and felt it was now their place to lead their lessers."

Tony snorted inelegantly, then muttered an apology. She merely smiled. "Exactly how I feel," she said.

A flicker of surprise crossed his face, but all he said was "Go on."

"He was the only son, and was catered to and fawned over from the day he was born. He was raised with a powerful sense of entitlement, that he was born to the elite and deserving of all their privileges. What started as a quick temper and a sense of superiority in the child became a brutal arrogance in the man."

"But he took it out only on you."

She nodded. "He limited it to inside his own home, yes."

"Which makes it worse," Tony said, his voice rough. "It means he had some control. He chose when and where. He chose…"

His voice trailed away, and she finished it for him. "Me. Yes, he did."

"Bastard." He didn't apologize for that one.

"Yes," she agreed calmly.

And she was calm, somewhat to her surprise. Tony Alvera was angry enough for both of them. And that not only surprised her, it warmed her in an odd sort of way. Enough that she was able to go on.

"I found out much later, thanks to Josh and John Draven, that he'd done the same thing to his first wife. But he'd managed to hush it up."

"Did he kill her?" Tony asked, his voice harsh. The possibility obviously didn't startle him.

"No."

"You're sure?"

"Draven is. He found her, talked to her. In her case they paid her off. She took the money and ran. I can't blame her. If I hadn't had Josh standing behind me, I might well have done the same."

He gave her a long, level look. "I don't think so," he said, and something in his gravelly voice touched her. "How did it start with you?"

"It seemed almost accidental. We'd been married six years. I forgave him that time. He'd had a horrible day, a big deal had fallen through, he'd meant to strike the wall, not me, it would never happen again, it was all a mistake…all the usual excuses men like that make." She gave him a wry smile. "He even cried. It was a nice touch."

"Croc tears."

"Yes. But from Daniel Lee Huntington, quite effective. He is—was—perfection personified, the man who had it all, looks, money, position. And I'm the one who destroyed his perfect position in his perfect world."

"He blames you."

It wasn't a question, so she didn't treat it as one. "It was really only thanks to the detective who worked my case," she said. "She devoted herself to taking Daniel down. And she did it, despite pressure from a lot of quarters. The Huntingtons can wield a lot of influence."

"And did?"

She nodded. "To this day, a lot of people in his world support him. Some because they honestly can't believe he would do such a thing, others because they can't afford to cross the Huntingtons."

"What happened? That got him arrested?"

"He had another bad day, nearly a year after the first. He again chose to take it out on me. That was it, for me. I waited until he left, then began to pack. He must have sensed something, because he came back. This time he used a weapon. A fireplace poker."

"Son of a bitch." The curse was whispered, but no less furious. And again Lilith felt that warmth. Silly, she thought. It didn't matter anymore to her who believed her and who didn't. It was the past, long past, behind her and as close to forgotten as it could ever be.

At least, it had been.

"I managed to trip him, and it gave me enough time to get away. I didn't get far before passing out from blood loss." She heard him suck in a breath, but finished it. "Someone found me and called the police."

She stopped there, as if that were the sum total of the story. And for these purposes, it was; the long, horrible nightmare of the trial was not something she wanted to relive in any form.

Tony sat there, looking at her steadily. He didn't prod her for more, or even look as though he had more questions. He looked as if he was seeing what she wasn't saying. And his next words proved her right.

"They put you through hell to put him away, didn't they?"

She saw no point in denying it, especially since that would require exactly what she was trying to avoid, reliving the experience. "They tried. But by then I had help."

"Josh."

"Yes." Then, knowing this was the part Josh would never tell him, she went on. "While I was in the hospital, I saw on the news that Josh was in town. I hadn't seen him in years. I'd spoken to him now and then, but…in any case, I called him. I'm not sure why."

She knew she didn't have to say anything more; no one knew better what it meant to be in trouble and have Josh Redstone on your side.

"You said he's been in for two years."

"Nearly, yes." Guessing what his next question would be, she answered before he had to ask. "His lawyers managed to keep him out for over three, but two years ago his appeals ran out and he was sent to prison. And he was just denied a parole hearing. He thought he should get one sooner than the sentence specified, because…he's special."

Tony smiled at that. It was a smile Lilith thought she wouldn't like to see aimed at her; there was nothing of civil discourse in it, and a great deal of that feral wildness she'd seen flash in his eyes before.

"Good," was all he said.

"So you see why he can't be behind this. I appreciate Josh's concern, but—"

"You can arrange for anything from behind bars. In fact, it's probably easier. A constant flow of people with criminal mindsets, it doesn't take much to find one who's about to get out and willing to do you a favor for a price. Or one who knows somebody who will. And I'm guessing your ex still has the price."

She wondered if he spoke from experience. She knew Josh hadn't pressed charges for his attempted robbery all those years ago, but it didn't seem likely that that had been the first foray into crime for the boy he'd been, the street gangster she'd heard about.

"Oh, yes," she said. "He still has all the assets of the Huntington family. His father died four years ago, and controlling interest in all their varied enterprises passed to Daniel."

"Somebody must be helping him run all that."

"I'm sure the family attorney is dealing. He's very efficient." She grimaced. "As was his criminal attorney. Anyone less than Detective Drake, and the trial might have had a very different outcome."

"Remind me to find her and thank her someday," Tony said, almost under his breath.

Lilith found that curious; it had nothing to do with the current situation, and certainly nothing to do with Tony himself. "Really, I can't believe—"

"If he was out, would you believe he could do this?"

Lilith didn't have to think about that. "Yes."

"And being denied even the possibility of early parole would really set somebody like him off."

Wearily now, she conceded the fact. "Yes. He could never accept that he'd been convicted. Couldn't believe a Huntington would actually be put in prison."

"The pendulum has swung a bit," Tony said.

Lilith's brow furrowed. "How do you mean?"

"The public perception of justice has shifted. Nowadays you're more likely to get hit hard the more prominent you are. Decade or two ago, he'd probably have gotten away with it. Or at least gotten a lesser sentence."

Lilith knew that was likely true. And wondered again just how he'd gained his knowledge of the legal system.

"I'll need to know what his weaknesses are. What will set him off, or oil his jaws."

She blinked. "What?"

"What will get him talking. Or make him mad, if I need to."

For the third time, that fierce, wild look flashed in his eyes. "I'd like that."

"You…you're going to see him?"

"Easiest way to find out if he's behind this. He'll deny it, sure, but if I rattle him enough, he might give himself away."

"He's a very practiced liar," she said.

"So am I, when I need to be," he said negligently.

I'll bet you are, Lilith thought.

The idea didn't please her much.

Chapter 6

Tony tapped a finger restlessly on the steering wheel of his car. As he had been since they'd left Redstone ten minutes ago. "This is a mistake."

"Perhaps."

"You don't need to do this. If you'd just tell me—"

"You said you wanted to rattle him. Make him mad." She gave him a wry grimace of a smile. "I can do that better than anyone."

"How can you want to see him?" Tony asked, barely masking his incredulity.

"Believe me, I don't. I have no desire to ever lay eyes on that man again. But I swore I would never cower from him again, either."

He admired her fortitude, but said, "It's not cowering."

"It is if there's anything to Josh's suspicions, and he's really behind this. If," she added, "there really is a 'this.'"

He didn't tell her that, while he'd been doubtful at first, the moment he'd learned about her ex he'd become as convinced as Josh that there was more to this than just a couple of accidents.

Or perhaps he simply wasn't willing to risk her life on the assumption they'd been mere coincidence.

"I'll handle this," he said firmly. "It's my job, remember?"

"And it's my problem."

He tried another approach. "Would you let me interfere with your work?"

"If it was your area of expertise, yes."

"Exactly." He thought she had just proved his point, but she'd said it too quickly and easily; Lilith Mercer was no fool, and her steely determination was well-known around Redstone.

She proved his unease well-founded with her next words. "And Daniel Huntington is my area of expertise, not yours. If you want to push his buttons, I'm the one who knows what they are."

And just that easily, she had him. And he was going to be stuck in a car with her on the drive that would likely take nearly an hour.

The Redstone name carried a lot of weight in most places, and between Josh himself, John Draven and Josh's mysterious right-hand man, St. John, Tony guessed there weren't many places where one of them didn't know someone. In any case, one phone call had netted them permission to see the prisoner Daniel Huntington as long as they got there within the next two hours. Tony guessed whoever the contact was, he got off duty then.

"You'll need to change," he told her.

She drew back slightly. "What?"

"Your jeans. You can't wear them to visit. Too close to prison blues."

She stared at him, clearly wondering how he knew that, and for some reason he didn't even try to understand he felt compelled to go on, as if in some perverse way he wanted her to be even more aware of the differences between them.

"You can't wear some shades of green, either, because it's too close to the guard uniforms."

"I…see."

"It's my world, Lilith." It hit him then, what he'd been trying to do, to make her keep the distance between them, because he wasn't sure he could. He didn't want to keep doing it, but he couldn't seem to stop. "I know a lot of people in Chino. Gangsters I ran with. Gangsters I ran against. A couple of them are there because they killed my little sister in a drive-by."

She looked at him just long enough to remove her next words from the category of automatic platitude. "I'm sorry."

"Yeah," he muttered, wishing he'd never started this. He hurried her along then, knowing it was going to eat up some of their two-hour window for her to stop and change clothes. But it would give him a chance to look at the scene of this morning's incident, something he wanted to do as soon as possible anyway.

He was surprised when she directed him to a condominium building that looked as if it had once been apartments. It was well kept, and nicely landscaped, but definitely older than the high-rise style buildings that were popping up in the area.

"Twice the space for half the money," she explained, as if she'd read his mind.

So despite her background, she had a practical streak, Tony thought as they started up the stairs to her front door.

"Who cut the wire?" he asked, gesturing to where the ends of the thin silver line were still wrapped around both newel posts of the stairway. He pushed out of his mind the thought of what a miracle it was that she hadn't taken that full tumble, and focused on the evidence left behind.

"I did. My neighbor is seventy-five years old. A fall like that could seriously injure, even kill her."

And a tumble down that flight of concrete stairs could have killed you, he thought.

He crouched to look more closely at the posts as she went inside to change. She was right. A fall like that would have been devastating for her older neighbor.

As if his thoughts had conjured her up, a woman who had to be Mrs. Tilly appeared at the bottom of the stairs, and he realized she must have gotten off the community Dial-A-Ride van that had just pulled out. She had a small bag of groceries and a handful of mail in addition to a capacious black leather purse slung over her right shoulder.

"Is this because of that wire?" the woman asked as she came up the stairs, very spryly for a woman her age, he noted. But she was having trouble with the groceries and the purse slipping off her shoulder, so he instinctively did what he would have done with his mother, who was about the same age; he took the bag. "Let me get that for you."

She looked at him with a touch of wariness he appreciated. "It's all right," he said gently. "I'm not a threat."

"I didn't think you were, or Lilith wouldn't allow you around."

So she knew Lilith well enough to make that assumption. He barely managed to stop himself from probing that knowledge, knowing asking questions would probably have the woman running to Lilith to warn her off.

She let him carry the grocery bag across the landing to her door, where she dug out her keys, opened it, set her purse and the mail inside, then turned back to him and took the bag; she might not be afraid, but she was still cautious. "Are you a policeman or something? Are you here because of what happened?"

"Or something," he said.

"I think it was that little scamp who lives downstairs."

"Lilith told me."

The woman looked thoughtful. "If it wasn't him, who could it have been?"

"I was going to ask you. Did you see anyone around in the morning?"

"Just the gardener," she said. "Although come to think of it, it was a new man, not Jose, who's been here for years."

"You talked to this man?"

"Yes. He said Jose was his cousin, or something like that. And he had all the equipment." She wrinkled her nose. "And tattoos. I don't care for those."

If you only knew, he thought, but managed not to smile. "So he was Hispanic?"

She gave him a wary look, as if she thought he was setting her up to insult him. "Yes," she finally said, and left him standing there on the landing as she went inside.

He was pondering the possible significance of an unknown Hispanic with tattoos when Lilith returned. She'd exchanged those jeans he'd admired for a pair of black twill pants that were almost as distracting, and a crisp, white blouse.

"Here," she said, holding something out to him.

It was a plastic baggie holding a coiled length of silver wire that matched the remnants he'd been looking at.

"Not sure why I saved it. It looks like something you could buy at any hardware store, but there it is."

"Good." He took the bag. "Can't hurt."

He pulled the small, red-handled pocketknife he usually carried out of his left front pocket and made quick work of freeing the two tied ends of the wire. He noticed there were flattened spots on the one end, as if the person tying them had used a tool of some kind, likely pliers, to tighten the wire. He added the ends to the baggie and stuffed it in his jacket pocket. He could have Sam verify whether wire had been sold to any of Lilith's neighbors, at least eliminate that possibility. Sam would love it, tied to a desk as she was....

They headed back down to where his car was parked at the base of the stairs. She didn't go with any more noticeable care than anyone would, clearly not about to let the incident make her afraid of every step. And again he thought of determination.

By the time they were on the freeway headed north, he was realizing the drive wasn't going to be quite the ordeal he'd thought. Whatever her reservations about him had been to begin with, she seemed to either be over them, or at least ignoring them for the moment. She seemed more than willing to just chat amiably.

Or maybe she's just looking for a distraction from having to face her brutal ex, he told himself.

He was still having a bit of trouble absorbing what she'd told him. He realized now how stupid he'd been, thinking that things like that didn't touch her world, but still, it was nearly impossible for him to think of this elegant, classy woman as a victim of such brutality.

And when he did, when he pictured her frightened and in that kind of danger, when he thought of her hurt and bleeding and alone, a rage he hadn't felt since his days on the street welled up in him. The kind of rage that had gotten him into far too much trouble in his life.

Only this time he'd asked for it. Hell, he'd demanded it, demanded to be the one to help her, even knowing it would mean time like this, alone in her company, fighting his tangled feelings every step of the way.

Great.

Masochist didn't even begin to describe it.

"I think," Lilith said when the conversation turned, as it inevitably did between people who had their particular boss in common, "you have to have the most amazing 'How I met Josh' story in all of Redstone."

"The most infamous, maybe," he said as he signaled for a lane change to get out from behind a truck spitting rocks off its uncovered load. They were in the Redstone car he drove on assignment, but he took care of it as if it were his own, she noticed.

"That, too," she agreed with a laugh, and was oddly gratified when that made him smile, perhaps because it looked as if it was in spite of himself.

"I owe Josh my life," he said simply. "And not just for not having my…butt thrown in jail back then."

She didn't miss the change of words, and wondered if it was because she was female, or older than he, or simply that she was Redstone and therefore deserved the respect Josh demanded for all his people.

"I heard he sent you to school."

Tony nodded, although he didn't look at her. It wasn't because there was a lot of traffic at this midday hour, but maybe he was just a careful driver, she thought.

"Yes." She saw one corner of his mouth quirk. "It was his price for staying out of juvie. I'd been there twice, and I didn't want to go back."

This, she hadn't known. Either part. "His price?"

"He told me I could go to this school he knew about, or I could go back in the system. My choice."

She laughed; she couldn't help it. "That's Josh. Giving you options but making the right one all but impossible to pass up."

He did glance at her then. "Well, I wasn't sure it was the right one. To me, then, school was just another form of jail."

"I'm sorry to hear that."

"I'll bet you loved school. Becoming a teacher and all."

"I did love school," she said. "At least, until I got old enough to realize that I was being fed somebody's particular version of the world, to be memorized and spewed back when required."

"Sounds like school to me," he said dryly.

"I wanted the truth," she said, "and to learn how to learn for myself. And that's why I thought I wanted to be a teacher. To teach that. But when the trouble with my husband began, he used his influence to have me laid off. He didn't want me working."

"Hurt his self-image?"

"No, teaching was acceptable. It was control. He couldn't keep me sufficiently under his thumb if I was out working every day."

A little bitterness had crept into her voice, and it startled her. She'd thought herself long past such a feeling. Determined to end this now, she turned the conversation back to him. "So Josh made you go back to school?"

He accepted the change with surprising ease; perhaps he had sensed her discomfort. "Not back. To a different school. A college prep academy. I thought he was crazy. Me, in some snobby, upper-crust college prep? I laughed in his face."

Since she had gone to such a place herself, Lilith had a full album of images to draw on. She couldn't picture the kid he'd been in any of them. Nor could she begin to imagine how hard it must have been for him.

"But he didn't give up," she said.

"No. I told him it was a joke, no place like that would ever let somebody like me in. He said that was his problem."

"And they did."

"Turns out it was run by a friend of his."

"He has them everywhere, doesn't he?"

"That's because he helps people everywhere."

"I've often thought," Lilith said, "that if Josh ever called in all the favors he's owed at once, he could run the world."

"And it'd be a better place," Tony said.

"That it would," she agreed. "So, after that college prep, what happened?"

"College." He said it lightly, a small joke. But she was looking at him, saw the expression that flitted across his face, and guessed he'd still not quite gotten over the unexpectedness of it. "Business major. Which," he said, still lightly, "as you can see, I'm not really using."

She could not for the life of her imagine him tied to a desk. "Where?"

"U.C.L.A."

She blinked; she hadn't known that. "Great school."

"Yes." He flicked a glance at her. "And I've paid Josh back. Every cent of the tuition he put into me."

Somehow that didn't surprise her, although she knew Josh

would never have expected it. She wondered for a moment what it had taken for him to get Josh to accept the payback. That, she decided, must have been quite a discussion.

As if he'd read her thoughts, she saw him smile. "He fought me when I started, so I put it all into an account I never touched. Then I handed it over. He finally took it, but only for the next person he decided to help. It became the Redstone Scholarship Fund."

She smiled in turn. "That is so Josh it doesn't even require a comment."

That it was Tony as well didn't escape her.

She studied him for a moment. His hands were relaxed on the steering wheel and one elbow was resting casually on the armrest of the driver's seat. Logic, and her knowledge that Redstone Security was known worldwide even in traditional law enforcement circles, told her he might be relaxed now, but if anything happened, he would turn into what he was, a trained agent. John Draven would have seen to that.

But there was something more in this man, something somehow more intense than even Draven, who had arrived at Redstone via the military, a veteran of battles in various parts of the world, including the one that had taken from Josh his brother and last surviving relative.

Tony Alvera had been in only one war, but it was an insidious one that claimed casualties in a way that seemed little different to her.

Except that it took place at home, where kids should have been safe.

It struck her then that it was no small miracle that this man was here, now, where he was. And while he might want to give all the credit to Josh, she knew better. It didn't take much imagination to figure out he'd had to fight every step of the way.

She suspected the thing he'd had to fight hardest was himself.

Chapter 7

She had acted, Tony thought as they waited in the visiting area, as if they were simply going for a pleasant drive. Totally at ease, as if he were a casual acquaintance she didn't mind spending time with.

Why not, since that's all you are? he told himself.

Of course, she wasn't feeling any of the internal tension he was feeling. She had no idea that he'd volunteered for—or to be honest, commandeered—this assignment, let alone why. So why should she feel anything but relaxed?

And if she did know?

His first thought was that she'd run, screaming. But his second thought was no, she wouldn't, she had too much class for that. She'd think of some graceful, tactful way to deflect his idiocy, and probably try to do it without being cruel.

But she wasn't happy to be here, that he could see. She kept looking around, the only sign of nerves he'd seen in her, which was a testament to her determination.

"Depressing," she muttered.

"Yes," Tony agreed.

"'In case of lockdown,'" she read off a posted sign on one wall that explained what visitors must do.

"Doesn't happen often, not during visiting hours. They're pretty much sacrosanct."

"I'm sure no one wants to lose a chance to see the people they care about."

"Not to mention that that's when they get their contraband," he said dryly. "Nobody wants to risk that."

She went still, then turned away from the posted sign to look at him steadily. "What is it you're after, Mr. Alvera? Am I supposed to assume you know all these things because you're Redstone Security, or because you're a badass yourself?"

He couldn't believe elegant Lilith Mercer had said that. Her casual use of the term startled him into gaping at her. As did her perceptiveness, realizing he'd done it on purpose.

He had no answer to her second question, at least none he wanted to share with her, so he took refuge in the first.

"It would be nice if you'd quit calling me 'Mr. Alvera.' We were at least on a first name basis before."

"You weren't digging into *my* life before," she said wryly, but she gave in gracefully and smiled at him as she added, "Tony."

That smile did crazy things to him, and he welcomed the arrival of a uniformed corrections officer to escort them to the visiting area.

While he'd asked for a private room, he'd made clear that in no way was this to be a contact visit. He didn't want Daniel Huntington anywhere within reach of the woman he'd once tried to murder, even with guards close at hand. There was a table, with chairs on both sides, and Tony guessed this room was usually used by lawyers visiting clients. Lilith stared at the setup, and he wondered if she was thinking of the kinds of people who had sat in these plastic chairs over the years. If she was wondering how on earth she'd ended up in a place like this, even for a moment.

He couldn't think of a place more contrary to who and what she was. And he couldn't imagine how she must feel, being here, for this reason.

Startling him, she reached for the back of one of the chairs, pulled it out from the table and sat down, crossing her legs at the knees and leaning back casually as if she were sitting in a friend's living room. As if this didn't bother her at all.

Tony realized she'd been contemplating what scenario she wanted her ex-husband to see when he came in: a nervous, frightened ex-wife who was still his victim, or a calm, cool woman who wasn't afraid of him at all.

Bravo, Lilith, he thought, wishing he had the nerve to say it out loud. He stayed on his feet; if he had to take Huntington down—an action he would savor to the max—he didn't want to waste time kicking a chair out of his way.

The sound of a door opening drew his attention, and he snapped to full alert. His first impression of the man they'd come to see was jumbled. As Daniel Huntington walked through the door, a guard close behind him, Tony wondered what the hell it was that let guys like him look sophisticated even in jail garb. Even now, he oozed upper crust in a way Tony knew, for all his acquired polish, he himself could only fake. There was just something in the way Huntington walked, the way he carried himself. Even his smooth, superior expression made his surroundings seem irrelevant. He didn't look as if this place had touched him at all, and Tony guessed he'd been able to buy his personal safety as easily as he'd bought his way out of charges from his first wife.

Even now, the man looked as if he'd walked off the cover of *GQ* or something, Tony thought. No wonder nobody had believed that he could do something as classless and crude as beat up women. It all fit—that perfect, chiseled face, the blond hair and icy blue eyes, the haughty air….

But not the fear that flashed in those eyes. It was there for only a split second—if he hadn't been studying the man so carefully he would have missed it, but he was certain it had been there. Certain in the way he'd once been able to judge whether guys on the street would run or fight.

This was the kind of guy who'd order a drive-by, but never do the dirty work himself. Not if there was a possibility the victim might be able to fight back.

The smirk that accompanied Daniel Huntington's first words made Tony want to smack him down right now.

"Hello, my sweet wife. Finally missed me too much to stay away?"

Tony didn't know if Lilith was going to answer—she was staring at the man as if he'd crawled out from some dark, dank place—but he spoke before she had the chance.

"Ground rules," he said, letting every bit of the animus he was feeling show in his voice. And in his face, since his back was to Lilith at the moment. "You sit. You stay on your side of the table. You keep your hands on that table. You don't so much as lean forward. If I don't like the way you breathe, I'll put you on the floor. Got it?"

Huntington looked him up and down. He was cool now, that moment of fear vanquished and likely forgotten; this was the man who'd nearly fooled a jury into believing Lilith was a disturbed woman who'd made all this up.

"Bought yourself a pit bull, have you?" he sneered, glancing at Lilith.

Lilith simply looked back at him, much as if he were some sort of ugly anomaly whose existence she was pondering.

"Charming, as always," Lilith said, and Tony marveled at the amusement in her voice. If she was faking it, she was doing a masterful job; Huntington's jaw tightened slightly.

"Fitting. Does he service you like the bitch that you are?"

Tony's hands wanted to curl into fists.

Lilith's smile only widened. "Poor, inadequate Danny. He's much, much better at it than you ever were."

It took all Tony had to keep his expression even and his mouth shut. He knew she was doing exactly what she was here for—pushing Huntington's buttons—but he wished she'd chosen a different one first.

He focused grimly on his job, ignoring the images her words had started cascading through his mind. She'd obviously been right about knowing their quarry, because for an instant sheer fury showed in Huntington's face. Tony guessed it stemmed from the insecurity that was at the base of many abusers, and from the possessiveness of a man like Huntington, who couldn't abide the thought of anything he'd once owned belonging to someone else.

"It's nice to know I can still get to you," Lilith said, as if she were discussing the weather.

"You never could," Huntington declared.

"Dear boy," Lilith said, in a tone Tony had always associated with society mavens, "then why are you so angry?"

"Bitch," he said.

"I must say, your vocabulary has degenerated since you've been here with all your fellow convicts."

Huntington started out of his chair. Tony sensed the action the moment before the man made it, and with a darting move he slammed his forearm across Huntington's upper chest, slapping the man back into the chair, nearly knocking it and him over like a beetle tossed helplessly on its back.

The guard coughed but never moved. Tony thought it was a quiet warning until he flicked the uniformed man a glance and saw approval in his expression. Then the man looked away, pretending he'd seen nothing. Tony straightened, towering over the seated man now.

Huntington looked startled and off guard, so Tony struck fast, spitting out the question with all the fury he himself was feeling.

"Who did you hire?"

"I don't know what you're talking about."

"You know damned well what I'm talking about. Was the plan murder, since you failed when you tried?"

Tony couldn't be sure if the man's sudden tautness was because he'd struck home with the truth, or merely at the accusation of failure; he was fairly certain the latter would get to the likes of Huntington more.

He pressed, leaning in until Huntington reacted, and wariness came into those icy blue eyes.

"You sent somebody after her, and I want to know who it was."

"After her? Why on earth would I do that? She's nothing. Less than nothing."

Then why the insults? Tony told him silently. That was not the reaction of a man to a woman who meant nothing to him. Even hatred was a form of saying someone mattered to you.

"I know you set it up. And I will find out how and who you sent. When I do, your life here is going to be even more miserable."

"I did nothing," Huntington declared. "Why don't you ask her who else she's made angry enough to want to give her what she deserves."

"Was it somebody who was getting out? Cell mate?"

Huntington glared at him. Tony leaned in.

"Maybe just *your* mate? Whose bitch are you?" Tony used the word purposefully, turning it back on the man who had thrown it at Lilith. He knew the moment he'd said it, however, that he'd blown it. He'd let his emotions override his cool.

"Go to hell," Huntington said. His face went tight and stubborn, and Tony knew he had shut down. He refused to say another word, and at last Tony had to signal the guard that they were through.

"That went well," Tony muttered under his breath as they cleared security and started out of the building. He gave her a sideways glance, but was unable to read anything in her expression. "I'm sorry. I blew it in there."

"It was worth it."

He stopped in his tracks. She halted a couple of steps later, and turned to look at him.

"I just made this whole thing harder," Tony pointed out. "He'll never talk now. So how is that worth it?"

"It was worth it to me," she amended. "Because I wasn't afraid of him."

Tony's expression softened. One corner of his mouth lifted in a crooked smile. "No, you weren't. You were iced. It was him who was nothing to you."

"Yes."

"Okay, it was worth it, then."

His abrupt about-face seemed to amuse her, and she smiled back at him.

He was contemplating the effects of that smile, a little amazed that she wasn't angry with him for having made a hash out of the interview. He'd always known, simply because of the kind of person who was Redstone, that there was much more to her than the polished, refined exterior. That had been proven to him during Logan Beck's case, when she had gone out of her way to allow Liana to help the ex-cop. She'd barely known her new assistant, hadn't known Beck at all, but she'd gone to the wall for them both, right along with Josh.

By the time they were outside in the spring sunshine he was feeling a little better, and he didn't think it was entirely due to getting out of the oppressive surroundings. They got to the car and he opened the door for her. She thanked him with another smile, obviously having no problem with having a door opened for her, and as he went around to the driver's side he was feeling much better.

He pulled the driver's door open, turned to get in. And the view he got of the California Institute for Men jolted him back to reality.

If not for the grace of Josh Redstone, there was a grimly real chance he would have wound up there, or someplace like it. Or worse, like Chaco Ramirez, who'd ended up in Pelican Bay, locked down twenty-three hours a day.

Instead, he'd been in school—although he wasn't sure the battle for acceptance there was much easier than the battle to stay alive and well in prison. And then college, and then further training under the wing of Redstone, in anything that had interested him. And some that didn't; his street brothers would have laughed as he learned about table manners and the right fork, but Josh had insisted.

He'd come a long way, true.

But no matter how far he'd come, he still hadn't reached the point where Lilith Mercer—or Daniel Huntington—had started.

He never would.

Chapter 8

Lilith sat in the Redstone car in silence, marveling a little over what had just happened. She felt a quiet, inner satisfaction that she had experienced only the tiniest of inner lurches when Daniel had walked into that room.

She knew nothing had shown on the outside, but that had never been a requirement; Daniel could always sense her fear. It told him how far he could go—when he knew someone was afraid of him, any boundaries fell away. But today, there had been nothing.

She had been, as Tony had so aptly put it, iced.

But to her surprise, the greater satisfaction came from something else, something that surprised her. She had never thought of herself as vengeful, but she couldn't deny that she had taken a certain pleasure in seeing suave, sophisticated Daniel Huntington treated like the dog he'd called Tony.

And even more pleasure that her "pit bull" had turned on him. The words played back in her mind, and she looked away, out the passenger window, not certain she could hide her odd reaction.

Does he service you like the bitch that you are?

Daniel had said it, of course, to insult her. It was crude, and coarse, and meant to convince her she wasn't good enough for his world.

Funny how, instead, the abusive words had sent thoughts and images roaring through her brain that now made her afraid to turn her face to the man Daniel had been speaking about.

He's much, much better at it than you ever were.

Her answer had been calculated to enrage him. And it had.

But it had also intensified those vivid images racing through her mind, until she had felt her heart begin to pound in her chest as her pulse picked up.

Because she had little doubt that the slap aimed at her ex-husband was true. Little doubt because, she told herself, Daniel had been a perfunctory lover when calm, and a painfully rough one when angry.

It had nothing to do with what kind of lover Tony Alvera was. That was something she'd never know.

She told herself that, given how many women probably already knew, that was a very good thing. And then she told herself again.

She steadied herself, forced herself to look at the man in the driver's seat, wondering why they were still sitting in the prison parking area, why he hadn't even turned the key.

Unusually for her, she felt the strain of silence and finally spoke. "So now you know."

"Now I know what?"

"How shockingly bad my judgment can be."

"Was, maybe back then."

She appreciated the assumption that it had improved.

"But that mask he wears is pretty good."

"I was hoping never to see it again. I had relegated all that to the past."

"The past," he said quietly, "is part of what made us who we are today. You may not think about it, but it's always there."

It wasn't a stretch to realize he wasn't just talking about her. And for all the painful experience she'd gone through with Daniel, it had been only a few years. She'd been an adult, and she'd enjoyed a fairly happy and secure childhood. For Tony Alvera, there had been none of that respite; he'd had to start fighting as a child, probably younger than she cared to think about.

"Did he always talk to you like that?" he asked.

She was almost grateful for the disruption of her thoughts. The tangle of imagining what this man had been through—and her own out-of-hand imaginings about him—were getting stickier by the minute.

"No. If he had, I would never have married him, no matter who he was or how happy it made my parents. It was only later on that that kind of thing started. I've often tried to figure out if there was something, some incident that set him off, because for the first six years of our marriage, he was…normal."

"But you never found anything?"

"No. Nothing that stood out to me, anyway. On the surface at least, things were…if not happy, at least pleasant. Then the insults started. My family, according to him, were latecomers to wealth, whereas his had been old money. Generations of old money."

"Built on what?" Tony asked, surprising her with how quickly he asked the key question.

"Smuggling," she said, confirming his guess. "Back in the day it gave them enough to buy their way into academia, politics, and they used the mask of public service to hide their origins. It worked. Now people either don't know—an ignorance I have to confess to—or choose to forget where the Huntingtons made their fortune."

"So now they're legit."

"Oh, I'm sure their fingers are in a few things that would raise eyebrows. The polish is only a veneer. A very thick one after all these years, but underneath, they're the same cutthroats that used to lure ships onto the rocks so they could steal the cargo, and the drowning crew be damned."

"Nice."

"And Daniel is the culmination of all those years of polish and wealth."

"And he tried to murder you. How can you be so calm about it? About him?"

She smiled at that. "I wasn't, not always. It took a long time to reach the assurance that one man was not all men, and my ex-husband was not worth becoming a frightened, timid person for."

Something shifted in his steady gaze then. His expression changed. It took her a moment to realize that what she was seeing was undisguised admiration.

An odd sort of warmth flooded her. She tried to gather her thoughts, to control this strange, unknown response to a simple look.

Except there was nothing simple about the look Tony Alvera had turned on her. And she was finally forced to admit that part of the satisfaction she'd felt had been because he'd lost his cool, on her behalf. He'd jumped Daniel in her defense. Somehow the fact that he'd lost his cool because Daniel had insulted her made it much more personal.

But personal was exactly what this couldn't become, she told herself. Still, she wanted to say something to him. She tried to put into words something she'd been thinking since the moment her ex-husband had walked into that visiting room.

"Daniel was born to a world of privilege, and that's the facade he presents to the world, but underneath it all, he's the worst kind of slime."

"That," Tony said, "goes without saying. I've seen street killers with more class. At least they don't hide what they are."

"And that's the world you were born to," she said, thoughtfully. "But you worked your way out."

"Josh gave me that—" he began, but stopped when she shook her head.

"You know as well as I do Josh doesn't believe in handouts. He may have given you the opportunity, the hand up, but you did it yourself. You worked, fought and probably clawed your way out. Now, *that's* something to be admired."

For a long moment he simply stared at her, looking stunned. She'd known his story—at least, the versions that circulated at Redstone—but never really thought of it beyond the surface. Now, after having been inside that prison and seeing where he could so easily have ended up, she felt an even greater sense of amazement.

In an odd, unexpected sort of way, she felt proud of him.

That's it, she told herself. You're proud of him. Proud of him like…like a doting aunt would be.

Because she was old enough to be his aunt, she knew. She wasn't sure exactly how much older she was, but enough.

At least you're not old enough to be his mother, she muttered inwardly.

She refused to think about why that small fact made her thankful.

"I blew it," Tony said at the end of his report, his voice grim as he faced his boss. He'd dropped Lilith off at Redstone Headquarters and come straight back to report.

John Draven looked at him in that cool, calculating way that made anybody with sense realize he was messing with somebody who could take him down in an instant. And would, if he thought he had to.

After a moment, Draven simply said, "Why?"

Tony blinked. "What?"

"Why did you blow it?"

Leave it to Draven to cut to the crux of things. "I just did," Tony muttered.

"You're one of the coolest agents we've got. You *never* lose your composure. Even when Lisa was killed, you stayed cool and finished the job."

Tony winced inwardly, as he always did at the mention of Lisa. She'd been the first woman he'd ever thought about forever with. And he'd gotten forever, all right. The only forever anyone was ever guaranteed—forever dead.

"Always a first time," he muttered. He shifted uncomfortably, as much because of Draven's scrutiny as from having to admit to his mistake.

"So why now?"

The only answer Tony had was something Draven wasn't going to want to hear, something that would likely get him pulled off the case.

"Is this something to do with why you lobbied for this assignment in the first place?"

He should have known Draven would make the connection. Knowing he had no real choice, he answered. Carefully. "I told you. I worked with her on Beck's case. We got along. I thought she might prefer somebody she knew, at least a little, rather than a stranger poking around in her business."

He was sure his demand to be assigned to this had been far more strident than that casual explanation made it seem, just as he was sure that fact was obvious to his boss. But he wasn't ready to go any further. In part because he didn't really have an answer to Draven's question.

Why now? Why lose it now, when he'd been fine working with her during the entire thing with Beck and Liana? Was it simply because then the focus had been on them, and not on Lilith? He'd felt the same way then, and working with her had only expanded his admiration. She was tireless, and more than once Liana had remarked that Lilith could wear *her* out. He could see that himself now; she never seemed to slow down.

Or was it something stupider? Had working with her, talking

with her, seeing her concern for Liana and her cop even though she barely knew either of them, weakened the barriers he'd built? Had he somehow lowered his guard, let impossible ideas into his head?

He jammed those thoughts back into that cage in his mind that seemed to be getting fuller and harder to close these days. And when he spoke again—as he had to, in response to Draven's silent, patient waiting—it was again the truth.

"Lilith is a classy, kind, generous lady. He talked to her like she was some twenty-dollar streetwalker. It pissed me off."

"I see." For an instant Tony thought Draven was fighting a smile, but that seemed so impossible he knew he had to be wrong. "I suppose I should be glad you left him alive, then."

"It was close," Tony muttered.

"Your tux clean?"

Tony nearly gaped at his boss, nonplussed by the abrupt non sequitur. "What?"

"Your tux," Draven repeated with an exaggerated air of patience.

Tony gambled on yes, because he always had it cleaned after the rare occasion when he was required to wear the thing. He wouldn't have one at all if Josh hadn't insisted there would be occasions when he would need it. "Uh…yes."

"Good. Because you'll be taking your…assignment to Josh's Back to Life prosthetics fund-raiser tonight. Under wraps, of course, so you'll have to act like an escort, not a bodyguard."

Automatically, Tony cataloged the reason for the event. Redstone R&D had been the leader in that field of research ever since Ian Gamble came up with the prosthetic foot that had revolutionized the entire endeavor.

Then the rest hit him.

Tux. Escort. Fund-raiser.

They all added up to formal. He groaned inwardly. It wasn't

that he couldn't dress up—he had, on several occasions, when the assignment demanded it.

He'd just never done it as somebody's escort before.

Lilith's escort.

He fought down the rising tide of heat that was building within him. God, what if she wore that red dress again? What if he had to look at her like that, sticking close to her side like a good bodyguard, all evening?

He opened his mouth to suggest someone else do it. He just wasn't sure who. Rand Singleton would be perfect—he could picture Rand, who was even blonder and almost as beautiful, with Lilith—but he and his wife, Kate, were still ensconced in the woods west of Seattle, keeping Redstone Northwest safe and running smoothly.

"This is a direct request from Josh, so if there's a problem, Alvera, tell me now. I'll put Taylor on the case and you can go get your head together, or whatever you need to do."

"No," he said instantly. The last thing he wanted was a brand-new headquarters agent, no matter what her outside experience, responsible for Lilith's safety. He would simply have to get his head back in the game, and fast.

"I know you hate these things," Draven said. "I'm not fond of them myself. But it's only a few hours. You can stand anything for a few hours."

I'd rather be tortured, Tony thought, but wisely kept that thought to himself; somehow he didn't think it would be well received by a man who wouldn't take it as a figure of speech. Draven had personal experience with torture, and the scars to prove it.

Still, Tony thought as he left the airport office of Redstone Security, there was physical pain, and then there was nonphysical. And sometimes the nonphysical kind was worse.

Problem was, he was very much afraid this could turn into both.

Chapter 9

"Josh, really, it's a public event, with a lot of people. I hardly need a bodyguard under the circumstances."

"Sorry, Lil. Not negotiable."

Josh's voice held that note she knew so well, implacable, immovable. The voice that so startled unsuspecting folk who took his regular speech at face value and assumed he was as slow as his lazy drawl. If he were here instead of on the phone, she knew exactly what expression he'd be wearing, only his eyes giving away the steely resolve.

"Don't worry," he said then, a glimmer of humor changing his tone, "he cleans up pretty nice. Better than I do."

Lilith chuckled at that; Josh hated putting his tall, lanky body into formal wear, and his usual lament was that he was much happier in jeans and cowboy boots. Even Lilith, who'd never been closer to a cowboy than a movie or TV screen, had to admit that the attire suited him, made her see the almost universal appeal.

It wasn't until they'd hung up that the other part of what he'd said really registered.

Don't worry, he cleans up pretty nice.

"Oh, I'm sure he does," she murmured under her breath.

He was amazing enough already. With that easy, practiced charm he seemed to turn on so effortlessly, he reminded her a little too much of Daniel. But unlike Daniel, where the veneer was all there was, where the charm dripped from every pore only in public, in Tony it was a striking counterpoint to his edgy, dangerous looks. Even if you didn't know his background, anyone could sense the edge was sharp and the danger real.

There was, she knew, a type of woman who was drawn to that particular paradox. She'd never thought herself one of them.

And you aren't drawn to Tony Alvera, of all people, she told herself firmly.

She even believed it. It had simply been a very long time since she'd had a man around with any regularity, and having this one practically in her pocket all the time was unsettling. That was all.

The problem was hers, she knew. He was simply doing his job, and doing it with the thoroughness and determination that was the Redstone hallmark. If he had the slightest clue she was even having these thoughts, he'd likely laugh in her face.

No, he wouldn't do that. That would be Daniel. Tony would never laugh at someone in the family. He was probably used to such things, given the number of those women she'd been speculating about.

However, he would also likely ask to be pulled from this assignment, and rightfully so.

And that would solve my problem, wouldn't it?

It would. But the image of how that request would sound, of Tony going to Draven, or worse, Josh, and explaining why he couldn't stay on this assignment, was so hideously humiliating that she couldn't even think it through.

Since asking Josh to call the whole thing off had been fruitless so far, she had no choice but to deal.

And deal she would. She'd stood up to Daniel Huntington,
so this should be nothing. She simply had to make certain that
the man Josh had glued to her never got the slightest clue that
the woman who was merely a job to him was having thoughts
that would mortify them both. If she was ten years younger…

But she wasn't. And that alone was enough for her to quash
those thoughts and get on with her day. At least here, in
Redstone Headquarters, she was allowed to be alone and focus
on her work.

So focus, she ordered herself silently.

Still, it took her a while before she could completely free
her mind of Tony's presence. But after she caught herself wondering what he was doing right now, she summoned up the will
to shut that part of her mind off. She had a job to do, too, and
she was as dedicated to doing it as her charming shadow was.

She called up the computer file she'd been reading when the
phone had rung and went back to searching for hints of any
more damage to the place that had become as much her home
and family as her blood one.

The raucous catcalls and whistles followed him down the
grim, graffiti-laden street. He plastered a cocky grin on his
face, held up his arms to show off the expensive leather coat
he'd purposefully chosen for this expedition, and spun slowly
as he walked, giving a slight bow when he was done.

The grins and shouts he got in response told him the show
had been effective; they were treating him like one of their own
made good. He knew they were likely assuming he'd made
good in ways the cops would like to know about, probably
thinking he was dealing in drugs or women, and that could only
help his cause.

It felt strange to be here. It wasn't that he hadn't been back before; he had. He'd been careful to see that no one here knew the real reason behind his disappearance all those years ago. For all they knew, he'd been in prison somewhere else, and he let them keep thinking it. There had been no one left behind to tell the truth, anyway; his little sister was long dead, and thanks to Josh he'd moved his parents out of this hell within weeks after his foolish yet fortunate attempt to mug the young then-millionaire.

Before, when he'd come back, he'd simply thought how lucky he was to be out. This time, his feelings were more tangled, and he wasn't sure why.

He kept going. This had been his neighborhood, once. And more than once he'd used that, because people on the street had a way of knowing things you'd never expect them to know. Including whether there was anyone recently out of jail or prison who had come out with a job to do. True, the possibility was tenuous—a new gardener who happened to be Hispanic wasn't much of a connection—but thanks to his misstep with Huntington, it was all he had.

He hadn't really planned on doing this today. He'd thought he would keep digging into Lilith's ex's past, see what he could find. As far as Tony was concerned, the man was still the prime suspect, although he was honest enough to realize he'd like nothing better than to add time to the charming, urbane, sophisticated and rotten-inside Daniel Huntington's sentence.

But after Draven had informed him what he'd be doing this evening, he'd changed his plans. And about then his self-honesty had fallen short; on some level he knew he'd come there intentionally, to pound home the differences between them by revisiting his past in a literal sense, but he wasn't admitting that up front.

Not yet, anyway.

But here he was, after dressing with care in the kind of clothes that he knew would scream *success* to the people he'd be encountering. And as he'd put on the clothes he'd also put on the attitude, the arrogant swagger he'd grown up emulating, wanting to have for real, because it was the only way out that he could see.

And he'd wanted out. Long before the day his little sister had died from a stray bullet fired by a drive-by shooter, and he'd seen his mother become a faint shadow of her former, vibrant self and his father, always a reserved man, shut down completely, he'd wanted out. Wanted *them* out.

He hadn't missed the irony that the only way out seemed to be using the very things that made him want to get out. Getting out took money, and the gangs and their hierarchy seemed the only option; if he rose high enough, and his cut of their illegal activities got big enough, then he could afford it.

Of course, if you got that high, you could never leave. They'd kill you first.

But he could get his parents out. And then, if he had to leave everything, including his family, to get out himself, he would.

He shook himself out of the swamp of memories; not paying attention on these streets could get you killed. He kept walking, noticing there weren't any familiar faces among those he passed. Some eyed him with suspicion, some with disgust, some with envy. The flashy coat, he thought wryly, was working. It was warm enough on this late spring day to make it clear he was wearing it either to show off or to hide something beneath it—a weapon, he was sure, most of them thought—and either reason contributed to the effect he wanted.

As he kept going, he wondered if the East Side 13s had all been killed off and he'd somehow missed it. Then he laughed inwardly at himself; the ones he'd run with were his age now, and a whole new batch had likely taken over, probably guys who were just toddlers when he'd been here.

Once he saw a woman he thought he recognized, but she darted away from him too quickly to be sure. He kept going, certain that whatever else had changed, the grapevine on the streets hadn't, and that whoever was running the ES 13s these days would know about this intruder sooner rather than later.

He was proven right about three blocks from the heart of their turf.

"¡Orale, vato!"

The "Hey, dude," hail from behind turned him on his heel. He was a little startled to finally see a familiar face. *"Rico. ¿Que pasa?"*

More than the casual what's-up inquiry, he wondered what Rico Morales was doing here. And even more than that, he wondered when his onetime friend had gotten out of jail.

"¿Tienes un cigarro, mijo?"

"Sorry," Tony said to the request, switching to English, "I quit smoking."

"You quit a lot of things, bro." Rico made the switch as easily as he did.

"Some," Tony said, "I never started." Thanks to Josh, I never had to.

Rico, however, had never shown any interest in getting out. His greatest aspiration had been to be a loyal ESer. And he'd gone to jail to prove it, taking the fall for the leader of the gang in a drive-by case like the one that had killed Lucinda.

But Rico had also had a bit of a teenage crush on Lucy, and therefore had never given Tony much heat on those rare occasions when he went back to the neighborhood.

"When did you get out?" he asked.

Rico frowned at him. "I been out six months, *vato.* You ever come around anymore, you'd know that."

"Been busy."

Rico eyed the leather coat. "Yeah, you have."

The man didn't ask at what, for which Tony was thankful. What he'd done since he left the streets wasn't known here, and he wanted to keep it that way. Let them think what they thought, that he'd made it dealing drugs or pimping whores, as long as the conduit for information didn't dry up. It was the one thing he had to offer Redstone that no one else had, and he knew it.

Someday he would come back here and show others there was another way, passing along what Josh had done for him in his own small way, but right now he was leaving well enough alone. "Anybody else local get out lately? Like in the last month or so?"

Rico lifted a brow at him. "Why you want to know?"

"Looking for someone."

"Who?"

"Don't have a name. Just heard he took on a job for a friend of mine, in Chino. Might have something else worth his while to do."

Rico eyed the coat again. "Hey, I can do whatever you need doing, my old friend."

"You find me this guy," Tony said with a grin, "and you can have this coat."

Rico laughed, but the sound faded when he realized Tony was serious. "What else do you know about this guy you are looking for?"

"Job was getting rid of my friend's ex-wife."

Rico laughed. "She cheat on him while he was inside?"

"No."

His answer was quick and certain. Too quick, he realized instantly; it would have been the easiest explanation. But it had been instinctive; Lilith would never cheat. That would be more Huntington's style.

"Before." He knew he'd have to get more specific, make something up that sounded real enough, and it made him edgy. "She's some wheel at that big-time place, Redstone, Incorporated. It was somebody there. That's why he's inside."

"He had to teach her a lesson," Rico said with a nod, accepting the story with complete understanding. In his world, it made perfect sense.

"Know anybody who took on a job like that, when they got out? Or anybody who knows anybody?"

"I could ask," Rico said. "I have a lot of friends."

Tony got the subtext, that after doing his time Rico had moved up in the ranks and could call on other gang members to do this for him.

"I know you do. Why I came to you," he said, paying the requisite respect. "Anything you find, anything about a job like that, or anything connected to that Redstone place, would be worth a lot to me."

"I would need to thank them for their help," Rico said pointedly.

"I'll make sure the pockets in the coat aren't empty," Tony promised.

Rico seemed to consider this for a moment, obviously wondering if he could trust this man who'd left them in the dust years ago. Finally, Rico nodded. "I will ask."

Tony reached into his pocket and took out a business card. It was blank except for a single phone number. He'd had them made for just such occasions. "My pager. Use it if you turn anything up. If it's the right thing, the right person, I'll make sure there's more than the coat in it for you."

Rico took the card, looked at it, then looked at Tony speculatively. "What is it that pays so well, *mijo?*"

"Pal," Tony echoed in English, "you wouldn't believe me if I told you."

Chapter 10

"Stop it!"

Lilith snapped the order to her image in the mirror as she fussed with her hair yet again. So far she'd had it down in a sleek fall, then curled into waves, then up, then down again.

She was acting, she thought with rueful self-awareness, as if this was a date. A first date. With someone she wanted to impress.

Disgusted with herself, she finally pulled her hair into a classic French twist, secured it quickly with the ease of long practice, tugged a few strands loose to soften the look and let it go at that.

And she was *not,* she told herself firmly, going to second-guess what she was going to wear tonight. She had a limited choice for formal occasions, having long ago gotten rid of the expansive wardrobe of gowns and shoes and bags she'd required as the wife of Daniel Huntington. She'd donated them to a charity the week she'd gotten out of the hospital, wanting nothing from that time in her life, no reminders except one—she kept the photographs the police had taken of her injuries.

At first, she'd kept them to remind herself of her near-fatal lapse in judgment. Later, she kept them to use when she spoke to groups at women's shelters. She knew the image she presented, knew it resulted in the kind of disbelief she so often encountered, that such things could ever happen in the world she had lived in. But one look at those photos, and the women she talked to knew that what she told them was true; she had indeed walked in their shoes. And then they listened to her, knowing she understood.

She brushed off the old memories, hating that they'd been stirred up again when she'd thought them safely and securely buried. She forced herself to focus on the task at hand, getting out the floor-length gown she'd chosen. It was one of two she owned in her favorite red. The other was more daring, lower cut and clingy enough to warrant some care about what she wore under it.

But tonight was a fund-raiser, and some decorum was called for, so she chose the second one, still sleek and elegant, but a little tamer. A strapless sheath with a beaded lace shrug, it hinted but didn't advertise and had the added advantage of being Redstone red.

The color was a declaration. It had been too bold, too assertive for Daniel's taste, and he'd ordered her not to wear it. Since the functions she would have chosen it for were for his work, she hadn't fought him on it.

Looking back, of course, she realized it had been a glaring sign of what was to come.

But now she wore what she pleased when she pleased. And wearing Redstone red appealed to her on that level as well, not to mention that she was rarely alone; many in the Redstone family made a point of showing their loyalty in that subtle way.

And that it was a color that looked exceptionally well on her was something she didn't allow herself to dwell on when she chose it for tonight over the other options in her closet.

She simply wanted to look her best for the cause, she told herself. It had nothing to do with the man who would accompany her.

She glanced at the thin gold watch on her wrist; she'd dispensed with her daily, utilitarian model for a more delicate one, with a small diamond at the twelve and the six, unable to make the break completely and go without one at all.

The watch, a pair of drop earrings in gold set with a single ruby each, and a thin gold chain around her neck completed the outfit; she'd always followed her mother's rule of no more than three pieces of jewelry. Others in Daniel's circle had worn much more on such occasions, some simply dripping with the diamonds that shouted their status, and had given her pitying glances for her lack of flash and sparkle.

Daniel hadn't pitied her. He'd been angry. He'd tried varying tactics to get her to change her style, from buying her bigger and better jewels, to asking, to outright ordering her to put on more or flashier pieces. When she'd refused, he'd accused her of trying to undermine him by making it seem among their friends that he couldn't match their show.

And if they truly were our friends, she'd told herself then, the thought would never occur to them.

Looking back, she'd realized that had been another sign. At the time she'd just thought him silly—and exhausting—for making it a competition. But then, for a Huntington, everything was, even the games of tennis he played with a ferocity that made it seem close to a blood sport.

She doubted if Tony Alvera had ever had time for such frivolous things. A long weekend spent at a country club tennis tournament didn't seem like something he would indulge in, even if his world had included such things.

"Now, what do you know about it?" she told herself sternly. "Nothing. Josh sent him to college, perhaps he joined the tennis team."

Lord, she was talking to herself. Not the inner voice she guessed most people had, putting thoughts into words to aid in the process of working something out, but out loud, question-and-answer talking to herself about ridiculous things.

When the knock on her door came, it was a surprise. Not because she wasn't expecting it, although it was a few minutes early, but because instead of the heavy, demanding rapping she'd half anticipated, it was a firm but polite tapping.

And no cutesy rhythm, not for Tony Alvera.

Because this is all business, and you'd best remember that, she ordered herself as she walked through her living room to open the door.

When he'd been up the first time, to look at the wire across the stairs, he hadn't come inside. They'd been in a hurry to get to Chino before the favor Redstone had called in expired. This afternoon, he'd merely seen her to the door, as if he'd sensed she was already about at her limit at his insistence on following her home.

This time she supposed he would at least be stepping inside, so she glanced around, although she'd made certain it was tidy when she'd first gotten home.

Because you knew this would happen? Straightening up for the bodyguard, Lil?

She smiled in spite of herself as she realized she'd used Josh's nickname for her. He was one of the very few who ever shortened her name, although it didn't particularly bother her when someone did. In fact, she'd grown to like it, since it had once irritated Daniel, who had also insisted on being addressed by his full name rather than the detested Dan or worse, Danny.

It was with that smile on her face that she pulled the door open and, as she'd practiced in her head, gestured him inside.

If she hadn't done that mental practice, she likely would still be standing there, hand on the doorknob and her jaw hanging open in shock, she thought wryly a moment later.

Tony Alvera made her spacious living room seem small with his edgy presence. He made even her straightforward, low-key décor seem fussy compared to his lean, pared-down style in a perfectly fitted tux with a wing-collared shirt and classic bow tie—hand tied, she noted.

He also made the air seem a little thin, she thought as she finally remembered to breathe.

Something about the way he was looking at her made her think there would be no more air outside than there was in here.

"I came early to do a security check on your place," he said, his voice sounding oddly gruff.

So much for the niceties, Lilith thought. But in fact she was grateful for the businesslike approach. It took things out of the realm of the personal.

She had to admit that her first sight of Tony Alvera in a tux had blasted her imagination into some very personal areas.

And blasted the doting aunt analogy she'd been clinging to into an astronomical number of pieces.

Okay, so he was gorgeous, in a dark, exotic way that literally took her breath away. That was a fact, and no amount of calling herself a fool would change it. Any woman with a pulse would find it picking up at the sight of him.

And she had to walk into a crowded room with him tonight. With every woman in the place no doubt wondering what he was doing with *her* when he could have one of them—younger, more innocent and baggage free—with one snap of his elegant fingers.

None of them, of course, would be wondering what she was doing with him. One look at him in that tux would make that question irrelevant.

She fought for control, while he seemed briskly professional as he checked all the windows in the living room, looking at locks, trying to open them both locked and unlocked and peering out through them, she guessed to check possible access.

She didn't know him well enough—and he'd said nothing

more than those few words of explanation—to know if that odd note in his voice meant anything.

Perhaps he didn't want to be doing this—going to this thing with her—anymore than she did.

She steeled herself, wondering what had happened to all her vaunted determination and resolve. Get over yourself, Lil, she muttered inwardly.

"I'm sorry you had to do the penguin suit," she said, trying to break the tension even as she wasn't sure she wasn't the only one feeling it.

He glanced at her as he headed toward the next room, the smaller den that served as her home office, his expression unreadable.

"It's just another disguise," he said, and kept going.

She wasn't sure what that was supposed to mean. Clearly he wasn't happy about being here, so she decided his was the best approach and kept things on topic from then on.

"No windows in the den," she pointed out.

He nodded, and indeed his check in there was quicker. Then came the small dining room, the same routine as in the living room for the single large window. The kitchen took longer; there was a sunny garden window in the breakfast nook, with sliding panels that opened for venting, and he frowned until he walked over and saw there was no easy way to access it from outside.

When he then headed down the hall toward the bedrooms, she realized with a jolt what he was going to find if he stuck his nose in the master bathroom. She'd left it quite a mess, including some sexy underwear she'd firmly decided against wearing, which she now wished she had put back in the drawer instead of leaving it until she got home.

Stirred now, she followed him as he opened the door to her only occasionally used guest room. If he was bemused by the bunk beds and animated character décor—her young niece and nephew were the most frequent occupants of the room—he didn't show it. He merely walked over to the single window, again checked the lock and looked out, then came back.

And headed toward the last remaining rooms, the master suite.

At least I made the bed this morning.

Not that it seemed it mattered; as he walked over to the sliding glass door that led to the balcony, he didn't even glance at the big, white, cottage-style bed she'd bought as compensation for living for so long with Daniel's heavier, darker tastes.

In fact, he seemed to be studiously avoiding looking at it, she thought. Which obviously had to be a silly assumption on her part, there was no reason—

"This won't work," he said.

No, it won't, she thought. She was having no luck at all in her effort to ignore the effect this dangerously elegant man was having on her, no matter how silly or ridiculous she told herself she was being.

But she hadn't expected him to say it, especially so baldly.

"That balcony is too easy to get to, from above or the side. You need something more secure than this lock."

For an instant she was more grateful than she'd ever been in her life that his back was to her.

"I do?" she asked, figuring she could manage the two simple syllables without giving away her stupidity; when she heard the slight quaver in her voice she knew she should have kept quiet.

He didn't miss it, either. He turned his head, his gaze narrowed as he looked at her. With one of the greater efforts of her life, she steadied herself.

"You mean like a burglar bar? I've been meaning to do that." She was proud of how she sounded that time. Business-like, cool, calm. Herself.

After a second he shook his head, apparently deciding he'd imagined whatever he thought he'd heard in her voice. Or in answer to her question, she wasn't sure which.

"No. Those are useless against a pro. He'll just pop this little hook lock and lift the whole door out of the track. I'll get a pin for it, put it in tomorrow."

"A pin?"

He pointed to the top of the slider, where the moving panel and the stationary panel overlapped at the center. "You drill a hole through both frames. Put a heavy steel pin through both. Then you can't lift the door out or open it."

"Oh. What if I want to open it?"

"It's on a short chain fastened to the frame, so you can take it out and not lose it. But," he added, "don't."

"Don't what?"

"Open the door."

She blinked. "Don't open the door?"

"Don't open it. Get some pots or something, put them all along that railing, so anybody coming over will have to make noise. Then stay off the balcony. In fact, stay away from this—" he gestured at the expanse of glass "—altogether."

"Excuse me?" Irritation was starting to spark in her now. She'd been tolerant so far, but this was starting to go over the top.

"You heard me. Stay away from all the windows, and at night keep your lights to a minimum or curtains and blinds closed."

He couldn't know the nerve he was hitting, she told herself. But that didn't stop her from lifting her head and resorting to her most imperious voice. "I beg your pardon, but are you implying that I should become a prisoner in my own home, and in the dark as well?"

"No."

"Well, that's a relief," she muttered.

"I wasn't implying at all. I was ordering."

That did it. She drew herself up to her full height—and augmented by three-inch heels, she was a respectable five foot eight, only four or so inches shorter than he.

"I'm sorry," she said coolly, "but I quit taking orders from anyone in my personal life the day I left my husband. And you," she added sourly, "are beginning to sound a bit too much like him."

He went still. Something flashed in his dark eyes, something hot, grim and dangerous. It was all she could do not to take a step back from him.

"I am," he said, his voice low and harsh, "*nothing* like your ex-husband."

No, he wasn't, Lilith thought, regretting her words. Tony would never take out his anger or frustration on someone weaker than he. She opened her mouth to apologize, but he'd already turned and walked away. She told herself she should be thankful; at least he'd blown her silly thoughts right out of her mind.

As she stood there, watching him go, she wondered where she'd gotten the idea that he'd meant much more than just that.

Chapter 11

"I didn't do it!"

It was the standard, instinctive answer of any kid who was caught doing something he shouldn't have done. Tony knew that. It had never done him much good as a kid; with him, his father had operated on the assumption of guilty until proven innocent.

Lucy, on the other hand, had been able to get away with almost anything simply by giving their father that look, those big brown eyes turned on him liked a beaten puppy. The old man would just melt. Tony had tried hard to be mad at her for it, but she had used it on him as well, and he hadn't been immune.

And ever since she'd been killed, he'd been hard pressed to be tough on a kid. Any kid. But he had to be a little tougher on this one. Until he was sure.

"I didn't do it, honest!" Billy Wells exclaimed again when Tony didn't immediately respond. "I heard my mom talking about how she fell, and I came up here to see if Lilith was okay."

"And why," he said, purposefully stepping close enough so that he towered over the nine-year-old, "should I believe you?"

"Because it's the truth!" Billy looked up at him, and the fear in his eyes was real. "I did that other stuff, the fire and the flat tires, but I didn't do that! Mrs. Tilly is a grumpy old bi—bag, but I like Lilith. She's nice to me, and my mom. I wouldn't try to hurt her."

He believed him. Whether it was the fear, or the urgency in his quavering voice, Tony believed him. But that didn't mean a warning wasn't in order, given the boy's admissions to other questionable actions.

"I'm going to find out who did," he said. "And if I find out you had anything to do with it, you're going to see me again, and you won't like it."

"I didn't," the boy insisted for the third time, but more calmly now. Then, as if sensing the immediate crisis had passed, he looked at Tony with a touch of curiosity. "You a cop or something?"

"Or something," he said, wondering about the change, wondering what had given the kid that kind of knowledge. "I work for Lilith's boss."

"Oh. That Redstone guy? My mom says he's a bazillionaire."

"Probably."

"Wish he'd give us some of it."

"He gives it to people who work hard to earn it."

The boy frowned. "Not to people who need it?"

"If they're willing to work for it. Then he'll help more than anybody you'll ever meet."

"Maybe my mom could go to work for him. She works hard. She's got like three jobs."

Tony's brow furrowed. "That's a lot."

"She's always tired. And worried. If she could get just one good job, then we could stay here, and not have to move all the time."

Tony heard a female voice call the boy's name. Billy's head turned, and he spoke quickly.

"I gotta go. I promised I'd be back in five minutes. She gets worried if I'm late. Like my dad could ever find us here."

Then he was scampering down the stairs, leaving Tony pondering those last words. It didn't take much to guess what was behind them. No wonder Lilith was considering getting his mother hired at Redstone. He could put in a word himself, he thought, even as he realized he was grasping for distraction from the night ahead, something he was anticipating with an odd sense of eagerness and dreading at the same time.

But his belief that the boy had been telling the truth also meant he was facing the greater possibility that Josh was right; if the boy hadn't strung that wire across this landing, if it hadn't been a childish prank that could have turned lethal, then the chances that someone was truly after Lilith rose dramatically.

And his gut-deep reaction to that put him even more on edge.

A few minutes later, when Lilith came out her door and he saw the way that damned red dress moved when she did, when they got down to his car and he watched her get in, saw the slim ankles above the red shoes she wore, imagined how her legs must look in those spiky heels, he knew the confused feelings were appropriate.

He was not, Tony thought, going to make it through this night. A night of rich, sophisticated, high-society types, and most of them would probably be gaping at him and Lilith, wondering what on earth a classy lady like her was doing with a guy like him.

Probably figure I'm after her money, he thought. And the fact that thanks to Harlan McClaren, one of Josh's first investors and the canniest financial adviser on the West Coast, he'd never have another money worry in his life, didn't change that. He still looked the way he looked, and he was going to stand out in this crowd like a wolf in the flock.

If it wasn't for Josh…

But it was. This was all for Josh, so he had no choice. That's how he had to look at this. It was for Josh, and therefore imperative. He'd shut off his feelings before, often, so he would do the same now. And he would handle this as if it were nothing more than any other security assignment.

It would work, he thought. As long as he never looked at the woman now sitting beside him in the car.

It had taken everything he had in him not to grab her and kiss her when she'd opened the door, standing there in that long column of vibrant red. Not the sexy number she'd worn to the Christmas party the first time he'd seen her, but an elegant, shimmering strapless dress with a lacy, short, jacket-thing over it that sparkled with crystals or something.

This was closer to the real Lilith, he supposed. He wondered if she realized what a dichotomy the two presented: the sexy, slinky, low cut dress, and this stylish, tasteful, screamingly chic gown. This was the cool, unflappable Lilith, untouchable in his mind.

Untouchable, except that that was the first thing he'd wanted to do. Touch. And more. A lot more.

The atmosphere in the car was a little tense. His fault, he thought, he'd snapped at her, and for no good reason. She had every right to be upset at this invasion of her privacy.

Not to mention your high-handed orders, he told himself ruefully.

He'd overreacted. Again. He'd been reeling from the sight of her, and when he'd seen the vulnerabilities in her home and visualized the worst happening to her, he'd gone over the top in addressing them.

And her.

But when she'd said that about him being like her ex, he'd lost it. And ironically, it wasn't even the comparison to a wife beater that hit him so hard; he knew it wasn't anywhere close to true, and he knew on some level that Lilith knew it as well.

It was every other way it wasn't true that hit him. He truly wasn't anything like Daniel Huntington. He wasn't smooth, suave, sophisticated, polished or anything someone born to the manor as Huntington had been was. Oh, he could act it, and put on a pretty good front, but that's all it was, an act. Underneath he was still Tonio from the streets, and he was beginning to think he always would be.

And now he had to walk into a roomful of people just like Huntington—hopefully most without his particular predilections—and pretend he belonged.

And he had to do it with the woman who personified that world to him. Also pretending he belonged.

Something, he realized, he hadn't explained to her yet. At least he was driving, so he didn't have to look at her. He drew in a deep breath and took the plunge.

"Since I've already made you so angry, I might as well finish the job. We have to talk about tonight."

"I'm not angry."

He flicked her a sideways glance. "You could have fooled me."

"Oh, I was angry. But it was a reflex, an old reflex I thought I was over. You didn't deserve it, you were only doing your job. That I feel that job is unnecessary is irrelevant. I'm sorry."

It was as pretty an apology as he'd ever gotten. And he had no idea what to say. Her ex probably would. He'd accept gracefully, charmingly and everything would be smoothed over with consummate skill.

Finally, he decided the only thing he could do was talk normally, as if they'd reverted to the time before tonight, and hope she'd understand. "Think of it as Homeland Security on a smaller scale. Parts are annoying, but the final result is safety."

He sensed her looking at him, but had to negotiate a turn.

"Interesting analogy," was all she said, but in the slightly more relaxed tone of her voice he read her understanding of his unspoken acceptance of her apology. For a moment silence spun out, until she asked, "What about tonight?"

He'd almost forgotten. And now he had to hit her with something that would likely be even more annoying than the orders given for her security.

"We—Redstone Security, I mean—try to maintain a very low profile," he said.

"I know," she said. "I know you try to keep interaction even inside Redstone to a minimum, in case you have to work on the inside."

He nodded. "Good thing bad apples at Redstone are about as rare as five-leaf clovers. You're cleaning up after the only one ever found at Headquarters."

"I know. But it must be exciting, to travel all over the world. Redstone is just about everywhere, in some form."

"It has its moments."

"Liana told me you returned only a few months ago from a job in Rio de Janeiro."

Beck, he thought. What was it about love that made you turn into a fount of information you normally wouldn't share with anyone?

"Yes," he said.

"She said you cleaned up a mess that even Draven had doubts that one man could handle."

"Logan Beck talks too much."

She laughed, and suddenly he understood why the ex-cop couldn't seem to keep anything from his redheaded siren. Who wouldn't say anything to keep a laugh like that coming?

"So, what about tonight?"

"That low profile means that tonight, I'm not Redstone Security."

"All right," she said.

He waited, silently, for her to get the point.

"What are you, then?"

He knew she was smart; hell, he knew she was damn near brilliant, so it had to be just that the possibility would never in a million years occur to her. He couldn't blame her. On appearances alone it was likely no one would believe it. A classy, pure lady like Lilith Mercer with a street thug like him?

"And to think I could have been an accountant, wrestling with spreadsheets instead of this," he muttered.

"You?" She almost yelped it. "An accountant?"

"Is that so impossible?" He wasn't sure whether to be offended or not. "I have a perfectly good business degree."

It must have sounded in his voice, because she hastened to say, "Oh, please. It's just that I can't picture you being happy behind a desk."

Since he'd used the same argument with Josh when he'd asked for the chance at Redstone Security, he felt his irritation fade.

"I wasn't. I tried, for nearly a year. In Marketing and Distribution, like a good little worker bee." He grimaced. "Don't get me wrong, that office at Redstone is a lot better than most places, but it just…"

"Wasn't you," she finished. "I can't imagine you being anything but miserable."

"I was. But I thought I owed it to Josh."

She shifted in her seat then. "All anyone he's helped ever owes Josh is to make the absolute most of the chance he's given them. That's all he ever wants or expects."

"I know. Now. Then I thought I was letting him down."

She was quiet for a moment. "I'm guessing he figured out how unhappy you were."

He flicked a glance at her again. She was smiling, knowing as all of Redstone did, what came first with their boss.

"Yes, he did." He turned his attention back to the road. "He asked what I really wanted. I told him."

"And thus a match made in heaven."

He didn't dare look at her again. "Something like that."

"And you've been happy?"

"Yes." Except when it cost someone I was just falling in love with her life.

That the feelings he'd had then were minuscule compared to what he was feeling now was something he didn't want to think about, didn't dare think about, not now.

And they still hadn't gotten to it. They had, however, reached the hotel where the gala was to be held.

"Sorry I can't have the valets park it," he said as he turned away from the booth outside the hotel lobby. "There are some things in this car we wouldn't want the hassle of explaining. All with permits, but convincing the police of that would be…time-consuming."

She merely nodded. He found a spot, parked, shut the car off, then turned in the driver's seat to look at her.

"Tonight," he began, determined to finish it now.

"You're not security," she repeated dutifully. "So what are you?"

"Your date."

She stared at him. To his chagrin, color flooded her face. He heard her take a quick, deep breath. Obviously he'd shocked her, although he couldn't help thinking she should have seen this as the most logical approach.

Her reaction needled him, and for the second time tonight he overreacted, knowing he was doing it even as he spoke.

"Or," he said, drawing the words out and accompanying them with the smile of invitation he used only when working, "if you'd rather, your lover."

Chapter 12

Lilith told herself it was her imagination, that not everyone in the room was going quiet and staring at them, but she was having trouble convincing herself when heads kept turning.

She was still a little breathless from that moment in the car when Tony had uttered the words that had stolen her breath in the first place.

She'd felt hot and cold and tangled inside, and only years of practice had allowed her to face him with any semblance of calm and ask levelly, "And just how should I introduce you?"

"Antonio Diego Alvera Bernard," he'd said, throwing the name out as if it were some sort of challenge.

As, perhaps, it was.

Now that they were inside and walking through the ballroom, she realized she was so off-balance from what he'd said that she was probably acting exactly as he'd wanted her to. And was fairly sure that had been his plan—to make her act like a woman out for an evening with a lover, perhaps a new one, on edge and a little uncertain. Which, she knew, was how most people would interpret the tension between them.

Except for those wondering what a guy like Tony Alvera was doing with a woman old enough to be…

She'd forgotten the demise of her doting aunt analogy, and she wasn't sure what to put in its place.

A woman old enough to be very foolish will probably do nicely, she told herself sternly.

If she'd known this was going to be the approach tonight, that they would be masquerading as two people on a formal date, she would have had time to think of what to say. But she hadn't, so now she had to think on the fly. The temptation to just play up the facade, to play it as if it were true, to act as if there was truly something between them, was so incredibly tempting that she knew it was dangerous.

…if you'd rather, your lover.

She felt a sudden rush of heat, and feared she must be as red as her dress.

"Lilith! You look wonderful."

She turned to see Alicia Cramer, a woman she knew from the organization this fund-raiser was for. The woman was a five-foot powerhouse who had done more to bring research money into the field than anyone except Josh himself, and for that Lilith was willing to overlook her somewhat haughty manner. Most of the time.

But right now she was eyeing Tony Alvera like a person who'd just seen something impossible. True, she had always come to this function alone, in fact had never brought anyone who wasn't a business relationship or someone she'd hoped would respond to the fund-raising aspect of the evening, but there was much more to Alicia's avidly curious inspection.

And so it begins, she thought.

"Alicia, how are you?" she said with every evidence of delight, hoping her tone would foster reality.

"I'm fine, thank you," Alicia said, but she was still eyeing Tony. And there was a hint of doubt in her gaze, something that wasn't quite puzzlement and wasn't quite distrust, but some combination leavened with a touch of fear that made Lilith feel defensive. She looked as if she were wondering if someone had left a door open somewhere, letting him wander in off the street.

As if, Lilith thought, he wasn't the hottest man in the room. The defensiveness sparked.

"Meet Antonio Diego Alvera Bernard," she said, rolling out his full name grandly and purposefully making her voice sound as if she were introducing visiting royalty.

Then she waited; Alicia was too smoothly polished to be rude, but Lilith expected at the least an arched brow as she contemplated the unlikely couple they made.

If Tony was surprised at her deferential introduction, he didn't let it show. Instead he played along with her perfectly, took the uncertain woman's hand and gave her a courtly bow.

"My deepest pleasure, madame," he said, in a formal voice and an old-world inflection Lilith had never heard from him. "It is an honor to be here on such a worthwhile occasion."

To Lilith's amazement, the supercilious Alicia actually blushed.

Why are you surprised? she asked herself. He's made you blush more than once. But for, she had to admit ruefully, very different reasons.

Or maybe not, she thought as she watched him work on Alicia as if she were any woman he'd set out to charm. His reputation in that arena was clearly well earned. Lilith remembered Liana's frequent jokes about the fact that all Tony's sources in official places seemed to be female. Now that she was seeing him in action firsthand, she understood why.

Which set her to wondering why he hadn't used the charm he obviously had in abundance on her. Not that she would be susceptible to it; she'd learned to distrust charm the hard way.

But he hadn't even tried to beguile her into cooperating with him. He'd just ordered. Arrogantly.

Of course, she worked for Redstone. Not that that stopped him from, however teasingly, exercising that charm on, say, Liana, even though her love for Logan Beck made her immune. And that had also been during a Redstone assignment, so that wasn't the difference, either.

Perhaps he just saved the charm for women closer to his own age. But then, he'd just turned it on full bore for Alicia, who was at least sixty-five.

So maybe it's just you, she thought.

She nearly laughed at the glumness of her own thought; she normally wasn't given to such absurdities. It was, she knew, most likely a combination of factors, probably including the fact that she apparently had the ability to make him angry. Why, she didn't know, but assumed it was because he knew this was a lot of wasted time, that no one was really out to get her, and while he was tied up doing this, no doubt agents dealing with real, serious situations for Redstone could be using his help.

But what she also didn't know, and what unsettled her even more, was why this even mattered to her. Now, *that,* she told herself, was the height of absurdity.

"Lilith?"

She snapped back to the present with such a jolt she thought it must have been obvious to everyone. Fortunately, while she'd been lost in silly contemplation, Alicia had moved on, obviously deciding against evicting the dangerous-looking man Lilith had brought into their midst. The man who was looking at her curiously.

"That effortless charm of yours is amazing," she said, hoping he hadn't read her foolish thoughts in her face.

"That *charm,*" he snapped, startling her, "is effortless because it's meaningless. I learned it just like I learned what fork to use. I honed it because it worked. It's as put on as this—" he tugged at one lapel of the expensive tuxedo "—is. I'm a fake, hadn't you realized?"

Lilith stared at him; clearly she'd finally hit a nerve. That it was this surprised her. Could he really think that learning such skills late made them any less real? Could he—

"Lilith!"

She turned at the hail, and found herself face-to-face with Grace O'Conner Draven.

True pleasure rang in her voice as she exclaimed, "Grace!"

The two women hugged genuinely. She hadn't seen Grace much since the wedding. Not only was she still one of Redstone's most important cogs, designer and builder of airstrips all over the world, but she had become a frequent spokeswoman for the Back to Life Foundation that was the beneficiary of tonight's fund-raiser.

As one of the first recipients of Ian Gamble's incredible prosthetic foot, she was the perfect choice. No one who looked at the slender, lovely woman with the short, wispy dark hair and the vivid blue eyes would ever guess she'd been through such hell. Trapped by tons of debris after a violent earthquake in Turkey, her right foot crushed beyond repair, Grace had survived. She'd hung on long enough for the man who would eventually become her husband to reach her.

And she'd survived what he'd had to do to her to save her life.

Of course, Lilith knew there were those who would say that being married to John Draven would require more courage than either of those. Lilith wasn't one of them; from the first time she'd seen them together she'd known they had what she'd never had, that magical, incredible connection of two people completely right for each other and deeply in love.

"Mrs. Draven." Tony spoke in that formal tone again, yet this time it was laced with a respect that made it sound very different than when he'd spoken to Alicia Cramer. Of course, this was the wife of his boss, the head of Redstone Security.

And Lilith realized he'd waited until there was no one in earshot to speak, no one to hear that he knew who she was. And that he addressed her by her married name, something only those inside Redstone ever used. To the world she was still Grace O'Conner, out of the need to keep her husband's position at Redstone as low profile as possible.

"Mr. Alvera," Grace answered, a teasing glint in her eyes. "My, but you do clean up nice."

Doesn't he just? Lilith muttered inwardly.

Before her thoughts could spin out of control again, there were others there, and Tony and Grace both put on a show of just having met. Grace obviously realized—or perhaps she knew, given whom she shared pillow talk with—that he was working, and had quickly caught on that he was here undercover. Lilith knew Draven would never share details of an ongoing investigation, but he was madly, crazily in love with his wife, and Grace was a smart, perceptive woman.

"And don't you two make a couple?" Grace added.

Lilith blinked. She sensed Tony going very still. Grace went on cheerfully.

"You so golden, him so dark, and both gorgeous. It's hardly fair to us ordinary folk. I don't know who people are going to think got lucky," Grace added with a teasing smile.

More likely they'll wonder how much I had to pay the young stud to escort me, Lilith thought dryly.

She tried to mentally slap herself for the thought. She knew she was attractive enough, and that people rarely believed she was in her mid-forties. She told herself her uncertainty about her personal appeal was a legacy from Daniel that she needed to be rid of, but that was easier said than done.

"I'd guess," Tony was saying easily, "they're all simply wondering why a classy, uptown lady like her is with a reprobate like me."

Grace snorted inelegantly, rolling her eyes at him. "Oh,

please. I can't speak for the males in the room, but no woman on the planet will wonder that."

Lilith barely stopped herself from echoing the opinion, since she'd thought it herself just minutes ago. She envied Grace her ease with the man, and supposed it stemmed from the fact that he worked for her husband. She probably knew him much better than Lilith did, although Lilith couldn't help wondering if anyone really knew this man.

When Grace walked away moments later, toward the raised dais where she would make her impassioned speech for the support of the foundation—and if asked, not hesitate to lift the hem of her sleek, blue satin dress to show the prosthetic foot that had, in its way, brought her here tonight—Tony spoke as if that moment of oddly still tension had never occurred.

"Anyone who didn't know would be stunned to learn she'd lost a foot."

"Which is," Lilith said, responding to his normal tone with the best one she could manage, "the point of the evening. Ian's work in prosthetics is cutting edge, and Josh will fund him endlessly, but getting the prosthetics to people who need them is what the Back to Life Foundation does best."

"Sounds like you could be up there touting," Tony observed.

"I could," Lilith said. "I have. Grace is a good friend, and I admire her. She makes this issue personal for me."

"And personal makes you passionate."

She didn't think he meant it as a double entendre but didn't dare look at him to find out. "Yes," she said simply.

And with that she pulled herself together and began to do what she was here for, to work the room. As a representative of Redstone, she knew her job; in a way she was working as much here as she did in her office.

But as she went around the room, greeting those she knew warmly, encouraging them to be even more generous than last year, greeting strangers even more warmly, welcoming them to this chance to make a difference, she couldn't help but be aware of the frequent looks they were garnering. She would have assumed the stares were for all the reasons she'd expected them, but Grace's words made her wonder now.

She introduced Tony by name only—forgoing now the full, grand introduction she'd given him to the haughty Alicia—and he took it from there. He was, it quickly became clear, quite capable of handling himself in this setting, of turning on that easy charm, although to her it didn't quite mask the edgy hyperalertness.

But after a while Lilith quit worrying and became almost amused at the way women responded with blushing pleasure and fascination, and men reacted with a wariness usually accompanied by a furrow between the eyebrows, as if they weren't sure this man was quite domesticated.

Occasionally she caught women—some she knew, some she didn't—glancing at her with an expression that was unmistakably envious.

…no woman on the planet will wonder…

No, Lilith thought, she didn't suppose they would. And as she gave him a sideways look, saw that unexpected dimple flash as he made another of his courtly bows, noticed yet again how devastatingly attractive he was in that perfectly fitted tux, how he managed to exude that charm and yet never lose that edginess, she caught herself wishing, for just the tiniest moment, that it was real.

Chapter 13

Tony smothered a yawn. He was on his third cup of coffee and it wasn't even nine o'clock yet. This did not bode well.

As he waited in the back of the small bodega, watching people—mostly older women or young ones with children in tow picking up groceries; later it would be men who migrated to the wine shop along one side—come and go, he tried to distract himself by remembering when he had come to this place himself, running errands for his mother. It didn't work.

He shook his head in an effort to clear it, knowing he was walking a dangerous line. The combination of endless tension and tiredness was hardly the best for someone in his line of work.

But sleep had not been in the cards for him again last night. In fact, he hadn't had much sleep since that blasted charity fund-raiser on Tuesday night. It was crazy, it made no sense, but going in there as Lilith's date, knowing everyone other than Grace and perhaps a few others from Redstone assumed they were together as a couple, had somehow changed everything.

And it wasn't simply that his imagination had run amok, leaping from what he guessed they were thinking to his own seemingly uncontrollable fantasies. It was more that he wanted them not to be fantasies. He wanted what everyone in that room was thinking to be true. He wanted their assumptions that when he and Lilith left that glittering affair, they would do it together, that wherever they went back to, it would be together, that when they went to bed, it would be together.

Need cramped him up yet again, and he fought it with the grim determination he'd learned at a very early age. But at that age, he hadn't known this kind of need even existed.

And he certainly never, ever would have pictured himself feeling like this over a woman like Lilith Mercer.

He should, he knew now, never have taken this assignment. When she'd been safely out of his sphere, he'd been able to deal, able to laugh at himself for his ridiculous feelings for a woman so far out of his reach. But now, now that he'd spent days with her constantly in his mind if not always his presence, that barrier of distance was shattered, and he didn't know if he could ever rebuild it.

That he would have to, he knew. Somehow. And sooner rather than later, since there hadn't been a trace of a problem since the trip wire four days ago.

When his cell phone had signaled a text message early this morning, he'd been getting ready to go pick Lilith up at her condo—and postponing figuring out exactly what was going to happen this weekend. At least for today and tomorrow she would be tucked safely inside Redstone Headquarters for the day; he hadn't even dared to ask if she had plans for the weekend.

A sudden vision of himself playing bodyguard to Lilith on a date with some nebulous upper-crust type slammed into him, making him feel as if he'd taken a roundhouse punch to the gut. He had to fight for breath, stunned at his own reaction.

The image played out. Dinner, maybe a movie, Lilith in that

sexy red number from the Christmas party—never mind that it was hardly something she'd wear out on an ordinary night—that unknown man who looked too much like her ex-husband holding her hand as they watched some chick flick that would inspire them to go home and reenact the love scenes….

How the hell do I keep from killing the guy?

He shook his head again, this time at least dispelling the remnants of the video loop his sleep-deprived brain insisted on running. He knew he was in trouble when he was thinking of murdering some imagined character that might not even exist.

The last time he'd felt anything like this, Lisa had died. And what he'd felt then hadn't had the chance to become what he was feeling now.

He made himself focus. Although there had been no sign or mention of a man in her life, he simply couldn't picture a woman like Lilith not having them constantly buzzing around her like flies.

Or fluttering, like that pompous, deceptively pretty butterfly Huntington.

He used those images, the memory of how the man had spoken to her, to jab himself back to the matter at hand. With a glance at his watch, he wondered if Rico was going to show up at all.

The text message this morning had simply told him to be here by nine. More accurately, it had said only, La Bodega—9:00 a.m. The implication being, of course, that Rico had something to tell him.

Or maybe it's a setup, he thought. Maybe they're finally coming after me to show me how you don't ever really leave the neighborhood.

He knew he was tired when he started having paranoid ideas like that. If they'd wanted him dead, he would have been long ago. But he'd never really been that active in the ES 13s, he'd pulled his stunt with Josh before he'd gotten in too deep. In fact, that stunt had been a sort of proving ground dare, to find some rich guy and rip him off, bringing the proceeds back to Chaco, who at the time was the leader.

Now he was in Pelican Bay, doing the hardest of hard time for killing three civilians and two cops in a shoot-out during a drug bust gone bad.

One of those civilians had been fifteen-year-old Lucinda Alvera.

Maybe that was why they'd let him go, Tony thought, taking a final sip of the coffee that was now cooled to lukewarm. They understood death and what it meant. Most of them had lost somebody, many of them somebody they'd loved as he'd loved Lucy.

He tossed the cup into the wastebasket beside him. The irony of that possibility, that Lucy's life had been the price of his ticket out, bit deep and hard, and his jaw clenched.

He'd just decided he'd had enough of hanging around this place that was haunted for him when the front door opened again, the jingle of the old-fashioned bell attached to it a cheerful sound amid the grim recollections. He looked that way.

Rico.

With the swagger typical of ES 13s, he called out an over-exuberant greeting to old man Martinez, who watched the gangster warily as he walked toward the back of the bodega. But, Tony noticed, the bluster vanished and Rico looked around carefully before he approached.

"You owe me a coat, man."

"If it's worth it, you got it." Tony cut to the chase. "What?"

"One of my guys, Carlito, he knows a guy who knows a guy who—"

"I don't need the history. Just give it to me."

"That's the problem with people these days, y'know? No respect for the rituals."

"Plenty of respect," Tony said. "No time. You want money in the pocket of that coat, *digame*."

At the order to just tell him, Rico shrugged. "A guy did time in Chino. Cell mate with a guy who did time with a guy—"

He stopped when Tony's gaze narrowed, then shrugged again and went on. "End of the string is some guy in one of those lightweight places, you know? Private, minimum security? Out in Baker. He knew some guy there who used to work for that place, Redstone. He talked a lot about payback, for them putting him in jail. Mentioned some woman who took his place."

Tony nearly stopped breathing.

"That your friend's ex?" Rico asked.

"Could be," Tony said, keeping it vague. "I'm not sure what she does. This guy got a name?" he asked, although he knew perfectly well who it had to be.

"My friend, he says it's Stan. Don't know any more than that."

Stan Chilton. The ramifications started to rapid-fire in Tony's mind, and he had to yank himself back to the present. "I need to talk to this friend of yours."

Rico pondered this for a moment, and Tony guessed he was considering just how much payment he could push for.

"Could be arranged."

"You just earned yourself a coat," Tony said. "With enough to buy another one in the pocket."

Rico laughed. "Don't need two coats, man. Lots better things to spend it on."

"Keep going," Tony said. "You find me more, you'll be able to buy a lot of them."

Rico grinned. "I find out more, I want that fancy car you drive, *mijo*."

Tony laughed, but his mind was already racing ahead. This turned everything around. If the person behind this was Stan Chilton, the former head of Redstone R&D, who had left in ignominy after being caught selling Ian Gamble's exclusive research, then the whole complexion of this had changed.

As soon as he was back in his car he would make the first call to Draven, using the hands-free Bluetooth system so he could be on his way to Redstone Headquarters at the same time. It suddenly seemed imperative that he get there as soon as he could.

Lilith was going to have to take this more seriously now; for the first time there was something more, however tenuous, than simply Josh's innate worry about his people. There was outside evidence that someone truly had it in for her, and while hearsay wasn't admissible in a courtroom, it was more than enough for Tony Alvera when it came to Lilith's safety.

He whipped the Redstone car quickly away from the curb as the phone rang on the other end. As he waited for Draven to answer, he found himself grimacing as he faced a thought he didn't want to analyze just yet but couldn't deny, either.

He'd been a lot happier when he'd been convinced the person behind the threat to Lilith was her ex-husband.

Chapter 14

"It's about ten times removed from firsthand hearsay," Tony said.

John Draven looked at him and nodded. "I got that."

"I'm just saying," Tony said, a bit uncomfortable under his boss's steady scrutiny.

"I know."

"It made more sense that it was her ex," he said, wondering if it sounded as lame as he felt it did. "Why would Chilton go after her? It's not like she had anything to do with him going to prison. She just came in to clean up the mess he left behind."

"If Chilton was man enough to come after the ones who really put him where he was, which would be Sam and Ian and me, he probably wouldn't have done what he did in the first place."

Tony couldn't argue with that cogent and concise argument, so didn't even try. "My contact's going to set up a meet with the guy who was in the slam with Chilton. Later today, I hope. I'll see if I can get any more."

Draven nodded. And then, in a way that even Tony knew

never would have happened before his marriage to Grace, he went on, almost conversationally. "Come in handy sometimes, those contacts."

It struck Tony, not for the first time, that it was rather amazing that Draven hadn't had using those contacts in mind from the moment he'd found out about him. In need of the distraction, he asked his boss something he'd always wondered.

"When you dug into my background sixteen years ago, how hard did you push Josh to toss me back where I belonged?"

Draven's legendary cool didn't waver. "Josh never asked me to do a background check on you."

"But you did," Tony said; he knew his boss well enough by now to know that unless directly ordered not to, Draven checked out everyone that might have access to *his* boss.

Draven's mouth twitched. "Of course."

"So?"

"I didn't. It's who Josh is, and it's not my place or desire to change that." He gave Tony a sideways look before adding, "I did push him to just give you that hand up, then let you sink or swim on your own."

"But when I finished school he took me into Redstone instead."

"I knew he would. I also knew you wouldn't be happy at a desk job, no matter how much business or accounting they crammed into your head."

"But you didn't figure I'd end up working for you someday, did you, *jefe?*"

Draven gave a one-shouldered shrug. "Josh is the real boss. I do what he wants."

Then, after a silent moment reminiscent of the old Draven, the onetime man of fewer words than anybody at Redstone except St. John, he again elaborated. "I didn't want you here just because of where you came from."

Tony's brow furrowed at the ambiguity of the statement. "You didn't want me because of that, or not *only* because of that?"

Draven's mouth twitched again. "Yes," he said. "The first because I thought that if I ever needed to send you back to the streets on a case, you might lose everything you'd gained."

Startled, Tony blinked. He'd heard the legends, of course, about this man before he'd ever come to work for him. You didn't work at Redstone long in any capacity before you heard about the head of the most famous and efficient private, company-run security team in the world. One of those legends— one Tony suspected was true—had both Josh and Draven approached by governments from various countries about privately contracting out for official security, but turning down the lucrative offers; they were Redstone, and that was enough.

The rest were the more common kind of thing, that Draven had more than once made a suspect confess just by the simple fact of his presence, that there was something in his eyes that made even the most brazen of bad guys quiver. Tony believed it; some combination of where he'd been, what he'd done and what he'd seen made him the most intimidating man he'd ever encountered, and he'd encountered a few on the streets of L.A.

But he'd always thought of Draven as focused strictly on that security; you didn't run a team as good as his, in as many places as Redstone had outposts around the world, without that kind of dedication.

But now it seemed Draven apparently subscribed to Josh's other doctrine as well—a hand up, not a hand out, to anyone willing to work for it.

"As for the other," Draven said, "I was afraid you'd be a loose cannon."

"And now?" Tony asked.

"You are a loose cannon," Draven said, and this time he grinned, a rare enough occurrence that it caught Tony off guard. "But I know you won't fire without just cause, so I don't worry about it much."

As a vote of confidence, Tony thought, it didn't come much

higher than that, not from John Draven. "You have Hill assigned to anything yet?"

"Not yet, it's been relatively quiet of late. You need her?"

"On call, maybe. In case that meeting comes up and I can't get back in time to see Lilith home."

Draven nodded. "I'll have her stand by."

"And stay with her until I get there."

Draven didn't ask, only nodded. And as he left the airport office of Redstone Security, Tony knew why.

Draven realized as well as he did now that the threat was real.

"Ms. Mercer?"

At the soft inquiry from the doorway, Lilith looked up, quashing a wince as her shoulder—and backside—reminded her of the tumble she'd taken.

A woman stood there, someone she'd never seen before, with straight, medium brown hair tied back and a quiet sort of face. Since Lilith knew almost everyone in the building that was odd, and if this was any place but Redstone she might worry that whatever threat she faced had found its way here.

But as she studied the plain, seemingly deferential figure before her, she couldn't imagine the woman doing anything in the least aggressive, let alone trying to hurt anyone. "Can I help you?"

"I'm Taylor Hill. Mr. Draven sent me. I'm here to see you home, whenever you're ready."

Automatically, Lilith glanced at the clock. It was a bit early for her to call it quits, although she'd been having trouble focusing this afternoon, ever since Tony had called her with the information he'd discovered about Stan Chilton.

She opened her mouth to ask where Tony was, but realized this young woman probably wouldn't know, anyway. Besides, she thought ruefully, with her luck lately, the question would come out sounding like a petulant whine.

She did wonder where he was, though. And with no small

qualm; it would hardly take a researcher—albeit that was pretty much what she was—to figure out that he hadn't come across the bit of information about Chilton at the local library.

She knew more about Tony now than she had; she'd rather delicately picked Liana's brain, knowing that Logan, and through him Liana, had to know a lot more than she did; she'd been merely a slightly involved bystander during the investigation of Logan's case. Tony had kept her in the loop, but their talks had been purely business.

Purely business, she thought again now. It struck her then that after that first day in her office, he'd never again turned upon her any of the oozing charm she'd seen him use to such effect on just about any other breathing female. Even Alicia, at the charity fund-raiser; if she hadn't seen it herself, she would have sworn the woman who'd been called a termagant more than once would be immune to such things.

The memory in turn made her think he'd been acting rather oddly ever since then. As if there were some kind of impenetrable wall between them.

Maybe that was why this woman was here instead. Not because Tony was busy, but because he didn't *want* to be here. Didn't want to be around her.

Perhaps he'd even asked to be taken off the case, she thought. Although now that it appeared there really *was* a case, that it wasn't just Josh's overprotectiveness, she found that hard to believe. Nobody who worked for Draven, or Josh, walked out in the middle of a job. Redstone simply didn't hire those kinds of people.

So she tried to find out, discreetly.

"Alvera afraid he's going to get sucked into another black-tie event?" she asked, with what she thought was a credible show of carefree good humor.

The woman never cracked a smile. "I wouldn't know, ma'am."

Ma'am.

Well, that put her solidly in her place, didn't it? Lilith thought. To this young thing, that's what she was. One foot in the grave. She refrained from asking Taylor how old she was. If her age started with a three rather than a two she'd be surprised.

Giving herself a mental shake, Lilith said briskly, "I won't be ready for a half hour or so, if you want to go find some coffee or something."

"That's fine. I'll be back in thirty minutes."

"On the dot," Lilith heard in her head, as if the young woman had said the words. Somehow she thought she probably would. If she'd said she needed thirty-two minutes, Taylor would have said and done exactly that. Lilith wondered what her story was. She'd have to ask Tony.

Assuming, of course, she ever saw him again.

Chapter 15

Alejandro "Loco" Degas wasn't going to be much more help, Tony thought. The man was of the sullen sort, marked by his life in ways that could never be changed. Since Tony guessed he was still under thirty, he'd apparently given up early. Not that he could blame him; at sixteen he'd been ready to give up himself, and if not for a knife, his own reckless decision and the intervention of Josh Redstone, he would have.

The only thing he'd gained from this meeting was the information that Chilton had apparently had help. Tony had figured that out himself already; Chilton didn't have the brains and hadn't been inside long enough to develop on his own the kind of network something like this would take. It was tougher to set up something like this in the minimum-security lockups, anyway; not many hit men or their ilk ended up there, unless they were undiscovered. In his experience, white-collar criminals, once they were caught, tended to crumple. They just weren't tough enough. Ruthless, yes, but prison tough? No.

Despite the lack of really solid information, he paid the man the agreed upon amount anyway and repeated the offer of more if anything else was turned up.

"I'm not a cop, and I don't have to go to court and prove any of this," he told both Degas and Rico, who had insisted on umpiring this meeting. "This is—" he almost stumbled and said the word *personal,* but recovered "—private, and even if it's second-hand hearsay or rumors, I want to hear it."

As he drove out of the neighborhood he'd once inhabited— he hesitated to say lived in—he wondered again if that help had been inside or outside. He wished he could somehow tie it back to Daniel Huntington, but Chino and the privately run minimum-security prison in Baker were different worlds as much as were these streets and the kinder, gentler streets of Bel Air or Beverly Hills.

Of course, Lilith wouldn't be happy if he did that.

And there it was again, just that quickly, eating at him, gnawing at a sore place somewhere inside him that no amount of effort could let him ignore.

She'd been relieved that it hadn't been her ex-husband.

At first, he'd tried to tell himself he'd imagined her reaction; after all, he'd told her over the phone about Chilton, he hadn't been there to see her face. But he knew, with every ounce of that gut instinct he'd developed, every bit of perception Draven had hammered into him in the past six years, that she'd been relieved. It had been in the tone of her voice when she'd said, "Not Daniel?" and in the tiny sigh he'd barely heard when he'd confirmed that.

He'd cautioned her about the source of the information, the tenuousness of the lead, but he knew that had been as much to try to convince himself as her. This lead felt right, and wishing it had been Huntington wouldn't change that.

He caught himself letting the speedometer creep upward far enough past the speed limit to draw any cop's eye. He backed off, wondering how he could be so eager to get to Lilith's and so reluctant at the same time.

He'd told Draven to have Hill stay until he got there, so it wasn't as though he had a choice. Besides, he wanted to do a check of her condo once more, make sure nothing had changed since the last time, and he was the only one who could do that.

Even the thought rang hollow; Lilith was a perceptive, observant woman, and if anything had changed she would notice. Especially now that even she was convinced there was at least some danger to her.

He rubbed his eyes as he drove, suddenly feeling much more tired than even his last few nights of little sleep warranted. Perhaps he should just let the woman handle it, take a break from all this.

But he couldn't. He didn't know Taylor Hill, and while if Draven said she was good, she was good, he didn't *know* that himself.

The realization that hit him then nearly stunned him. He trusted John Draven with his life. Anyone at Redstone would, knowing there was no one better at keeping himself and those in his charge alive and safe. And yet here he was, doubting Draven's faultless judgment in this. Why?

The answer was painfully clear.

Because it was Lilith. And when it came to Lilith, he didn't trust anyone but himself to keep her safe.

"Right," he muttered to himself. "And who's going to keep her safe from you?"

"That," he said aloud into the silence of the car, "is up to you as much as keeping her alive is."

He nearly groaned at the realization he was not only talking to himself but answering himself.

When he pulled into the parking area at the condo, he spotted the car Hill had driven right away, since it was one of the cars from the pool security had access to. It was parked next to

Lilith's dark gray coupe, which had remained in its assigned spot since all this had started.

She'd told him that the other spot was her neighbor's, but since the woman didn't have a car, it wasn't used, and that Mrs. Tilly had offered it to her any time she needed it. It was where he usually parked, but now obviously he'd be relegated to the visitors' section.

Visitor. Yeah, that's what he was, all right. Just a temporary presence in her life, and one she'd like to be rid of as soon as possible, no doubt. As she would be, as soon as this was resolved. She'd go back to her busy, productive, pleasant life, and he'd go back to his busy, productive, empty one, and they'd both think of this as nothing but an interruption in those lives.

Right.

He'd be thinking of this for the rest of that miserable life. Thinking of how close he'd been to the impossible, how he'd had a taste of being with her, only to learn for good that his world, no matter how it had changed, did not blend well with her world.

Because it wasn't really his world that was the problem.

It was him.

He glanced down at the newel posts as he reached the top of the stairs. The grooves from the tightly strung wire were visible, but not glaring.

Kind of like you, he thought wryly. Strung tight but hiding it.

At least, he hoped he was hiding it. From Lilith, anyway.

After he knocked it seemed to take forever for the door to open. He told himself to rein it in, it should take a couple of minutes if Hill was doing her job. And when it did open, it was indeed the new Redstone agent.

Except…she was smiling. Laughing, actually, and it transformed her. No longer was she a plain, ordinary, fade-into-the-background woman. Her eyes fairly sparkled, and for the first time he noticed that they were an unusual shade of hazel flecked with gold. Odd, he thought, he was usually pretty good at details like that.

"Something funny I missed?" he asked as she stood back to let him in.

"No," Hill said. "We were just talking."

"About?" he asked before he could stop himself.

She laughed, and he sensed it was a continuation of the one that had left her face so animated. "Men," she said pointedly.

His mouth twisted wryly. Great. Men, or one man in particular?

As soon as he thought it, he nearly laughed, too. Get over yourself, Alvera. It's not all about you.

He stepped inside and immediately spotted Lilith, who was coming out of the kitchen with a coffee mug in her hand. She, too, was smiling, in a way he hadn't seen since all this had started. As if she, too, had just been laughing and the glee lingered.

He'd never seen her look like that. Even at the Christmas party where he'd first seen her, she'd been restrained, polished...regal had been the word that had come to his mind then.

But then, he told himself as he stood there staring at her, unable to help himself, she'd been two years closer to the hell her ex-husband had put her through. Perhaps that was the answer.

Or perhaps it was just that she and Taylor Hill had hit it off.

Or perhaps, he told himself with an inward grimace, she just doesn't like being around you.

"—asked if you wanted coffee, there's some left."

She was standing in front of him now, a faintly puzzled expression on her face, and he realized she must have already asked him once.

"No."

It sounded abrupt, almost rude, even to his own ears, but it was all he could manage.

"You can leave now, Hill," he said, without looking at the woman.

Lilith blinked. Then she looked at the other woman. "Or you can stay, Taylor. I was enjoying your company."

The implication wasn't lost on Tony, and his jaw tightened.

"You're relieved," he said, more fiercely this time, making sure she realized it was an order, gambling she was too new at the job to want to risk arguing with him. That this was bubbling up out of some silly resentment that Lilith was so relaxed and able to laugh was something he knew on some level, but refused to think about.

To his surprise, Hill stood her ground. "I'd say that's up to Lilith. This is her home."

The two women exchanged a look that made him exceptionally nervous. And made him wonder again exactly what men—or man—they'd been talking about.

"It's all right, Taylor," Lilith said. "We do have some things to discuss."

We do? Tony thought, but said nothing, not wanting anything to delay Hill's quick departure. Why he wanted her gone, and right now, was another thing he didn't want to think about.

Hill hesitated, then nodded. She closed the door quietly behind her as she left.

"Well, that was sufficiently rude."

Stung, he answered before he thought. "What did you expect from somebody like me?"

She drew back slightly. A furrow appeared between her brows as she studied him. The silence spun out long enough to make him uncomfortable, long enough for him to wonder where the hell his professionalism had vanished to.

"I expected," she said finally, "the courtesy anyone from Redstone shows anyone else from Redstone. I expected you to be polite, perhaps even use a little of your famous charm. Not to charge in here and practically throw out a young woman who was only here because you asked her to be."

He felt the jab of guilt because he knew those first and last words were true. But somehow the only thing he could focus on was the other thing she'd said in between.

Famous charm?

He knew it was absurd to get hung up on that amid everything else. But something about the way she had said it was poking at him, and he didn't know why.

It wasn't that he didn't realize what she meant. He'd learned charm at a time when he still wasn't certain he was really going to escape the streets for good. So he hadn't hesitated to use it, justifying it with the excuse that he had to use whatever tools he had if he was going to truly get out.

He had gotten out. And then had come Lisa. And what had happened then had changed everything. Including his use of his *famous charm.*

But Lilith didn't know about Lisa. Even Josh didn't know, not all the details, anyway. No one did, except St. John. And perhaps Draven; St. John might have told him if for no other reason than he'd be thinking maybe Draven should keep an eye on him, see if it was going to affect his work.

But he'd shown them it wouldn't, and now, all these years later, he was sure they'd forgotten all about it.

It was only he who couldn't forget that he'd as good as killed Lisa with his own hands.

Chapter 16

"Sorry to interrupt your little party," Tony muttered, apparently just noticing that there were dishes and Chinese takeout cartons on the coffee table.

"Were we not supposed to eat without your permission?"

Lilith's expression was sweet, her tone deadly. She saw that Tony didn't miss it. But then, it should have been obvious to even the most muddled male mind that he'd crossed a line. And she knew he was very far from stupid, and it didn't take a genius to realize what that line was.

"I am not your ex," he said, seeming to try for a calm, even tone, although he didn't quite achieve it. As if the gruffness had merely been a rough throat, he gave a halfhearted cough. She wondered why he even tried.

"No," Lilith said after a moment. "No, you're not. You were right, you're nothing like him."

"You think I don't know that?"

He was snapping again, as if he couldn't help it. She

could almost see the effort he made as he tried once more to rein it in.

"I'm glad for you," he said.

She wasn't sure what he was talking about, but she knew he didn't mean it. It was so obviously a forced lie that she drew back in puzzlement. "Glad?"

"That it's not him. Obviously that made you…happy."

She stared at him. "Happy?"

"Obviously you still have feelings for him, so of course you'd be relieved it wasn't—"

"Are you out of your mind?"

"Completely," he muttered, so low she wasn't sure she was supposed to have heard it.

"That's a lot of 'obvious' you're throwing around there, and *none* of it is obvious to me. Relieved? Yes, I was relieved. Do you think I want to have to deal with him again, in any way?"

"I—"

"What's wrong?" she asked bluntly, cutting him off. "You've been acting odd ever since the fund-raiser, and you've been behaving worse ever since you got here tonight. Is there something you're not telling me?"

"Yes."

He looked as if he regretted the word the moment it was out.

"What? Tell me."

"Never mind."

"I don't play that game, Tony. Not anymore."

She stood there, toe-to-toe with him, not even close to backing down. It took every bit of the nerve she'd gained in the years since Daniel, to stare down this man who had likely seen and done things that would make her quail.

"You opened this door, you can't slam it again and pretend you never did," she told him, still refusing to back off. "What have you learned? Is it about Chilton?"

"No. Nothing more than you know."

"Then what?"

To her amazement, he looked away, as if he were dodging her. What on earth could make this man, who as a child had faced days when he would see certain cars turn down what had once been a quiet, residential street and had known a hail of bullets was about to start, be afraid to face her?

"I'll have Draven assign Taylor Hill to you," he said, turning away from her now.

"What are you talking about?"

"It will be easier," he said. "She's a woman."

"I noticed."

"You liked her, right?" he said, indicating the dishes and half-empty cartons.

"Yes, I did. She's a bright, very nice young woman."

"So it's no problem, then."

"*What* is no problem?"

She was starting to sound exasperated, while he was desperately trying to avoid saying the one thing he most didn't want to say.

"Having her take over," he finally said.

"Take over?" Comprehension dawned. "You're *quitting?*"

She was astonished; this went against everything she knew of him, of Redstone Security, and of the people Draven selected and trained.

"You're Redstone," she said. "We don't quit."

"I'm not quitting, not really." It sounded like an excuse even he didn't believe. "I'll keep digging, I'll find out what's really going on, I just…can't do this anymore."

Oh, God. Lilith's stomach knotted, and her skin went suddenly clammy and cold.

She had betrayed herself. Somehow. Some way. He knew. She thought she'd successfully hidden her silly, unruly, impossible thoughts about him, but somehow he knew, somehow he'd guessed. And he was trying to extricate himself from a hideously embarrassing situation as gracefully as possible.

She told herself to keep quiet, to just accept and let it be, but she was so mortified she couldn't hold back the words that rose to her lips.

"I've made it impossible for you to go on."

He winced, and she groaned inwardly at her own inability to keep her mouth shut. She turned away then, wishing more than anything that she could run, hide from this, from him. But her days of running and hiding were over.

And then, suddenly, his hands were on her shoulders, turning her back to face him. "It's not you!"

The quick, almost fierce words caught her by surprise.

"It's…me."

She blinked, her gaze drawn unwillingly to his face. His eyes, usually dark, were even darker now, and troubled. On some deep level of her mind she was thinking inanely how exotically beautiful he was, how timeless, how easy it was to picture him in another age, an aristocrat riding the endless miles of his rancho, in charge of all he surveyed.

"I made a mistake, Lilith. I thought I could do this, that I could ignore how I feel enough to do my job."

She went very still. "How you feel?"

"How I've felt," he said, his voice so tight and grim it was more suited to delivering a death notification, "since the first time I saw you."

He released her and turned away, as if unable to meet her eyes after that startling declaration.

Lilith stood there, frozen. To her knowledge, the first time they'd ever met had been at a Redstone Christmas party a couple of years ago. He'd been there to shadow Quinn Rafferty, a high-profile guest of Josh's who had received death threats after the release of his novel, which stepped on some famous toes.

She'd told herself at the time that she remembered him so

vividly because it was unusual for a Redstone Security agent to attend this function in a job capacity; they tended to keep their true function out of view. Lilith guessed that many Redstone people knew members of the security team without realizing it. And perhaps not all of them realized why Tony had been there.

But now she was wondering if perhaps she remembered him so vividly for other reasons entirely.

"I don't understand," she said, knowing it was imperative that she do just that, understand exactly what he'd meant. But she couldn't think of anything else to say, because the only thing it seemed possible he was saying was…well, impossible.

"Of course you don't," Tony said, his back still turned. "Why would you? You're everything I'm not." He laughed, and there wasn't a touch of humor in it. "Maybe that's why I practically fell at your feet."

Lilith's breath caught. "Are you saying—?"

She couldn't finish the question. Tony whipped around then, so quickly she almost took a step back.

"I'm saying I wanted to meet you the minute I saw you in that damned red dress. I wanted to find out all about you. I wanted to know about your work. I wanted to know what you liked, didn't like. I wanted to know who your friends were, and why." His voice broke, went almost unbearably harsh. "I wanted…you."

She stared at him, stunned.

"So," he said, pulling back visibly after that astonishing outpouring, "now you can see why you'll be better off with Hill."

"Past tense."

He went still. "What?"

"You said all that in past tense." She didn't point out the obvious, that if it were truly in the past, there would be no problem now.

His mouth twisted into a wry grimace. "Wishful thinking."

Lilith tried to take a deeper breath, wondering what it was called when you had to remind yourself to do things your body normally did automatically.

But there was nothing normal about this, or her reaction to his words. She didn't know what to feel. Her quick, usually reliable mind seemed to have completely shut down on her. All this time she'd been battling her silly imagination, thinking how humiliated she would be if he had any idea how many times she'd thought of him in a far from professional way, and he hit her with this?

He just stood there, looking at her, as if trying to read her mind from her expression.

"Tony, I'm too old for you," she said, the only thing she could think of when the silence became too much to bear.

"I know you're older than I am."

"Much older."

He frowned. "You can't be *that* much older."

"I met Josh when he was in high school. I was on staff."

That got his attention, as she'd thought it would. "You were really his teacher?"

"I was a teaching assistant. My first year in college. But I could see he was something very special, even at fifteen."

She looked up at him then, smiling almost sadly as she read his expression. "Don't bother with the math. I'll tell you. I'm three years older than Josh. Which makes me, what, fifteen years or so older than you?"

He blinked. "I'm thirty-two."

"Are you?" She'd thought him even younger. Not that it helped much.

"Yes. So it's only twelve years."

"Only?" She managed a laugh that was better than his of moments ago, but not by much.

"When you're on a roll," Tony said, with an odd sort of sternness, "you could run me into the ground. Or Liana, who's almost my age. Nobody at Redstone keeps longer hours than you do, except maybe St. John."

"Thank you. I think. I'm flattered. Really."

"To hell with flattered. I would have preferred interested." Interested. If you only knew….

"This is…" she said, then stopped, trying to gather her courage. "This is impossible."

"You think I don't know that? Why would you look twice at someone like me when you're used to the Daniel Huntingtons of the world?"

And look where that got me, she thought. "Do you think I'm a fool, Tony?"

He frowned. "You? Hardly. You're one of the smartest people I've ever met."

"Smart doesn't necessarily mean not foolish," she pointed out. "But I would be foolish indeed to fall for the same kind of man twice. I know what that kind of surface charm is worth. Exactly nothing."

He winced, and she realized he was thinking that was at least in part aimed at him.

"I'm not accusing you of that," she said.

"Are you sure?" he said, sounding rueful.

"Yes. I know now you're nothing like him. Daniel's charm masks the fact that there's nothing beneath it. Yours…masks that there's too much."

He drew back slightly, his dark eyes widening as if in shock. "Lilith…"

"Josh rarely makes mistakes about people," she said. "And if I forgot that for a while with you, it was because of the unpleasant shock of having my ex-husband shoved back into my world. I reacted as I once did, defensively against any man. I'm sorry about that."

The shock she'd seen gave way to something else, something she couldn't quite name, as he stared down at her. The only word she could put to it was pride, but that made no sense at all.

"You are…amazing," he said softly.

To her astonishment, she felt her cheeks heat. She rarely blushed; it happened only when her emotions were running too high to control.

Like now.

"Does that mean if it weren't for those twelve years, you'd be…?"

"Interested?" She nearly laughed out loud again. But somehow she couldn't bring herself to lie about it. "Oh, yes. I'd be interested. You're fairly amazing yourself, Mr. Alvera."

The look he gave her then was one of such heat that she nearly recoiled from it.

"Good," he said. Sharply. Succinctly.

And Lilith suddenly realized she'd made a serious miscalculation. She'd thought she was firmly closing a door that should never be opened.

She hadn't taken into account that Tony Alvera was not the kind of man to let a mere closed—or even locked—door stop him.

Chapter 17

He went over her condo inch by inch but found nothing. No sign that anyone had tried any windows, no new marks on the doors or the locks.

He still didn't like that damned balcony, not when anyone with decent balance and a bit of strength could get to it from the landscaping wall below, or even more easily from the neighbor's balcony.

Out on the landing he checked the front door and its serviceable dead bolt once more. Then, as if there were some clue there he'd missed, he crouched down again to look at the grooves in the wood newel posts.

His thought about the neighbor's balcony coming back to him, he took a look at the door at the other end of the landing. Lilith had told him Mrs. Tilly was like a one-woman neighborhood watch; she had a lot of spare time and didn't miss much. Except when she got on the phone with her daughter in Arizona,

Lilith told him; then the world could cave in and she wouldn't pay any attention.

An old lady like that might seem like a tempting pathway to her neighbor, he thought. It wouldn't take much to break in, overpower her and simply wait on that balcony for Lilith to arrive home.

But there was no sign of tampering there, either—although he would ask to inspect the inside, later, to be sure—and he went back to those infuriating grooves in the wood again.

Apparently the neighborhood watch aspect was in full force, because it wasn't long before Mrs. Tilly opened her door and stepped out onto the landing.

"Lilith told me it wasn't the Wells boy after all," the woman said without preamble. "Is that true? I thought she was just being soft. Why, she's even thinking about getting the boy's mother a job at that Redstone place."

"No, I don't think it was him," he said, thinking again how like Lilith that would be. "But it was someone."

"Is what happened why you've been coming here with Lilith all the time?"

Whether she fell into the nosy or concerned category, he wasn't sure. Lilith said concerned, but then she was a generous soul.

He gave himself a mental tug when he felt himself start to veer down the road of all the other things Lilith was. "What makes you think that? Maybe I'm…a new boyfriend."

Mrs. Tilly snorted incredulously. Tony tried not to be insulted. When the woman went on, it was easier as it became clear what she'd meant.

"Lilith? That girl barely takes time to breathe. Told her for years she needs a man in her life, but she just laughs and says work is safer."

Safer.

The word made him wince inwardly. A memory of his mother, crying in the rocking chair that had been her mother's in turn, because she no longer felt safe in her home, burned through his mind. But at least that threat had been from outside.

He couldn't imagine how it must feel to have the threat come from inside, and from the very person whose main concern should be keeping you safe.

So now that's your concern, he told himself. Get to it.

When the woman had gone back inside—and quickly secured her dead bolt lock—Tony continued downstairs and headed for his car. Lilith was safely inside now; he could think. He would call Hill, have her come back, then…

Then what?

He had no idea.

He yanked the driver's door closed with more energy than was necessary, and the slam settled his nerves a bit. He *did* need to focus on this. Anything else—if there was anything else—would simply have to wait.

It was dark enough now that the automatic sensors turned on the headlights. He drove slowly down the row of covered parking stalls. He didn't like the things, didn't like the vehicles being outside and vulnerable. Most people didn't, he supposed, but their concerns were usually limited to weathering and the occasional vandalism.

He tried not to glance over at Lilith's car, at the now empty parking spot beside it. Ridiculously, his hands tightened on the wheel, and he realized he was fighting the urge to turn in and park there.

And do what? he asked himself. Go back up, confront her, start one of Those Conversations any man in his right mind tried his damnedest to avoid?

She'd already made it pretty clear how she felt. She thought she was too old for him.

Or maybe that you're too young for her, he amended silently, finally giving in and glancing at that tempting empty space as he went slowly past.

He hit the brakes sharply.

For an instant he just stared, wondering if he was imagining things because he'd just been thinking of the hazards of unsecured parking. But he knew it was there, that gleaming bit of fluid creeping out from under Lilith's car, reflecting the headlight's glare.

He was out in an instant, the flashlight from his glove compartment in hand, kneeling beside the drying puddle. In the fading light it was difficult to tell, but it didn't look like the greenish color of coolant, or the red of transmission or steering fluid, not even the darker shade of engine oil. It looked almost clear, just faintly golden.

Suspicion bit deep, and he reached down to touch the wettest part of the small seepage. He rubbed the liquid between his fingers.

Not just wet. Not oily. Slippery.

Very slippery.

Brake fluid.

He was on his back and under the car in seconds. He traced the brake line with the beam of light. He found no visible drip, but after a moment spotted a point on the line that looked cleaner than the rest. He touched it, and his fingertip came away once more slick and slippery. He focused the flashlight there, saw a barely perceptible puncture. Slightly elongated, as if it could have been made with the tip of a pocketknife, just enough to cause a very slow leak.

He swore viciously under his breath, wondering how he could have missed this. That Hill had apparently missed it as well registered, and he thought it was a good thing the woman was gone or he might have chewed a piece off her, and that was Draven's job.

The puddle was dry enough that it likely had been there awhile. It was just barely visible beyond the edge of her car's shadow, and they hadn't really gone near her car all week, but that, to him, was no excuse.

Not when it was Lilith.

Not when this might well have succeeded in killing her. They obviously had every reason to think she'd have continued to drive this car, and the results eventually could have been disastrous.

The thought chilled him much more than the cool asphalt at his back.

It was time to get his freaking head back in the game.

Chapter 18

She opened the door hesitantly.

"I'd ask if you forgot something, but I know you didn't," she said.

Just my mind, he thought as he stared at her. She'd changed into some bluish-looking outfit, loose pants and a sweatshirt-type top, but it was in a fuzzy material he just knew would feel like warm velvet. The sheen of it seemed to ripple over her, changing with her every move, every breath. Her hair was pulled back into a tail at her nape, and he thought for all her concern about being older than he, at the moment she looked about twenty.

He stepped inside, pushing past her, unable to resist the slightest brush of his fingers over that fabric; it felt even better than he'd imagined.

And she felt more tempting beneath it than anything he could ever remember.

"Put some clothes on," he said, hating the snap that had come into his voice. "We're getting out of here."

"I believe I have clothes on," she said mildly.

Put something on that won't drive me insane, he amended, then held his breath, half-afraid he'd said it out loud. When she just continued to look at him with that cool, assessing expression, he pulled his thoughts together.

With an effort, he presented her with a concise report of what he'd found. Then he got back to his original order.

"Get what you need, while I figure out where we're going."

"I am not leaving home," Lilith said firmly.

"That wasn't a request," Tony retorted.

"You said yourself it probably happened some time ago," she pointed out with annoying reasonability. "The spot was nearly dry, you said."

"Never mind what I said. It's still twice they've come after you here."

"Maybe, but couldn't it just as easily have been the same time? The brakes as backup in case the wire didn't work? I haven't driven the car since that day, and you said it was a small leak."

"Stop repeating what I said," he snapped.

He knew she was right, but he didn't want to admit it now that it was helping her avoid doing what he wanted her to do.

"So there's no reason to assume the threat has suddenly become more…immediate," she said. The fact that she wasn't denying that there indeed was a threat mollified him a little. But not much.

"Reason," he muttered, "doesn't seem to have much to do with it."

"What?"

"Nothing. You can't stay here."

She smothered a sigh. "You're not listening."

"I heard you."

"Tony—"

"You want to die to prove me right?"

The sharpness of his tone got through to her. But she didn't buckle. He wondered—if her life had been different, if she hadn't had to learn to stand up to her ex, would she have given in by now? Ironic that, without even trying, Daniel Huntington was still affecting her.

"I'm through running," she said. "There has to be another way. If you must, have Taylor come back."

He took a breath, amazed that it took conscious effort. "No. If you won't go, I'm staying."

Lilith simply looked at him, as if she were pondering the ramifications of his decision—one that he hadn't even realized he'd made until this moment—not to call back the other agent.

Whatever her thoughts were, they didn't show. But then, she'd likely had a lot of practice hiding her thoughts from her ex-husband. That she would use that skill with him rankled, but he supposed she felt she had to. Now that he'd blurted out his idiot attraction to her.

He thought she was going to argue with him, insist that he leave, that she'd be fine here alone.

"I'm staying," he said again. "Damned if I'm going to face Josh and have to tell him I let something happen to someone who matters to him as much as you do. So I'm staying. Whether it's in here or out in my car is up to you."

There. He'd put it nicely in the context of it being his job. And bringing Josh back into it had been a master stroke, he told himself. She couldn't—wouldn't—argue with that. Nobody from Redstone would.

And she didn't.

"There's a lot of Chinese left," was all she said. "You might as well eat, then."

He blinked. "What?"

"I'll warm it up."

She was merely being polite, he knew; she had the leftover food, so he might as well eat it. There was nothing about her capitulation or her manner to indicate they were going to head into any deep, emotional discussion of his unwise confession.

And what about hers?

Oh, yes. I'd be interested. You're fairly amazing yourself, Mr. Alvera.

Her words echoed in his head, replaying in an audio loop that seemed endless. The part of him that wanted to seize on those words and go after what they implied was warring with the part of him that told him this was a job, and he needed to focus on that until he was sure she was safe. She was Redstone, and therefore his responsibility. She was one of Josh's oldest and dearest friends, which made that even more imperative. He'd told the truth about that.

When he'd finished the meal, or at least as much as he'd been able to force down, he sat at the cool granite bar in her kitchen, poking the last grains of rice around with the fork she'd given him when he'd told her chopsticks weren't part of his milieu. He knew he had yet another battle in front of him, and he didn't even know how to start.

"I have some work to do," she said as she opened the dishwasher and put in the plates she and Taylor had used. He set down the fork and picked up both it and the plate he'd used, then walked around the end of the dining bar to add them to the collection in the rack.

At her glance, he shrugged. "I'm housebroken. My mother never had a dishwasher when I was at home, but she made sure Lucy and I cleaned up after ourselves."

"Lucy?"

"Lucinda. My sister." He got it out evenly enough. "My mother cleaned up after my father. It was their way."

"I didn't realize you had a sister. Where is she now?"

"Dead," he said shortly, wishing he'd never let the name slip out. Something about this woman made him lose his usual care about speaking without thinking. He'd never really been aware how much of a buffer that studied flattery, the surface flirting created between him and every woman he dealt with, until he'd stopped using it on her. It hadn't even been a conscious decision, it just hadn't seemed right. Those practiced words and gestures were for casual acquaintances, for friends who didn't mind the teasing nature of it, and for those he needed to finagle something from. Lilith wasn't any of those.

He just wasn't sure what she was.

"I'm sorry, Tony."

Her words were soft, and the long, silent moment she'd waited before saying them somehow took them out of the realm of automatic platitude.

"It was a long time ago." He was sounding gruff again, but he couldn't help that.

"She must have been very young, then."

"Fifteen."

"That's horrible," she said. "Was she ill?"

He blinked. Then laughed harshly. "Of course you'd assume that. In your world, if a fifteen-year-old dies, it's illness, or maybe an accident. In mine, the first possibility that comes to anyone's mind is a drive-by bullet."

To her credit, although she paled, she didn't back away. "Is that what happened?"

"She wasn't even out on the street. She was in her bedroom, trying on her new dress for her fifteenth birthday. We buried her in it, instead."

"I am sorry, Tony. There's no excuse for that."

"They paid," he said succinctly. He waited for her to ask, realized he was angry, wanted her to say something silly about the law and vengeance so he could unload all his tangled emotions. But instead she simply nodded, a little sharply, and said just one word.

"Good."

She left him there, staring after her, as she went into the den that she used as an office. For a moment he couldn't move. He so rarely talked about Lucy, he was a little stunned that it had come out so easily.

Only one secret left, *vato,* he told himself.

Since it was the one most likely to actually send her running, he didn't know if he would ever spill it.

Finally he walked to the door of her office, watching as she waited for the desktop computer to finish booting, then picked up the small flash drive that sat beside the keyboard and plugged it in.

"You don't get enough of this ten, twelve hours a day at Redstone?" he asked.

"Josh brought me in to clean up this mess, and until we're sure we've found everything that Stan Chilton might have tampered with or sold, then no, I haven't done enough."

"Josh wouldn't expect you to drive yourself into the ground."

"Yet he would, for me. Or anyone else Redstone."

Tony couldn't argue with that. And since he had another unpleasant surprise for her later, he left her in peace for the moment. He couldn't help her with what she was doing, apparently searching some huge database that had been on that little USB drive; he was competent enough using a computer, but this kind of process was out of his league. She'd probably laugh at him if she knew he sometimes resorted to plain old pen and paper, with a small notebook he carried in a jacket pocket, but sometimes he felt better being able to be sure sensitive information had been destroyed. A computer file seemed to exist in some form forever.

He went back into the living room, sat down on the couch where she and Hill had been sharing dinner and that talk about men, or whatever it was that had had them laughing. He couldn't relax and was soon back on his feet, wandering around the room, checking windows he'd already checked and the front door he'd already made certain was securely dead-bolted.

He paused as he passed a large bookshelf at one end of the room. It was full, not just with several shelves of books—mysteries, biographies and, he noted with a bemused inward smile, apparently the entire *Harry Potter* series—but a shelf of DVDs in a similar vein. CDs took up another shelf, everything from country to alternative rock to Beethoven. Eclectic, he thought, wasn't the word for it. There was much more to Lilith Mercer than that polished exterior might suggest.

He barely stopped himself from making another tour of the condo, checking all the doors and windows yet again. The only thing that allowed him to rein in the urge was the fact that she was trying to work. Instead he paced the living room, trying to halt his careening mind instead. Here he was, at home with the woman who'd captured his imagination so thoroughly that he'd never forgotten her even though, before Beck's case had come up, he'd barely ever seen her. And he couldn't do a damn thing about it. He was here to protect her, keep her safe.

And that included from him.

Almost desperately he picked up a book at random; he would have chosen the TV, but didn't want to disturb her work. He sat down in the chair closest to the window that looked out on the front landing; he didn't expect a repeat of the wire trick, but he also didn't take anything for granted. There was an ottoman next to it, and he stretched his legs out and settled in; he didn't know how long she planned on working, only that she never seemed to stop.

He started to read, but found himself having to go back and reread a section every few pages. The more he thought about what Lilith had said, the more he thought she was probably right; the brakes and the wire had been rigged at the same time. He had no idea if the cut in the brake line had been purposely small, making for a slow leak that would gradually drain the system, or if the culprit had just been in a hurry. Either way, it was sloppy if the intent was murder.

Then again, so was the wire. True, a tumble down the full flight of concrete steps could have proved fatal, but just as likely, had her reflexes not been so good, Lilith could have been just badly injured.

He cringed inwardly at the thought of her broken from such a fall, or from some horrible crash when her brakes finally gave out at just the wrong moment....

So was that the goal? he wondered. Was it to injure rather than kill? And if so, why? If it had been her ex, he could have understood it; that kind of emotional involvement sometimes required inflicting lasting pain, and shied away from the death that would also mean the absence of someone to hate. He'd seen it before, people who were so focused on the object of their hatred that once it was removed, when they by rights should have been happy, they instead lost their driving force and drifted, rudderless, unsure what to do with themselves now that the hate that had defined them for so long had no object.

But Stan Chilton didn't even know Lilith, from all he could determine. There was nothing personal involved; she was nothing more to him than the person brought in to clean up his mess. So why not just kill her outright?

Except that that wasn't logical, either. As Draven had said, it was he and Ian and Samantha Gamble who had brought Chilton down. Chilton should be after them.

So why Lilith? It made no sense to him.

Which was, he admitted, probably the problem; looking for logic in screwed up minds like Chilton's was a mistake to begin with. If the man had been merely after money—although with what Redstone paid that was hard to believe—it would have been cut-and-dried. But he'd been nursing a fierce case of envy—envy of Ian's brilliance and success under the Redstone wing—and that had contorted his existing sense of entitlement into something twisted and evil.

He grimaced, both at the tangled mess this was, and at the

irony that it made street gang violence seem simple. Ugly, yes, but simple; you hit us, we hit back, harder. Stray onto our turf at your own risk. Black and white, it was what it was.

"Problem?"

Jerked back to the present by her quiet query, Tony gave up any pretense of reading and slammed the book closed; even magic wasn't enough of a distraction at the moment. He sat upright, surprised at how long he'd been sitting here unraveling; it was full dark now. A glance at his watch told him it was nearly ten.

"Same old," he muttered. He didn't explain whether it was her situation or just her, and she thankfully didn't press him.

She sat down on the edge of the ottoman his feet had just vacated. Close. Too close. "I can't make any sense out of it, either."

That her words could apply to either thing he'd been wrestling with didn't escape him, but he took the more prudent route. Especially with her sitting so damned close.

"Somebody told me once that every mind, even a sick one, works out its own logic," he said.

She pondered that for a moment. "Draven?" she guessed.

He shook his head. "Actually, St. John."

Her brows rose. "The mystery man?"

It was an appellation applied frequently to Josh's enigmatic right-hand man, the man rarely seen by anyone outside—some speculated because he never left his penthouse apartment on the top floor of Redstone Headquarters—and not all that often by Redstone people themselves.

"I don't know what his life has been, but I have a feeling it just might make mine look tame."

"Hard to believe," Lilith said.

"I don't have the corner on dubious pasts."

She gave him an odd little smile he couldn't quite interpret. "Funny, I never thought of your past as dubious. Heartrending, yes, and painful, but not dubious."

He swallowed against the sudden tightness in his throat. He'd long ago gotten over the fact that almost everyone at Redstone knew where he'd come from, just as they knew the story of how he'd been given a way out by Josh. But until now, he hadn't really considered the logical fact that some had actually spent time thinking about it.

That one of them had apparently been Lilith unsettled him.

He barely managed not to leap up just to put some more space between them. He could smell her, that rich, luscious scent he'd come to associate with her. He'd seen a bottle of perfume in her bathroom, something gardenia, so he supposed that's what it was. Whatever the name, it was driving him crazy, and he knew that whenever he smelled anything like it, he was forever going to think of her.

"Doing a pretty good job of that now," he muttered to himself.

"I'm going to bed," she said.

At least he'd armored himself for that one. Not that the simple words didn't conjure up a host of vivid images he could have done without. Or at least, could have done without just now; if he were alone, he wouldn't mind dwelling on each one in turn at length.

"Fine. Move what you need in there." He gestured toward the second bedroom.

She took a step back, her eyes widening. "I beg your pardon?"

So polite, he thought. Always so polite. "You're not sleeping in that bedroom with the balcony."

She stared at him as if the only thing she could think of to say was what she had just said, so she wasn't going to say anything. But he also saw her delicate jaw set, and knew he was going to have a fight on his hands. He wasn't in the mood.

So instead of trying to persuade her with convincing arguments, he cut straight to the one he figured would win the quickest.

"You have two options," he said evenly. "First, you sleep in the guest room without the balcony."

She arched a brow at him. "Or?"

"Or you sleep in your bedroom, in your bed…with me."

He watched the color flood her cheeks. Watched her lips part as if she were having trouble taking a breath.

And he held his own, trying not to admit to the simple fact that, no matter how insane, no matter how impossible, he wanted more than anything for her to choose the second option.

Chapter 19

There were women she knew, Lilith thought, who could take such a statement and handle it coolly, with a blasé sort of acceptance—of course men made offers such as this, it was their due—that she'd always admired but never been able to perfect herself.

Then again, she doubted any of them had ever had an offer—or ultimatum—like this given to them by a man like Antonio Diego Alvera Bernard.

She wondered if any woman he really set his sights on had ever, could ever, refuse him.

She wondered if, had he been serious instead of obviously trying to goad her into doing what he wanted for her own safety, she could have refused him.

But it was clear that was what he was doing. Despite his earlier, surprising confession, she knew that he was simply using this to provoke her into doing what he thought best.

It was, she thought, a form of manipulation. He'd said it just to get her to recoil and do as she was told. He couldn't really—

"Don't," he said, his voice no longer provoking but quiet, almost imploring, all challenge gone, vanished. "Whatever you're thinking, whatever you're telling yourself, don't. I meant what I said."

Her breath caught in her throat and it was a moment before she regained enough of it to speak. All of her umbrage at the transparent manipulation vanished. If he'd meant it…

"Tony, you can't—"

"Don't tell me what I can't think, or feel, or want. And you don't have to tell me you're out of my league, I know that."

"I don't believe in that tripe, and I would never say such—"

"I know you wouldn't. You don't have to say it, it's obvious. But I just tonight realized that even though I know it, I don't care."

She stared at him, seeing something in his dark eyes that she'd never seen before, never thought to see, not in this man. Not a softness, that word could never apply to him, but just a hint of vulnerability, as if she had some sort of power over him. And that he was expecting her to use it.

Realization flooded her. He did mean what he'd said. All of it. Including that he thought her out of his league, as he'd put it. She tilted her head slightly as she explored the revelation that had struck her.

"After I left Daniel," she said slowly, "it was weeks before I stopped jumping at any sound behind me."

He grimaced, and she held up a hand before he could say the terse opinion of her ex-husband she sensed was on the tip of his tongue.

"It took longer for me to be able to view the approach of any man without suspicion. And longer still before I could make the change from expecting the worst to assuming others meant me no harm."

"I would never hurt you."

She doubted that, although she knew he never would in the way he meant it, physically, as Daniel had hurt her. Emotionally, she wasn't so sure. But she also wasn't sure whose fault that would be, if she were to be so foolish as to give free rein to tangled emotions.

"I know that. Because I've left that past behind. It shaped me, yes. But it doesn't rule me." She looked at him steadily. "Can you say that?"

He blinked. Drew back slightly. "What?"

"Aren't you letting your past rule you? You've come so far from those mean streets, and yet they're never that far away in your mind."

"I don't want to forget where I came from."

"Of course you don't. Nor should you. You should be proud that you survived, prouder yet that you got out. It can't have been easy, even with Josh's help."

"Then your point?" He said it stiffly, as if she'd offended him somehow. But she slogged on, anyway.

"Do you really want to live like you're still there?"

He stood up then. Instinctively she rose as well, unwilling to let him tower over her. This was important, she sensed, or he wouldn't be reacting like this.

"You say I'm out of your league," she repeated quietly, "but the only one keeping you in the league you think you're in, is you."

He stared down at her. She stood her ground. It was a hard-learned lesson that took hard-won nerve, but she didn't, couldn't falter, not now, not here, not with this man at this time.

The hush spun out so long she didn't know if she could stand it. She'd never been one who felt she had to fill any silent moment with chatter, but this was different. She couldn't help imagining that if only her hearing were a tiny bit more acute, she'd be able to hear the crackle of electricity between them.

Finally, in a voice that sounded strung almost as tight as the tension in the room, he said, "Are you choosing option B?"

She opened her mouth to say "Of course not!" But the words

didn't come. Because she wasn't sure it was true. Had she, on some level, been saying yes?

For a moment, just a moment, her heart jumped to her throat, her pulse began to hammer, and an odd combination of heat and chill gripped her.

But then reality flooded back, taking with it the urge to leap that she'd been so close to.

"I…I'm flattered, really," she said, hating the sound of the words even as she said them. But the cold truth still remained. "But I'm still old enough to be your…aunt," she finished lamely, falling back on the old analogy she'd been clinging to since the day she realized this man was going to be in her pocket for the foreseeable future.

"I have three aunts, all of them are years older than you and I don't need or want another."

His voice was harsh, and she suddenly realized he'd put his hands on her shoulders. Gently, with none of the bruising grip Daniel had used, but still firmly. She had the oddest feeling that if he weren't doing that, his hands might be shaking. That image, of this man, so tough, so strong, sent ripples of that chilling heat through her all over again.

"We're going to continue this discussion," he said, his voice barely above a whisper now, "but first…"

She knew before he moved what he was going to do. Common sense told her to stop him before he started, but the combination of that rising heat, the tingling of every nerve and the lack of air to breathe drowned out her own warning.

When his mouth came down on hers she nearly gasped at the sweet shock of it. It felt as if she'd been waiting for this for years. It wasn't that she hadn't been kissed since Daniel; she had. But never by anyone she'd wanted it from more, and that was a fact she only now admitted, even to herself.

She had thought she might never truly trust a man again. She had accepted that possibility and gone on, thinking that if she

ever came across a man who could accept that limitation, she
might even venture into a relationship of sorts, the best she
could hope for under the circumstances. And there had been a
couple of men who had been willing to try, but in the end had
given up, unable to stick it out for the length of time it had taken
her to get around to trusting them.

But she trusted this man. Maybe it was because he was
Redstone, maybe it was because Josh had trusted him first and
he was so rarely wrong. But whatever the reason, in this case the
trust had come first. Perhaps that was why, in this moment, all
the feelings she'd kept banked and under wraps for so long burst
free at the first touch of his lips on hers, heedless of all the reasons
why this was probably the least wise thing she could ever do.

And then thought fled, burned away at the testing flick of
his tongue over her lower lip. She heard an odd little moan,
realized it had come from her and almost pulled away. As if he'd
sensed her retreat, he pulled her closer, deepening the kiss,
giving her more of the hot, incredible sensation. Things seemed
to spin around her, and she wondered if he truly had somehow
sucked all the air out of room.

When he finally broke away, she nearly let out that moan
again, at the loss of his heat, his touch, his taste. When he let
go of her shoulders, she thought she might fall. She was almost
afraid to open her eyes, afraid to see what would be in his face,
afraid to look up and see the Tony Alvera she'd seen in action,
the incurable flirt his reputation held he was, afraid she'd see
some kind of smug satisfaction in those dark eyes, as if he'd
proven she was as susceptible to his charms as any woman.

But she did; she'd long ago quit avoiding the things she was
most afraid of, another hard-learned lesson.

He was staring at her, that much was true to her imagining.
But she could never have envisioned the look of wonder that
she saw now on his face; she wouldn't even have begun to guess
he could look that way.

She wasn't ready for this. She wasn't even sure what it was, this fierce, hot feeling. But that she was even experiencing it at all, in terms that hinted that at some point she might be ready, shocked her.

She saw him swallow as if his throat was as tight as her own. "Aunt?" he whispered. "I think not."

Tony stared at the closed bathroom door. She'd retreated to her bedroom as if it were some sort of sanctuary, then to the bathroom to do whatever it was women did to get ready for sleep.

He'd have thought she was running from him, if he hadn't known she never ran from anything.

Sleep was the only thing that was on the agenda tonight, he knew. He'd expected no less. He'd already gotten more than he ever expected, in the way she'd responded to him, the way she'd gone soft and warm, the way she'd kissed him back.

And even if it never went beyond that kiss, he'd carry the sound of that tiny moan she'd made to his grave.

But it was that tiny moan that also gave him hope, hope that maybe, just maybe, she wasn't quite as far out of reach as he'd thought.

...the only one keeping you in the league you think you're in, is you.

Her words came back to him as he stood in the doorway of the bedroom he still wasn't going to let her sleep in. Was she right? Did he truly carry his past around with him like some baggage loaded with graffitied bricks? Had this woman, who had a different but just as heavy a load of memories to carry, in fact done a better job than he had of getting past them?

You should be proud that you survived, prouder yet that you got out.

He was proud, he thought. He'd never taken Josh's generosity for granted. He'd worked hard, he'd been determined, had fought for this chance, knowing full well it would likely be the only one he ever got. He'd just never thought it had earned him the right to move in her kind of world.

But was he wrong? Was it possible that it didn't really matter, at least to her?

He flicked a glance at that closed bathroom door, trying not to let his mind career down the dangerous path of wondering what she wore to bed. Some elegant, lacy thing? Some swath of shimmering satin that would glide over her like that damned red dress he'd never been able to get out of his head? Or, aware of his presence, would she instead armor herself in something heavy and concealing? Not that it would matter; after that dress he was too well able to imagine the body beneath for camouflage to have much effect.

He made himself turn his gaze to the sliding glass doors that led to that damned balcony. He was tempted to go over and open it, leave it open not for the cool breeze but as an irresistible temptation to whoever was after her. If she wasn't here, he would do it.

Grateful for the distraction as he waited for her to finish, he turned the idea over in his mind. He could enlist Mrs. Tilly; she clearly liked Lilith and would likely help. And Hill, although she probably wouldn't be thrilled to work with him after he'd summarily dismissed her tonight. But she was Redstone, and she'd help, no matter what.

He'd send Mrs. Tilly off to visit her daughter for a few days, he thought, courtesy of Redstone. Few people could resist a free trip, especially when it was on one of the Redstone fleet of Hawk jets. He knew that if he said it was necessary, Redstone would foot the bill for the whole trip without a question; it was part of the extreme trust Josh had in his people.

That would give him a base to work from. Lilith could come home with Hill, as she had tonight, he thought. He would be next door, and would help Lilith make the too-easy climb from her own balcony to Mrs. Tilly's. And then Hill could make a show of leaving, waving and talking as if Lilith were still inside, indicating she was now home alone.

It might take a couple of days, but sooner or later that fish was going to bite. And he'd be waiting. He could take up a position here, or just stay on Mrs. Tilly's balcony and wait.

He was still considering all the possible facets to this plan when he heard the door open. He braced himself, then turned his head.

No lacy, sheer thing. No sweep of red satin. Not even the flannel-type armor he'd imagined.

Lilith Mercer, high-class, elegant, polished Lilith Mercer apparently slept in a hockey jersey.

He nearly laughed at the incongruity of it. Would have, if it hadn't bared so much of those long, luscious legs he'd imagined so often. Would have, if he hadn't been able to tell, when she moved, that her breasts were free beneath the slippery fabric.

Would have, if it hadn't made her look so tiny, almost fragile.

A sudden image of Daniel Huntington snapped into his mind. The man was as big as he was, and the idea of Huntington hitting this woman, of him using a crude, brutal weapon on her, striking what could so easily have been a fatal blow, made a protective urge that dwarfed everything he'd felt before nearly swamp him.

No matter what it took, he would keep this woman safe. He couldn't let himself be distracted from that task. Not by anything. And if that meant he had to keep his own feelings on a tight leash, so be it. He'd done harder things.

Maybe.

Chapter 20

When the phone rang at three in the morning, it didn't wake Tony. He was already awake. Had been, most of the night. It had nothing to do with the sofa in the living room he was lying on—it was actually comfortable—and everything to do with the visions of the woman sleeping just down the hall that he couldn't seem to get out of his head.

But when the phone stopped abruptly in the middle of the third ring, a different image of her suddenly flashed through his mind, the image of her picking up the cordless phone from her nightstand in the master bedroom and taking it with her to the guest room.

He hadn't said anything; she wasn't arguing with him about sleeping in the other room, so he'd decided to leave well enough alone. Whether she just couldn't bear to be out of touch, or whether she got late night calls from someone he didn't know about, was something that was going to have to wait.

But 3:00 a.m. didn't qualify as simply late night.

He was on his feet, kicking aside the blanket she'd given him. In seconds he was at the door of the guest room. He paused for a moment, listening, but heard no sound of voices through the closed door. There was, he'd noted earlier, no lock, as there was on the master, so he hadn't had to bring up the possibly touchy subject of her locking it or not.

He gave a courtesy tap on the door but didn't wait to open it.

The room was dark, but his eyes were adjusted; he hadn't been foolish enough to turn on a light and destroy that. She sat up in the double bed that was the lower bunk of the childishly decorated room, looking sleepy and puzzled. He could see that the phone receiver sat quietly on the bedside table. If he hadn't been certain, he might have thought he'd imagined the ring.

And then her expression changed, and she pulled the covers closer around her, as if they were that armor she'd not put on. And he realized she was wondering exactly why he was in her doorway.

In her room, he corrected himself silently, only now realizing he'd taken a couple of strides past the door.

"Who was it?" he said.

She moved then, reaching up to click on the bedside lamp. He instantly missed the intimacy of the darkness, then wondered if that was exactly why she'd done it.

She squinted against the flare of light, looking up at him. "No one."

"Lilith, I can't do my job if you—"

"It was a hang-up call," she said with an air of strained patience.

He didn't like that answer, either. "Were you planning to tell me about it?"

She lifted a brow at him. "At a decent hour in the morning, yes. Wake you up to tell you at 3:00 a.m.? No."

"I was awake."

"I'm sorry it woke you."

"I was already awake," he amended.

"I offered you the other bed," she pointed out.

She had. If she was going to sleep in here at his order, he then was welcome to her bed, she'd said. The only conditions under which he'd make it to her bed, he was sure.

Fortunately for his sanity, his newly discovered masochistic streak hadn't run to subjecting himself to a night in her bed without her. He could only imagine what it would be like to slip between those sheets that likely smelled of that damned gardenia stuff. His dreams were out of control enough already.

He looked at her now, sitting there in that jersey, looking a world removed from the woman she was during the day. Whatever she'd felt when he'd kissed her, she was obviously over it now.

Which fit neatly into his new resolve to keep this hunger he had for her on its chain.

"It's not the couch," he said. "It's fine."

He stopped himself from adding, "It's you." That wouldn't fit at all into his new resolve.

He yanked himself back to business. "They said nothing? At all?"

"No. Not a word."

"Could you hear anything?"

"I could tell it was an open line, that's all. No background noise if that's what you mean."

"Breathing?"

"No. Heavy or otherwise."

If it was an attempt at a joke, he didn't smile. But neither did she, so perhaps she was merely reporting.

"Caller ID?"

"Restricted number," she said. He frowned. She picked up the phone and held it out to him. "Check for yourself."

He believed her, but he took the phone anyway. When he didn't even glance at it she gave him a questioning look.

"The next middle-of-the-night caller is going to get me, not you," he said.

He half expected a fight over this, too, but she merely shrugged. "Fine. But if you decide to answer it in daylight, let me know first. The shock might kill my mother when she calls."

He blinked. That *had* to have been a joke. Didn't it? He couldn't seem to stop himself from asking, "Would the idea of a man answering her daughter's phone really be such a shock to her?"

"It would."

He studied her for a long, silent moment. Then, against every bit of his better judgment, he asked softly, "Have you been…with anyone since your ex?" He saw her go still.

"Are you asking that professionally or personally?"

"Whichever will get me an answer."

"Is that how it works? That charm of yours? If you can't get the answer asking honestly, you make it seem personal and hope no woman can resist?"

He frowned again. This frontal, almost snappish attack wasn't her usual approach. It occurred to him to wonder if it was his question, or simply the setting, being alone with him in a bedroom, while he was fully dressed and all she had on was that silly jersey with the big 66 on it, that had her on edge.

"I still need that answer," he said, ignoring her dig. "Make it a professional inquiry if you want. Because it is that as well. If there's somebody else in this mix, like a disgruntled ex-boyfriend, I need to know."

"How convenient," she muttered.

"Lilith," he began, but stopped when she held up a hand as if she were too weary to argue with him.

"No," she said. "There's no one. Beyond a lunch now and then, or a date for an official function, there hasn't been. Satisfied as to the pitiful state of my social life?"

I was more concerned about your love life, he thought.

Did the two even intersect, in her world? Or did women there keep a very presentable man like Daniel Huntington around for show, and then turn elsewhere for sex? He couldn't imagine

Lilith doing that, but some of the others he'd seen at that fund-raiser? Absolutely.

Hell, maybe he was wrong about all of them. Maybe Lilith was right, and even his perceptions were weighed down by all that street-level baggage he seemed to be lugging around.

And maybe all his thoughts were clouded by the gut-level realization that even if Lilith were like that, he'd want to be the one she turned to for sex. Even if she would never be seen with him in public.

It was going to be, Lilith thought, a very long weekend at this rate.

After that 3:00 a.m. interruption—and the unsettling con-versation with Tony Alvera—she hadn't gone back to sleep until nearly five. She'd then slept until just after eight, and still felt groggy.

At least, she had until now, but Tony's calm announcement that he was glued to her hip for the remainder of the weekend shocked her out of the fog and left her gaping.

"I have plans," she snapped. "Not everything requires a man around, you know."

"Fine," he said, unruffled. "Continue with them. I'll drive."

"I'm going shopping," she threatened, although she'd had no such plan.

"I'll carry bags."

She thought of adding "for lingerie," in the hopes of embar-rassing him, as it would many men, but she had the sinking sus-picion he'd just grin at her and give her an enthusiastic "Good!" Instead she went for the worst female cliché she could think of, even though it was one she'd never been prone to.

"Shoes," she said. "I'll be trying on dozens of shoes."

"I'll wait."

Lord, the perfect man, she thought. For many women, anyway. She didn't find the idea at all appealing, but then, she didn't find the idea of an entire day spent shopping appealing, either; she'd often been teased about being a disgrace to her gender.

Desperate, she tried another tack. "I'll be getting my hair done." Another ruse, she'd just gotten a trim, but worth a shot. "The smells of a salon. You'd hate it."

The grin she'd thought of before unexpectedly popped out now. "Grew up with it. My mother was a hairstylist for years."

She blinked. Distracted, she asked, "What does she do now?"

"Manage my father. Tries to manage me."

"Tries?"

The grin widened. "If I let her, she'd have nothing to complain about."

It sounded so normal, she couldn't help smiling back at him. And realized that this was Tony Alvera's real charm, not the surface teasing that made Liana call him an incurable flirt.

"I really wasn't planning on doing any of that," she confessed.

"I know."

She drew back slightly in surprise. He shrugged.

"You were just trying to scare me off."

"And with most men," she said dryly, "I would have succeeded."

"I'm not most men."

"No," she said, "you're not." And then, as the reality of their connection flooded back, she added, "You're a man on a mission."

"That, too," he said easily.

He'd meant it when he'd said he'd be glued to her for the weekend. He'd been looking forward to it, despite—or perhaps because of—the fact that it made her nervous. He wanted to probe that reaction, wanted to poke at it until she admitted again that if not for all the things that made it impossible, she'd want him.

He was editing what she'd actually said, of course, jumping ahead a step, but he didn't care. The next step would be editing out those things that made it impossible.

Yeah, right, he told himself as he drove, like you're suddenly, magically going to fit in her world?

But here he was now, on Saturday night, headed back into those mean streets. True, they had spent the day together, but it had been impossible to needle her about anything when she was working. He had a suspicion she did that a lot on her weekends; her devotion to Redstone was as deep and genuine as his own, and for similar reasons. And her focus on her work was…well, admirable, he supposed. She'd barely seemed aware he was there after she'd gone into the den, booted up her computer and logged on to her office workstation.

"Why don't you just go in to Redstone?" he finally asked when she emerged after a couple of hours for a cup of coffee.

"Because Josh told me not to on the weekends."

"So you work here instead? Do you really think that's what he meant?"

"I'm not there, am I?"

"So you're a letter-of-the-law kind of person?"

She had looked at him over the rim of the mug she was sipping from. "I am a person who owes Josh Redstone more than I can ever repay."

As am I, he'd thought.

"I thought you'd understand that," she'd said, and moments later returned to her den and her work, leaving him to spend an afternoon doing what little work he could from his cell phone, including arranging to have her car towed and repaired, and then trying again to read while the woman who seemed able to distract him from anything was in the next room.

They'd ordered in—she loved pizza, another surprise from the elegant Ms. Mercer—for dinner, and he'd met the delivery car down in the parking lot, after having given them a bogus address that was close, and his own cell number. They'd barely talked as they ate, and after they'd cleaned up—why was he working so hard to show he was domesticated?—she'd finally left her home office long enough to settle in and look at a magazine that had been in the mail he'd picked up late this morning.

A gardening magazine, he'd noted, and wondered why a woman who lived in a condo without a square foot of dirt would subscribe to such a thing.

She hasn't always lived here, he reminded himself. She'd probably lived in some huge, fashionable house with carefully landscaped grounds. He could just picture her with one of those straw garden hats he'd seen in photographs of women showing off their prized…gardenias, he finished on a sour note.

He'd been left to do nothing but try not to stare at her; she seemed determined to pretend he wasn't there.

Or rather, to treat him like what he was, her bodyguard, worthy of politeness, but nothing more.

And then just after dark Rico had called, saying he'd come up with something else. Something worth another face-to-face, and maybe, Rico had suggested, even more money than before.

He'd called in to Draven, who had sent Hill out to stay with Lilith. Tony had waited for her, and while not chewing her out as he once might have, had pointed out what she'd missed with the brake fluid. The young woman was properly chagrined, and Tony knew she'd be hypervigilant now to make up for it. Which had been his point.

She'd also handed him an envelope from Draven; paying for information was getting expensive, and he'd already given Rico most of his cash kept back for just that purpose.

"I'll be back, and then you can go home," he'd told her.

"I can stay tonight, if you want a break."

He'd nearly snapped at her then, but stopped himself, wondering what had made her say it. Her expression was utterly guileless—too guileless, he wondered?—and he finally gave it up. He was walking too close to the edge when such a simple thing could set him off, he thought.

"I'll be back," he repeated, and left.

So here he was, at nearly midnight, with a pocketful of hundreds that any number of guys likely within ten yards of him at this moment would slit his throat for without a second thought, working his way through foreign turf to what had once been his own. He'd been an ES 13 once, and that alone would have gotten him killed on Cholo turf even then; now that he was long out of the life, he had no armor at all except his own skill and training, and the instincts that were on high alert at the moment.

And the Glock 21 he'd pulled out of the hidden compartment in the panel of the driver's door of his car. It was nestled at the small of his back, a comforting presence.

He pondered, not for the first time, if this was a trap. Rico had no real loyalty to him, not since he'd left the gang, and only respect for his former membership had kept him alive before. But right now he was a cash cow for Rico, and that wasn't something the man would give up on easily.

Then again, the wad in his pocket might be thought of as a last bit of milk from that cow, after which you might as well slaughter it for the meat.

Rico had suggested an out-of-the-way building for the meet. Tony had insisted on a more public place, but still on ES 13 turf.

"You don't trust me, *vato?*" Rico had asked in indignant tones.

"As much as you trust me, *vato,*" he'd replied, earning a laugh.

He made the turn and spotted Rico, pacing rather nervously just out of the halo of light from the one unbroken streetlamp on the block.

Otherwise the street seemed deserted, but he knew better than to assume. He drove slowly but saw nothing. Rico spotted him, gestured sharply, as if urging him to hurry.

He pulled over, checked the Glock, settled it again and got out of the car, every sense tuned to his surroundings.

"Hurry up, man!"

Rico was very nervous, and the possibility of a setup went through Tony's mind again.

"You do something stupid, Rico?" he asked softly as he neared the man.

"Christ, man," Rico retorted. "You want what I got or not?"

"Talk to me."

"That friend of mine. He says that Chilton dude, he buddied up in the city jail before he got transferred to that country club place. Gave me the other guy's name. I checked him out on Google."

Tony blinked.

"What?" Rico sneered, "you think we don't got our own kind of network? Think we're stuck in the old days? You been gone too long, *pendejo*."

Tony ignored the slur on his ancestry. He had been gone a long time, but it would never be long enough, not in his mind. "And?" he prompted.

"A guy Chilton was buddied up with was the same guy they sent up for buying what Chilton was selling."

"Santerelli?"

"That's what—"

The scream of car tires on asphalt split the night. That meant only one thing in this neighborhood, and no matter how long he was away, Tony knew he'd never forget that.

Yanking out the Glock, he dove for the cover of his parked car, while Rico took off running back into the darkness. He heard the yelling from the racing car.

When the shots came, as he'd known they would, it was as if he'd never left.

Chapter 21

Lilith found herself holding her breath as Taylor closed her cell phone, breaking the connection. She made herself take in air. She already knew it had been Tony, from the side of the conversation she'd heard, but Taylor confirmed it with her first words.

"He's on his way back."

Lilith nodded, but something about the way Taylor wasn't meeting her eyes set off an alarm in her mind. That and the fact that he'd left hours ago, and that now it was nearly two in the morning. Taylor had told her to go to bed, but she hadn't even tried, knowing she wouldn't sleep.

And what that said about the state of her feelings for this man was something she wasn't sure she wanted to face.

"What is it, Taylor?"

"Nothing."

"He's a better liar than you are, and I still know," she said.

Taylor sighed. "There was…an incident."

"An 'incident'?" When Taylor didn't respond, Lilith asked, "Did he tell you not to tell me?"

"No."

"Then tell me."

Another sigh. "It was a drive-by shooting."

Again Lilith forgot to breathe. And she realized in that instant, the instant before she asked the question that could change everything, that she was face-to-face with those feelings whether she was ready or not. "Is he all right?"

Taylor blinked, as if the very idea that Tony Alvera could be hurt had never occurred to her. Was the woman naive, or did she just see him as invincible? Many thought of Redstone Security that way, she knew, and she supposed to some extent they had to think of themselves that way, to do the jobs they did.

"I…assume so," Taylor finally said. "He didn't say otherwise."

As if he would, Lilith thought. And then, belatedly, it occurred to her to ask, "Was someone else hurt?"

"Yes," Taylor said, reluctantly.

…they killed my little sister in a drive-by.

Tony's words rang in her head, and her throat tightened as she imagined how he must be feeling, no matter who it was who'd been hurt tonight.

Taylor got up off the couch where they'd been sitting, trying to watch a movie that had captured neither of them. She gathered cups and dishes—Lilith had discovered to her chagrin that Taylor shared her weakness for all things butterscotch—and carried them back to the kitchen.

Taylor would leave when Tony arrived, Lilith supposed. And then she would be facing another night with the man who so unsettled her, she didn't know whether to wish the guest bedroom had a lock on the door or be thankful it didn't.

Now she knew.

The very realization that something could have happened to him, that he could have been hurt, or worse, had brought slamming home into her mind the simple fact that she would be devastated. And no amount of telling herself she was a silly female falling for the big, strong man protecting her could change that.

Besides, she knew perfectly well that it wasn't that. She wasn't afraid, she'd never been afraid during this time, only angry. The only person who had ever been a threat to her was in prison, and she refused to live her life in fear. Doing that would mean Daniel had won, and she absolutely would not give him that satisfaction.

So where did that leave her? Besides lusting after—she couldn't kid herself about that any longer—a man twelve years her junior?

…you don't have to tell me you're out of my league, I know that.

His words came back to her, along with her sense of the absurdity of it. Her "league," as he called it, consisted of a man who hid behind the facade of refinement and upper-crust gentility, denying he would ever hurt so much as a flea, while his wife lay in the hospital bed he'd put her in. Tony Alvera had more honesty and honor in his little finger than Daniel could muster in a lifetime.

"He's pretty…intense."

Lilith snapped out of her reverie to find Taylor standing a few feet away, watching her, assessing.

"Yes," she agreed; there didn't seem any point in denying it.

Taylor seemed to hesitate, then shrugged. "You do know this was never just a job for him, right?"

Lilith frowned. "What do you mean?"

"I was in Mr. Draven's office when he burst in, demanding this assignment."

"He…what?"

"I think the boss was about to assign me, thinking you'd be more comfortable with a woman. Then Tony arrived, saying the job was his." Taylor gave her a faint smile. "I never would have thought anyone would have the nerve to talk to Mr. Draven like that."

"He's mellowed a bit," Lilith said, barely aware of her own response. The vision of Tony charging into Draven's office demanding to be the one to protect her broke down the last bit of that crumbling wall she'd tried to keep around her response to his overpowering, larger-than-life presence.

She made herself focus on the woman watching her. "Why did you tell me that?"

The shrug again. "Seems to me you're a little…conflicted about him. I thought it might help."

Lilith laughed despite herself. "Conflicted. Yes, that's a good word for it."

Or it had been, she thought. Because she wasn't sure she was in the least conflicted anymore.

When a few minutes later she heard strong, quick steps on her stairway, she let out a compressed breath. Whether it was an ebbing of worry—he was obviously well enough to move in his normal manner—or an increase in anxiety at his return, she wasn't sure.

She seemed unable to move and just stood there as Taylor and Tony held a quiet exchange in the doorway. Then the woman left, with a backward glance at her and a smile that Lilith would have sworn said "Good luck."

Lord, was it that obvious?

When Tony turned to face her, her breath shot out of her yet again; he was spattered with blood. His hands looked as if he'd been swimming in it. Instinctively she reached out to touch him.

"Are you hurt?" she asked urgently, suddenly disbelieving Taylor's earlier assurance.

He gave her an oddly assessing look before he said quietly, "It's not mine."

She stared up at him. "The man you went to see?"

He nodded.

"Is he…?"

"Dead. Yes. There was nothing I could do for him."

And he would have tried. Lilith knew that as surely as she knew he was standing here. No matter what manner of man it had been, even had he been the worst that ran those streets, Tony would have tried.

"I'm sorry. Was he…a friend?"

Tony's mouth twisted. "Once, he would have been a brother to me, simply because we both belonged to the same gang. But no, he wasn't really a friend. Didn't make it much easier to watch him die."

Lilith shook her head, slowly. "I can't imagine. It must have made you think of—"

"Yes. It did."

The edge that had come into his voice warned her to veer away from that subject. She stared at him, still unable to look away from the stains on his shirt, his hands. Finally she lifted her gaze to his face. "You're really all right?"

She didn't know what had changed in her voice to make his expression shift. But it did, and he looked down at her with a sudden ferocity that left her no doubt what he was referring to when he bit out, "No."

He reached for her, then stopped abruptly, and she saw his gaze flick from her to his bloodied hands, then back. And slowly he lowered them, but his eyes, those dark, hot eyes, told her this was only a temporary respite.

A sudden panic filled her, and she wanted nothing more than to retreat. "I'll…get you some towels, a washcloth, so you can…wash that off."

It was inane, it was so far from what she was feeling she almost laughed at herself. And half expected him to laugh out loud at her. But he let her retreat, although she again had the feeling she was only buying herself a few minutes. Something had changed about him tonight, something was there that hadn't been before, something that warned her the wolf was about to slip the leash.

She heard him in the guest bathroom, wondered what it must feel like to have to clean another human being's blood off your skin. What it must have felt like to be back on those streets where he'd grown up, once more hearing shots fired like the one that had killed his little sister.

"There's something I need to tell you."

She gave a little start; she hadn't heard him come out of the bathroom. For a big man, he moved like a cat. When she looked at his face, it was set in such grim lines her stomach knotted. He'd seen so much, done so much, she didn't want to think about what could make him look like that.

"What?" she asked, even though she was positive she didn't want to hear whatever it was.

"There was…someone, once. Nine years ago. Lisa Marquette. She was someone I'd met in college, but we ran into each other again and…hit it off."

Lilith found herself holding her breath, and had the inane thought that no one had ever interfered with her normal breathing the way this man had.

"I was working a case then. One of my first, and a nasty one. One of Redstone's marketing guys was being extorted with threats to his little boy. I knew him, he was my old boss in fact, so I was…seriously invested."

"Of course," she said when he paused.

He was silent so long she wondered if he was going to stop altogether. Wondered why he was telling her in the first place, it was so obviously painful for him. He couldn't even look at her anymore; he was staring down at the floor as if the diagonal pattern of the slate tiles was the most fascinating thing in the world.

"It got ugly," he said at last. "Very. And I couldn't seem to get a handle on it, couldn't track the suspects even though I had a decent idea who they were. Then just before it all came to a head, it became clear *they* knew who *I* was. Things got dicey, and I got…pretty wound up."

Lilith listened silently now, but with a growing curiosity as to what the two seemingly divergent stories had to do with each other.

And then he told her.

"I got wound so tight I blew up at Lisa. I couldn't talk about the case with her, but I was worried she might be in danger if they knew enough about me to follow me. So I ordered her to stay locked inside. Because I couldn't explain, she got angry in turn."

Lilith took in a shallow breath. She couldn't help thinking of her own reaction to his imperious orders. Was that what this was about, was this some convoluted apology for how he'd acted, for his high-handed manner and arrogant insistence?

"It…escalated."

His voice had dropped. Odd, she thought, that he had started this here, standing in her hallway. Odder still that he was now leaning against the wall where they stood, as if he needed the prop.

"And I didn't have time to fix it, not then. I thought I would later. I had to go out because there had been another extortion call. The call was a setup. To lure me out. She was angry enough that when I left…so did she."

He fell silent again for a long moment. His expression didn't change, nor did his own breathing, but she knew the punch line was coming.

And that it was going to be ugly.

"I don't think they meant for her to die. They just wanted to scare me off. They kidnapped her, restrained her and covered her mouth with duct tape, tossed her in the trunk of a car. The medical examiner said she…suffocated. She had gotten so scared she vomited."

Lilith shuddered, understanding what he wasn't saying. And he still wasn't looking at her. She was grateful for that, at least for a moment. She was trying to wrap her mind around the scope of the tragedy this one man had had in his life. As if living the way he'd had to as a child hadn't been enough, then the senseless death of his sister, and then…this? She couldn't imagine what it must be like to live with such memories. In her mind, they made her own painful ones seem almost clean.

Finally, slowly, he lifted his gaze to her face. "She died, horribly, because of me. Because I slipped back into the old days, the old ways, the old machismo my father lives by."

A protest rose to her lips, but she stopped it, making herself wait until she could speak calmly, gently. "It wasn't your fault, Tony."

"So they say."

"She made the decision."

"But I pushed her to it." He eyed her steadily. "Would you have stayed, if it had been your ex ordering you around?"

"No," she admitted. "But there's a big difference. Daniel would have imposed his orders with brute force. You would never do that. You would never…hurt me."

"You were angry enough, last night, to walk out. If this hadn't been your home, you might have."

She couldn't deny that, either. Didn't want to deny it. Somehow she knew honesty was imperative now; this man wouldn't want or accept any banal, insincere platitudes. This was Tony Alvera stripped down to the bone, and she didn't dare trifle with that.

"I might have. More likely I would have just thrown your sorry…backside out."

He looked startled, but the tiny beginnings of a grin tugged at the corners of his mouth.

"So next time," she said, "just ask. Don't try to bully me."

His expression shifted again, turned slightly sardonic. "Just ask?"

"If you'd just said 'Lilith, I need you to do this,' I wouldn't have fought you. And one little 'please' goes a very long way."

She studied him for a long moment before asking what she'd

wanted to know since he'd first started his grim story. "Why did you tell me this? About Lisa? Was it to explain why you acted like that the other night?"

"Partly."

"And the other part?"

"Because you should know the worst thing about me."

Her throat tightened almost unbearably. "Why?"

"Because I'm going to ask you again."

She stared up at him, knowing what he meant, knowing this was the moment she'd known was coming, the moment some part of her had been thinking about even as she tried to force it out of her conscious mind.

"Only this time," he said, with a quiet acknowledgment and admission that was as much apology as anything else, "it has nothing to do with my job."

"I…see."

"I hope so. So once more…your bed, or that silly bunk bed?"

She'd wondered how it would feel, to make this decision. Now she knew she wouldn't find out, because on some level, some part of her mind, the decision had already been made.

"You can say it better than that, Mr. Alvera."

She thought she heard him suck in a breath. And then a slow grin curved his mouth, making that unexpected dimple flash. There was nothing of the practiced charm in this, only the genuine, unexpected sweetness she'd seen sparks of before. And when he spoke, it was with a voice so full of gentle teasing and boyish dutifulness that she nearly grinned back at him.

"Lilith, I need you to do this. Please."

"All right, then," she said.

And the moment she spoke the words, the instant she saw the heat flare in his eyes, she knew she'd taken an irrevocable step. She might someday regret it, the impossibilities were all still there, but right now, as he pulled her into his arms and lowered his mouth to hers, she truly didn't care.

Chapter 22

He'd known it would be sweet. He'd known it would be hot. He'd even known, on some level, that it would be unlike anything he'd ever experienced.

But he hadn't known it would be like this. Because he hadn't known *anything* could be like this.

The moment he realized she was trembling, he reined himself in with one of the fiercest efforts of his life. He undressed her gently, letting out the tender side of what he was feeling, the emotions that he had no words for. He wanted her now, right now, but he also wanted her for the rest of his life, and he wasn't going to get that if he scared her, rushed her now. Even with her bed right here, a step away, he had to go slow.

When she tentatively reached for him, helped him tug off his shirt, his belly tightened fiercely, knotting with a heat and tension he'd never felt before. He treasured every move she made, every quickened breath she took, every tiny sign that she wanted him, too. He had to fight down the urge to take her now, hard and fast, before she could change her mind.

He'd wondered if her concern about the difference in their ages was based on something more than the calendar, if it stemmed from what she saw in the mirror every day. He'd known he wouldn't care—the thought of looking, of having the right to look, at her naked body, in a mirror or otherwise, told him that—but he'd made up his mind she wouldn't care, either. As it turned out, he didn't have to work very hard at it.

She was beautiful. As beautiful as he'd imagined. More. In a womanly way, with luscious, taut curves that made his fingers curl with the urge to trace every one. He'd meant to tell her he thought she was just that. Now that it was here, now that she stood before him, he couldn't say a word.

But when he lifted a hand to touch her, he saw he was trembling himself, and had to hope that that would tell her what he couldn't find the words to say.

He stopped, unable to move his hand that last, critical inch. In this final moment, when what he'd ached for for so long was within reach, all he could see were those faintly lighter patches across his knuckles.

I shouldn't even touch you, he thought, frozen, staring at his own past as if it were alive and here.

He didn't realize he'd spoken the words, whispered them aloud, until she followed the line of his gaze, then looked back at his face.

"I had them removed," he said, "but that doesn't change—"

He sucked in a breath as she touched him, traced those reminders on his skin with gentle fingers.

"Badges of honor," she said softly. "A permanent reminder of the courage and determination it took to get out. You should be proud."

He swallowed tightly. And he of the quick repartee, the easy flirtation, still couldn't think of a thing to say to her that didn't sound hollow and false to his ears.

Finally, he went with a gut-level truth that left him feeling as if he'd bared his throat to a blade.

"The only thing I want more than you right now, is for you to be sure."

"I'm sure," she whispered. "I've been sure since that endless second before I knew you were all right."

He wasn't sure exactly what she meant, but was positive he didn't care. He leaned forward and kissed the top of her shoulder, the spot he'd seen her rubbing on occasion, where it was no doubt sore from her near fall on the stairs.

He'd get to the other sore spot, that beautiful, lusciously curved backside, later.

He touched her then, cupped and lifted her breasts just as he'd imagined so many times. But the reality far surpassed the fantasy; the feel of that soft fullness rounding into his hands sent a jolt of fire through him that left him reeling, and wondering if there would be anything left of him but ash when this was over.

He rubbed his thumbs over her nipples. They hardened and she let out a gasping moan. The sound and feel answered his own question; there would be nothing left and he didn't care. He couldn't think of any way he'd rather go out than with this woman in his arms.

She reached for him then, urging him to shed the rest of his clothes.

"You do it," he said harshly. "I don't want to let go."

He caressed her again, savoring the way she moved at his touch, arching, shifting restlessly. When he felt her hands slide across his belly, fingers reaching for the buttons of his jeans, he sucked in a breath so quickly it was audible.

She stopped.

He was so achingly hard he thought he would die right here and now if he didn't have her hands on him soon.

"Lilith," he whispered, the first time he'd spoken her name since they'd come into her bedroom.

"I…it's been a long time."

"I know. Just don't stop."

Freed of his clothes at last, he had a moment to be aware of the contrast between them, her creamy skin and his own darker bronze. He saw her look at his hand on her, wondered if she was thinking the same thing. But then she smiled, a soft, wondering smile, and slid her own hands down to his hips, pulling him toward her. Rigid flesh met soft curve, and his usually agile brain went into free fall.

And suddenly nothing was as he'd expected, or thought it would be. Elegant, poised, collected Lilith Mercer responded fiercely, arching to him, her muscles fairly rippling beneath his touch. And she touched in turn, exploring until he was gritting his teeth with the effort to hold back. But she stroked, caressed, with just a hint of tentativeness that reminded him it had been a very long time for her.

It was a reminder he needed, to keep himself slowed down. And he wanted to go slow, wanted to trace every single, glorious inch of her. He wanted her with him every step of the way, wanted her to want it as ragingly as he did, and set about making sure that happened. He set his jaw against the urgent demand of a body so hard he thought he might die from it, and coaxed her to the edge again and again, until he was certain.

And then she was urging him on. He slipped a testing finger between her legs and found her hot and slick and ready, and the anticipation of easing this damned ache in her sweet heat was more than he could resist.

When he began to inch into her he thought she cried out; he couldn't be sure because her name ripped from somewhere low and deep in his chest. It was a long, nerve-wrenching slide as her unaccustomed body adjusted to take him, but once he was in her to the hilt, only one word echoed in his pleasure-drugged mind.

Home.

He knew in that instant he wasn't going to be able to go slow. He of the infinite control and careful uninvolvement was lost.

"I can't," he whispered to her. "Sorry, I can't go slow."

"Don't. Oh, please, don't," she said, breathlessly, stunning him more than a little.

He began to move, savoring every tiny sound she made, every lifting movement that drove him deeper. And just when he knew he couldn't hold out another instant, he heard her cry out, and felt the first clenching squeeze of her muscles around him. He let go then, slamming into her twice more, and then a shout of gasping triumph broke from him as his body erupted in an explosion of pure, sweet pleasure.

And when she held on to him, even when he would have moved to relieve her of his weight, he thought again of that single word.

Home.

When she awoke, he was gone.

She supposed she should have seen the inevitability of that. What had happened between them last night had probably been ordinary to him. Not that she doubted he'd truly wanted her. There was no way she could question that, not after the way he'd held her, touched her, and taken so long to caress her she'd almost screamed at him to finish it.

She'd expected something hot and fast. She'd gotten instead a tenderness and gentle insistence that had steadily pushed her higher than she'd ever gone in her life.

She'd expected demands and fierceness. She'd gotten soft, sweet persuasion and looks of such wonder she almost forgot all about the fact that her body was twelve years older than his, with all the extra wear and tear that entailed.

She'd also expected a casual aftermath, from a man much more experienced in this sort of thing than she was. That, she had apparently gotten.

She resisted—barely—the urge to curl her satiated body up in the fetal position to ponder what she'd done, to open the door to the morning-after regrets she sensed were hovering just on the edge of her consciousness.

But how could she regret something that had been so overpoweringly glorious? How could she regret waking up feeling like a woman who had been loved to within an inch of her life?

How could she regret the simple fact that never again would she think of Daniel first when she thought of the few men she'd shared a bed with?

Then something else that had been hovering finally penetrated the fog: coffee. She was smelling coffee.

On the thought she heard footsteps. And then he was there, in the doorway, painted dark and golden by the morning light. Beautiful, tall, strong and unabashedly naked. She watched him walk toward her, two mugs of steaming coffee in his hands. It gave her the chance to really look at him, in a way she hadn't been able to in the dark of the night.

He moved, she thought, like that big cat he'd put her in mind of last night. She supposed that was because he was so perfectly put together. Her cheeks heated as she noted the dusting of hair on his chest, remembering the rough caress of it against her nipples, and the way it had made her arch her back, wanting more. And the small patch of beard beneath the center of his lower lip made her smile; she'd never even kissed a man with so much as a mustache before.

He reached the bed too soon; she'd wanted to keep looking, to work up the nerve to give that part of him that had driven her to madness last night more than a quick glance. Not that she needed to; she knew all she needed to know—he fit her perfectly.

He sat on the edge of the bed and held out one of the mugs to her. It was, she noticed as she took it, exactly as she liked it, just enough milk to take it from near black to creamy brown.

She was grateful for the distraction, since she had absolutely no idea what to say to him. *Thanks for the most amazing night of my life* seemed a bit cliché.

And all the thoughts that she supposed inevitably followed a night like last night were now tumbling around in her head, the most prominent being *Where do we go from here?*

Assuming, of course, they went anywhere except straight back to business.

Even as she thought it, he did just that.

"I'm going to go see Joe Santerelli."

She blinked. "Now?"

He nodded. "It's Sunday. He'll be…relaxed."

"Unsuspecting, you mean," she said, thinking she was oddly thankful he'd not started by talking about last night. Realizing he'd probably done it on purpose, sensing her unease.

"If you like," he agreed easily. Then, with a touch of wariness, he added, "You're not going."

"I wasn't planning to. I never met the man, I wouldn't be of any use."

He looked relieved. "You were, with your ex," he admitted. "It was me who blew that."

"I…appreciated the way you treated him. He deserved it. It did me good to see it."

He smiled. "In that case, I forgive myself."

She hesitated, then asked what had been bothering her all night. "Last night—" he tensed, and she realized he thought she was going to bring up what had happened between them, in this bed, and quickly went on "—are you sure the man who died was really the target?"

He relaxed, and she realized how out of whack things were when talking of a drive-by shooting where someone had died was easier than talking of a night of passion. Out-of-control passion, yes, but still…

"Yeah. They were Cholos, a rival gang, and they yelled his

name. They were after him. He knew it—he'd been acting twitchy."

"Oh." It seemed wrong, to be relieved, but she was.

He took a sip of coffee, then said briskly, "Hill is on her way over."

Uh-oh, Lilith thought. Here we go. But she tried to keep her response calm, reasoned. "I'm just going to stay here this morning, do some work."

"Fine."

"I'm sure Taylor will be glad to get her Sunday morning back."

He frowned. "She's still coming."

"I don't need a babysitter."

"You're getting one."

She tried to ignore the high-handedness. "In fact, Taylor would be a distraction, since I do need to work."

"I'll tell her to leave you alone."

"That would be rude."

"Rude," he snapped, "is a word that only works in your world. And you're not in your world at the moment, you're in mine."

Just like that it was between them again, that barrier between worlds he couldn't seem to get past. And now, looking at him, at that lovely expanse of golden skin over taut muscle, she wondered if she truly had lost her mind. Because the morning light only brought home the reality that she'd dodged last night.

And she guessed the morning light was bringing home the reality to him as well, showing the faint lines around her eyes and mouth that advertised the difference in their ages.

"Did you think," she asked, her voice tight, "that because we slept together, you now own me?"

"I thought," he said, his jaw set, "that you would agree to letting me keep you safe. But your agreement isn't required."

"Back to ordering instead of asking, are we?" she snapped.

Of course, he'd gotten her into bed, so now maybe he thought it wasn't necessary anymore. But the fact that he had reverted to the very behavior he'd confessed he felt had gotten Lisa killed bothered her more than she cared to admit. Because it told her she was in this much deeper than she'd allowed herself to acknowledge.

And there's no one to blame but yourself.

The problem wasn't just the difference in their ages, although she felt that more than ever this morning. She drew herself up, refusing to clutch at the bedcovers to hide behind; it seemed ridiculously pointless after the night they'd spent.

"I can tolerate a great deal," she said quietly. "I can even tolerate overprotectiveness. What I can't tolerate is someone making the same mistake over and over again."

She got up then and escaped to the bathroom, where she tried valiantly not to weep and succeeded, for the most part.

When she finally emerged, Taylor was sitting at her kitchen bar and Tony was gone. Lilith put on a smile with that practiced ease her world—and her life with Daniel—had taught her.

Maybe Tony was right. She belonged there, in that world.

Because she certainly wasn't doing very well venturing into his.

For at least the fifth time since he'd left the condo, Tony had to force himself to focus on what he was going to say to the disgraced, imprisoned CEO of JetCal. His mind kept wanting to go backward, and no amount of telling himself Lilith was just being stubborn could erase the sting of her last words.

What I can't tolerate is someone making the same mistake over and over again.

The words stung because there was no denying the truth of them. He had done exactly what had set her off before. If it were only that, it would be bad enough. But it wasn't.

Because he'd done exactly what had sent Lisa out of their apartment to be kidnapped and die.

Again.

He tried to tell himself it was because he was worried, and that made him edgy. That much was true. He even admitted he'd reacted that way for the same reasons, that desperate need to keep the woman he loved safe.

The woman he loved…

It didn't even hit him with a jolt. He'd gone into this knowing he was halfway there already, but he'd counted on the impossibility of it, the hopelessness of trying to blend her world and his, to keep the feelings at bay, to keep him at that harmless halfway point.

It hadn't worked. And he knew that he'd been beyond that point even before last night; that incredible, powerful, life-changing night that he suspected had been as intense as it had been because he was in love with her.

And maybe that was why he was taking so long to learn, to stop himself from reacting from the gut, making the same mistake with her he'd made with Lisa. He'd never loved anybody like this before and it was distracting him.

None of which changes a damned thing, he told himself.

The minimum-security facility where Joe Santerelli was being held was much different from Chino, where Daniel Huntington was. And Santerelli was going to get out a lot sooner. Sooner than Stan Chilton as well, since Chilton had threatened lives and Santerelli had only been convicted of cooking his own books; buying industrial secrets, suborning corporate espionage was a nebulous area to convict anyone on. But Redstone influence was huge and Josh had a lot of friends, and the investigation into other areas of JetCal had netted its CEO a home away from home for quite some time.

It was also why Tony thought approaching Santerelli was the way to go; the man had a lot more to lose and therefore could be pressured. He'd already run afoul of Redstone when he'd thought he'd get away with something he told himself every business-man did, and Tony hoped he'd want to avoid that mistake again.

Of course, if he was behind the plot against Lilith, Josh would want to crush him.

You're going to have to get in line behind me, boss, he thought.

Tony watched carefully as Santerelli walked toward him. He was short and a bit rotund, although Tony guessed he'd lost a bit of weight since he'd been inside, given the way his clothes hung on him. He also walked with a hint of a strut; it had likely been a swagger when he'd started, but prison life—even at what were laughingly called country-club prisons—would take some of that out of just about anyone. Especially someone used to living large, as Santerelli had been.

Tony had asked them not to tell the man who he was, just a visitor. He didn't have many, they said, family and his attorney mostly. And as usual, the Redstone name got him what he wanted.

Tony saw the man's forehead crease when he saw him. Trying to figure out who he was, Tony guessed. Saw the puzzlement change to a frown, and guessed the man's thought process had gone from wondering who this was to realizing what he looked like. He'd chosen his clothes carefully for this visit, forgoing his usual for the kind of street attire Rico had died in last night. And he saw Santerelli realize it, saw the sudden wariness in his demeanor as he sat across the outdoor picnic table from him.

"Do I know you?"

The attitude fit, too. Imperious, superior, just like the head of some medium-wanting-to-be-big company speaking to someone he didn't think could be any help to him. Tony couldn't help but contrast this man with Josh, who treated everyone with the same respect he demanded. The respect that kept Redstone at the top of any list of best places to work, the respect that meant Josh had never had to face a group of disgruntled employees.

"You don't," Tony finally answered when Santerelli began to look uncomfortable. "But I know you. My brothers on the street, they know you."

He wasn't sure Santerelli was smart enough to pick up the hint, but the way he pulled back slightly told Tony he must have. But he pretended ignorance anyway.

"I don't know what you're talking about."

"I think you do."

"I have no idea. What is it you want?"

The still imperious tone told Tony he wasn't scared. Yet.

"The job got trickier. You're not paying enough."

Santerelli's frown deepened. "Trickier?"

And there it was, Tony thought. Of all the things Santerelli could have said, that was the one that convinced Tony he was on the right track. Not "What job?" or "Paying?" as anyone truly ignorant would have said.

"It's going to cost your little cabal more."

"We already—" He stopped, as if realizing what he was about to admit.

"Paid? Yes. But not enough."

"I don't know what you're talking about," he said again.

Tony had had enough of the silly game. "It might be wiser if you did."

The frown again. "Wiser?"

Tony stood up. Heightwise he towered over the shorter man, and the contrast was even greater with Santerelli seated. He put his palms flat on the table and leaned in, letting every bit of the menace he was feeling toward this man show in his body language, his face, and his voice. The man reacted before he even spoke, quailing slightly, pulling back.

"Stealing from Redstone was one thing," Tony said icily. "Trying to hurt one of the family, and a close personal friend of Josh Redstone himself, that's something else."

"Redstone?"

The gulped exclamation said it all, and Tony finally saw what he'd wanted to see—fear.

"What do you have to do with Redstone?"

"I," Tony said, leaning in, "am the man who will decide if you simply continue to serve your time here in relative peace, forgotten as you deserve, or if the entire force of Redstone comes down on you."

Santerelli squirmed on the seat. Tony knew in that instant the man would break.

"If you think he can't make your life a living hell even in here, you're wrong."

He paused, then leaned in even farther, until he was barely inches from Santerelli's face, sensing the man was on the edge. He had no qualms about what he was going to say next, not after this man had conspired to hurt or kill a woman he didn't even know.

His woman.

Lilith.

Because she was his woman, even if he would never in his life have any more than he'd had last night.

"You have a wife, Santerelli. A son."

The man paled. He squeaked. He literally squeaked, before managing to get any words out. "You…wouldn't."

"Josh would never countenance hurting them. It's not his way. And it would put him on your level, hurting an innocent to get to someone else."

Santerelli took a breath, clearly relieved. The man wasn't just a coward, Tony thought, he was a fool. But it was the cowardice that was going to get him what he wanted right now.

"*Josh* wouldn't," he said ominously. "But I run on different rules."

Panic slammed into the man, visibly. Santerelli looked around wildly, as if for help.

"No help here. If you want to wake up from this nightmare, there's only one way to do it. Tell me everything."

Santerelli broke.

Chapter 23

Lilith looked at her reflection in the mirror. Again. She wasn't one for overindulgence in checking her own appearance, but this morning she seemed driven to it. As if what she'd done must have forever imprinted itself on her face.

But there was no sign, except for a new weariness in her eyes, that she was forever changed. The reflection that looked back at her was the same; younger than she was on the calendar, and much younger than she felt just now. She had always been passingly grateful that she didn't look her age; now she wasn't sure it was a blessing. If she did, she might not be in this painful place now.

"You knew," she whispered to herself. "You knew you shouldn't, and you did it anyway."

She made herself turn away and start to dress. She'd already spent enough time hiding in her bathroom, and too much just standing there doing nothing. Even the simple decision to take a shower had seemed too difficult; did she want to wash away any trace of Tony Alvera, or savor the scent of him on her skin because that was all she had left?

She wondered what had happened to her usual calm, decisive self, wondered if she had been burned away last night, replaced by that eager, hungry woman she didn't even recognize.

Hungry for a man who, in his way, was as high-handed as Daniel had been?

She'd assumed the biggest barrier between them was her age, or his own hangup about the differences between their worlds. She'd never thought it would be this. Although she knew perfectly well that Tony's actions stemmed from genuine concern, and not Daniel's bone-deep need for total control, she wasn't sure how much it mattered if the end result was the same.

"Ms. Mercer? Are you all right?"

Taylor's voice came through the closed door. She supposed the young woman thought she'd slipped and fallen in the shower, she'd been in here so long.

"I'm fine, Taylor. I'll be out in a few minutes."

She moved hurriedly then, dressing in faded, comfortably soft jeans and a Redstone shirt that made her feel somehow stronger.

"There's a cinnamon bagel left," Taylor said as she came into the kitchen for the second time; the first time she'd lasted only long enough to determine Tony was really gone before retreating to the bathroom, mumbling about taking a shower.

"Thank you," Lilith said. It sounded as perfunctory as it was, and she added with more life, "I like cinnamon bagels."

"I remembered," Taylor said, and Lilith recalled then that she had mentioned it when they discovered their mutual butterscotch addiction.

She warmed and ate the bagel, then went into her Saturday routine, general tidying up, sorting mail that had accumulated, cleaning the kitchen. Normally she would have stripped the bed by now and tossed the sheets into the laundry, but she hadn't. Somehow making that decision was even harder than the decision to take a shower.

She nearly laughed aloud at herself, and the only thing that stopped her was the realization that explaining it to Taylor would be impossible.

"So, how long have you and Tony been together?"

Lilith whirled, nearly dropping the plate she'd been about to put into the dishwasher. Lord, did it show after all? Was it somehow obvious that she'd spent the night having passionate, wild sex with a passionate, wild man she had no business being with?

"I beg your pardon?" she asked when she could speak.

Taylor blushed. "I'm sorry, I don't mean to pry. It's none of my business."

Lilith steadied herself. She didn't want to ask, had to ask. "What makes you think we're 'together' at all?"

The younger woman blinked. "Uh…superhot chemistry?" It was Lilith's turn to blink. Taylor shrugged then, before adding, "I mean, seriously, you two, like…sizzle. So I assumed…"

Seized by an urge she tried and failed to combat, Lilith took advantage of likely the most unbiased opinion she could get on the matter. "Don't you think we'd be a bit of an…odd couple?"

Taylor gave her a sideways look. "I don't know either of you that well."

"I meant…appearancewise." At Taylor's wary look, she added, "It's all right. I really want to know."

"Odd?" Taylor repeated, as if considering the word. "No. Dramatic, yes. Head turning. Opposites attract and all, I guess. I mean, he's dark and you're so fair, he's exotic, you're classic. Both beautiful, but different." She smiled then. "I think you look amazing together."

And there you have it, Lilith thought. Not a word about what bothered either of them the most.

With the feeling there was a lesson there, Lilith turned back to her chores.

And wondered why Taylor's observations didn't make anything seem any easier.

"So Chilton and Santerelli hatched this together?"

Tony looked away from his hands, where the paler spots along the knuckles showed where he'd once worn the badge of the ES 13s. He raised his gaze to Draven, who was leaning on the edge of his desk at the airport hangar office of Redstone Security. "Yes."

"This was their idea of taking revenge on Redstone? Hurting or killing someone who had nothing to do with their downfall?"

"Apparently so." Tony grimaced; the knowledge that Lilith had been in genuine danger still made him queasy. Afraid of what he might betray to the too perceptive Draven, he added quickly, "But then, if they were smart, they would never have tried to spy on Redstone to begin with."

"Truer words never spoken," Draven said. "Well, at least it's over now. Our end, anyway, the officials can handle it from here. Good job, Tony. I'll let Josh know."

"Yes."

It's over. Truer words never spoken.

Funny how just a change in sentence order spoke an even more definite truth.

Because it was over. It had to be. He looked again at the discoloration on his hands, thought of the one he couldn't see, at the back of his neck.

If he'd had half the class Lilith had, he would have stopped last night. He would have stopped the moment he'd glanced down and seen these hands on her creamy, delicate skin. But he'd been wild with need, and then she'd touched him back, as if she thought his darker, scarred skin was as beautiful as her own, and he'd been lost.

Badges of honor, she'd called those marks, the faint discolorations and the actual scars. Badges of courage, and determination.

Maybe. But that didn't move him into her world. Nothing could do that. You had to be born into it.

"What's brewing?" he said suddenly. "There must be something on your plate by now."

"Where?" Draven asked, looking as startled as he was capable of looking.

"Anywhere." Draven frowned. Tony dug in. "I want to work. Send me somewhere. The farther away the better."

"You just got back from Caracas, then Beck's case and before that you spent months in the jungle in Brazil. Then you jumped right into this. Don't you want a break, or at least to stay home for a while?"

Home. Right. He'd found home last night, in Lilith's arms. Problem was, it wasn't *his* home. And if he tried to make it home, he'd just end up making her angry all over again, eventually.

What I can't tolerate is someone making the same mistake over and over again....

That, he thought bitterly, would be me. "No. There must be something, somewhere. Didn't you mention Australia a while back?"

"Yes, but that's all done except for the mop-up."

"Fine. Let me do the mop-up."

"Australia?"

"Perfect," Tony said, thinking that the entire planet between him and Lilith might just be enough.

"Why don't you just take a vacation?" Draven suggested dryly.

"I'd rather work. But either way, I want out of here."

Back in his apartment overlooking the harbor full of expensive boats—a place he'd consciously chosen so that every day he would remember how far he'd come—he began to toss things into his battered suitcase; the trip to Austria and that mess in the village near the Redstone ski resort in Innsbruck four years ago had been hard on the thing.

It had been hard on him, too; skiing and the cold had never been in his repertoire, and he'd rarely felt so out of place as he had there. His cover had been a visiting, wealthy playboy of unspecified Latin descent, and he'd played it to the hilt, the facade the only thing that let him function at an altitude intimidating in reality and in his mind.

He was, he realized, thinking about such things to avoid thinking about what was in fact taking up most of his mind. The realization that he was running came as a bit of a shock. And from a woman. He who had never run from anything or anyone in his life, and had the scars to prove it, was running like a scared kid.

But then, it was the scars, both physical and otherwise, that were the reason he was running. Because he couldn't deny any longer that Lisa's death had scarred him in ways he hadn't even understood until Lilith.

"Think about something else, damn it!"

That he'd said it out loud, to an empty room, nearly made him groan. But he tried to follow his own order anyway.

He should be feeling satisfied at the quick wrap-up to this case. Draven had been pleased, at least. The fact that he *didn't* feel satisfied was just further proof that he'd gotten in way over his head. It was over—all of it—and the best thing he could do was get himself out of Lilith's life and on with his own.

Such as it would be, now that he'd had a taste—God, such a sweet, hot, incredible taste—of her.

It's over, he repeated as he tossed a pair of socks into the bag. As soon as Draven called to say that the flight was arranged, he'd be on his way, leaving the wheels of Redstone to grind Chilton up for him.

And then there it was again, that niggling feeling that he'd missed something, that there was something that just didn't feel right about the whole thing. It wasn't that it had been too easy—cases actually were easy, sometimes—but something else, something he couldn't quite bury.

You just wanted it to be her ex-husband, he told himself sourly. Or worse, you're just looking for any excuse to see her again.

And neither would change anything. However good they'd been together—and the passion that had exploded had shocked even him—it was still impossible. She clearly knew that, it was him who was having the problem swallowing the inevitable.

But he couldn't seem to let it go.

When he caught himself standing over the open suitcase with a shirt in his hand, uncertain how long he'd been there staring into space, everything that had happened in the last week tumbling through his mind, he swore under his breath.

He tossed down the shirt and began to pace, needing the physical movement to try and get a grip. But it didn't work, and before long, even knowing he was likely being seven kinds of an idiot, he was sitting at his notebook computer, logging on to the Redstone network and pulling up the report he'd filed just hours earlier.

He read through it all again. He sat for a while, staring at a rushing, star field screen saver as if the answer was somehow there in that random pattern.

Then he made two phone calls, one to Redstone's in-house tech genius, Ryan Barton, who quickly found and e-mailed him the software program he'd written at Draven's request a few months ago; Tony had used it, but hadn't yet installed it on his home computer.

The second was to a woman he knew at the county sheriff's office. She was his most reliable unofficial source, had been since the day she had laughingly told him he'd get a lot further with her if he turned off the automatic flirting device and simply asked.

So next time, just ask. Don't try to bully me.

Lilith's words echoed in his head. He *had* tried to bully her, since he couldn't bring himself to try and charm her, not when he knew how superficial, how shallow those efforts were. Not when he knew how she despised the tactic, thanks to her ex-husband.

"Is that what you wanted?"

Tony yanked himself out of the reverie and read back the data she had given him.

"Yes," he said, "thanks."

"Just dates? That's all you need?"

"That's all," Tony said absently, hanging up without really saying goodbye, his eyes scanning the numbers he'd scrawled on the notepad.

He called up the newly installed program Ryan had sent him. He entered the dates he'd just gotten. Then he switched to his own report, took the dates and locations from there and entered those as well. There were a lot of them, so it took a while. Then he activated the program's compare function and waited.

Nothing. No match, no correlation that hadn't already come to him and been checked out.

For a moment he sat there, telling himself to give it up, that his instincts couldn't be relied on when his heart kept interfering, making him want to look for something that wasn't there. He got up and started pacing again, shaking his head at himself; he felt edgier than he could ever remember, since he'd left the streets.

Maybe he was simply losing his mind.

But then something else struck him, that he hadn't entered quite all the data he'd collected. He got up, went over to the half-packed suitcase, where he'd tossed his jacket. He dug into the pocket for the small notebook he used to scribble notes in. Primitive, yes, but for some things he still preferred media that could be literally burned afterward.

He found what he'd been looking for, entered it into the program, made one more call for one more date and entered that. Then he ran the program again.

In moments, a single line of data in common appeared in the search box. A single line consisting of a date, a time and a place. A single line that changed everything.

Chapter 24

The anger he'd felt when confronting Joe Santerelli was nothing compared to what he was feeling now. Stan Chilton's betrayal was so much worse, because he'd been Redstone.

Tony would be willing to bet you could count on one hand the number of bad apples that had slipped through since the founding of Redstone. Josh's instincts about people were rarely wrong. It was part of what had changed him from a young man with nothing more than drive and a plan into the head of a multinational corporation that dwarfed most privately held companies in the world. He'd built Redstone into something that to those who didn't understand seemed impossible: even a total stranger was family if they were Redstone.

And Stan Chilton had turned on that family.

He was where he belonged because of it, but that wasn't good enough for Tony right now.

When he was brought out, Chilton took one look at Tony and stopped. He tried to tell the guard he didn't want this visitor, tried to turn back, but the man was already gone. The Redstone name reached even here; Josh believed fully in supporting his local police. And since Redstone was just about everywhere, that was a lot of support.

"Who are you?" Chilton asked, a quaver in his voice.

"Redstone," Tony said simply.

Chilton drew back, eyes widening as he gave Tony a fearful look up and down. Tony knew he had him then. And it was a matter of only minutes before he had the confirmation he needed.

Next stop, Chino, he thought.

When he was face-to-face with Daniel Huntington again, Tony realized that he'd long ago surpassed anger. He was enraged. He wanted the pure, physical pleasure of his hands around this man's throat. And he didn't bother to hide it as the urbane, elegant man clad in the baggy jumpsuit sat down. He had the satisfaction of seeing a touch of wariness mar Huntington's supercilious expression. And although Huntington's words belied it, Tony didn't forget it.

"Well, well. If it isn't my wife's pit bull."

Tony didn't rise to the bait this time. "I don't work for your *ex*-wife."

Huntington lifted a brow. "No? Then who? Whoever's screwing her at the moment?"

Tony grinned, knowing it would infuriate the man. "It must really humiliate you to realize you weren't man enough for her." He remembered the man's own words. "You're less than nothing to her."

Huntington swore crudely, cracking the smooth facade for a moment. And with a sudden flash of insight, Tony realized something about the first time he'd seen this man. He remembered the moment when he'd seen fear flicker in Huntington's eyes. The moment when he'd seen Lilith, in her purposefully chosen pose, seated as relaxed and casually as if she were sitting in a friend's living room. As if he didn't bother her at all.

That flash of fear hadn't been of him. It had been of Lilith. Because she hadn't been afraid of him anymore.

And Tony knew he could break him, here and now.

"Of course," he said with a laughing contempt he knew would rankle beyond anything else, "any man would be more man than you are, you twisted, useless—no, wait. I'm sure you have your uses in here."

"We're done," Huntington snapped, starting to rise.

"Like hell we are," Tony said. "Sit. Down. Like the bitch you are. And if you think I can't make sure you're used like one by half the inmates here, think again. All your money won't save your sorry ass."

Huntington was naturally pale, but Tony didn't think he was wrong in thinking the man just went a shade lighter. And he sat.

"Who are you?"

There was more than a touch of wariness in Huntington's voice now, there was fear along with the confusion. Tony could smell it. He could smell it, with instincts honed on the dangerous streets where smelling another's fear could be the one thing that kept you alive. This man was an amateur in this world, and a coward in his own.

"I'm the man who's going to haunt you until your dying day. You'll never be free of me. You'll never again take an unworried breath. Ever. Because I'll be there. Every time you turn around."

He knew he probably looked like Huntington's worst nightmare. Should have kept the tats, he thought, knowing the sight of spidery gang tattoos would have sent Huntington over the edge a lot quicker.

But then a sudden memory of Lilith last night, tracing the faintly lighter places on his skin, declaring them badges of honor, shot through his mind. The image of her, delicate, fair, beautiful, in the arms of a man wearing the declarations of the life that would have eventually killed him, was impossible, and he'd never been more glad he'd had them removed.

Huntington's fear was rapidly escalating, and Tony pressed.

"I have resources you can't even begin to imagine. Your own are nothing compared to mine. And I'll use them all against you. You can't hide. There's no place you can go that I can't find you."

"Who *are* you?" The fear was uppermost now, above even the confusion.

"I'm Redstone."

Huntington blinked. His puzzlement vanished, but the fear only increased. Good, thought Tony.

"Yes," he said. "Be afraid. Very afraid."

"I'm not—"

"Then you should be."

"Why? Is my wife sleeping with Josh Redstone now? I always suspected there was more to that—"

Again, with an effort, Tony didn't rise to the bait. "You should be afraid because being Redstone makes my life so much easier. I don't have any of those annoying rules to follow. I don't have a civilian board looking over my shoulder all the time, no one to scream about brutality, or to care if you end up in the hospital. Or worse. And I have a boss who cares about results and won't second-guess my methods. But then, you know that."

Tony was guessing that Huntington knew quite well the reputation of Redstone, and of their security team. He'd been a mover and shaker at nearly the same level; he'd know how much pressure Redstone could bring to bear.

"What you don't know is that I came from exactly where you think I came from. A place where life is cheap and payback is truly hell."

"You can't come in here—"

"Yet I have. Because the Redstone name will get me in anywhere. And once I'm there, the game is played by my rules."

"What do you want?" Fear was gaining the upper hand, Tony noted with satisfaction.

"My rules," Tony said in a near whisper, "say you get more than what you ask for. Not an eye for an eye, but an eye for an eyelash. And for attempted murder…"

He let the words trail off, saw Huntington's eyes widen, saw him suck in a gasping breath at the clear implication.

"I owe Josh Redstone my life." Tony went for that fear. He lowered his voice again. "I would *kill* for Josh Redstone."

A tiny whimper broke from Huntington, and Tony guessed what he was feeling had shown in his face. "Call for a guard, and I'll do it right here and now."

He was trusting the man was scared enough not to realize that a visitor committing murder here was insane. Or that Huntington believed Tony was just that, insane. The man was trembling now, a barely perceptible shiver beneath the urbane exterior, but it was there.

"You made four crucial mistakes, Huntington. First, you're a bigot who assumed anyone in prison, especially if they're Mexican, had the capacity to commit murder for hire. Second, you chose incompetents—but then, how would you know, when you don't even realize how incompetent you yourself are?"

Huntington's temper flared. At the accusation of incompetence, Tony noted, not of murder for hire.

"Go to hell."

"From where I sit, you're the one in hell. But where you are now is paradise compared to where you're going."

"You can't—"

"Third," Tony ticked off on his fingers. "You went after someone who matters to Josh Redstone. And he is a man who knows the meaning of friendship and loyalty. A man who wouldn't hesitate to use every bit of the worldwide power he holds to defend one of his own. He'll crush you, your reputation, and toss the debris into the sewer where it belongs."

The bluster vanished. Huntington was starting to look like the cornered rat he was. Tony got up and walked around the table. He sat down next to Huntington, who tried to scuttle away sideways on the bench. Tony clamped his fingers on the back of the man's neck, wondering if he would have the willpower not to break it.

"But your worst mistake," he whispered, so close to Huntington's ear, "was crossing me."

Huntington whimpered again, trying to pull away. Tony tightened his grip, thinking how easy it would be to snap the vertebrae beneath his fingers. But death was too clean, too easy for this man. He deserved worse.

His worst nightmares come true.

"I have brothers in this place, *pendejo*. Lots of them. And unlike the bumblers you hired, they *have* killed. They're in for life already, and they have nothing to lose."

"What do you want?" This time the question was a plea, and Tony knew Huntington was crumbling. But he didn't stop.

"You'll never know which ones they are, or when I'll tell them to strike. And they won't kill you right away. They'll just torture you. And I don't mean that pansy-ass stuff you people think of as torture. I mean the real thing."

"What do you want, damn you? A confession?"

"I'm not the police. I don't need a confession. And your partners already rolled on you. Not only did you pick incompetents to try to kill her, you chose cowards as your accomplices. Santerelli and Chilton couldn't wait to toss it all in your lap."

"Santerelli?" Huntington looked genuinely blank, but Tony had expected that.

"The other incompetent Stan Chilton sucked into this. After you had your little chat with him while he was awaiting transfer to Camp Cupcake west."

"I didn't—"

"You did. You were on the work detail in the yard when he was waiting for the bus. You heard him swearing to get even with Redstone, with Josh. And offered him a way.

Offered him any personal information he needed to get to the woman who'd taken his place. Even though she had nothing to do with taking him down."

"The bitch had it coming," Huntington spat out, giving up the pretense at last.

Tony's grip tightened, and for a brief moment, he truly wondered if he was going to be able to stop himself.

"All right, all right!" Huntington yelped. "I did it. Just back off."

With one of the greatest efforts of his life, Tony released his grip.

"You think this makes any difference to me?" Huntington sneered. "I'll deny all of this. You'll never prove a thing."

"And who's going to believe a convicted felon?"

Huntington paled further; he obviously still hadn't accepted that.

"Besides," Tony went on, "who said anything about proof?"

Huntington blinked then. "What?"

"I told you, I'm not the police. I don't need proof. You're mine now, Huntington. Until I get bored with toying with you. Then I'll decide which of my brothers gets the honor of putting an end to your misery. And believe me, you'll be begging for it long before then."

"But…you got what you wanted!"

It was small of him, perhaps, but Tony took great pleasure in seeing this man's fear escalate to terror. The terror of knowing that all his money, all his social standing, couldn't save him now. It made him smile. That it wasn't a pleasant smile was made evident by the cold sweat that broke out on Huntington's forehead.

"I told you what you wanted to know. Call the guards, the cops, whoever, but leave me the hell alone."

"And where," Tony said in that deadly casual tone, "did you get the idea this was a bargaining session?"

"But I gave you what you wanted." Huntington was whining now. "You have to call them off!"

"I don't have to do a thing. I told you, I have my own rules. And I never promised you a thing, now, did I?"

Pure horror spread over the man's already pale face.

"I don't understand," he whispered, shaking visibly now.

"You never did." With an image in his mind of Lilith facing her worst nightmare, this man, with more courage than this coward had ever dreamed of having, Tony added, "And that will be your fatal mistake."

He left Daniel Huntington a broken, terrified man who would spend his future shaking at every turn, forever looking over his shoulder.

It was almost enough.

Chapter 25

"So it was Daniel all along," Lilith said, feeling more than a little dazed.

"Yes."

Tony's voice was flat, emotionless. As it had been through his entire explanation. She'd heard business reports given with more emotion. Even Liana, who had been in her office when Tony and Josh had arrived, gave him a curious glance. She'd told the young woman to stay; after all, it had been her concern that had started all this in the first place, and it would save Lilith repeating it all later.

Even when Tony had explained what he'd done, what he'd left hanging over her ex-husband's head, he'd shown no sign of anything personal, no hint that this had ever been anything more than a job to him.

Of course, perhaps he couldn't, with his boss standing right there.

Or didn't want to, she thought. Didn't want Josh to know

he'd gotten involved with the woman he was assigned to protect? Or did he not even consider what had happened between them involvement? Was he that casual about sex?

Just because it was life-changing for you…

She pulled herself together, aware Josh was watching her with that steady look that meant his agile mind was pondering, weighing, considering.

"I…thank you." She barely managed to stop herself from saying *Mr. Alvera.* "I appreciate you sticking with this."

When Tony only grimaced, Josh spoke.

"We'll piece together a case that will stand up. He's got good lawyers, but I've got better. He's going to be inside a lot longer than he'd planned," Josh said. "And he's going to be terrified for most of that, thanks to Tony. It's not enough, but…"

"It's enough."

"Sorry for you it was him," Tony said, and for the first time since he'd begun his explanation, emotion crept into his voice. "I know that's not what you wanted to hear."

That jabbed her into a sharper response. "What I *wanted* was to find out who was really behind it. You did that. Thank you," she added again, yanking her voice into a formal, business-like tone; if that's what he wanted, then that's what she'd give him. Apparently he wanted nothing else from her.

Including what she'd already given him.

"Yeah. Great. See you around."

Tony stalked out without another word, so abruptly even Josh looked startled. Her boss, the man who'd given her and everyone at Redstone so much, turned back to her, brows raised in inquiry.

She couldn't do this now. Damn Tony for leaving her to explain. He had to know Josh wouldn't just look the other way after an exit like that.

But she couldn't do it now. She just couldn't.

"Excuse me," she muttered, "I have to…talk to Ian about something. Now."

"Lilith," Josh began.

"Later. Please," she said.

Maybe she could think up a story by then, something he would believe, something close enough to the truth that she wouldn't feel as though she was lying to someone she couldn't bear to lie to.

But as she walked out the door she heard Josh say quietly, "Liana?"

And she heard her assistant, still new enough to Redstone to respond with a formality Josh never required, sigh. "Yes, sir. I think I can explain."

Let her, Lilith thought. It would only be guessing. Although Liana was very perceptive, and didn't miss much. She continued her escape, for one of the few times in her life grateful to have someone else do something she should be doing.

"Wish I could fly you myself," Josh said. "I could use a long stretch in the air, nothing hammering at me but weather or turbulence."

Tony glanced at his boss, who was standing beside him on the tarmac, looking up at the Hawk V, the latest in the Redstone fleet. Tony had seen and heard about the sleek little jet, but hadn't flown on it before. So far only two had been built, and rumors were running rampant that the Hawk V surpassed its nearest competition in range, speed and fuel-efficiency, thanks to Josh's design and Ian Gamble's genius with materials.

"L.A. to Australia, nonstop," Josh said proudly as he ran his gaze over his latest creation. "I wish Elizabeth could see this."

Tony's gaze shot to Josh's face; he rarely spoke about his late wife, and when he did, it wasn't casually. Tony had always known, instinctively, that it was a pain Josh carried deep inside, and he knew enough of such pain himself that he recognized it in this man to whom he owed so much.

"Her family disowned her when she married me," Josh said

quietly. "They ranted about what a mistake she, a Hampton, was making, to throw her future away on a penniless drifter with nothing but a dream to his name."

"Obviously she didn't listen," Tony said, for something to say.

"But I nearly did. All I had to give her was my heart, and I knew she deserved so much better, so much more."

Knowing how it had ended, that his beloved Elizabeth had died after ten short years together, Tony didn't know what to say and his discomfort was growing.

"But she loved me. She swore my heart, my love, was enough. And the day the Hawk I flew for the first time, she was the one who cheered the loudest. She sent her father a photo of the takeoff, the first time she'd communicated with him since she told him she wasn't going to let his ridiculous idea of proper social hierarchy ruin her life."

Tony was utterly speechless now. Josh was looking at him with a quiet understanding that Tony was at a loss to explain.

"Have a good flight," Josh said, and was gone before Tony managed to find his voice.

I could have done without that, he thought as he stared after his boss. It had been unsettling, to say the least. Because, Tony realized, in the entire sixteen years he'd known Josh Redstone, he had never once talked about his late wife like that.

Tony started toward the jet. Obviously, Josh had had a reason. And the only one Tony could think of was the one he most didn't want to think about.

He went up the gangway steps, wondering if Lilith had told Josh about them, if that's why he'd opened up about Elizabeth. He'd obviously been making a point. But the analogy didn't really apply; while Josh might not have had much to recommend him to Elizabeth's patrician parents, he hadn't been starting from negative ground. He might not have been a blue blood, but he hadn't been a gangbanger, either. He hadn't—

Tony stopped dead two steps into the cabin of the jet. Stared. And for the first time in sixteen years, he swore at the man who'd saved him.

"Damn it, Josh!"

Lilith looked up at him, clearly as surprised as he was. "I should have known," she said. But she didn't say it angrily. "When Josh said he needed me to leave in the middle of my work and go to Australia, of all places…"

The gangway slammed shut behind him. A man in the Redstone polo shirt stuck his head out from the cockpit. "Need you to belt in now, folks. We'll be starting to taxi in a moment."

Tony didn't even look at the man. His gaze was fastened on the woman in the luxurious leather reclining seat, with the open, inviting second seat beside her. He knew he had only seconds to decide; if he wanted out, it had to be now, before they started rolling.

She just kept looking at him, and something he saw there in the sea-blue depths of her eyes had him moving to the empty seat and sitting down. Belting in, as instructed. Less than a minute later, the jet began to roll.

"What did he tell you?" she asked softly.

"About Elizabeth. How she went against her upbringing and her parents to marry him. You?"

"He said, 'You've got a fourteen-hour flight. Work it out.' I had no idea what he meant. Until now."

"Work it out," Tony muttered.

"He told me something else," Lilith said slowly. "I didn't realize until just now how he'd meant it. He said sometimes it's better to quit looking at the obstacles and look at the possibilities."

"How do I stop looking at where I came from and where you came from?" he asked, fighting down the hope that was flickering deep down, trying to catch.

She was silent for a moment. Just when he thought she had no answer, either, she said quietly, "Maybe by looking at who you are, and who I am. Now, today. We've both been through some ugly times. We survived."

He couldn't argue with that. "That doesn't change where you came from."

"But it changed where I want to be," she said. "I'm not some perfect, untouchable ice queen."

The memory of her in his arms, crying out as her body convulsed around his, the sweet grip sending him into a fiery explosion unlike anything he'd ever known before, swamped him with fresh heat.

"No," he said, sounding hoarse even to himself. "No, you're not."

As if she'd read his mind, color tinged her cheeks. Her lips parted. Her gaze lowered, but only for a second, as if she had wanted to look away but wouldn't let herself.

And suddenly all the lessons he'd learned, all Josh had taught him about fighting for what he wanted, for never letting others shape—or stop—him, came flooding back.

"And despite that calendar you're so worried about," he said, holding her gaze steadily, "in some ways I'm much, much older than you are."

She didn't flinch. "Yes. In some ways you are. You're also an incurable flirt."

"Was," he said. "I found the cure."

She smiled at that. "I almost believe you."

"Flirting only in the line of duty for me, from now on," he said, meaning it. Then, hesitantly, he went on. "About the other…I know I was out of line. What happened with Lisa, it…"

"Haunts you?"

He didn't like admitting it. "Yes. No matter what anyone says, I will always feel her death was in large part my fault."

"How old were you then?"

He blinked, not sure what that had to do with anything. "It was my first year with security, so…twenty-three."

"Are you the same man you were then?"

He grimaced. "I was a kid."

"If you were in the same situation now, what would you do?"

"Apparently," he said grimly, "I'd tick her off all over again."

"Why did you then?"

"I was too stupid to realize what she'd do."

"So how is it your fault?"

"The law of unintended consequences."

"A harsh law to live by. Didn't one of Merton's causes state that a person's basic values may require certain actions, even if the result is unfavorable?"

His mouth quirked. "We're going to discuss sociology now?"

"It's not what you did, Tony. How you did it, perhaps."

"If this is your way of asking why I didn't learn my lesson, I don't have an answer."

"Maybe it's my way of asking if you're going to keep doing it that way. You can't force someone to do what you want just because you say so," she said. "At least, not anyone with a spine. That's Daniel's way."

"I'm not—" He cut off the fierce protest that he wasn't anything like her ex; they'd been through that before.

"You can, however," Lilith went on, "generally get a reasonable person to do what you want, when it's your area of expertise, and you ask…reasonably."

"How about pleading?" he said, a bit sourly.

He saw one corner of her mouth twitch. "Pleading has its uses."

He steeled himself, knowing it was time, that it was now or never. "It's gut-level, Lilith, to protect someone I love."

He said it purposefully, watching her. She didn't even blink. But she smiled.

"And that's the key, isn't it? I told Liana, just recently, that I try not to get angry with people who care enough to worry about me. I lost sight of that, with you. I think…love got in the way."

He stopped breathing.

"But I do know, really, the difference between wanting to control someone and wanting to keep them safe is love. Just like the difference between resisting it and accepting it is love."

She said it so easily it made his head spin.

"I can't promise I won't make you angry again."

"Oh, I can pretty well guarantee you will. No one said mixing our worlds would be easy. But if Ian and Sam could do it…"

He stared at her, searching for words, wishing that he'd spent less time in his life on the charm and more on the kind of direct honesty this woman required.

"Possibilities, not obstacles, Josh said."

"Yes," she said. "He's built an empire on that principle."

"I love you." He felt a little reckless, blurting it out like that, but reckless seemed in order just now. "I love your nerve, your loyalty, your brains, your grace."

"And I love you," she said, so without hesitation that his heart slammed in his chest. "I love your strength, your determination, your courage and your achievements. And when you take all that and weigh it against the obstacles…"

"They don't matter," he whispered.

"No. What we've found is precious, Tony. Worth fighting for."

"And I'm not one to give up without a fight."

"I know."

"So it can be done. Mixing our worlds."

Lilith gave him a smile that made him shiver in reaction. "We're Redstone. We can do anything."

"Why do I get the feeling Josh expected this?"

Tony laughed, cradling her in his arms. Lilith hovered on the edge of satiated exhaustion; this more than made up for the morning after they hadn't had before.

"Perhaps because the stateroom was fully equipped and prepared?" he suggested.

"It's a Redstone plane. Of course it was."

"Then how about because the usually solicitous and attentive Redstone flight crew vanished after takeoff and we haven't seen or heard them since?"

She laughed. "Now, that I'll believe."

He kissed her, gently, thoroughly, completing her visit to more levels of passion than she'd ever known existed; he had been by turns fierce, ardent, near wild and incredibly gentle, and she loved every one.

"And we," he said with the grin that never failed to make her pulse skip, "still have eight hours to kill."

Lilith knew the obstacles that faced them hadn't vanished. But she also knew that they could be conquered. Especially by two people who had been through fire and come out the stronger for it.

"You were right," Tony said quietly as he nuzzled her ear.

"Of course I was," she teased. "But about what?"

"We're Redstone. We can do anything."

* * * * *

BECOMING A CAVANAUGH

BY
MARIE FERRARELLA

Marie Ferrarella has written more than one hundred and fifty books, some under the name Marie Nicole. Her romances are beloved by fans worldwide. Visit her website at www.marieferrarella.com.

To Jaren Sterkel
Hope you like this one

Chapter 1

Too much.

It was just too damn much to handle at the same time, Detective Kyle O'Brien thought as he walked out of his lieutenant's office.

His late mother used to be fond of saying that God never gave you more than you could handle. Obviously, this had to be the new, improved God heaping all this on him. Either that, or his mother wasn't really as close to the Man upstairs as she thought. All this was more than he could put up with at one time.

It had been hard enough dealing with his mother's recent death without finding out that she had lied to him, to his brother and to his sister for the last twenty-five years.

All of their lives.

Their father hadn't been a Marine who had died overseas for his country. Their biological father had actually been the late, malcontented Mike Cavanaugh, a police detective who had never married their mother because he already had a wife and family. From what Kyle had managed to gather, unlike his older brother Andrew and his younger brother Brian—both high-ranking officials on the Aurora police force—Mike Cavanaugh selfishly preferred the company of a bottle to that of anyone around him.

The revelation, made by his mother on her deathbed, had hit Kyle like the full swing of a sledgehammer right to his gut. What made it even worse was that they were the last words his mother uttered.

Angry at the immediate world and feeling deprived of his mother and the illusion of the father he'd *thought* he had and his very identity, Kyle had gone storming over to Andrew Cavanaugh's house to confront the former chief of police with this information.

At the time, Kyle had believed that everyone else in the vast Cavanaugh clan had known about Mike's indiscretions. As it turned out, Andrew Cavanaugh and the rest of the family were just as stunned by this latest twist as he and his siblings were.

None of the Cavanaughs were angered by this information, and he, Ethan and Greer suddenly found themselves welcomed into the family with open arms.

Well, almost everyone. It had taken Mike Cavanaugh's son, Patrick, a little while to come around.

But eventually—thanks to his wife and his sister—he had. The whole of the Cavanaughs had come around a great deal faster than he, Ethan and Greer had. Barely two months later, Greer was still a little in shock but coping. As for Ethan, he seemed to be acclimating to the reality of who his father was.

Funny, when you're part of triplets, you expect the other two-thirds to feel exactly the same way as you do. He supposed he couldn't fault them and in a way, he envied Ethan and Greer the peace that seemed to be coming into their lives.

But here he was, still trying to work through his hurt, his anger and his confusion, not to mention his grief. And if that wasn't enough on his plate, his partner up and quit the force.

Oh, he hadn't called it quitting. Eric Castle called what he was doing *retiring,* saying something about wanting to enjoy his life before his luck ran out. Whatever the hell he chose to call it, it felt like desertion.

Castle had been his first and only partner and he'd worked out a system with the older detective. One that served him pretty well. Now he was supposed to just skip off happily into some other partnership? With a Cheshire cat?

That was apparently what the lieutenant thought when he'd called him into his office.

Kyle sighed. He should have known something was up when he walked in and saw the woman sitting there in front of Lieutenant Barone's desk. A petite, pretty blonde, with lively blue eyes and a mouth that kept pulling into a smile as easily as she drew breath. Also as often. At first glance, he'd just assumed she was a friend of the lieutenant's. Maybe even his daughter, given the age spread.

The last thing she could be was his new partner. But then, he hadn't noticed the telltale bulge of her weapon.

His new partner.

The words stuck in his throat the first time he tried to repeat them. Finally, he managed to ask, his voice low, the words coming out almost on a growl, "You're replacing Castle?"

By the tolerant smile on the lieutenant's face, it was obvious that he'd expected resistance and had decided to be amused by it rather than annoyed. "Well, given that the man's on his way to Lake Arrowhead…" The indulgent smile widened as the lieutenant cocked his head, as if he was trying to read him. "Did you miss Castle's retirement party? Wasn't that you I saw giving the toast?" he prodded.

Kyle blew out an angry breath, but kept his expression blank. "Yeah, I know he's retired. I just thought you were going to let me go it alone for a while."

"I was," the lieutenant replied. "I believe my exact words were, 'You can go it alone until I can find you another partner.' And I did." He gestured toward the young woman in the other chair. "Detective Rosetti," he emphasized.

Kyle kept his unfathomable eyes on the lieutenant. "It's only been a week."

Barone inclined his head. "So it has. I didn't want you

to get too used to being on your own. You need someone to watch your back." There was no arguing with the lieutenant's tone. "Rosetti's a transfer from the Oakland PD. As luck would have it, she's from the homicide division, so there won't be a breaking-in period." He ended with a smile aimed at the young woman.

"As luck would have it," Kyle murmured under his breath.

Right now, he wasn't feeling particularly lucky. Just the opposite. He didn't have the time or the inclination to babysit a novice, no matter what Barone claimed. The woman couldn't possibly be a seasoned detective. Not with that face.

A glimmer of Barone's temper surfaced. He tolerated a little stubbornness, but only for so long. "Look, it's not as if we're some bed-and-breakfast township where arguments are resolved by going, *rock, paper, scissors.* People have hot tempers here and they kill each other. We need all the good men—and women," Barone amended, nodding his head at the new detective by way of a semi-apology for his near oversight, "we can get. Am I right?" he asked Kyle.

He knew there was no fighting this. "Yes, sir, you're always right."

Barone nodded his head. "Good of you to remember that. All right, I'll leave it up to you to show Detective Rosetti her desk and introduce her around to the others." Barone was already turning his attention to the next matter on his desk.

"Right." Kyle eyed his superior. "Is that all, sir?"

There was humor in the brown eyes when they looked up at Kyle. "For now," the lieutenant allowed.

Kyle turned on his heel and walked out. By the rustling noise behind him, he knew that his new albatross was shadowing his tracks.

"It's Jaren," he heard her call after him.

Kyle stopped, and turned around. The woman stopped an inch short of colliding into him. "What's Jaren?"

"My first name," she told him cheerfully. "You didn't ask."

"No, I didn't."

Because he didn't care. He'd been working with Castle for three months before he learned the man's first name. Things like that weren't necessary to do a good job. He wasn't looking for a relationship or a friendship, he was just looking to execute his job to the best of his abilities. Knowing her first name didn't figure into that.

Looking just a little at a loss as to how to read him, Jaren said, "So, now you know."

"Now I know," he echoed, his voice utterly emotionless.

Her eyes met his. He could swear he saw a bevy of questions forming and multiplying. It was like looking into a kaleidoscope as it rolled down a hill. "Can I know yours?"

Several retorts came to his lips and then slipped away. It wasn't her fault that he'd been saddled with her, he argued. Wasn't her fault that his mother had lied to him, and then chosen not to go to her grave with the secret that he and his siblings were bastards, fathered by a man who didn't care enough to form any sort of relationship with them, or their mother. Wasn't even her fault that his partner had left the force, leaving him exposed for just this sort of thing.

But damn, the perky little blonde was the only one here and he had no place else at the moment to discharge his temper.

"It's Kyle," he finally said. "Look—Rosetti is it?" Her eyes still holding his, she nodded. "You'd better know this up front. I've got my own way of getting things done."

Her smile was more amused than anything else. Why did that annoy him?

"I kind of figured that out. Don't worry, I won't get in your way, Kyle," she promised, her voice so cheerful it instantly grated on his nerves. "I'm just here to do my job, same as you."

He sincerely doubted that. Rosetti didn't suddenly have a *name* to live up to, didn't have to prove that she was every bit as good as the others who legitimately bore the name of Cavanaugh. He was no one's poor relation and the only way he could show his newfound *family* that he was just as good as they were was by being faster, better, smarter than all of them.

Hell of a tall order considering that the other Cavanaughs on the force—practically an army of them— were all top-notch cops, every last one of them. Still, he swore in his heart he was more than up to the challenge.

He and his brother and sister were up to the challenge, Kyle amended. Sometimes he tended to forget that he didn't need to feel as if he was the leader of the group. Just because he'd been born a full five minutes first didn't mean that he was the big brother. He'd always felt as if he was the protective one, the one who had to take care of everything for his siblings and his widowed mother.

Widowed. What a crock, he silently jeered, his heart hurting even as he did so.

Why the hell didn't you trust us enough to tell us the truth when we were kids, Ma? Why build up a legend for a man who never even existed? Was it to make us feel better? Or did you make up those lies to make yourself feel better?

He had no answer, only anger.

Kyle realized that his so-called new partner was looking at him as if she was waiting for an answer to something.

"What?" he snapped out impatiently.

They were out in the squad room and without thinking, he'd walked over to his own desk. Castle's had faced his. The surface was wiped clean. Hadn't been that clean since the first day he'd walked into this room.

"Is this my desk?" Jaren asked. There was no sign of impatience in her voice.

What was she, a robot? Just what he needed, someone who was always sunny. "That was Castle's desk," he answered.

"Your old partner."

It wasn't a guess. Jaren had done her homework. She always did. As bright and chipper as a cartoon character, she knew that people tended to underestimate her, and initially assumed that she probably had the IQ of a freshly laundered pink sock. Not wanting to surrender her natural personality and force herself to appear more somber than she was, she worked hard to negate that impression in other ways.

One of those ways was to be a walking encyclopedia on a great many subjects. The other was to be the best damn detective she could. This included being up on almost everything, including weapon proficiency. She mentioned none of this, preferring to surprise her detractors with displays when they were called for. It usually put them in their place after the first couple of times or so.

O'Brien, she decided, was going to take a bit of work.

"Yeah," Kyle answered grudgingly. "My old partner."

It wasn't that he felt lost without the older man, who'd been a decent mentor. It was just that Castle understood that he liked to keep his own counsel unless he had something important to say. Silence was a great part of their working relationship.

This one struck him as someone who only stopped talking if her head was held under water. And maybe not even then.

She nodded her head, curly, dark blond hair bobbing. "Then I guess that makes it mine."

"For now," he qualified. Despite what he'd said to the lieutenant, he was still very far from committed to this so-called partnership.

Her smile made him think of a mother indulging her child's fantasy. But only so far.

"I'm not going anywhere," she informed him pleasantly. "Unless, of course, they decide to move us. *En masse.*"

He grunted in response as he took his seat. Hitting a few keys, he appeared absorbed by what he saw on his monitor. His question took her by surprise, especially since she didn't think he asked questions, not of the people he worked with. She'd heard he was a pretty terrific detective, though, and she was hoping to learn something from him.

"Why'd you leave Oakland?"

"Personal reasons." When he merely nodded at her answer, Jaren asked, "Don't you want to know what they were?"

His eyes answered her before his words did. "Not particularly. Someone says something's personal, I figure they want to keep it that way."

She shook her head, allowing a small laugh to escape. It almost sounded lyrical. She would have a melodic laugh, he thought darkly. They'd hooked him up with a wood nymph.

"No, I was just labeling them. Personal as opposed to professional." Then, before he could cut her off, she filled him in—whether or not he wanted her to, she thought. "I left because my father died, and there was suddenly nothing left for me in Oakland. I have no family," she confided. "So, I sold my house and applied for a job down here."

I've got too much family, he thought. *Want some of mine?* Out loud he asked, "You're kind of young to be a detective, aren't you?"

She all but radiated pride as she answered. "Youngest to make the grade in Oakland," she confirmed. "The Chief of Ds said I was an eager beaver."

"Terrific."

Jaren waited for a moment. When her unwilling new partner said nothing further, she took the initiative. "So, what would you like me to do?"

"Stop talking, for one," Kyle answered without skipping a beat, or looking up from the folder he'd opened on his desk.

Rather than back away, she asked another question. "I take it you're the strong, silent type?"

He made a mental note to stop at the hardware store and buy a roll of duct tape. The clear kind so people wouldn't immediately notice that Rosetti's mouth was taped over.

"Something like that."

He heard her laugh softly to herself. "I've run into that before."

"I bet you have."

Jaren leaned over her empty new desk in order to get closer to him. "Don't worry, O'Brien, you'll find that working with me won't be such a bad thing."

Abandoning what he was trying to read, Kyle finally raised his head. He gave her a long, penetrating look. Had he met her off the job and a year ago, when he thought he knew who and what he was, and when the world was still recognizable to him, he might have even been attracted to her—once she learned not to talk so much. But now, well, now he had a feeling he would count himself lucky if he didn't strangle her by the end of the day.

"We'll see," he said, his voice showing no glimmer of hope in that direction.

Suddenly, his new partner was on her feet again like a Pop-Tart escaping a toaster. "I'm going for coffee," she told him. "Can I get you any?"

"No, thanks." She took five steps before she stopped and turned around again. He had a feeling that she would. "What?"

"Where is the coffee machine?" she asked, her demeanor so sunny it just blackened his mood.

Kyle sighed and began to point in the general direction where the machines were located, then remembered that they had been moved last week. If he were still a churchgoer, he would have thought of this woman as penance.

Reluctantly, he pushed back his chair and rose to his feet. "C'mon, I'll show you."

He didn't think it was humanly possible for her to brighten, but she did. "Thank you, that's very nice of you."

"No, it's not," he denied, walking out of the squad room and into the hallway. "For the record, it's called self-preservation. If you're drinking, you won't be talking."

His sarcastic remark earned him yet another grin. "I'll try to keep it down," she promised.

"If only," Kyle murmured to himself under his breath. He had a feeling she heard him because she slanted an amused look in his direction.

The vending machines' new location wasn't that far

away from the elevators. They were almost there when he heard a woman call out his name. They both turned around, Kyle almost unwillingly, and Jaren with the bright enthusiasm of a newcomer who was eager to absorb her surroundings as quickly as she could.

He found himself facing Riley McIntyre, newly attached to the Cavanaugh clan herself, as were her two brothers, Zack and Frank, and her older sister, Taylor.

At this rate, the Cavanaughs were going to be able to populate their own small city, he thought cynically.

He saw her giving the woman beside him a quick, scrutinizing look. This almost constant sharing of his life was new to him and he didn't much like it. "Heard you got a new partner, Kyle. This her?"

She obviously waited for an introduction, but was never one to stand on ceremony. "Hi, I'm Jaren Rosetti," Jaren said, extending her hand to the woman.

Riley wrapped her fingers around Jaren's hand. "I'm Riley McIntyre, Kyle's stepcousin." Riley's eyes danced as she made the introduction.

Okay, that was a new one, Jaren thought. She looked from the blonde to Kyle. If any explanation was coming, Riley would do the honors. Getting words out of Kyle O'Brien was like pulling teeth. Very strong teeth.

"Stepcousin?" Jaren repeated.

Riley nodded. "My mother recently married Brian Cavanaugh. He's the chief of detectives here. And Kyle's his nephew. That makes me his stepcousin. There're four of us on the force—stepcousins," Riley qualified, flashing a grin at the younger woman. "Don't worry, it gets easier as time goes on," she said.

"Not hardly," Kyle muttered to himself. Looking for a way to garner a few seconds of peace and quiet, he decided to do what he ordinarily never did—ask for a favor. "Riley, can you show her where the coffee machine is?"

Riley shrugged. "No problem. I was on my way there myself."

And the next minute, Jaren found herself being taken under the wing of a Cavanaugh by marriage. Any misgivings she might have entertained about transferring to Aurora's police department quickly faded away in the face of Riley's sunny disposition and easy manner.

She was going to like it here, Jaren decided.

Chapter 2

"I brought you some coffee."

She was back, Kyle thought. So much for peace and quiet.

He glanced up from the report he was finishing. He hated the paperwork that went along with the job, and it was hard enough tackling it when he was in a good frame of mind. This was going to take him all day.

His new partner, Mary Sunshine, stood there, holding in each hand a container of what passed for coffee at the precinct.

"I don't remember asking you to," he said, making no attempt to take either container from her.

"You didn't," she answered, keeping a smile on her face. "I just thought you might like to have a cup. Newest studies say that three cups of coffee a day help keep your memory sharp."

Part of him knew he was being unreasonable and ornery, but he just didn't feel friendly at the moment. And for her own good, Rosetti had better understand his moodiness early on.

"And just why would you think that you have to appoint yourself the guardian of my memory?" he asked.

Jaren placed the container she'd brought back for him on his desk, then sat down at hers. She studied him for a moment.

"You know, I'd say that you got up on the wrong side of the bed today, but I've got a feeling that today, there wouldn't have been a right side." She paused to take a sip of her coffee, then asked, "Or is that just a given?"

Kyle didn't bother giving her an answer. Instead, he just looked back at the paperwork on his desk.

She sighed, but refused to give up. "Look, I'm trying to make nice here."

He raised his eyes, meeting hers for a fleeting second. "Don't."

There was no such thing as *don't* in her language. Jaren tried again, relying on logic, something she felt probably appealed to him. "Until one of us transfers or dies or they rearrange the room, we're going to be stuck facing each other like this five days a week. Don't you think it would make things a little easier on both of us if you stopped acting as if I'm the devil incarnate?"

"Nope."

She sighed and shook her head. "I think you should know I don't give up easy."

She wished he didn't look so damn sexy as he raised his eyes again and said, "You do what you have to do, and I'll do what I have to do."

She had no idea if she was being warned, put on notice or dismissed. But she wasn't about to put up with any of that.

Before she could think of something to say in return, she saw the lieutenant walking toward them. Barone held a slip of paper with writing on it in his hand.

"Dispatch called to say a hysterical receptionist just got in to the office to find the doctor she worked for— a Richard Barrett—dead." The lieutenant held out the slip of paper that contained pertinent information, including the address. "You two are up."

Mentally, Kyle winced. He wasn't ready to work a case with Little Miss Perky, but there was apparently nothing he could do about it. Resigned, Kyle pushed himself away from his desk. But by the time he got to his feet, Jaren had taken the slip of paper from Barone.

"We're on it," she assured Barone as she slid her arms through the sleeves of her jacket.

Frowning, Kyle confiscated the slip of paper from her and glanced at the address. He spared the lieutenant a look as he shoved the paper into his pocket. "Pricey part of town."

"Rich people get killed, too," Barone replied. "The details are a little freaky, so get back to me on this as soon as possible."

"What do you mean by freaky?" Jaren asked before Kyle could voice the same question.

The woman had a mouth set in fast-forward, he thought darkly.

"You'll see," was all Barone promised.

"*Freaky* doesn't begin to cover this one," Kyle commented under his breath as he looked down at the slain doctor. Parts of the expensive Persian rug he lay on was discolored. Blood oozed from the man's chest.

Dr. Richard Barrett was a respected, well-known neurosurgeon whose skill was only equaled by his ego. Said to be almost a miracle worker, his services were sought from all over the country. Consequently, he had an incredibly long waiting list.

According to what Barrett's receptionist told them in whispered confidence, as if the dead surgeon could still somehow hear her, he'd had the bedside manner of Attila the Hun.

"Care to be more specific about that?" Kyle prodded the nervous young woman.

"He always made you feel as if you were beneath him," Carole Jenkins told them. She averted her eyes from the slain figure on the floor. The sight of him had made her turn a very unbecoming shade of green. "To be honest, I think Dr. Barrett even felt he was above God."

Jaren glanced down at the man's face, frozen in horror. That kind of an attitude would have won the neurosurgeon no friends.

"So, you're saying that Dr. Barrett had a lot of enemies?" Jaren asked.

The receptionist backpedaled a little, as if she didn't want to speak ill of the dead. "He had a lot of grateful patients," she assured them hastily, and then relented, "but yes, he did have a lot of people who didn't like him. I don't know if you'd call them enemies, but he had a tendency to rub everyone the wrong way. But I never thought…" Her voice trailed off as she glanced at the body on the floor and then shivered.

Kyle squatted down beside the body, his attention focused on the large wooden stake protruding from the man's chest.

"Death by wooden stake. Don't think I've ever come across that before," he said more to himself than to his partner. "This does seem to be a little extreme."

"I'll—I'll be in the next room if you need me," Carole stammered, already backing away from them—and the corpse. "I—I just can't—"

Giving her a comforting smile, Jaren took the woman's arm and escorted her out of the doctor's study.

"You just sit down at your desk and we'll get back to you if we have any more questions," she said kindly. Turning around, she appraised the slain surgeon. The stake had been driven into the middle of his chest. Deeply. "Think it's a statement?"

Kyle glanced at her over his shoulder. "That someone hated him?"

She was going for something a bit more colorful. "That someone thought of him as a vampire."

Kyle stared at her as if she'd lost her mind. "Come again?"

"Are you baiting me?" she asked. A frown was the only answer she received. Humoring the man, she went into detail. "Everyone knows that the only way to kill a vampire is to drive a stake through his heart."

It didn't make any sense to him. They weren't living in the Middle Ages, they were living in an enlightened society. "So, someone was calling Barrett a vampire?"

"Blood sucker, most likely. Maybe they were protesting his fee. Or a surgery that went wrong," she suddenly guessed. In her opinion, those could have all been viable reasons for murder, given the right person.

Kyle wasn't ready to grant that she'd had an interesting theory just yet. "Don't you think that's a little off the wall?" he scoffed.

"To you and me, yes," she agreed. "But maybe not to the killer." And it was the killer's mind they were attempting to assess.

Jaren had pulled on a pair of rubber gloves the minute they'd gotten off the elevator on the third floor. As Kyle examined the doctor more closely, she went through the surgeon's things on his desk and shelves, looking for a lead.

When she came to a black-bound, hardcover book, she paused. There it was, in plain sight on the shelf behind his desk.

"Well, how about that."

The bemused note in her voice caught his attention.

Though he wanted to pretend he hadn't heard her, something about the woman was hard to ignore.

"What?"

Jaren turned from the shelves, holding a thick volume in her hands. "The good doctor's reading material might have given our killer the idea."

Damn but he missed his old partner's monotone, straightforward voice. When Castle talked, it wasn't in circles. "What the hell are you talking about?"

Jaren held up the book she'd found.

"The Vampire Diaries," Kyle read and then scoffed. "Who reads trash like that?"

His reaction to the book didn't surprise her. "Apparently, enough people to put this on the *New York Times* bestseller list for several weeks."

Few things caught him off guard, but she'd scored a point. "You're kidding me."

"I don't think it's possible to kid you," she added when he eyed her curiously. "But to answer your question, no, I'm not kidding. *The Vampire Diaries* has been on the list for close to five weeks now." She flipped some of the pages. "Not a bad story, as far as things like that go."

Kyle stared at her as if she'd just announced that she was an extra terrestrial, sent down to conquer Earth. "You read it?"

If he was trying to embarrass her, he was going to have to do a lot better than that, Jaren thought wickedly. "Yes, I did. I wanted to see what the fuss was about. I like leaving myself open to new experiences—like getting along with a partner who acts as if he's constantly got a bur under his saddle."

Kyle didn't appear to hear her, or, if he did, he was ignoring her comment and focusing on what she'd said before that. He circled the dead man, taking the body in at all angles.

"Vampires, huh?"

Jaren shrugged. "Some women find fantasizing about vampires romantic."

He laughed shortly, letting her know what he thought of that. "Some women marry prisoners who have no chance of getting out."

"Takes all kinds," she agreed. "Besides," Jaren quipped, "the woman who marries a lifer always knows where he is at night." He looked at her. "And before you ask, yes, I'm kidding."

"You guys mind taking this to the next room?" asked a tall, gangly man wearing what looked like paper scrubs over his regular clothing. He was one of three crime-scene investigators who had been sent to go over the doctor's office, preserving it just as it had been when the receptionist found Barrett.

"No problem. We need to ask Carole for a list of the doctor's most recent patients," Jaren told the investigator agreeably. She leaned over and extended her hand. "I'm Jaren Rosetti, by the way."

"Hank Elder," the investigator responded, shaking her hand.

"Carole?" Kyle asked as they exited the doctor's study.

"The receptionist," she told him.

He stopped short of the woman's desk. "I don't recall her giving us her name."

"That's because she didn't," Jaren told him. "She's wearing a name tag."

He'd been too interested in the weapon used to kill the surgeon to notice all that much about the woman who had called the murder in.

"I tend not to look at a woman's chest area," he said. "Avoids problems."

"It's okay, that's what you've got me for."

Kyle suppressed another sigh. "Knew there was a reason."

Carole obliged them with an extensive list of the names of the neurosurgeon's patients in the last six months.

"When did this man sleep?" Jaren wondered out loud as she scanned the names.

"I don't think he did," Carole confided. "According to what I heard, the doctor was burning the candle at both ends."

Kyle took the list from Jaren and folded it, putting it into his pocket. "Was he married?"

The receptionist pushed her glasses up on her nose before she shook her head. "Divorced. Twice."

Kyle nodded as if he'd expected to hear something like that. "We'll need his ex-wives' addresses, as well," he told the receptionist.

Carole caught her lower lip between her teeth. She was obviously thinking.

"I'd have to get in touch with one of his colleagues at the hospital to get those for you. Dr. Barrett doesn't

have that kind of information accessible on his computer." Her expression was apologetic. "He is—was—
extremely private that way."

Jaren looked toward the study. The three crime-
scene investigators had left the door open. They were
combing the area but all she could see was the body
on the rug.

"Could be a crime of passion," she speculated. She
turned back to Carole. "You wouldn't know if Barrett
had any current girlfriends, would you?"

Carole's short brown hair swung from side to side
as she shook her head. "Like I said, Dr. Barrett was
very private."

"That's okay, we'll ask around. And if you can think
of anything else—" Jaren reached into her pocket to give
the young woman her card, then stopped. She flashed
an apologetic smile. "I'm afraid I don't have any cards
printed up with my cell number on them yet." She
turned toward her partner. "O'Brien?"

"Yeah, I got one." Reaching into his pocket, he took
out a card and handed it to the receptionist. Despite the
gruesome scene in the other room, Carole smiled up at
him. For a moment, she seemed to forget about the circumstances that had brought them together.

"Thank you," she murmured.

"Guess I'm due for a hearing test," Kyle commented as they walked out of the office several minutes later.

"Excuse me?" Jaren asked.

"Well, I'm obviously not hearing as well as I should

be." Reaching the elevator bank, he pressed the down button. "Because if I were, I would have heard Barone say that you were primary on this."

The elevator arrived. She stepped inside and turned toward the front. They were the only two people in the car. "Sorry. I tend to be a little enthusiastic."

He laughed as the doors closed again. "Is that what you call it?"

She knew she was going to hate herself for this. "What would you call it?"

"Being a pain in the butt."

The best way to deal with things was through humor. She reverted to it now. "Potato, po-ta-to," she replied with a quick shrug of her shoulders. She saw him taking the list that Carole had given them out of his pocket. She nodded at it. "So, how do you want to do this?"

What he wanted to say was *alone,* but he knew that wasn't going to get him anywhere. She apparently had the sticking power of super glue. Still, he decided to give it one try. "We could divide the list between us."

"I'm still new here," she reminded him. "I would have thought that, since you're primary on this," she deliberately emphasized, "you'd want to question these people together—to make sure I don't mess up."

He wasn't in the mood for sarcasm. "Rosetti, I don't want to do anything together," he told her, "but it looks like I have no choice."

The elevator came to a stop and they got out on the ground floor. She followed him out of the building.

"Tell me, is it just me who sets you off, or is it having a partner in general?"

"Yes."

The single word hung in the air. Jaren took a breath. This had the makings of one hell of a long day. "Okay," she declared, as if she knew where she stood.

And she did. Barefoot in hell. But she'd survived worse and she was going to survive this. She made herself a solemn vow that she would.

Their next stop was the hospital where Richard Barrett performed his mini miracles—skillfully reattaching nerve endings against defying odds. Everyone they spoke to on the floor attested to the fact that the surgeon had no equal. On a scale of one to ten, he was a twelve.

But when it came to being human, that number dropped to a two.

The woman in the administration office was able to provide them with the names and addresses of both the former Mrs. Barretts.

Armed with both the list of patients and the addresses of his ex-wives, Kyle made the decision to interview the latter first. Sixty percent of the time, whenever a homicide victim was married or estranged, the search for the killer had to go no further than that person's spouse or former lover.

As it turned out, spouse number one was immediately dismissed. According to the doorman at the apartment building where she lived, Wanda Barrett had become Wanda Davenport a little over a week ago and was currently in Spain on her honeymoon with her brand-new husband. The doorman said he'd never seen the woman look so happy. For the time being, they believed him.

Spouse number two wasn't out of the country, she was in her apartment. Once Kyle identified himself and his partner and told the woman the reason they were there, Alison Barrett, a slightly overweight brunette with scarlet nails and a mouth that formed a wide frown, became livid.

"That bastard!" she shrieked. With a swing of her hand, she knocked over a statue of Cupid that had been perched on a pedestal. It hit the marble floor, shattering. In her fury, she appeared not to notice. "He finally found a way to get around paying me alimony."

Jaren glanced at Kyle to see his reaction to this display of unbridled temper. "With all due respect, Mrs. Barrett," she said, "I don't think that death by wooden stake would have been his first choice to avoid making payments to you."

"You didn't know Richard," she fumed, pacing. "Life with him was hell and I thought that now, at long last, I'd be compensated for it." Her eyes flashed with unsuppressed fury. "But he found a way to wiggle out of it."

"Your grief is touching," Kyle commented.

Her eyes blazed. "You want grief, Detective? Grief was being married to him and being treated as if I was some sub-intelligent species. He thought he was God and should have been worshipped accordingly."

"If you felt that way about him, why did you marry him in the first place?" Jaren wanted to know.

Alison sighed, frustrated. "Because Richard could be very charming when he wanted. The problem was, once we were married, he didn't want to be. He was out all day, out all night. Like some damn werewolf."

Jaren's eyes met Kyle's. The exchange was not missed by the victim's ex-wife. She quickly backpedaled.

"Not that I thought he was one," she assured them. "Or a vampire," she added for good measure. "What he was—and everyone who knew him knew this—was a self-centered bastard."

That made the opinion unanimous, Kyle thought. He had a feeling that they were going to have their hands full with suspects.

"Just for the record, Mrs. Barrett, where were you this afternoon?"

"Where I am every afternoon," she replied haughtily. "Shopping. It's one of my few pleasures."

"Anyone see you shopping?"

She blew out an angry breath, as if this was a huge inconvenience. "I went with friends. I have receipts," she volunteered. "I didn't want to see him dead, Detective. I wanted to have him pay through the nose."

"Thank you for your time," Kyle told the woman once she produced the time-stamped sales receipts to back her up. "We'll see ourselves out."

As they left the opulent apartment, they could hear Alison Barrett heaping curses on her ex-husband's dead head.

"Woman makes a good case for the single life," Kyle commented more to himself than to Jaren as they closed the door behind them.

So do you, Jaren thought, but she decided to keep her observation to herself.

Chapter 3

Kyle glanced at his watch after he buckled his seat belt. He'd more or less promised to be somewhere. His exact words, when he'd received the invitation, were, "We'll see." The look on Andrew Cavanaugh's face had told him that he was going to wind up coming. He supposed it wouldn't do any harm to give this family thing a try.

"It's after five," Kyle announced, addressing his words more to the windshield than to the woman next to him. "Why don't we call it a day and get a fresh start in the morning?"

The suggestion surprised her. She would have thought that O'Brien would have wanted to push both of them to the point of exhaustion—probably just to see what she was made of.

She was relieved to find out that she was wrong. "Sounds good to me."

Like all first days on the job, this one had felt endless, going on much longer than eight hours. It would feel good to go home and unwind, she thought, even though *home* right now was an apartment filled with boxes waiting to be unpacked. Towers of boxes that made maneuvering around the premises a challenge.

But at least she'd get the chance to chill out for a few hours.

Despite a minor traffic snarl due to a two-car collision on the next block, they got back to the precinct in a fairly short amount of time. Getting out on her side, Jaren paused. The ride back had consisted of her talking in between the silences. O'Brien's contributions to the conversation had been limited to occasional grunts, and even those she had to prod out of him.

Still, Jaren thought it might be worth a try to ask. The worst that could happen would be another grunt. "You know anywhere around here where I could get a decent meal? I'd prefer take-out, but if I have to sit at a restaurant, that's okay, too."

Kyle peered at her over the top of the car for a long moment, debating. And then, because he knew he hadn't been a joy to work with and the days that were ahead probably wouldn't be any better, he made an impulsive decision, something he didn't ordinarily do.

"Yeah," he finally said, "I do."

Maybe he got more human at the end of the day, she thought. "Really?"

Kyle frowned. "You sound surprised."

"Well, I guess I am," she confessed. What surprised her even more was that he seemed to actually be willing to tell her about the place. She'd half expected him to snap out a *no*.

"If you didn't think I knew of a place, why did you ask?"

One slim shoulder rose and fell in a gesture that he found, if he were being honest, oddly appealing. Kyle forced himself to focus on her face instead.

"There was always an outside chance," Jaren replied. "And to be honest, after dragging almost every word out of you today, what I'm really surprised about is that you're willing to share the information."

He didn't make it an outright invitation. Instead, what he said was, "Best meals in town are at Andrew Cavanaugh's house."

"Andrew Cavanaugh," Jaren repeated, processing the name. It seemed to her that every third law enforcement officer at the precinct was named Cavanaugh. It took her a second to place this one. "Isn't that the name of the old chief of police?"

To her delight, she heard Kyle laugh. It was a short, quick sound, but it was a laugh nonetheless. "Don't let him catch you calling him old."

"I didn't mean old as in old," she explained quickly. "I meant old as in former. Anyway, he's a person, I'm looking for a restaurant."

He knew Andrew's philosophy. The more, the merrier. He'd thought it was a myth—before he ever had a blood connection to the man—that Cavanaugh had what amounted to a bottomless refrigerator. The myth was that Andrew never ran out of food no matter how many people showed up at his table. Now that he'd been witness to it several times, Kyle knew this was actually a fact, as incredible as it seemed.

Having Rosetti come along with him would provide no hardship for Cavanaugh. The opposite would probably be true. "I thought maybe you were looking for a memorable meal."

At this point, she'd settle for something that didn't repeat endlessly on her throughout the night. "Well, yes, but—"

His voice had a disinterested ring to it as he told her, "Doesn't get any better than what Andrew Cavanaugh can whip up. Even his throwaways are better than most restaurants' featured specials of the day."

He really did think she was pushy, didn't he? "That might be, but even if I did know where the man lived, I couldn't just go barging in and show up for dinner." He surprised her by laughing in response. She looked at him in confusion. Was he pulling her leg? "Did I say something funny?"

"From what I've gathered—and I've only interacted with the man a handful of times—that's exactly what you can do."

"I don't understand."

"The chief likes to cook and he really seems to like

having his family around him. In his opinion, the best way he can get them to keep coming back is to keep feeding them."

O'Brien had missed one very important point, she thought. "I'm not family."

The glimmer of a smile intrigued her. Or was that a sneer? With him it was hard to tell.

"You are if you're a cop," he told her.

He had no idea why he was extending the invitation or saying any of this to her. The entire day, all he could think about was getting into his car and going home— to silence. At the very most, maybe he'd call Ethan or Greer to see how their day went. He'd already made up his mind that he wasn't going to show up at Andrew's tonight for the party.

But for some reason he couldn't quite fathom, he'd changed his mind. He knew that the former chief of police felt personally guilty for the way Kyle and his siblings had been physically and emotionally abandoned by the man responsible for bringing them into the world in the first place.

Ordinarily, someone else's guilt was none of Kyle's concern, but Cavanaugh had tried to do right by them. He supposed that not showing up tonight would be an insult. It'd be tantamount to throwing the man's hospitality in his face.

That he felt a certain obligation to go was understandable. The real mystery was why he was asking Rosetti to come with him.

Maybe it was as simple as just feeling sorry for her. And then again, maybe not.

"I was thinking of dropping over there tonight. He's having some kind of gathering," Kyle explained vaguely. "If you wanted to tag along…" He left the rest unsaid.

There was silence for exactly two seconds.

"Sure. Yes. That would be very nice." Eagerness increased with every word she uttered. And then she shook her head. "You know, O'Brien, you're a damn hard man to figure out."

Kyle had a perfect solution for that. "Then don't try."

"Now that sounds more like you," Jaren responded, grinning. "Look, I just have to get my car. I'll follow you over to the house."

He took out his worn notebook, vaguely realizing that there were only three empty sheets left. Kyle turned to a fresh one and wrote something down, then tore it out and held it out to her.

"Here's the chief's address. In case you get lost," he added when she raised a quizzical brow.

There was no chance of that, he thought as he drove to the chief's house. Jaren Rosetti followed closer than a heartbeat, leaving hardly enough room between his car and hers for a thin mint.

When he pulled up to the curb, she was right there behind him, matching movement for movement. "You know," he said as he got out of his car, "if there'd been an eager cop around, you could have gotten a ticket for tailgating."

"Lucky there was no eager cop around," she countered, amused. They both knew that uniforms didn't issue tickets to detectives unless gross misconduct was involved. Jaren examined the house number they'd parked in front of and turned to him. "This isn't the address you gave me."

"That's because there's no space left to park in front of the chief's house." He nodded toward the middle of the street. "It's one of their birthdays and he's throwing a party. Everyone was supposed to come."

That stopped her dead. "Birthday?" Jaren echoed. She suddenly felt awkward, not to mention empty-handed. "But I don't have anything to give."

"Why should you? You don't even know Callie." Callie was the chief's oldest daughter, married to the judge whose kidnapped daughter she'd helped rescue.

He had a point, but he was missing the main one. "But if I don't even know her, why am I—?"

"You hungry or not?" he demanded.

"Hungry," she confirmed. Hungrier for company than she was for anything that could be served on a plate, she added silently. While she was comfortable enough in her own skin, she had to admit that she did like the sound of people's voices and she *really* enjoyed interacting with them.

"Then stop arguing and come on," he ordered.

Jaren hurried to catch up as he walked quickly down the block.

He was right. The entire way from where they parked to the front of Andrew's house was jammed with cars, all going nose to tailpipe. She didn't envy the owners when they attempted to free their rides in order to go home.

Music greeted them before they ever reached the house, as did the sound of laughter. Andrew Cavanaugh's house seemed to exude warmth.

Walking up to the front door, Kyle didn't bother ringing the bell. Instead, he knocked on the door. Hard.

When there was no response, he tried the doorknob and found it wasn't locked.

"He leaves his door unlocked?" she asked, stunned. The neighborhood where she'd lived with her father had slowly gone downhill. By the time she'd sold the place, the front door had been outfitted with double locks coupled with a chain.

Kyle glanced at her over his shoulder just as he opened the door. "If you were a thief, would you walk into this?"

This was practically a wall of people, mostly detectives with their spouses and children. There was also a smattering of uniformed officers who'd come straight from work.

"Not unless I had a death wish," she agreed. It looked as if half the precinct had gathered here. There wasn't a solemn face in the lot.

This was it, Jaren realized. This was exactly what she'd longed for all of her life. Enough family stuffed into a house to make the very walls groan and bow. As far back as she could remember, there'd only been her parents and her. And, from the time she turned twelve—when her mother had decided that she'd just had enough and walked out, never to be heard from again—there'd been only her and her father.

Officer Joseph Rosetti had been a handsome man, quick to smile, quick to tell a joke and quick to raise a glass in a toast—even if he was the only one in the room. Most of her childhood had been spent either taking care of her father, or searching the local bars for his whereabouts in order to bring him home. Despite his shortcomings, Jaren loved him dearly and she knew that, in his own way, her father had loved her, too.

Just not enough to conquer the grip that alcohol had on him.

More than once when she was growing up, she'd found herself wishing that there was someone she could turn to—an aunt, an uncle, a sibling or grandparent—just someone with a few good words to cheer her on and buoy her up. But the only family she had was a man who seemed intent on pickling his liver one bottle at a time.

Eventually, he had. Liver failure claimed him, taking him, in her opinion, years before his time.

Lost in thought and wishful thinking as she scanned the large group of people, she suddenly felt a large hand on her shoulder. Turning, she saw a tall, smiling man with the kindest blue eyes she'd ever seen. He'd placed himself between her and her new partner.

Instinctively, she knew this had to be Andrew Cavanaugh.

"You came!" he exclaimed, his booming voice echoing with both pleasure and surprise. He turned approving eyes toward the young woman with his brother's son. "And you brought someone with you."

Kyle nodded. "This is my new partner, Andrew. She's

new to Aurora and she asked me if I knew anyplace that served really good food."

"And you brought her to me," Andrew concluded, pleased. "Well, young lady, I hope you don't come away disappointed. By the way, Kyle forgot to introduce us. I'm Andrew Cavanaugh."

"Yes, I know," Jaren said, shaking his hand. His grip was firm and warm. She noted that he didn't insult her by weakening his grip in deference to her softer gender. She liked that. Nothing worse than a limp-wristed handshake. "My name is Jaren. Jaren Rosetti."

"Rosetti," Andrew repeated. His eyebrows drew together as he thought for a moment. "I used to know a Joe Rosetti. He was on the Oakland police force. Had an occasion to work with him early on. Great guy. Any relation?"

A spark of pride ignited. Until the end came when he had to be hospitalized, her father had somehow managed to be a functioning alcoholic, never drinking on the job, just continually from the moment he was off duty. He'd fooled a lot of people, she remembered.

"He was my father."

"Was?" The concern in Andrew's eyes was genuine. She liked him immediately.

Jaren nodded. "He died a couple of months ago." It was still hard for her to say that. Harder still to imagine a world without Joe Rosetti.

"Well, I'm sorry to hear that, Jaren. Your father was a good cop." Somewhere in the distance, a timer went off, but Andrew continued talking to the young woman his nephew had brought into his house. "He must have been proud to see you follow in his footsteps."

By the time she'd made it to the rank of detective, her father had retired from the force and been too wound up in his daily ritual of emptying wine bottles with Black Russian chasers to take much notice of anything.

Jaren knew that her smile was just a wee bit tight as she said, "I'd like to think so." Was it her imagination, or had the chief's eyes softened just a shade, as if he understood what wasn't being said?

Andrew turned toward his nephew. "Why don't you introduce Jaren around, Kyle? By the way, in case you're wondering, your brother and sister are already here. You were the last holdout," Andrew said with a soft laugh, as if he'd known all along that it would just be a matter of time before he was won over by the family. He clapped Kyle on the shoulder and said warmly, "Glad to see that you decided to make it. Wouldn't have been the same without you."

Kyle looked back into the house. The living room, the family room and parts beyond, including the back-yard, were teeming with people.

"And how would you have noticed?" he asked dryly.

"Trust me," Andrew assured him, "I would have noticed." The timer sounded a second time. Andrew checked his watch. "If you'll excuse me, I've got to see to the main course."

"He really does cook, then?" Jaren asked.

Kyle laughed. "You don't know the half of it."

She had never really mastered the kitchen. The best

she could do was work with things that came in boxes and had the word *helper* in the title. Cooking for its own sake was a foreign concept to her. She'd been too busy juggling school, jobs—part-time and full—and caring for her delinquent father to spend any real time in the kitchen beyond cleaning up.

"He seems like a very nice man," she observed as she watched the former chief retreat into his state-of-the-art kitchen.

"Yeah." No matter how he felt—or didn't feel—about becoming part of this close-knit clan, there was no denying the fact that Andrew Cavanaugh had done his damnedest to make the transition easy on all three of them. But he still wasn't completely convinced that he wanted in.

He became aware that his new partner was studying him. When he glanced over at her, she asked, "And you're actually related to him?"

He could see how she might doubt that, given their natures. "Yeah."

"How?" The single word had launched itself out of her mouth before she could think to stop it.

He blew out a breath. "Do you ever stop asking questions?"

"Sure. Once I get the answers."

Just because—in a moment of weakness he was beginning to regret—he'd felt sorry for her and brought her to this gathering, didn't mean that he was going to bare his soul to her.

"If you get all the answers," he told her, "then there's nothing to look forward to."

"Sure, there is," she contradicted. "More questions—and answers."

He wasn't about to be cornered into a game of truth or dare with this woman. "Don't make me regret bringing you here."

Jaren knew when to back off. "I'll do my best," she promised.

They stood in the doorway of the living room for perhaps ten seconds before they were approached by another one of the Cavanaughs. This time, it was Patience, the only Cavanaugh besides Janelle who wasn't a law-enforcement agent. Patience's vocation lay with curing animals. Her involvement with the police department, other than through her sibling, cousins and uncles, was by being the official vet for the K-9 unit. Which was how she'd met her husband.

She was also Mike's daughter and thus Kyle's half sister, a connection she more than readily embraced. As she came toward them now, there was the same mixture of pleasure and surprise evident in her face that her uncle had displayed.

She brushed her lips against Kyle's cheek, catching him off guard. "I didn't think you were going to make it," she confessed. Her eyes darted to Jaren's face, then back to her newly discovered half brother. "And you brought a date?" It was more of a question than an assertion.

"I brought my partner," Kyle corrected. "She was hungry and it's a known fact that Andrew's the best cook in town, so I just thought—"

Why was he even explaining himself? Kyle wondered. Maybe he shouldn't have shown up at all. More than that, a part of him regretted pushing for recognition as Mike Cavanaugh's son. He wasn't even completely certain why he'd pushed the way he had. What had he hoped to accomplish? It wasn't as if the man was still around to acknowledge the connection.

When he'd undertaken this little mission, he'd been prepared for fierce opposition. Just the opposite had occurred. He'd had dealings with the Cavanaughs before. Anyone who was on the force had had dealings with a member of the clan at one time or another. He'd always thought that they were a decent bunch of people. But even so, he'd expected them to be hostile to the idea that he and his siblings cast a shadow on Mike Cavanaugh's name by turning up and claiming to be his offspring.

Nothing could have been further from the truth. He still didn't quite understand why.

Patience hooked her arm through Jaren's. "So, his new partner, huh? This should be interesting," she prophesized. "By the way, I'm Patience, Kyle's half sister. We shared a father," she said matter-of-factly. "Let me take you around and introduce you, Jaren."

Jaren felt her mouth curving, reflecting the smile she felt inside. "Works for me."

Her smile didn't even fade as she heard Kyle instruct Patience, "Take your time. There's no hurry."

"He takes getting used to," Patience confided with a comforting smile. "But in the long run, we figure he's worth it."

"I've kind of figured that out myself," Jaren told her.

Patience looked at her for a long moment, her smile warm and welcoming. "My money's on you, Jaren."

"Nice to know," Jaren replied, the sentiment warming her heart.

Chapter 4

"C'mon, Callie, tell us. How old are you?" Riley McIntyre teased as they all gathered around the birthday celebrant and the huge, three-tiered cake Andrew had baked, the last strains of an off-key rendition of "Happy Birthday" fading away. "You've got to be older than one."

One large white candle, a pink rose winding around its thick base, was all that stood atop the third tier. Callie had made her wish and blown it out to the sound of cheers, applause and laughter.

"Older than you," Callie responded with a toss of her head. Her eyes shone as she added, "That's all you need to know."

"My wife is ageless," Brent Montgomery informed Riley and anyone else who cared to make inquiries about Callie's chronological age. "Like fine wine, she just gets better with time."

Slipping her arm around Brent's waist, Callie inclined her head, resting it against his shoulder as she gave him a quick squeeze. "Knew there was a reason why I married this man."

"Yeah, 'cause he was the only one who wasn't fast enough to run for the hills," Clay, her younger brother and Teri's twin, chimed in. It earned him a swat to the back of his head from his wife, Ilene.

"I suggest we begin cutting the cake before someone gets tempted to start throwing it instead," Andrew told the gathering. He placed one of his prized knives in Callie's hand, moving the plates closer to her.

"You heard the man," Callie said to the rest of her family and friends. She made the first cut. "Line up if you don't want to be left out."

No one had to be told twice. Riley was first in line, but rather than take a plate and walk away, she began to pass out the slices as Callie cut them and placed them on the plates.

"Are they always like this?" Jaren asked. She was standing off to the side with Kyle, waiting for the crowd to thin down a little.

Kyle shook his head. "I wouldn't know. I'm new to this."

She slanted a knowing look in his direction. "That would explain it."

"Explain what?"

"Why you didn't sing 'Happy Birthday' when everyone else did." She'd been standing right next to him and had wondered why he hadn't joined in with the rest.

"I sang," he protested tersely.

"No, you moved your lips," she corrected. "But no sound came out of your mouth." She grinned at Kyle. "So, what we had was video, but no audio."

He was one of those people who couldn't carry a tune in a bucket and he knew it. He didn't particularly like calling attention to the fact.

"Maybe that was because I figured you'd take care of the audio all by yourself," he retorted.

She was a guest here and since he was the one who'd brought her, she wasn't about to get embroiled in an argument, no matter how innocuous it was. So she nodded. "Glad to pitch in."

Riley handed him a plate. He, in turn, passed the slice of vanilla fudge cake to Jaren. "I've got a question for you," he said.

That surprised her. He seemed more inclined *not* to ask any questions, and she was certain that he was given to the philosophy: the less you know about a person, the less likely you are to get close to that person.

"Okay," she responded, drawing the single word out.

Accepting the slice that Riley handed him, Kyle moved over to the side. Seeming to devote his attention to the cake on his plate, he asked, "Are you *always* this cheerful?"

There were times when a sadness threatened to overwhelm her, but she always fought it off. She'd seen

what an innate sadness could do. It had eventually destroyed her father.

"I do my best."

"Well, stop it," Kyle ordered just before he took a
bite of cake.

She glanced in his direction. There was a tolerant
smile on her face that he found annoying and yet, still
oddly attractive. Whatever else her faults were, she had
an aura of sorts.

"You don't mean that," she replied. "You might think
you do, but you don't."

"Oh, so now you think that you're a psychiatrist?"
he scoffed.

"No, but I did take a few psych courses in college,"
she answered glibly. "Everyone is better off thinking
positive than dwelling on the negative."

"I don't *dwell* on the negative," he corrected her
tersely, "I accept reality for what it is."

"Or what you make it out to be," she countered.

"When I figure it out, I'll let you know," Kyle told
her darkly and with that, he turned away and put
distance between them. Her cheerfulness was *really*
starting to get under his skin.

Feeling awkward was not something she ever allowed
herself to experience for long. Left alone, Jaren made
her way over to Andrew. The latter stood with his wife,
Rose, as well as Callie, her husband and their children.

Callie smiled at her, then, excusing herself, she ushered her family away.

"What can I do for you, Jaren?" Andrew asked.

That he remembered her name amid all these other people, even if they were his family, told her the kind of man he was. She wondered if his family appreciated him.

"Chief, I just wanted to tell you that this has to be the best cake I've ever had."

Andrew allowed himself a moment to bask in the compliment. He knew exactly what he was capable of and had the utmost confidence in his abilities. But every once in a while, he relished hearing someone say it. His own family had become so accustomed to having their taste buds romanced. For the most part, the Cavanaughs took their meals here for granted.

"Thank you, Jaren. And it's Andrew," he corrected. "It hasn't been *Chief* for a very long time."

"If it's all the same to you, sir, I'd still like to call you Chief. You're my dad's age and it just doesn't seem respectful for me to call you by your first name."

He was nothing if not flexible. Raising five children single-handedly while searching for his missing wife had gone a long way in teaching him how to bend. "Then *Chief* it is," Andrew allowed kindly. As he spoke, he refilled her plate with another slice. "So, tell me, how long have you been in Aurora?"

It began simply enough, with her answering his question. That led to another question and another after that. Before she realized what was happening, Jaren found herself pouring out her heart to this man who had once known her father.

By the time she finished, Jaren confided to Andrew that his was a family that most people dreamed of having.

Andrew grinned broadly, surveying the room. "Yes, they did turn out pretty well, didn't they? And the most amazing part was that every last one of them found soul mates who blended well into this mix." He thought of the events of the last few months. "And just recently, the family expanded again when we gained Brian's four stepchildren, plus my late brother's trio." He glanced over his shoulder toward the room where he spent a good deal of his time each day—the kitchen. "We've had to expand the basic table that's in the kitchen. Again," he added with a soft chuckle.

"Not to mention that the kitchen's been expanded twice," Rose Cavanaugh told her, then confided, "You'd think with all that extra room, the man would let me in once in a while to experiment."

Andrew kissed the top of Rose's head, the deep affection he had for her evident in his eyes. "Experiment's the word for it all right," he agreed, humor curving the sides of his mouth. "I love you with all my heart, Rose, you know that, but you have to face the fact that you really can't boil water."

Rose gave an indifferent shrug. "I guess it's lucky for me, then, that I found you," she quipped.

"Very lucky," he agreed. The wink he gave her separated them from the rest of the room, creating their own little haven.

Wow, Jaren thought as she quietly stepped back to give the chief and his wife a private moment. After all these years, the two were still very much in love.

Maybe if her mother had felt that way about her

father, he might have still been around rather than seeking to decimate his liver a lethal ounce at a time.

But then, she reminded herself, her mother had initially left because of her father's drinking. Nora Rosetti's departure hadn't been the cause of her father's descent into the bottle. That had come about because of his inability to deal with the realities of his job, among other things—things that he took with him to the grave.

"Kind of makes you believe in love, doesn't it?"

Startled, Jaren turned around to see a young woman standing almost at her elbow. The woman bore a striking resemblance to Kyle.

"Yes," Jaren said with a sigh, "it does."

The young woman extended her hand to her. "Hi, I'm Greer O'Brien. Or Cavanaugh. I haven't quite decided yet," she admitted honestly. Her smile widened. "I hear you're my brother's new partner."

"I am," Jaren answered. Her curiosity piqued, she couldn't help asking, "Are you getting married to a Cavanaugh?"

Greer laughed. "No, turns out I am one. As are my brothers." Not nearly as private a creature as Kyle, Greer focused on the positive side of this latest development. "All information the three of us received via a deathbed confession from my mother."

Kyle had mentioned his mother's passing. But she'd had no idea that it had been this traumatic. "Oh, I'm sorry. I just recently lost my dad."

"Stings, doesn't it?" Jaren nodded in response. "It's

even worse when you find out that the parent you worshipped was keeping things back from you."

She could see why that would hurt. In the woman's shoes, she would have had trouble dealing with that herself. She tried to think of a reason that might be acceptable to Kyle's sister.

"Maybe your mother was just afraid that you'd think badly of her if you knew the truth," she suggested. "From what I hear, parents care deeply what their children think of them."

The look in Greer's blue eyes told Jaren that she hadn't entertained that idea previously.

"Maybe you have something there," Greer commented, rolling the idea over in her head. And then she flashed a quick smile. "Makes it a little easier to deal with," she admitted. "But Mom should have known we wouldn't have sat in judgment of her."

That terrain was sensitive. And there no longer was a way to ever resolve this, now that her mother was gone. "Maybe she wasn't all that sure about Kyle," Jaren speculated.

A knowing look came into Greer's eyes. "How long did you say you've been my brother's partner?"

"This is my first day."

And rather than run off screaming, she had come here with Kyle. To a family gathering. There just might be hope for her brother yet, Greer thought. God knew she'd come close to giving up on him more than once.

"You just might last," Greer told her, a glimmer of

admiration in her very blue eyes. She pulled out a card from her pocket. "Here, this is my cell number on the bottom. Feel free to call me if he gets to be too much of a pain in the butt for you."

Although she'd been fighting her own battles now most of her life, Jaren decided to play along. There was no need to turn Greer down and hurt her feelings.

Taking the card, Jaren tucked it away in her pocket. "Thanks. I just might take you up on that."

She liked them, Jaren thought as she watched Greer weave her way back into the crowd. She liked each and every one of the Cavanaughs that she'd met.

That was reason enough for her to be determined to make her partnership work. The challenge would help her get over the gnawing loneliness that she sometimes felt inside when she considered her own situation. Alone was a terrible way to be.

"Thanks for letting me tag along last night," Jaren said to her partner the following morning as they headed out to begin the first wave of interviews with the dead neurosurgeon's patients.

He hated to be thanked, hated to be in the position of having someone feel beholden to him. It made him as uncomfortable as hell.

"No big deal. You looked like you had a rough day and could stand some good food. It's no secret that Andrew enjoys taking people under his wing."

Jaren noticed that he talked about her rough day as if he wasn't responsible for it. But then, maybe bringing her with him to the birthday party had been his way of making up for it.

In either case, she wasn't about to get into a discussion with him about that, certainly not first thing in the morning. They needed a good working relationship in place before she felt confident enough to raise contrary points. So instead, she merely smiled appreciatively. After all, Kyle O'Brien was certainly under no obligation to make any kind of amends.

"The Cavanaughs seem like really nice people," she commented.

Getting into his Crown Victoria, he waited for her to get in on the passenger side. "They're a decent lot," he allowed.

Jaren wondered if that was a ringing endorsement in *Kyle-speak*. Getting in, she buckled up and adjusted the shoulder strap.

"I met your sister. Greer," she added in case he thought she was talking about his half sister, Patience. "She told me that she was debating changing her last name."

Although he was grateful for the hospitality that Andrew Cavanaugh and his younger brother, Brian, had shown him and his siblings, Kyle felt it was a little too early in the game to think about changing the name on the top of his dance card.

"Yeah, well, Greer always was the one who was quick to forgive and forget."

"But you're not like that?" She raised her voice as he started the car. The question was rhetorical.

"Like I told you, I'm a realist." His tone tabled the discussion.

They drove the rest of the way in relative silence—his, not hers. Nothing, he was beginning to believe, stopped this woman from chatting away. He missed his old partner more than ever. The two of them could spend almost the entire day in silence and it didn't get old.

Pulling up to a closed gate, Kyle identified himself and his partner to the disembodied voice that came over the callbox. The gates parted and they drove on through until they reached the building in the distance.

The word *mansion* would have been an understatement, he thought, bringing the sedan to a halt in the winding driveway. This was home, or at least one of them, for Jackson Massey, the wealthy founder of Massey Enterprises, a corporation that had holdings in a dozen and a half international companies around the globe.

"Wonder what it costs to run this place," Jaren murmured.

"Like the man said, if you have to ask, you can't afford it." Kyle rang the bell and heard what sounded like a funeral dirge come through the door. A moment later, the door was opened by a solemn-faced older woman with white hair and a pale complexion.

Kyle held up his ID. "Detectives O'Brien and Rosetti to see Jackson Massey. Is he in, ma'am?"

"No, Mr. Jackson's not in," the housekeeper replied, her voice quavering.

"When will he be in?" Kyle pressed.

"Never, I'm afraid." The woman paused to dab at her eyes. A huge sigh escaped her lips. "Mr. Jackson's gone," she added.

"Gone?" Kyle echoed. Dr. Barrett's former patient had houses and offices all over the world. Had he decided to suddenly move? "Gone where?" he asked her.

"Why, to God, of course. Mr. Jackson died a little more than a week ago," the housekeeper answered, her eyes welling up. Tears began to slide down the soft face.

Well, that gave Jackson Massey an airtight alibi, Kyle thought. But he believed in tying up loose ends. "Is there anyone in his family we could speak to?"

The woman pressed her lips together, clearly struggling to regain control over herself. "There's Mr. Finley, his son. But I'm not sure if he's up to having visitors."

"We'll be quick," Jaren promised. It earned her an annoyed look from Kyle, but her reassurance seemed to put the housekeeper at ease.

The woman took a deep breath before nodding. "All right, but please be gentle with him. Mr. Finley's always been rather fragile."

Following the housekeeper through the huge residence that could have easily contained several families whose paths never crossed, Jaren turned toward Kyle. "Would you like me to handle this?" she offered. "No disrespect intended, but I really don't see you having the patience to coddle someone."

He didn't bother disputing that with her. He had plenty of patience, but not when it came to men with no backbones. Besides, it might be interesting to see the woman in action.

"Go ahead," he told her. "Let's see what you're made of."

Finley Massey was in the study. Grief over his father's death had left his eyes red-rimmed and his wheat-colored hair in disarray. Of medium height and slight build, he appeared to have slept in his clothes and gave the impression of a man struggling to rise above his grief with only partial success.

Greeting them, Finley apologized for his appearance. He gestured for them to take a seat on the sofa, then proceeded to answer their questions.

"Your father was one of Dr. Barrett's patients," Jaren began.

"He was," Finley replied, a haunted look in the man's bloodshot eyes.

There was no genteel way to put this. "Dr. Barrett was found murdered in his office yesterday."

"Murdered?" Finley repeated, as if chewing on the word. "What happened?"

"That's what we're trying to piece together," she said, deliberately omitting the detail about the stake being driven through the surgeon's heart. Finley Massey didn't look as if he could handle that kind of information well. He'd paled at the mention of the surgeon's murder.

"Maybe it was karma," Finley volunteered.

"Karma?" Kyle asked uncertainly.

Finley nodded. "He wasn't a very nice man. Despite his exorbitant fees, he acted as if he was doing you a favor by taking on your case. He wasn't very nice to my father. His receptionist told me he was like that with everyone." He blew out a breath, as if talking tired him. "Maybe someone took offense at his attitude."

"It's possible," Kyle agreed.

Several times during the short interview, Massey's son appeared to drift away. This was, he explained, his father's study and contained a great many memories for him.

"I wish you could have known him. He was larger than life," Finley said proudly. "And I'm not ashamed to say that he was always my hero." He looked down at his hands. "I'm not sure just how to get along without him."

"Take it one day at a time," Jaren advised. "It's all you can do."

"I suppose you're right." Finley sighed, then glanced up from his folded hands. "Are there any other questions I can answer for you?"

"None that we can think of right now," Kyle replied, rising. "If we do, we'll be in touch."

The minute they walked out, Jaren eyed her partner. "Where do I know his name from?"

"Jackson Massey? He was a big deal with—"

"No," she stopped him. "I mean his son. Finley Massey. His name is really familiar. Like I've heard it or read it somewhere before." Jaren pressed her lips together, thinking as they walked back to the car. And then she shrugged. "It's probably nothing," she admitted. "But I know that it's going to drive me crazy until I remember where I came across it and figure it out."

Kyle spared her a look. She'd be the one to know about crazy, he thought. "Welcome to the club," he murmured.

Chapter 5

The following day, Kyle and Jaren were walking away from their first interview of the morning when his cell rang.

Digging the phone out of his pocket, he flipped it open. "O'Brien."

Lengthening her stride to keep up, Jaren slanted a glance at her partner. It was impossible to gauge the conversation just by looking at his face. The man had to be one hell of a poker player, she surmised. She stopped next to the passenger side of the car.

"No, we're not that far away. Right. We should be able to get there within the half hour."

"What's up?" she asked the second he ended the conversation. She had to wait until he closed his phone and slipped it back into his pocket.

Opening his door, Kyle got in behind the steering wheel. "Looks like vampire slaying seems to be in season."

Jaren was quick to get in. "Come again?"

"Someone found the chairman of the board of Massey Enterprises in his corporate suite this morning. Edward Cummings was lying on the floor—"

"—With a stake driven through his heart?" Jaren cried in disbelief.

Turning his key in the ignition, Kyle pulled away from the curb. "Not much on letting people finish their sentences, are you?"

Jaren let his comment slide. Something a lot bigger was going on here. She tried to wrap her mind around the concept. Everyone talked about serial killers, but in actuality, they were relatively rare. This killer had the makings of one.

"Do you think that we have a serial killer on our hands?"

Kyle laughed shortly as he got onto the freeway ramp. "What, a vampire slayer?" he asked, repeating the term he'd glibly used.

His tone made it sound like a grade B movie made around a forgotten comic book or video game. "Not a real vampire slayer, there's no such thing," she said, in case he thought she believed in something so preposterous. "But if the M.O. is the same…"

Kyle refused to go down that road. He tended to be conservative in his thinking. Less mistakes that way and less embarrassment.

"Most likely, whoever did this read about the first

murder in the paper and decided to make use of the publicity—which is why I have absolutely no use for the media," he added with feeling. Signaling, he sped up and got in front of a produce truck. "Or maybe the same person killed both, but only wanted to kill one of them and used the other for cover," he theorized.

Stranger things had happened and that was still more likely than jumping to the conclusion that a deranged serial killer was loose, determined to rid the world of vampires.

Sitting back in her seat, Jaren exhaled. Her mind was going in twelve different directions at once. Both O'Brien's theories made sense, as did her own thoughts on the matter.

"Hell of a lot of possibilities," she murmured more to herself than to Kyle.

"You think?"

She wasn't sure if he was agreeing with her, or mocking her. But something had just occurred to her and right now was no time to take offense. That was for after the case was solved.

"You think this might be a coincidence?"

There she went again, plucking something out of the middle without a proper preamble. He didn't know what was worse, her talking all the time, or her beginning in the middle of a thought.

"What's a coincidence?"

"That the head of Massey Enterprises died last week and now the chairman of the board of directors gets killed? Do you think that someone might have it in for Massey Enterprises?"

"Jackson Massey died of complications from his surgery," Kyle reminded her. "This latest victim died of complications arising from having a stake driven through his heart. Besides, what you're suggesting doesn't take the doctor's murder into account—"

"It might if the doctor suspected something was wrong, or had uncovered criminal activity at Massey Enterprises and had started asking questions."

"Why don't you hold off coming up with any more theories until we get a look at the scene of the crime?"

"Okay." Jaren did her best to curb her outward enthusiasm, but there was no way she could properly curb her mind, which continued examining the possibilities.

The second they entered the incredibly spacious, 1800-square-foot suite that belonged to the chairman of the Massey Enterprises' board of directors, Kyle felt his breath back up in his lungs.

"What is that smell?" He looked around for the source and then stopped dead. Someone had thrown up next to the body.

A short, dark-haired man in an off-green jumpsuit that identified him as one of the building's cleaning crew was on his knees, wiping away the visual display of Edward Cummings's personal assistant's weak stomach. Roxanne Smith had been the one who'd walked into the suite this morning and found the body.

"Hold it right there," Kyle called out to the man as he pulled on a pair of rubber gloves. Small dark eyes looked up at him quizzically. "Don't touch anything else," Kyle instructed.

"Okay," the man replied meekly. He rose to his feet and stepped aside, waiting for further orders.

Jaren looked at him in surprise. "You think CSI is going to want to process vomit?"

"CSI processes everything. It's a simple give-and-take relationship. I don't tread on their feet, they don't tread on mine," he told her. "And everyone gets along."

The man really was full of surprises. "I didn't think you cared about getting along."

Scanning the spacious office, Kyle made a few notes to himself, then flipped the small notepad closed. "When it helps solve a case, I can be the soul of cooperation."

She'd believe that when she saw it, Jaren thought. "Call my attention to it when it happens, please. I'd like to film that for posterity."

She'd gotten pretty damn cocky in the three days she'd been with the department, he thought. He hadn't made up his mind whether it irritated the hell out of him, or amused him.

Most likely, it was a little of both, he decided. "Who found the body?" he asked one of the two officers on the premises.

"The chairman's assistant. According to her, the chairman likes to have his coffee waiting for him when he arrives at exactly nine o'clock."

"A little anal," Kyle commented.

"But punctual," Jaren added.

"Always the bright side," Kyle muttered under his breath. "Where is this assistant?"

"At her desk," the officer replied, pointing to one of the three doors that led out of the suite.

Roxanne Smith had been at her job longer than the now-deceased chairman. Thin, with understated makeup and a subdued brown suit, the assistant was still visibly shaking. Her hands were clasped tightly in her lap in an effort to still them. So far, she was failing.

"I'm sorry. I never saw a dead person before." She looked from Kyle to Jaren, bewilderment in her eyes. "Who would want to do such a gruesome thing?"

"That's what we were hoping you could tell us," Jaren said kindly. "Did Cummings have any enemies?"

Roxanne swallowed to hold back the tears. "Of course he had enemies. He was a rich, powerful man. You don't get to be the chairman of the board of such a large corporation without making a few enemies." And then, because she seemed afraid of generating the wrong impression about her late boss, she quickly added, "But most of the people he worked with liked Mr. Cummings. As far as CEOs went, he was fairer than most."

Roxanne shivered and it was obvious that she struggled to hold herself together. "I'm going to have nightmares about this for the rest of my life," she wailed.

"Is there anyone we can call for you? A relative, a spouse, a friend?" Jaren offered.

Roxanne shook her head as she ran her hands up and down her arms, attempting to stave off a bone-deep chill. And then suddenly, a look of renewed anxiety surfaced. "Someone has to tell Mrs. Cummings."

"We'll take care of that," Kyle told her matter-of-factly.

"According to what we heard, he was pretty punctual, arriving at nine each morning. Do you have any idea what he was doing in the office early?" Jaren asked.

There was confusion in the assistant's eyes. "He wasn't early. That was the suit he wore last night."

Jaren exchanged looks with Kyle. Had the man been entertaining someone after hours and the visit had gone sour? But then, they were back to the stake through the heart M.O. Would a woman have the strength to do that?

"Do you feel up to giving us a formal statement?" Jaren asked the woman kindly.

Roxanne pressed her lips together and nodded. Her breath was shaky when she released it. "Yes, I—I think so."

"Good, I'd like you to go with this officer," Jaren beckoned over the policeman who was closest to her, "and tell him everything you can think of that happened last night before you left." Jaren raised her eyes to the tall officer. "Would you mind taking Ms. Smith's statement, please?"

It was a rhetorical question, but the officer nodded in compliance. For a flicker of a second, a grin curved his mouth until he seemed to realize that his reaction was totally out of sync with what was going on. He sobered quickly.

As she ushered the personal assistant toward the officer, Jaren glanced toward Kyle. Her partner was silently watching her. It didn't take her long to realize why.

She'd usurped him. Again.

"I'm doing it again, aren't I?" It wasn't intended as a real question. "I'm sorry. I'm used to being the primary on cases," she confessed. "It's going to take a little adjusting for me to hold back."

He watched her for another long moment, his eyes holding hers. He couldn't picture her in a position of authority. Just what kind of a homicide division did they have back in Oakland? And then he said, "Work on it."

"Absolutely," she promised.

Kyle squatted down beside the body to get a closer look at the victim and the wooden stake that had ended his life. He'd just begun his hands-off survey when he heard the M.E. arriving. In his wake were the other crime-scene investigators.

Wayne Carter had opted to become a medical examiner because the patients on his table didn't argue with him, and didn't challenge his rulings. He felt the peace and quiet was worth the knowledge that he would never be able to cure anyone.

Walking into the suite, the M.E. wrinkled his large Roman nose. "What *is* that smell?"

"Something we hope your people'll process quickly." Kyle addressed his remark to Hank Elder, the CSI team leader who entered directly behind the M.E.

Dr. Carter sighed when he got a good look at the latest victim.

"Another stake through the heart?" He looked up at Kyle. "Has everyone lost their minds?"

"Looks that way." Kyle rose to his feet. As he did so,

he noted that Jaren had gone wandering through the room. She seemed to be taking everything in, like the personification of a mobile, roving camera. "Anything strike your fancy, Rosetti?" Kyle asked, raising his voice.

"Come here," she requested in a subdued tone that seemed completely out of character for her.

Jaren was standing by the chairman's desk. A number of papers were scattered about, but in general it appeared rather neat. Which was why Jaren saw it. The book that lay on the corner of the desk looked out of place.

"What?" Kyle demanded impatiently.

"You have to see this," she told him. And then she turned around to see if he was coming. "Guess what Cummings was reading?"

That got Kyle's attention. Because of the stake through the man's heart, he immediately thought of the book they'd found in the surgeon's office.

Kyle was at her side in a minimum number of steps. "You're kidding."

Jaren shook her head. She held up the bestseller. "I never kid about a murder."

He took the book from her and looked at the cover in disbelief. "This is a hell of a way to get publicity for a book," he commented.

She looked at him, stunned. "You don't really think the author is behind this?"

"One thing I've learned is that you don't rule out anything automatically. But it would be pretty stupid of him—"

"Her," Jaren corrected.

He looked down at the book he was holding. "It says 'Mackenzie Carrey' on the cover."

Jaren smiled. She had a feeling that he was only tuned in to police work. Everything outside of that, including pop culture, didn't exist for him. "In this case, Mackenzie is a woman."

He merely sighed and shook his head. "All right, whatever. Right now, we'll go see Mrs. Cummings and go from there."

"So, we're finished here for now?" she asked.

He glanced toward Cummings's assistant. The woman appeared a little more composed than she had a few minutes ago. "See if you can get a list from his assistant of people Cummings might have stepped on in his ascent to the top."

"I'm on it," she said, crossing to Roxanne Smith's desk.

Unlike the neurosurgeon's ex-wife, Jane Cummings all but came unglued right before their eyes when she finally accepted the fact that this wasn't some elaborate hoax that her husband, a habitual practical joker, had instigated.

Jaren sat down beside the woman, putting her arm around her as if she were a friend. Watching her, Kyle silently acknowledged that he didn't have that kind of capability. He'd always had trouble relating to people, preferring to keep a safe emotional distance between himself and them. Made things far less complicated.

"Did your husband do that often?" Kyle finally asked Mrs. Cummings when her sobs had quieted down. "Play practical jokes?"

She nodded. The tissue in her hands was completely shredded. Jaren leaned over and pulled another out of the box on the coffee table. She handed it to the woman.

"I used to tell him that they'd backfire on him someday. Edward would only laugh. But he had been tapering off this last year, hoping to present a more serious image of himself to Mr. Massey."

"Because he'd been promoted to chairman?" Jaren guessed. The woman nodded. Fresh tears gathered in her eyes.

"With your husband gone, who's next in line?" Kyle asked.

Jane Cummings looked up at him blankly and shook her head. "I don't know," she admitted, her voice hollow. "Edward never liked me asking about his work. Said as long as his position fulfilled my every wish, I didn't need to be made aware of all the tedious details." The thin, angular woman shrugged, as if the arrangement had been fine with her. "I don't really have a head for business, anyway. Oh, God." Jane Cummings covered her mouth with her hands to keep back a fresh sob as a new thought occurred to her. A frantic look entered her eyes. "What am I going to tell the children?"

"How old are they?" Jaren asked.

Dazed, it took the woman a moment to remember. She looked, Jaren thought, as if she was going into shock. "Matthew is ten and Edward, Jr. is twelve."

"Try to break it to them as gently as possible. The

media is going to be all over this by the evening news," Jaren warned her.

"The media?" Jane repeated numbly, as if her thoughts hadn't taken her that far yet.

"Are you aware that Dr. Barrett was killed in the exact same fashion?" Kyle asked.

The expression on her face told them that he might as well have pulled any name out of the air. "Dr. Barrett?" she repeated without comprehension.

"Richard Barrett," Kyle elaborated, studying her face. Either the woman was an accomplished actress, or she really had never heard the name before. "Did your husband know him?"

She shook her head. "I don't know. He knew a lot of people, but we never entertained the man socially. I do know that there was no Dr. Barrett on the board. I know all the people on the board." Fresh tears were sliding down her cheeks again. "They come to our parties," she explained.

They remained with Mrs. Cummings a little longer, asking a few more questions. But for now, Kyle decided that they'd gotten as far with the woman as they could. She wasn't telling them anything that shed any light on the crime.

She did, however, give them one piece of information that could possibly be relevant. The bestseller they took from Cummings's desk belonged to her, not him. She'd met her husband for lunch yesterday afternoon and had accidentally left the book behind.

Because of the way Cummings had been killed, Mrs.

Cummings looked nervously from Jaren to Kyle. "You don't think that book had anything to do with my husband being killed, do you?"

"No, of course not," Jaren was quick to assure her. "We're just tying up loose ends, that's all."

They left Jane Cummings sitting on her sofa, looking more like a lost child than the wife of the late head of one of the most influential corporations in the country.

"You seemed pretty sure of yourself back there," Kyle commented as they walked out of the custom-built house. "Saying the book had nothing to do with it. Changed your mind about it?"

"No, I still think there's some kind of connection. What I said was for her benefit—and for her kids. If that woman thought that her leaving the book behind was in any way responsible for her husband's death, she would have completely fallen apart." Jaren found herself heading for the driver's side. Habit, she thought, retracing her steps and coming around to the passenger side. "So, until we find out otherwise, why make her suffer?"

He thought of his old partner. Rosetti didn't have a thing in common with Castle. Compassion had never been one of the retired detective's failings. As for him, well, he found that compassion could get in the way.

"Just what made you become a cop?" he asked out of the blue as he got into the vehicle.

She thought for a moment. "My father was a cop and I like helping people."

He didn't look at his job that way. He thought of it

as a chance to put away the bad guys. "You're a little too touchy-feely for this kind of work, don't you think?"

She gave him one of those smiles that were beginning to get under his skin and definitely on his nerves. "The way I see it, people like me balance out people like you."

He decided it was better all around if he just kept silent as they drove to interview the first name on the list of people Cummings's assistant had given them. He knew a no-win situation when he saw one.

There was no shortage of people to talk to. Most of the people on the list Roxanne Smith had put together had an alibi for the previous evening. The ones who didn't went on a short list that Kyle thought was none too promising.

No tangible connection existed between the two murders, other than the method used and the book found at both crime scenes. Initially, Kyle had guessed that the killer was leaving a calling card. But since the second book had belonged to the victim's wife, that possibility was ruled out.

They saw twelve more people that day, some connected to the neurosurgeon, some to Cummings.

They even went back to reinterview Finley Massey since his father had founded the corporation that Cummings had briefly headed, but Jackson Massey's heir could shed no more light on the chairman's murder than he could on the surgeon's. About the only information the younger man could offer was to point them to the next possible successor to the deceased Cummings.

"How about you?" Kyle asked Finley before they left. "Don't you figure into the setup somehow?"

Finley laughed as if the idea struck him as absurd.

"I just cash the checks when they come. My father was the thinker, the one who could make things work. He always called me the dreamer." When he spoke of his father, there was a fond note in his voice, a softness that was hard to miss. "He didn't want me in the business. He wanted me to find my own destiny, said he didn't care what I was doing or what I became, as long as I was happy." There was the soft sheen of unshed tears as he looked at them and concluded, "He was that kind of a man."

"And were you?" Jaren asked. "Happy?" she added when he didn't answer.

"I was." There was a heaviness in his voice, a sadness that sounded as if it would never leave. "Until he died. Now I'm not sure I'll ever be able to find my way again. He was my compass."

Jaren's heart went out to Finley. She knew what it was like to feel alone.

Chapter 6

They were asking too many questions.

Were they agents sent to lure him out and kill him the way they couldn't all those years ago? They would have succeeded back then, if it hadn't been for his Protector.

The Protector didn't come in time to save you, D, but he saved me.

But now, there was no one. Not the Protector, not D. No one.

He was alone and defenseless. Who would be there to save him when they came again?

And they would come. They already had. They'd killed his Protector and they would kill him. Unless he killed them first.

Oh, but there were so many of them. So very many. For each one he destroyed, another came.

He had to keep fighting.

With a deep, shuddering sigh, he looked out at the darkness beyond the window. This was their time.

He was tempted to stay inside and bar the doors. But they would find a way to get in. To get at him.

He had to keep moving.

To fool them.

To stay alive until the dawn so that he could be safe for another day.

They were afraid of the light. His Protector had told him so when he'd rescued him.

Even though it was dark, he needed to get out. To clear his head. To think even though it was getting harder and harder to do. Thoughts didn't want to penetrate the wall of pain that wrapped around him.

It was almost unbearable.

Arming himself against the forces that seemed always just a heartbeat away, he went out the front door.

Praying.

Jaren simply didn't remember closing her eyes—she really didn't.

The last thing she recalled was staring at the chart she'd compiled. A chart comparing the two victims' vital statistics. She grew steadily disheartened because she found far more differences between the two than commonalities. The only thing that linked the two victims was that both had higher degrees from prominent universities. And both were worth a great deal of money.

Was that what it was about? Jaren couldn't help wondering as she struggled to focus. Money? Was there someone out there with a vendetta against rich people in this time of tense economic strife?

But then why these two men and not some other two? she silently asked as she looked at the photographs she'd laid side by side.

And what in heaven's name did the stake through the heart mean? It had to mean something. People just weren't killed that way.

Jaren spent the better part of the night trying to wrap her mind around the question or more precisely, the lack of an answer. And then suddenly, she found herself tuning in on a sharp ache at the back of her neck. A cottony, sickeningly sweet taste exploded in her mouth and an annoying noise came from directly behind her.

Lifting her head, Jaren discovered that she was the not-so-proud owner of a killer headache shooting out from her jaw to the top of her head via her right temple.

She also found she could place the annoying noise. It came from Kyle.

Somehow, it had gotten to be morning without her knowing it.

As she blinked away the cobwebs from her eyes, she saw Kyle moving around to stand directly in front of her. The detective was laying claim to a section of her desk with his very tight butt.

When had she noticed that he had one of those?

"Didn't you go home last night?" Kyle asked, looking at her face.

She didn't respond right away. Feeling just this side of warmed-over death, she took a breath, then asked him, "What time is it?"

"Eight."

"In the morning?" It was a rhetorical question. The sun had moved into the squad room full force, causing her to squint.

"Yes," Kyle answered patiently.

"Then I guess I didn't." Why was he asking her dumb questions?

Shifting so that several parts of her back whispered protesting noises, Jaren took another deep breath and then looked down at the papers and photographs spread out haphazardly on her desk. She'd slept on two of them and was fairly sure they'd left their imprint on her cheek.

She dragged her hand through her hair. "I was looking for some kind of connection between our victims and I guess time just got away from me."

"Did you find a connection?" he asked, pretty certain he knew the answer. If she had found one, she would have called him no matter what time it was. It was just something that he sensed about her.

Jaren shook her head, fighting off a feeling of frustration. "Not unless being rich is a connection."

Kyle tried not to notice how her hair seemed to swing back and forth rhythmically. And hypnotically.

"Some recently laid-off person taking out his frustrations on strangers?" he guessed. "Might have worked if our killer had indiscriminately sprayed the crowd with a shotgun, but he didn't. He picked them out one by one and then drove a stake through their hearts." Kyle looked down at the two photographs, each taken at the scene of the crime. They were chilling and yet macabrely comical at the same time. "Some nerd trying to make the world safe from vampires?"

"Right, that'll fly in court," Jaren cracked wearily.

She ran her hand along the back of her neck, trying to will away the crick she felt there. The next moment, she stiffened as Kyle's strong fingers moved beneath her hand and began kneading the tight knots. She tried to turn around and found she couldn't. He had *very* strong fingers.

"What are you doing?" she demanded.

"Being nice?" He made his answer sound like a question.

Jaren managed to pull back, shifting her chair around quickly so that she wound up facing him. She pushed aside his hand. "I'm okay."

He made no attempt to continue to massage her. "The jury's still out about that one." Straightening, he moved over to his own desk. "You look like hell, Rosetti. Why don't you go home and catch a few hours' sleep? I'll cover for you."

That was all she needed, to go home at the start of the day. She knew how it would look, accepting preferential treatment after being here only a few days. Her butt would be out on the street in a matter of hours.

"Thanks," she said icily. "But I don't need covering."

Woman was too stubborn for her own good, Kyle

thought. That gave her a lot in common with Greer. "Don't you have a dog or something at your place, waiting to be fed?" he prodded. She'd do him no good dead on her feet.

"No," she answered crisply. "There's nothing waiting for me at my place."

Which was one of the reasons she'd opted to work on the case after everyone else had gone home. As the last of the detectives had taken their leave, the precinct slipped into a soft silence. There was an aura of safety about it that made her feel good as well as warm. There was no such feeling at the apartment yet. There might never be.

Kyle looked at her in surprise. "You're kidding. I thought for sure you were the dog-waiting-at-the-door-for-the-sound-of-mistress's-footsteps type."

She laughed softly, shaking her head. "Sorry to disappoint you. No dog." And then she paused for a moment, debating whether or not to say anything further. She decided it would do no harm. "I had a dog," she finally admitted.

He could tell by the sound of her voice that he'd accidentally opened up an old wound. "What happened to him?"

"*She* died," Jaren answered, purposely emphasizing the animal's gender. Why was it that everyone automatically assumed that all dogs were males and all cats were females? Propagation would have come to a screeching standstill long ago if that scenario were even remotely the case. "Less than a week after my father passed away."

"I'm really sorry to hear that."

Jaren shrugged carelessly, as if Annabelle's death had made no difference to her. As if she hadn't cried the entire night after finding the Yorkie's rigid little body on the kitchen floor. "All just part of life, right?"

"So they tell me," Kyle allowed. "But I can still be sorry."

She didn't want his sympathy—or pity. "That is your God-given right," she agreed flippantly, her tone closing the subject. Standing up, she unconsciously stretched, then caught Kyle smiling as his eyes washed over the length of her. The expression in his eyes both annoyed her and warmed her. "Look, give me a few minutes and I'll be ready to roll."

His desk was littered with work and as far as he knew, they had questioned everyone connected to one or the other of the two victims. "Are we rolling?" Kyle asked innocently.

Before she could say anything in response to the assumption she'd made, the lieutenant stuck his head out of his office.

"O'Brien, Rosetti, you're up."

At this point, that could only mean one thing. They both turned toward their superior.

"Another one?" Kyle asked before Jaren had a chance to.

The lieutenant nodded. "Another one," he echoed, then rattled off the address as he crossed to them. The location wasn't that far away. The man handed Kyle the notepaper he'd used when he'd taken down the information just now.

"Guess the coffee'll have to wait," Jaren said more to herself than to Kyle. She really needed coffee in the morning. Nothing strong, just hot and sweet. But she'd get by, she told herself.

"We'll pick some up on the way," Kyle promised, grabbing the jacket he'd just shed a moment ago. He pulled it back on as he led the way out of the squad room.

"So much for my theory about a rage against rich people," Jaren said with a sigh as she squatted down beside the newest victim.

The coffee Kyle got for both of them had more than done the trick. Nine parts caffeine, one part liquid, it brought every nerve ending in her body to attention. Overtired and wired, her body was at war with itself. But all that went on hold the moment she had approached the inert body of the latest victim.

From initial appearances, the so-called vampire slayer's newest victim was a homeless man. And not just any homeless man, but one who had gained a small bit of notoriety over the last few years. The dead man had a long, flowing gray-white beard. His skin was the color of aged parchment, yellowed long before its time by a harsh sun and an even harsher environment.

But the most noticeable thing about the victim was the dark, flowing cape that he wore over his black, shabby clothing. Winter, summer, no matter what the weather or the season, the Count, as he had been dubbed by an amused journalist who had once done a human-interest story on the man, always wore his cape. With his broad shoulders and his body almost in constant movement—like a symphony that would not end—the Count gave the appearance of being larger than he actually was.

He didn't look so large right now, Kyle thought, looking down at the lifeless man.

The Count lay in an alley behind one of the restaurants he was given to frequenting. Busboys and swing-shift cooks would feel sorry for him and set aside leftovers for the man, which was one of the reasons the Count looked so well fed rather than gaunt. He didn't sing for his supper, but in exchange for the leftovers, the Count would spin entertaining, elaborate stories about his life as a citizen of the night. No one ever took the man seriously.

"You know," Jaren said thoughtfully as she rose up to her feet again, still eyeing the victim, "this one actually looks the part."

"What part?" Kyle asked.

"Of a vampire."

"So, you're saying someone's going around, thinking they're killing vampires." The whole thing sounded even more ludicrous out loud.

She waved a hand at the body. The cape was twisted around the Count like a cocoon. At a quick glance, it looked as if he was attempting to undulate his way out of it.

"Certainly looks that way," Jaren said, "but I'm open to a better theory. You got one?"

Kyle shook his head. "Not at the moment," he sighed.

And then he shook his head angrily. "Damn it, the Count never hurt anyone."

Her eyes widened as she glanced at her partner. "You knew him?" That hadn't occurred to her.

"Everybody *knew* him," he told Jaren. "At least by sight. He's been hanging around this area for years." To his knowledge, the Count moved around a four-block square area, making it his domain.

"You keep calling him *the Count*. What's his real name?"

Kyle shrugged. "Haven't got a clue. Neither did he, I think."

If the Count had a family, as far as he knew, the man never mentioned them. He'd stopped to buy the man a meal or give him money for one on several occasions. And never once had he seen or heard of the Count imbibing anything alcoholic. He was just a poor, disoriented man who never did anyone any harm. Kyle couldn't help wondering if his death meant anything to anyone. *Did* he have a family looking for him even now?

"We can have his prints run through the system, see if he's a government employee or former military man." Give him a name in death even if he never used one in life, Kyle thought.

"His thumb print might give us a driver's license and a former address," Jaren suggested. "It would be a start."

A start. It was a little late for that, Kyle thought. But he nodded in response to her suggestion. "Everything but a reason why he's lying here like that and why someone would have wanted to kill him like some comic-book character."

Jaren made no comment. Instead, she squatted down again beside the body, taking care not to accidentally step into the blood that pooled beneath him. Behind her, the CSI unit was just arriving.

Her attention was focused on the stake that had been used. It looked identical to the other two stakes. "What kind of wood is this?" she asked Kyle.

Kyle looked over her shoulder. Damn if he knew.

"Sorry, but that's not within my field of expertise," he told her. He thought a moment. "But we can get someone at CSI to find out. Why?"

She was grasping at straws but straws were all they had. "If it's unusual, or found only in one place, then maybe it might lead us to the killer."

No harm in asking, he thought. "Worth a shot," Kyle agreed. And then he smiled at her. "Nice to know you can think on your feet."

"I'm lucky to be able to think at all," Jaren countered. She'd been feeling nauseous for the last twenty minutes. Ever since she'd finished her cup of coffee. "Where did you get that coffee from?" she asked.

"I picked it up at the coffee shop." And then he looked at her. "You were there. You saw me."

It had been more or less a rhetorical question. "You drink that on a regular basis?"

"Whenever I can. Why? What's wrong with it?"

He drank it and he had to ask? The only reason she'd consumed it was because she'd been hungry as well as thirsty and had hoped that the thick liquid would temporarily satisfy both needs.

"Nothing, if I had a huge pothole to fill," she told him, then added, "I've chewed on softer asphalt."

There was just no pleasing some people, he thought. Served him right for trying to do a good deed. "Next time, you pick up the coffee."

"I will," Jaren retorted, turning on her heel and walking away from him. She took exactly three steps before her conscience got the better of her. With a sigh, she turned around again to face him. "Sorry. I didn't mean to bite your head off. I tend to get cranky when I don't get enough sleep," she confessed.

"Thanks for the heads-up." There was just the slightest hint of sarcasm in Kyle's voice.

It was on the tip of Jaren's tongue to tell him what she thought of him *and* his crack. But that would only lead back into an argument and she was in no shape to hold up her end. So, rather than parry back, she swallowed her retort and continued to examine the scene of the crime.

This time, there was no copy of *The Vampire Diaries* left lying around. But in this case, it was obvious that the victim's appearance was more than enough to convey the message.

Someone was slaying vampires, whether real to the killer or just a sarcastic comment on something that was currently eluding the rest of them, Jaren didn't know. But they had to find this person and quickly because the ante seemed to have been stepped up. The time between slayings was decreasing.

They canvassed the immediate area to no avail.

No one had seen or heard anything. The Count had apparently died as silently as he had lived.

While the other two deaths might have had some kind of motive attributed to the executions, the Count's death mystified Kyle.

"As far as I know," he told Jaren, "other than being a little off his nut, the Count never offended anyone. Why would someone want to see him dead?" He posed the question as they drove back to the precinct.

"Maybe whoever did this didn't see him." Kyle spared her a quizzical glance as he made a right turn. "Maybe what the killer saw—or thought he saw—was a real vampire," she explained.

"You really believe that?" he asked incredulously. He'd tossed it out himself, but he'd been teasing.

She shrugged. "I believe everything until a theory is discounted. Most serial killers are off balance anyway."

"But why now?" he queried.

With a frustrated shrug, Jaren took a stab at it. "Maybe seeing *The Vampire Diaries* triggered him. Or maybe something happened in his personal life that set him off. All we have to do is find out what and we have our killer."

"*All,*" Kyle echoed with a short laugh.

She nodded her head. "I know. Pretty big word," she agreed. She just hoped that it wouldn't turn out to be too big for them to handle.

Chapter 7

Bone weary and not wanting a repeat performance of last night, Jaren went home at the end of the day.

She called in an order at the pizzeria located in the center of the strip mall she'd just discovered the other morning. On her way home, she swung by the restaurant to pick up what was going to constitute her dinner as well as her breakfast for the next couple of days—one extra-large pizza.

The thin-crusted, extra-cheese-and-meat offering was still warm and resting on the passenger seat beside her, filling the interior of her small vehicle with a comforting aroma. She could almost feel her salivary glands kicking in and going into overdrive. She was tempted to take a piece and start eating as she drove, but she managed to refrain.

After bringing the pizza inside her second-floor garden apartment, Jaren deposited the large box on the kitchenette table. Determined to exercise control, Jaren went to change, putting on a pair of comfortable jeans and a T-shirt. On her way back to the kitchen, she turned on her TV set. The two things she'd done on the day she'd moved in was have the electricity turned on and have the cable company hook up her set.

The channel that came on now didn't matter. She kept the TV on for company, wanting something besides silence to fill the room. As she returned to the kitchen, Jaren also turned on most of the lights in the apartment.

Usually, the dark didn't bother her, but this case, with its eerie details, was getting under her skin. Until she could come to some kind of logical conclusion about the nature of the killer, she preferred seeing into all the corners of her apartment.

Not that that was an easy trick. There were towers of opened and unopened boxes scattered throughout the two-bedroom apartment. She'd been in Aurora a full two weeks now and so far, she'd only unpacked necessities.

Admittedly, Jaren thought ruefully, she wasn't much of a housekeeper these days, but then, those weren't the skills that the police department required of her. Her years of caring for her father, of being the adult to his child had caused her to shun all vestiges of that sort of behavior when it came to her own living space.

Picking out the largest piece, she brought her plate

with her into the crammed living room. Jaren sank down on the floor, sitting cross-legged in front of the TV. A local news station was on, but her attention was primarily focused on appeasing her growling stomach.

She'd just systematically worked her way through the slice to the end crust when the bell rang. Frowning, she glanced in the door's direction, as if that would be sufficient to make the bell cease trying to claim her attention.

It didn't.

The doorbell rang a second time.

With a sigh, she got up, picked up her plate and walked back to the kitchen. The front door was just off to the side. Setting her plate down on the table, she paused. She hadn't actually made any friends and as far as she knew, no one outside of the Human Resources Department at the precinct even *had* her home address. This had to be a stranger.

For a second, she glanced at her service revolver casually lying on the table beside the pizza box where she'd put it.

Better safe than sorry, she told herself, picking the gun up.

Just then, her cell phone rang. Holding on to her weapon with her right hand, Jaren dug the phone out of her back pocket with her left.

"Hello?"

"Are you planning on opening the door anytime soon, or are you just going to keep staring at it for the rest of the night?"

Startled, Jaren looked around, searching for a hidden

camera. Then, chagrined, she realized that the window over the sink looked out on the space just a few feet shy of her door. Anyone coming up the walk could look in and see her in the kitchen.

Added to that, the voice was familiar. "O'Brien?" she asked even as she told herself she was wrong. They'd just spent the whole day together, basically getting on each other's nerves. There was absolutely no reason for him to be here.

"Good guess," the deep voice on the other end of the cell said. "Now open the damn door."

Still holding her cell phone in her hand, she tucked the service revolver into the back of her jeans and flipped open the lock. She stepped back as she opened the door.

Jaren started to ask if there'd been another vampire slaying and if that was what had brought him to her door when she realized that he was holding something wriggly and caramel-colored in his hands.

All paws and ears, her partner's companion was a puppy—of the mongrel persuasion.

What the hell was O'Brien doing here with a puppy?

Since she was still partially blocking access to her apartment and not saying anything, Kyle asked coolly, "Mind if we come in?"

Jaren cleared her throat and took another step back, clearing a path for him. She was still staring at the extremely animated ball of fluff in his hands. "Who's your friend?"

"She doesn't have a name yet," Kyle told her, struggling to keep the dog close. The puppy seemed just as determined *not* to be kept close. From what she could see of the situation, Jaren mused, O'Brien was the one destined to eventually lose the battle. "I figured you might want to take care of that little detail."

Jaren's eyebrows drew together as she tried to make sense of her partner's answer. "Why would I want to do that?"

"Because she's your dog," he replied simply.

Jaren stared at him. "I don't have a dog."

"You do now," he informed her matter-of-factly. Kyle twisted around, foiling the puppy's attempt to escape by climbing up his shoulder and then diving down to the floor. "My sister's dog, Hussy, had a litter a couple of months ago and she's been trying to find homes for the puppies now that they're weaned."

"Hussy?" she echoed. That seemed like a rather callous name for a pet.

"She gets around," Kyle explained, giving her Greer's reason for selecting the name. "Despite all of Greer's pre-cautions," he added. Greer had given in to the inevitable and was having the dog spayed before she had a chance to beget yet another litter. "Interested?" He seemed to move the puppy toward her as he asked the question.

It was on the tip of Jaren's tongue to politely but firmly refuse the offer. She even got to utter the first few words.

"It's very nice of you to think of me—"

But her refusal got no further. With a little help from Kyle, the puppy took matters into her own paws. Its tongue working faster than a windshield wiper set on High, the puppy began to lick every inch of Jaren's face.

Any resolve Jaren had melted away on the spot. She wasn't even sure just when the transfer was undertaken, when the puppy went from Kyle's hands into hers, but suddenly, there she was, holding on to a wiggling mass of tongue and fur, trying not to laugh as the puppy tickled her earlobe.

But still she valiantly tried to turn away the gift. She had no time for a dog in her life, especially not a puppy. Puppies required care and attention she just didn't have to give—no matter how adorable this one was.

"O'Brien, I can't—"

Kyle didn't let her get any further. "Yes, you can," he insisted. "You'll be doing my sister—and yourself— a favor."

"I don't know your sister and how would this be doing me a favor?"

This was harder than he thought. When he'd stopped by Greer's to pick up the puppy, he'd been fairly certain this was going to be a piece of cake, a win-win situation. Greer would have gotten a good home for one of her puppies, and he wouldn't have to apologize for getting on Rosetti's case. The puppy's very existence would do that for him.

"You said you had a dog that died."

"Yes?" Jaren pressed.

He spelled it out for her. "According to pet owners, once you've been there, once you've had a pet in your life, there's a void that opens up when they're gone that nothing else except another pet can fill."

Okay, he was right, but she had no desire to open

herself up to being hurt again and dogs didn't live nearly long enough.

"I had no idea you had a degree in psychology," she commented wryly.

"Just a student of human nature." A careless shrug accompanied his words.

For her part, Jaren was doing her very best to resist but even she sensed that it was doomed to failure. The puppy was winning her over by the moment.

"In case you haven't noticed, I'm a cop, and as such, I'm out all hours. That wouldn't be fair to the dog. I can't give her the kind of attention she needs and deserves."

Rather than argue, Kyle dug into his back pocket and pulled out a folded, colorful ad. He handed it to her. Jaren opened it and she saw that it was an ad from a local dog walker. The woman had ten dogs of varying size with her and Jaren could have sworn some of them were smiling.

"You have her walk your dog for you, and you'll have a contented and warm friend to come home to. Greer can help you housebreak the dog if you want." Looking around, he broke down. He'd held it back as long as he could. "I thought you said you moved in a couple of weeks ago." It was one of the pieces of information she'd tossed at him during their time together.

"I did."

Two weeks was plenty of time to settle in. It wasn't that big an apartment. "Did the moving van break down?"

What was he getting at—besides her one last nerve? "No, why?"

He peered into the next room. "These things have been here as long as you have?"

"Give or take a day." And then, as he slipped into the next room, it hit her. She thought men felt comfortable around unorganized chaos. Jaren sighed. "You want to know why I haven't unpacked."

"Question did cross my mind." His voice floated in from the second bedroom as Kyle undertook a survey of the rest of the apartment. All the rooms had boxes crowded into them. He thought of his sister and his late mother. "Most women I know are nesters." He walked back into the kitchen. "They like to keep things organized."

"Well, now you know one who doesn't," she told him nonchalantly. "I even hate unpacking groceries," she tagged on.

Kyle peered into the refrigerator, then closed the door. He shook his head. "I guess that would explain it."

"*It?*" she echoed.

His gesture took in the refrigerator and the tiny pantry he'd already looked in. They contained a bottle of water between them. "The lack of foodstuffs."

"Most take-out places cook better than I do," she replied without an iota of self-consciousness.

She would have liked to sound indignant at his prying, but it was hard being indignant about this assault on her housekeeping abilities when her neck was being tickled by a tiny, lightning-fast pink tongue.

Jaren noticed that Kyle was eyeing the pizza.

At least he didn't just help himself, she thought. "Would you like a piece?"

It was all the invitation he needed. He had a weak spot in his heart for pizza.

"Twisted my arm," he declared, flipping open the lid and claiming a large slice for himself. It was only after he'd taken two good-size, healthy bites of the pepperoni-and-sausage concoction that he asked, "So, what's the verdict?" When Jaren looked at him curiously, he nodded toward the puppy that was attempting to scramble up her shoulder. She had a lock of Jaren's blond hair in her mouth.

Using two hands, Jaren drew the puppy back down to chest level. "You mean I have a choice?"

His eyes held hers for a moment. "Everyone's always got a choice."

That was what she'd tried to make her father understand when he'd told her that he just couldn't get himself to quit drinking, that the alcohol just had too strong a hold on him. She'd loved her father dearly, but she'd hated that weak side of him with a passion. The side that hadn't fought to keep her mother in his life, that hadn't fought against the addiction that eventually had destroyed his liver and stolen him from her.

She couldn't think about that now, Jaren silently chided and forced herself to refocus. If there was any doubt in her mind about keeping the dog, it was completely demolished as the puppy all but washed her face with rapid, darting kisses.

Jaren sighed, surrendering. "I guess if it's doing your sister a favor—"

"It would be."

He said it so solemnly, she almost believed him—if it hadn't been for the glint in his eye.

But it was a way not to seem as if she was in his debt, which she knew she was. "Then I guess I'll keep her."

"Good choice." Standing closer to her, he scratched the dog behind her ear. The puppy's panting became audibly loud. "What are you going to name her?"

Jaren held the dog up and away from her for a moment, as if seeing the puppy from a different angle would decide the matter for her.

It did. "Kyle."

Kyle raised an eyebrow as he looked at her, waiting. "Yeah?"

She realized that Kyle thought she was addressing him. Jaren shook her head adamantly. "No, I'm going to name the puppy Kyle."

He'd deliberately picked out the only female in the litter because Jaren had mentioned that her previous dog had been a female. He'd referred to the dog as *she,* but Jaren had obviously missed that.

"That's a guy's name," he pointed out.

Jaren grinned. "Not these days. A lot of names are crossing over. Besides, this way when she chews through my shoes or the bottom of the curtains, I'll think of you."

Kyle shrugged, not entirely displeased at her choice—and that surprised him. "Whatever works for you."

He glanced at his watch. He'd promised his newly acquired cousins, Dax and Clay, that he'd join them and some of the rest of the family for a round of poker tonight at seven at Andrew's house. It was getting close to that time now.

But there was no clock to punch and he knew for a fact other people would be at the table. Hanging around a few more minutes wouldn't matter. No one would miss him for a hand or two.

Wiping his fingers on the back of his jeans, he nodded toward the cardboard towers that were closest to him.

"You want any help with those?"

Jaren looked over her shoulder at the boxes. When she'd packed, she'd just haphazardly thrown everything in without making any discerning choices, telling herself she could do that when she opened the boxes again. But now the day of reckoning was at hand and she didn't feel like facing it.

"You mean like helping me unpack?" she asked, tugging the puppy back down into her arms.

He laughed. "Well, either that, or helping you throw them into the Dumpster."

The second choice was not without appeal. She didn't want to have to deal with memories.

"Don't think I hadn't thought of that," Jaren commented. Shaking her head, she turned down his offer, rather mystified that he actually would offer. There was obviously more to this man than she thought. "No, unpacking is something I'm going to have to get to on my own." She saw the skeptical expression on his face and grasped at the first excuse she could think of. "You wouldn't know where anything went."

"I could ask," he told her pointedly.

He was actually serious, wasn't he? "That's okay. I don't believe in putting guests to work."

"How about friends?" Kyle countered.

She watched him for a long moment, not sure what to make of him or what he'd just said. On the first day they'd worked together, she would have said that he didn't want any part of her.

"You volunteering?" she asked.

He absently petted his namesake. "Makes life easier," he told her.

She laughed softly in disbelief. "Funny, you don't strike me as the warm and toasty type."

"I'm not," he said honestly, then added, "But I've had to make some changes recently." Changes in the way he'd perceived himself, his mother and his siblings. It shook a man to the core to discover that everything he'd believed to be true was actually a lie. "Got me a little ticked off for a while," he admitted, "but I'm starting to handle it."

He'd done it. He'd hooked her. "Do I get to know what *it* is?"

Kyle wasn't the type to share his feelings or private information. That much still remained true despite the changes his life had undergone. Changes that had, at the time, shaken the ground beneath his feet with more force than any magnitude 6.9 earthquake.

But he was still standing and that, he knew, was a good thing. "Maybe when I get to know you better," he qualified.

Curiosity, the intense variety, comprised approximately eighty percent of Jaren's makeup. She *hated* not knowing something. But she was also bright enough to understand that pushing in this case would have the absolute reverse effect.

So, resigned, she nodded in response to his answer and said, "Good enough," even though it wasn't. Shifting the puppy to her other side, she moved toward the door and rested her hand on the knob. "You'd better get going."

Amusement lifted the corners of his mouth. "Throwing me out?"

"More like giving you a way out," she corrected. "You've looked at your watch twice in the last five minutes. That tells me that you have somewhere else you have to be and I don't want to keep you from it."

He hadn't realized that he was being that obvious. "You know, you might just turn out to be a half-decent detective after all."

She laughed briefly. "You're going to wind up a lonely old man if that's an example of the way you flatter a woman."

Opening the front door, Jaren stepped back to let him pass. Kyle, the puppy, burrowed her head against her chest. Jaren smiled. She'd picked the right name after all, she mused.

"Oh, and O'Brien?"

About to cross the threshold out, Kyle turned to look at her. "Yeah?"

"Thanks."

He was completely unprepared for what accompanied the single word of gratitude.

Standing on her toes, Jaren leaned over to brush a quick kiss on his cheek. At least, that had been her intention.

But he'd turned his head too sharply and she'd missed her target.

Her lips brushed against his mouth.

Chapter 8

Startled, Jaren pulled back as if her lips had come in contact with a hot surface.

She didn't want Kyle to misunderstand and she grabbed onto words to form an apology. But the ones that rose to her lips were never given voice. Something had definitely been triggered—inside of him, as well, if that unguarded look in his eyes was any indication.

So, instead of talking, Jaren found herself leaning into Kyle again.

At the same moment that he leaned into her.

She was surprised and yet, not really. Because, although they were still relative strangers, that *thing* that sizzled between them was older than time. The only one who seemed oblivious was the puppy that Jaren still held in her arms. The dog wiggled, its warm body and whisper-soft fur only adding to the flash and fire that had been inadvertently ignited.

Jaren drew in a deep breath but that in no way managed to stop her head from spinning. It didn't even begin to properly stabilize the room which suddenly tilted.

His mouth was pressed against hers. The kiss was deepening.

Jaren heard herself moan.

Kyle wasn't sure just what he was thinking when he took hold of Jaren's shoulders. Most likely, he'd intended to gently but firmly create a separation between them. But somehow, the gesture was never completed. His hands remained on her shoulders and instead of pushing her back, even a little, he anchored her in place. And struggled against the very real urge to pull her into him. To charge through the door that this unintended kiss had unexpectedly opened.

The impulse was so strong that, for one unsettling moment, Kyle even considered following through. But then the puppy suddenly yelped. The sound drove a wedge between them, returning Kyle to his senses. It apparently did the same for Jaren, he noted, because she pulled back again.

The look in her eyes told him that she felt as unsettled as he did.

Granted, when he'd first met her, he had felt a rather strong attraction to Jaren. That was only natural. She was a knockout. But he had always been able to separate the physical from the emotional, work from his private life.

This moment had blurred the lines rather badly.

Jaren managed to find her tongue—and her wits—before he did. Stepping back into her apartment, one hand holding the puppy as she stroked its soft, furry head with the other, she heard herself murmuring, "Thanks again for the puppy."

It took him a second to realize what she was talking about.

"Don't mention it," he finally answered. Kyle found himself talking to her door. She'd closed it rather quickly at the end of her sentence.

Kyle stood there for a moment, staring at the closed door, his mind a blank for possibly the very first time in his life. And then the question, What the hell had just happened here? echoed in his brain.

No answer came to him.

Shaking off the bewildered feeling, he turned on his heel and walked to the vehicle he'd left standing in guest parking.

Standing a few inches away on the other side of the door, Jaren looked down at the puppy. In the distance, she heard the distinct sound of a car being started up and then pulling away.

O'Brien.

He was leaving.

She let go of the breath she was holding and then drew in another. She released that slowly as she tried to collect herself. Tried to go on with her evening as it had been before everything had been upended.

"Okay, Kyle," she said, addressing the dog, "what was that all about? Do you have a clue?" The puppy began to nibble on her fingertips. "Yeah, me, neither," she admitted with a sigh. "C'mon, let's watch some TV and pretend this never happened. All except for you, of course," she added, leaning her cheek against the top of the puppy's head.

Her heart continued hammering. Hard enough almost to crack her ribs.

When Jaren walked into the squad room the next morning, Kyle wasn't sitting at his desk. Setting down the cardboard tray that held four coffee containers and the box of doughnuts she'd brought in, Jaren looked around the area. No one was around.

It wasn't *that* early, she thought.

Had there been another murder?

No, she decided, someone would have called her.

A moment later, two of the detectives she'd met the other day entered. There was a heavyset man who'd only been introduced to her by his last name—Holloway—and his partner, Diego Sanchez, a ten-year veteran with a quick smile and sharp, brown eyes. Sanchez was half of Holloway's size.

"I brought doughnuts and coffee from the coffee shop down the street," she announced to the two detectives, gesturing toward the offering. "You're both welcome to them."

Holloway, in the process of lowering his girth on to his chair, straightened instantly. For a man his size, he seemed incredibly light on his feet. He crossed from his desk to hers in the blink of an eye.

"Knew I was going to like you the minute I saw you," the detective declared, grinning as he selected a dough-nut that was hemorrhaging strawberry jelly.

Jaren returned the smile as she looked around the room. "Have you seen O'Brien around anywhere?" she asked him.

Holloway shook his head, but Sanchez, helping him-self to a doughnut with a light dusting of sugar, told her, "He called in this morning and said he had to run an errand first and that he'd be just a little late coming in."

Very little, she thought because, even as Sanchez finished giving her this information, Jaren saw her partner walking into the squad room. He had something tucked under his arm.

"Your partner brought doughnuts," Holloway an-nounced in between appreciative, good-size bites. "How come you never do that?"

"Maybe it's because I don't want to go broke," Kyle answered, deliberately patting Holloway's puddinglike stomach. Opening a drawer on the side of his desk, he dropped whatever he'd brought with him into it and then closed it again.

Holloway pretended to take offense. He did his best to tense his stomach, then patted it. "That's solid muscle, boy."

Kyle laughed. There was nothing solid about it, but he didn't want to point out the fact that Holloway looked like the runner-up in a Santa Claus body-double contest.

"If you say so," Kyle murmured, dropping into his seat.

"I also brought coffee," Jaren said when it was obvious that her partner wasn't going to browse through the large box of doughnuts for a selection. "Asphalt, just the way you like it," she added. She paused to pick up a container that sported a large, red *X* on its white lid. "This one's mine," she told him, removing the lid. The creamy beige surface testified to its composition: one part coffee and two parts pre-sweetened creamer.

Getting up, Kyle glanced at her container and shuddered. "You're welcome to it," he commented. Selecting another container, he removed the lid and looked down at the inky contents. One hearty sip later, he allowed a contented sigh to escape his lips. And then his eyes met hers. "Thanks."

Was it her imagination, or was there an awkwardness shimmering between them? Did he feel it, or was it just her?

Jaren chewed on the inside of her cheek, debating her next move. They were either going to go through the motions of an awkward dance, or move on, placing last night's kiss behind them.

She'd always prided herself on being a direct person. "Look, about last night," she began.

Holloway's desk was a good half room away, but apparently the detective had ears like a bat. He scooted his chair around, *walking* it across the length of the separation until he was all but in her face.

"There was a last night?" he asked with keen interest shining in his small brown eyes.

"There's always a last night," Jaren answered, her voice crisp and detached. "Tonight will be *last night* tomorrow."

Holloway's small eyes narrowed even more. "You've got a college degree, don't you?" he guessed. "In one of those disciplines that don't do you any good, like literature or liberal arts."

She heard the slight note of dismissive disdain. She would have to win her place here. And it wasn't going to be a piece of cake, either. She'd need more than pastries and hot coffee to get into their permanent good graces, Jaren decided. So be it, she was up to it. This wasn't the first time she'd been on the outside, looking for a way in. But she always found one.

She smiled warmly at the big man. "As a matter of fact, my degree's in criminology and I plan on putting it to good use here."

Holloway took the last bite of what was to be just the first part of his breakfast. "Sounds good to me," he told her, selecting another doughnut and then making his way back to his desk.

Jaren picked up a napkin and crossed to the older man's desk. She held it out to him with a smile.

Taking the napkin, Holloway asked, "Where?" She pointed to the corner of his mouth and he wiped away the streak of strawberry jelly that had somehow eluded his consumption.

Kyle observed the interaction with a mixture of amusement and something he couldn't quite identify.

He would have to be careful, he decided. He liked keeping his private life as uncomplicated as possible, and what he'd felt ever so briefly last night was far from uncomplicated. It had all the earmarks of something that could become *very* complicated if he dropped his guard. The shapely lady was trouble. It remained to be seen just how much trouble.

Biding his time, he waited until Jaren looked in his direction. When she did, he shifted his eyes from her face to the door and then back again. The next moment, he got up and crossed to the threshold, walking out.

Jaren waited a couple of minutes before getting up to follow him since that was, she surmised, what he wanted. But just as she pushed her chair back, the phone on her desk rang.

"Rosetti," she announced into the receiver.

"Detective, this is Dr. Carter. The M.E.," the raspy voice on the other end of the line added when she made no response. "You and O'Brien want to come down to the morgue for that autopsy on the latest guy to get a stake through his heart, or do you just want me to send it up when it's typed?"

She tried to think like O'Brien. In his shoes, she would have wanted the autopsy five minutes ago. Preferably written. But in this case, a verbal one was going to have to do.

"We'll come down," she said.

But even as the words came out of her mouth, she couldn't help wondering if O'Brien was going to be bent out of shape that she made the decision for them. After all, any way you looked at it, O'Brien was the senior detective on this and she didn't want him to think she was trying to usurp him, especially after last night. Some men would see what happened as calculated on her part, trying to exercise control over the man by means of sex. The only thing was, that spontaneous combustion reaction between them had caught her by surprise just as much as it had him.

Jaren hurried into the hallway, only to find Kyle leaning against the wall closest to the door. He was obviously waiting for her.

But before he could say anything, she started talking. "The M.E. just called. He wants to see us at the morgue. He said he just completed the autopsy on the Count and thought you might be interested in getting the verbal report."

Kyle wondered if there was something unusual about it—other than the cause of death. Most likely, it was just Carter's way of getting a little attention. Being a medical examiner seemed like a lonely choice of a career, considering all the choices the man could have made with a medical degree. But he'd heard that Wayne Carter wasn't much of a people person and *patients* who couldn't answer back suited him just fine.

"Morgue it is," Kyle agreed, straightening. He took the lead, heading for the elevators.

Jaren fell into step beside him. Kyle still hadn't said anything when they reached the elevators. "Did you want to say something to me?"

Pressing the down button, he glanced at her. "Like what?"

"I don't know. In the squad room, you looked at me

and then indicated the door so when you got up and walked out, I thought you wanted me to follow you."

Kyle debated yanking her chain a little more—after all, she was the one responsible for his sleepless night—then decided there was nothing to be gained by playing games. He was ordinarily above that. He shrugged now, as if what he'd intended on telling Jaren really wasn't all that important.

"I was just going to warn you about Holloway and Sanchez. They like getting on the new kid's case. Right now, that happens to be you." They arrived in the basement and the doors opened for them. "But you seem to be holding your own."

She stepped out before Kyle, then turned to look at him. "Thanks."

He brushed off her gratitude. "Still, if I were you, I wouldn't give them any loaded lines, at least not for a while."

The smile that curved the corners of her mouth was rueful. "You mean like *about last night*."

He struggled to suppress the smile that automatically came to his lips as the memory of the unsettling kiss feathered through his brain. "That phrase does come to mind."

"Okay, since we're alone," she began, lowering her voice. "About last night—" Jaren took a breath. Kyle said nothing as he went on watching her. Jaren moistened her lips. With just a little imagination, she could still taste him. "I don't want you to think that I—"

She was squirming, he thought. Initially, he'd expected that this might amuse him a little, but it didn't. He didn't want her to feel uncomfortable, not about that. He didn't want to hear her make any protests about the kiss that had caught them both by surprise. Some things were better left alone and unexplored.

"I don't," he told her briskly, cutting Jaren off.

Jaren stared at him. She opened her mouth to ask Kyle just exactly what he thought she was going to say, then decided that maybe, in this case, it was better to let sleeping dogs lie. Besides, it would never happen again. She didn't believe in getting involved with coworkers.

"Okay. By the way, why were you late?" she asked, putting the sensitive topic to rest.

He started walking. Since she had no idea where the morgue was, Jaren fell in just a half step behind him, letting him lead the way.

"I went to the evidence room and checked out one of the copies of the book we found at the first two murders. It was the neurosurgeon's copy," he added before she could ask—not that it made any difference whose copy he had. Both were pristine, with no markings on the pages.

Jaren looked at him in surprise. "You mean *The Vampire Diaries?*"

He couldn't help the condescending frown that rose to his lips. He still didn't understand how anyone would want to read that kind of drivel. For that matter, he couldn't see how a publishing company would want to place their logo on the spine of something so demeaning.

"That's the one."

"I could have given you my copy last night."

"It didn't occur to me last night," he told her honestly.

"Why did it occur to you this morning?" Jaren asked.

He continued leading the way down the winding hallway. Jaren looked around, trying to take note of the numbers on the closed doors they passed. Right about now, she regretted not bringing bread crumbs with her to mark her path.

He shrugged casually. "Thought it might help me get into the killer's mind."

Score one for her side, Jaren thought. "So you *do* think the book has something to do with the murders," she said.

"I haven't made up my mind about that, but it can't hurt to get familiar with the work, just in case it *is* tied into the murders."

Even as he said it, it still sounded utterly ridiculous to his ear. Someone was slaying vampires, or people that he or she *believed* to be vampires. It sounded like a bad plot hastily thrown together for some movie-of-the-week program on one of the lesser cable channels.

Kyle looked at Jaren just before he pushed open the door and walked into the morgue. "I like covering all my bases."

Jaren surprised him by nodding. Her expression was completely serious. "So do I."

Chapter 9

Jaren expected the morgue in Aurora to be similar to the one she'd been to in Oakland: an eerily quiet place where the attendants moved around like wraiths on rubber-soled shoes. If they spoke at all, they kept their voices at a low level out of respect for the dead. Should music be part of the scene, something classical or very low-keyed would be piped in.

What she definitely did *not* expect was to walk into the middle of a rousing John Philip Sousa march.

Startled by the blaring rendition, Jaren halted right before the door and looked at Kyle. "Are we in the right place?"

Pushing the door open, Kyle gestured toward the wall comprised of closed, large metal drawers, behind which rested the latest group of homicide victims and deceased people whose manner of death raised questions.

"It's the morgue all right," he told her. Kyle raised his voice to be heard above the crash of cymbals. "The M.E. likes to counterbalance the solemnity of death with a little cheery music."

"There's cheery and then there's deafening," she pointed out.

This was downright weird, she thought. But not at all creepy. Looking around, Jaren saw the man who had summoned them a few minutes ago.

There was no one else in the room—if you didn't count the body he was presently working on.

Rail-thin, Dr. Wayne Carter seemed taller than he actually was. A welcoming smile curved his mouth when he glanced up and saw them entering the morgue. He waited until they'd both crossed to him.

"You must be the new homicide detective," he said to Jaren.

Her smile felt tight and forced. So-called cheerful music or not, this was definitely not her favorite place. "I must be."

"You'll forgive me if I don't shake hands," Carter said, nodding at her and then at the man standing beside her.

Jaren looked at the M.E.'s rubber gloves. They, as well as his blue paper smock, were covered with blood. He'd obviously just concluded the autopsy right before he'd called them.

"More than forgive you," she assured him.

Kyle got down to the reason they were there. "What's wrong with this one, Doc?"

Carter eyed the ragged clothes and black cape neatly folded on the counter behind him. Until several hours ago, they had been all but hermetically sealed to the vagrant known as the Count.

"In this case, it would be easier to say what wasn't wrong," Carter responded.

Kyle was amenable to playing along—up to a point. "I'll bite. What *wasn't* wrong?"

Carter's voice grew more expansive, as if he was conducting a lecture in a classroom. He milked the moment.

"Given the kind of life the Count had to have led on the street, his liver is in remarkable condition." He looked at Jaren, addressing the words to her as if he were in charge of her personal edification. "Most people on the street tend to have livers that are on the way out, thanks to incredible alcohol abuse."

Expecting some sort of litany, Kyle waited for more. There wasn't any. "That's it?"

The M.E. spread his hands. "That's it."

"Cause of death?" Kyle pressed. Carter raised his eyes from the body he had just now finished sewing up again and gave him an incredulous look. "I have to ask," Kyle explained.

"A wooden stake driven through his heart," Carter replied and then he paused, as if debating whether or not to ask the next question. "Is there *really* some nut out there running around and trying to make the world safe from vampires?"

The question was for both the detectives in the room, but Carter ended it by shifting his quizzical eyes toward Jaren.

It was Kyle who answered. "It's shaping up that way," he conceded reluctantly. The idea still didn't sit right with him. He felt he was being deliberately played.

Jaren, he noted, looked preoccupied. The next moment, she moved over to the dispenser on the wall and pulled out two rubber gloves. Slipping them on, she picked up the dark, wooden stake that the M.E. had placed on the counter next to the current victim's clothing. She examined the stake carefully, then addressed the M.E.

"What kind of wood is this?" she asked Carter.

The M.E. nodded. "O'Brien said you'd want to know so I had the guys at CSI run it for you." He paused, as if waiting for some kind of a drumroll. He had to settle for another crash of cymbals instead. "That is Brazilian hardwood," he told her, raising his voice again. "It's pretty rare around here."

Jaren turned the stake over in her hand. Did that have some kind of significance, or had it just been handy for some reason when the killer had murdered the neurosurgeon?

Looking up at the M.E. she asked, "Are you saying that someone went all the way down to Brazil to carve the stakes?"

Thin shoulders moved vaguely up and down beneath the blue paper gown. Carter pulled it off and deposited the cover into a nearby wastepaper basket. "I'm saying that your killer is a very organized, didactic person, maybe even superstitious." He regarded the table at the latest victim. "This has all the earmarks of a ritual slaying."

Jaren tried to make sense out of what Carter was saying. "So, you think he stalked them and then killed them?"

"Sounds like a theory," Kyle allowed noncommittally. He heard the doubt in her voice. "Why, what's your take on it?"

She didn't have a definite take on it. She felt like someone stumbling around in the dark, knowing that there was a light switch somewhere. If she only could find it.

"Maybe he's just prepared," she guessed, thinking out loud. "He has the stakes in his car just in case he comes up against another *vampire*." And then an idea hit her. "Maybe he's just a slayer, not a hunter." She saw the skepticism in Kyle's eyes. Not that she blamed him. "Protecting himself preemptively rather than just looking for a fight."

Kyle wasn't sure where she was going with this. "So, we do what, get on TV and tell everyone who bought that stupid book to get rid of it? And not to wear any clothes that might be mistakenly identified as something a vampire might wear?"

"Does sound pretty stupid when you say it out loud like that," she agreed. "Although we are dealing with someone who's a few cards shy of a full deck."

"Or wants us to think that he or she is," Kyle countered.

So many ways to go with this, Jaren thought, frustrated. Just exploring the options made her tired. She looked down again at the stake in her hand. Was this a clue, or a red herring? Most of the time, killers were just ordinary people trying to get away with their crimes. But once in a while, they turned out to be far more diabolical than anything found in a novel. Which one was this?

"So, if I wanted more of these hardwood stakes," she said, turning back to the M.E., "I'd do what, go off to Brazil?"

Carter thought for a moment. "Or check with some of the exclusive landscapers and nurseries. See if anyone recently either purchased a Brazilian hardwood tree—"

"Or had one cut down and ground up," Kyle interjected.

Was he humoring her, or was he serious? She still had trouble reading Kyle's expression. "Sounds a little out there," she admitted.

They were past the point of *a little out there.* It was more like *a lot out there.*

"So is driving a stake through someone's heart," Kyle answered. He turned to Carter. "So, how soon can I have the official report?"

"All in due time, O'Brien, all in due time." Carter stripped off the gloves he'd used for the autopsy and threw them into the trash after his paper gown. "By the way, who do I release the first victim to?" he asked. "I'm all done with the autopsy and I sent the report over yesterday." He waved a hand around the area. "I've got a storage crunch going on."

"Who asked for the body?", Kyle asked.

"That's just it," Carter told him. "Nobody requested the remains."

"Nobody?" Jaren echoed. This was a man who interacted with a great many people every day. He wasn't some hermit found by the wayside like the Count. "But he was married."

"Divorced," Carter corrected. He picked up the file he'd comprised from his desk and waved it for emphasis. "And I tried calling his ex, but she said she didn't care if I turned the good doctor into fertilizer and sprinkled him around in some park—preferably an out-of-state one." Carter opened the folder and glanced down a page to check his facts. "His receptionist told me that there was no next of kin, no parents, no kids and she has no idea if the man had any siblings." Closing the folder, he dropped it back on his desk. "He never mentioned any, and there were no burial instructions."

"That's because he thought he was immortal," Jaren surmised quietly, voicing the thought more to herself. She looked over toward the wall of drawers. "Which drawer is his?"

After removing the face mask that still dangled about his neck, Carter tossed it onto the counter and crossed over to the extreme left of the room where the drawers were. They housed the bodies either waiting for an autopsy or a ride to the funeral parlor.

He pulled open the bottom one.

Following him, Jaren gazed down at the surgeon's lifeless face. The vampire slayer's first known victim was already turning blue.

From everything they'd learned about the surgeon, he was insufferable, if exceedingly talented. A lot of people were probably glad he was out of their lives. But somehow, having him lying here, unclaimed like a forgotten lump of clay just didn't seem right. At least, it didn't sit right with her.

"What do you do with bodies that no one claims?" she asked Carter.

But it was Kyle who answered her. Intrigued by the expression on her face, he moved a little closer to her. "The city comes up with a little cash to bury them in Potter's Field."

She shook her head. "Not right," he thought he heard her whisper. "It's just not right." It wasn't as if the surgeon lacked for money. He just had no one who cared. Impulsively, she turned toward Carter and said, "If no one turns up to make arrangements for him, let me know."

Kyle exchanged glances with the M.E. "If you don't mind my asking," he inquired of Jaren, "why?"

"Because if no one else comes forward, I'll make the arrangements for the funeral," she told him.

"But you don't know this guy from Adam," Kyle pointed out. "I mean, other than the fact that we caught this homicide, you have no connection to him. Do you?"

"No," she told him firmly. "But it's just sad that no one cares enough about him to step forward." She turned to face her partner and noticed that both he and the M.E. were watching her as if they thought she'd lost her mind. But dealing with her father had shown her that there were always two sides to everything, if not more. "What does that say about the sum total of the man's life?"

"That he reaped what he sowed?" Kyle put in archly.

"Maybe so, but it still doesn't make it right."

Kyle had another guess for her. "How about *what goes around, comes around?*"

This time, Jaren smiled. "I'm counting on it."

Kyle didn't understand immediately, and then her meaning dawned on him. "You're hoping that when your time comes, that—"

Jaren waved away the rest of his words, not wanting to hear them. Somehow, hearing the sentiment spoken made her sound calculating, and she'd never been that.

"Yeah, yeah, yeah, okay, you've proven your point. You're good at guessing and piecing things together," she granted him. Turning toward Carter, she said, "Don't forget, call me if no one turns up to take care of our neurosurgeon."

"You're almost as good as called," Carter told her as she walked out.

Jaren walked slightly ahead of Kyle on the way back to the elevators. One arrived almost as soon as she pushed the up button. Stepping in, she was keenly aware that her partner studied her. The fact that he wasn't saying anything just seemed to make it worse.

She pushed the button for their floor.

"What?" she finally asked, unable to figure out if she'd said the wrong thing, or if something else was on Kyle's mind. Was he thinking about last night? Because she was, no matter how much she tried to shut it out of her mind.

The shrug was vague and dismissive. "Just trying to figure you out, Rosetti."

"Do yourself a favor and don't," she suggested, echoing the same sentiment he'd expressed on their first day together. "Just enjoy the ride," she instructed glibly.

The lazy smile that whispered over his lips told her that Kyle was already doing that.

"Okay, now what?" she asked.

The elevator doors opened and they walked toward their squad room. "You up for some more canvasing?" he asked.

"More than up for it," she told him.

Being downstairs in the morgue made her feel restless and unsettled. She didn't think she could concentrate if confined behind her desk right now. At least out on the street, she had an excuse to move around.

Grabbing her jacket from the back of her chair, Jaren said, "Lead the way."

They went back to the scene of the latest slaying. Jaren was both surprised and pleased to see that the area where the Count had been killed was now commemorated with a small collection of prayer candles of varying sizes and colors. Their flames flickered in the afternoon breeze like so many minions paying their last respects.

"I guess people really did like him," she commented to her partner.

Maybe if they'd shown the man this kind of attention when he'd been alive, he might have been able to turn his life around, she thought. But then, according to what she'd heard from the handful of people she managed to interview last night, the Count was content with the life he'd chosen for himself.

Maybe he actually was happy.

Kyle's next words confirmed her suspicions. "He was a character, part of the decor. I think a lot of people tried to help him over the years, but he wouldn't have any of it." Bending over, Kyle picked up a card that had fallen over and righted it. "He liked being the eccentric figure, leaning on his staff and spinning lies, reciting them as if they were pure gospel."

"Anyone else like him around?" Back in Oakland, all they'd had were the usual collection of homeless people. No one stood out the way the Count had.

"Not to my knowledge, but then the Count left a void. Somebody'll be along to fill it soon enough," Kyle speculated. "Why, think that'll be the next victim?"

"You never know," she replied, then shrugged. "Just trying to stay one step ahead of the killer."

He laughed a little. So far, three murders and they hadn't been able to catch a break. "And how's that working for you?"

"It's not," she admitted ruefully. Standing beside the restaurant Dumpster, Jaren scanned the area. There was an apartment building not far off whose back windows looked down into the alley.

Eight stories, she counted. And a lot of windows. That made potentially a great many people to interview.

"How do you want to do this?" she asked him.

He was already walking out of the alley. The building's entrance was on the opposite side. "We'll go floor by floor."

We. As in together. "I thought you might want to divide up the apartments." She was irked he didn't suggest it but made her feel as if she needed supervision. "I'm not a rookie, you know."

"I know," he answered mildly. He could sense her agitation. He just wanted to observe her a little more.

Strictly for work purposes, he silently added, then grew annoyed with himself for feeling that was even necessary. "Maybe I believe that two heads are better than one."

And if she believed that, he had a bridge he wanted to sell her, she thought. He didn't trust her yet, but that was okay. She was patient, she could wait him out.

Besides, she was accustomed to having to prove herself. There had been a few tough sells on the force in Oakland, but by the time she left, they had all been won over. And—she slanted a glance at her partner— she intended to do the same thing here.

Eventually, O'Brien was going to have to admit that she did more than just a decent job. God knew she was ready to run with the ball—if only he'd give it to her.

Until he did, she would go along and play his game. Nothing would be gained by crossing him or going behind his back. Those were plays she had reserved for desperate times, when her gut told her she could succeed and there was no other way left to go.

The canvas yielded nothing.

Almost no one looked out their window the night the

Count had died, not even out of boredom. The one man who had gone to the window when he thought he *heard a strange noise* hadn't seen anything. Fortunately for the killer and unfortunately for them, it had been a moonless night.

They kept at it for hours, until they'd interviewed every one of the tenants who were home.

"That went well," Jaren said sarcastically as they left the pre-1960s building. "What's next, fearless leader?"

He led the way back to his car. He'd left the vehicle parked by the curb. Two other cars had pulled in, one in front, one behind. Between them they'd left half an inch of space. This was going to take maneuvering, he thought, annoyed.

"Next you start calling landscapers and nurseries to see if anyone ordered or cared for a Brazilian hardwood tree in the last five years."

She didn't bother to ask why he'd given her the assignment. She knew. "My idea."

"Your idea," he answered. "Start with the phonebook and work your way to the Internet."

"Why don't I do it the other way around? Might save some time," she suggested. "Everyone advertises on the Internet these days."

"Not if they want my business," he commented.

"You don't like the Internet." The remark was accompanied by an amused smile.

"It's an annoying invasion of privacy," he said dismissively.

"It's also a hell of a fast way to locate things."

The look on Kyle's face told her he far preferred the old-fashioned way of information gathering—applying shoe leather to the pavement.

Jaren smiled to herself. It was nice to know that her partner had flaws.

Chapter 10

"You look dead on your feet," Kyle commented the next morning as he came in and sat down at his desk.

He'd deliberately come in early to get a jump start on things and was surprised to see that Jaren was there ahead of him. Unlike the previous time, she'd changed her clothing so she obviously had gone home the night before. Since their desks butted up against one another, he had an unobstructed view of her face. While disconcertingly attractive, she definitely looked like a woman in desperate need of a nap.

Kyle cocked his head and peered at her face now. "You get any sleep last night?"

The truth was that she'd only beaten him here by about ten minutes. She'd come in early because she was afraid she'd oversleep if she stayed in bed that so-called extra five minutes. Ringing alarms had no effect on her when she was sleeping. One of the few comments she could remember her mother making was that she could probably sleep through a grade 8 earthquake.

Jaren shrugged in response to his question. Picking up her mug of coffee, she held it in both hands and took a long sip before answering. "Some."

"Puppy keeping you up?" Kyle guessed.

"Indirectly," she allowed. Taking another hit of almost black coffee—hating the taste but thinking it would help make her come around—she elaborated. "I came home to find that she had chewed the corners on most of the boxes in the living room and bedroom."

Jaren's mouth curved in a small, fond smile. No doubt about it. It was love at first sight between her and the puppy. She supposed that she owed O'Brien for that.

"I think that was her subtle way of telling me to unpack, so I did. I hate stopping anything in the middle," she admitted, "so I was unpacking until one this morning." Leaning back in her chair, Jaren sighed and shook her head as if she couldn't quite believe it. "I didn't realize that I had so much stuff until I had to try to find a place for it all in the apartment."

He'd never had that kind of problem. Unlike Greer, he'd always been a minimalist. "Maybe you need a larger apartment."

Jaren's eyes widened and she appeared completely awake for the first time since he'd walked in.

"You mean move? Uh-uh, this is it," she swore vehemently. "I'm staying in this place until I die. No more packing and unpacking for me."

This had been her first experience with moving. In Oakland, she'd continued to live with her father even after she'd hit the age when most people moved out of their childhood homes. Afflicted with a failing liver and kidneys, her father had needed care. Jaren had seen no point in trying to maintain two separate households.

"I'm not going anywhere until someone finds a way to transport my apartment from one location to another—intact—without me having to do anything," Jaren added with feeling.

He laughed, amused because she sounded so serious. "You finished moving in, then?"

"Not yet," she confessed. "But almost."

There were still a few more boxes in the spare bedroom, but she'd been too exhausted to open them. Those she planned to get to tonight—if her puppy didn't beat her to it and chew her way through them.

Kyle debated volunteering his sister's help. Greer was a whiz at organizing things and she liked nothing better than doing just that. His thought was interrupted when he saw the lieutenant walking out of his small office.

Barone came directly to Kyle's desk.

The man wasted no words. "The Chief of Ds wants us to put a task force together before the city starts to panic that there's some kind of vampire-slaying weirdo out there."

"So now, instead of two of us being up against a dead end, we'll have company?" Kyle asked archly.

The lieutenant frowned. "That *dead end* had better crumple soon," he warned. "You know what happens when the public feels their police department isn't looking out for them—they start taking the law into their own hands." That was the last thing any of them wanted. And then he got back to business. He glanced at the notation he'd made while on the phone with Brian Cavanaugh. "Okay, you've got Holloway and Sanchez, plus McIntyre and Chang."

"Which McIntyre?" Kyle asked.

The lieutenant's expression indicated that he had assumed Kyle knew which one before the call came in. "You're related to them now, don't you guys talk?" he asked.

"Haven't seen any of them lately," Kyle admitted grudgingly.

Jaren had the impression that the last time he interacted with any of his new extended family was when he'd taken her to dinner. She simply didn't understand that. If she were part of a large family like that, she'd find opportunities to hang out with them.

"I think it's Riley," the lieutenant answered. "And, if that's not enough, the Chief of Ds said the money to bring in more detectives will be found. He wants results. As in yesterday," Barone emphasized. He gestured beyond the squad room. "You can use the conference room to get organized," he added, then looked from Kyle to Jaren. "Any questions?"

"None that I can think of," Kyle said.

The lieutenant nodded. "Keep me in the loop. I want

daily updates," he said, obviously anticipating that he would be quizzed daily about the progress himself. With that, he walked back into his office.

"And the fun and games continue," Kyle murmured under his breath. "C'mon," he urged Jaren as he rose to his feet. "Let's go get set up in the conference room."

Holloway and Sanchez had just come in, the former juggling a take-out breakfast housed within a large foam container.

"You two are with us," Kyle said, walking past them. "Lieutenant's orders."

"We get to work the vampire slayings?" Holloway asked.

"You get to work the vampire slayings," Kyle affirmed, leading the way out and down the hall to the conference room.

The conference room appeared relatively cheery, thanks to the invasion of the morning sun. It contained just a conference table with its accompanying chairs and a single white bulletin board, a holdover from the last time a task force had made use of the room. At the moment, the board was empty except for the handful of colorful magnets that were clustered in the upper right hand corner.

Hopefully, it wouldn't be filled up, Jaren thought. As far as they knew, there were only three victims.

Only she silently mocked herself. Since when had that word become part of the equation? Even one life so callously lost was too many.

Behind her, several technicians entered, some push-

ing carts with landlines, others bringing in slim comput-
ers to hook up and get running.

This was taking on all the characteristics of a major
operation. Even though it was her first of this propor-
tion, Jaren prayed it would be closed down soon and that
the case would wrap up.

Opening up the folder she'd thought to bring with
her, Jaren took out the three eight-by-ten photographs
of the victims as they had appeared in life, before
they'd met the business end of a wooden stake. She'd
gotten the Count's from the human-interest newspaper article that had been written about him a couple
of years ago.

She placed the photographs at the top of the board
in chronological order, then carefully wrote in their
names with a red marker just below the border of each
photograph.

Behind her, she heard one technician begin to open
up the tip lines. It was only a matter of time before they
were inundated with *helpful* information. Crazies would
start phoning in, people who lived humdrum lives and
tried to infuse them with a little drama by convincing
themselves that they had caught a glimpse of the vampire slayer. She wasn't looking forward to that.

But she knew that if they were patient enough,
somewhere amid the hundreds and hundreds of calls
destined to come in, someone just might have a genuine sighting.

That's all they needed, just one legitimate tip. One
thing to get them on their way to tracking down the

killer. In the interim, they would continue sifting through the information they had, trying to gather more and somehow make sense of it.

Once the other two detectives who were assigned to the task force arrived, Kyle addressed the group, handing out assignments and urging follow-ups to the calls they'd already gotten via regular channels. Everything had to be checked out and nothing—no matter how off-the-wall, trivial or preposterous—could be dismissed. Time and again, they'd discovered that truth was stranger than fiction.

When he finished, Kyle turned toward Jaren. "You get anywhere with those landscapers?"

She shook her head. "Not so far. Everyone I've contacted hasn't done any landscaping with a Brazilian hardwood tree. Some of them didn't even know what I was talking about," she added.

But even as Jaren volunteered the information, she knew that she could have been lied to. If she'd spoken to someone who actually knew something, they might have elected to remain silent for their own reasons. A lot of police work boiled down to simple luck. Luck that the killer would slip up, luck that they would stumble onto a clue. Luck that, if she actually found the killer, he could be captured without taking out one of them.

Despite the fact that she had been the one who advanced the theory in the first place, Jaren wasn't a hundred percent convinced that the killer actually saw himself with a mission to slay vampires. It could, after all, just be a clever cover. The killer might want to create a general panic and hide the one—or two—murders behind an incredible smoke screen so that his true intent was not discovered.

How could she decide which was the truth?

Jaren looked at Kyle and sighed. "There are just too many possibilities here, too many forks in the road that might or might not have been taken." She supposed she could draw up a flowchart, playing out the various different scenarios. Maybe seeing it in front of her would help her decide which theory to advance.

"That's why they pay us the big bucks," Riley McIntyre quipped as she walked into the squad room, bringing in her own giant container of coffee. "To sift through all the information and come up with some kind of conclusion." She grinned at Jaren. "Nice to be working with you." She looked around at the other detectives. "For once, I won't feel so outnumbered here."

"Playtime is later, ladies," Kyle informed them. He gestured over toward the bulletin board. "Right now, we've got work to do."

"That's why we're here," Riley answered, a bright, wide smile on her lips.

After two weeks, Jaren felt like she'd been working the vampire-slayer case forever.

Without any tangible result.

Although she liked to think that she was patient, the lack of headway was definitely getting to Jaren. Every call that had been received on their *tip* line was dutifully logged in and investigated. Because of the nature of the murders, she had spoken to a number of men and women whose souls, she was firmly convinced, had been sold or had gone missing in action. People who unwaveringly believed that they had a true connection to the dark side. Detective or not, it was hard for her to reconcile herself to the fact that these people existed.

And then there was the matter of the book. Instead of a drop due to fear, sales of *The Vampire Diaries* had gone through the roof.

"Why?" she murmured to herself under her breath as she read the latest sale figures on the Internet.

"Why what?" Kyle asked, hearing her mutter the question as he walked by her desk.

She raised her eyes to look at him, then waved her hand at her monitor in disgust. "That book we found at the scene of the first two murders, *The Vampire Diaries.* We still don't know what connection, if any, the book had to the actual murders. Maybe it even triggered the attacks, we don't know. You'd think that people would avoid having it in their possession, just in case. Instead, the bookstores can't keep that damn book in stock. It's literally flying off the shelves. What the hell is the matter with people? They're all acting like it's the forbidden fruit and they all want a bite."

Except when it came to his job, Kyle had long since given up trying to understand the workings of the average mind. He shrugged now.

"They want to live dangerously," he concluded. "For most of them, this is the closest they'll come to walking on the wild side and they all crave that thrill of danger, that rush that comes with a vicarious ride—because at the bottom they're certain it *is* a vicarious ride. Why do people go to slasher movies geared to scare them?" he posed. "Same reason. They want to experience that adrenaline rush without really endangering themselves."

She supposed that made as much sense as anything. "You still have the copy you got out of evidence?" she asked.

He shook his head. Looking the book over had proved to be a waste of time. "No, I logged it back in."

The book was over four hundred pages long. "You're that fast a reader?"

He laughed. He tended to skim, but he'd never managed to become one of those speed readers who absorbed everything.

"It wasn't so much a matter of being fast as it was of being bored." In his opinion, it was all purple prose, overdone and badly written. "I still don't understand how that kind of drivel gets published—or manages to gain a legitimate audience. If it wasn't for these murders giving it publicity, I'm sure the sales would have been abysmal." And then he recalled that she had a copy. "What made you buy it?"

"I didn't," she informed him. "Someone back in Oakland gave it to me as a going-away gift." The book had come from Delia, the chief's administrative assistant, a flighty woman who meant well but was far from being a student of human nature. "Someone who obviously didn't know me well enough to know what holds my interest."

Kyle grinned. "So, you don't find it exciting to have a lover who likes to sink his teeth into your neck and can sprout wings at the first sign of dusk?"

She watched him for a long moment. "In my experience, lovers don't need to see the first signs of dusk to take flight so much as hear the word *commitment*. In their language, they hear the word *trapped* and they can't wait to put distance between themselves and the object of their former affection."

There was a significant enough amount of passion behind her words for Kyle to make the logical conclusion. "Someone take off on you, Rosetti?"

She raised her chin and in so doing, dropped a curtain down between them. Her frustration had made her sloppy, she told herself. "I was thinking about a couple of my girlfriends."

He watched her expression, not fully buying into her explanation. "But not you."

"But not me," she affirmed with feeling. While friendly, she still didn't believe in allowing people into her private life until she trusted them. She didn't know O'Brien well enough. "I'm too busy to lay any foundations for a relationship that would frighten off a lover," she told him matter-of-factly.

It wasn't often that his curiosity was aroused when it came to something other than a case. But Rosetti had succeeded in making him curious. "Recently, or always?" he asked.

"Are you interrogating me, O'Brien?"

A careless shrug prefaced his answer. "Nope. Just

taking time to get to know the new kid," he told her with sufficient disinterest.

They'd all been putting in extra time, trying to solve the case before another victim turned up with a piece of wood driven through his chest. Every spare piece of energy was dedicated to finding the killer. Why was O'Brien suddenly wasting time with personal questions? And why, given her friendly nature, did that make her squirm inside? "And just how's *getting to know* me going to help solve this case?"

"It won't solve the case," he told her seriously, his voice low. "But it's good to know a little about the person who's supposed to have your back."

He had her there. She could understand the validity of his reasoning. But, since he opened the door, she had a question of her own, one that had been knocking around the back chambers of her mind.

"Okay, I'll buy that," she granted. He was about to get up when she stopped him with her question. "Why did you bring me a puppy?"

The question had come out of nowhere. He thought they'd already settled that the evening he gave her the puppy.

Kyle sank back down in his seat. "Excuse me?"

"Kyle. The retriever," Jaren specified, in case he thought she was referring to him by his first name. Lately, she only did that in the privacy of her own mind, where she could get intimate without consequence. "Why did you bring her to me that night?"

The expression on his face was meant to tell her that

what he'd done was no big deal, just a matter of logic, nothing more. "I told you, my sister was trying to find homes for her dog's puppies."

No, he'd gone out of his way to get her address and to be deliberately kind to her. This, after making her feel like an outsider. She just wanted to understand which the real Kyle O'Brien was. "I couldn't have been the only dogless person you knew."

He rose again, signaling the conversation was over. "You'd be surprised."

It wasn't over for her. "You always avoid answering questions this way?"

"No. Sometimes I don't say anything at all." He paused. He hadn't meant to sound so curt, but lack of sleep was getting to him, as well. "Okay, you want to know why I brought over the puppy? You looked like you needed a friend and I figured that I'd been kind of rough on you that day. It just seemed like a good match at the time." He had a feeling that Rosetti was the type who never let up so he diverted the conversation away from his motives. "Speaking of which, how's it going?"

"You were right," she admitted, allowing a fond smile to surface. The smile was actually meant for the puppy they were discussing. "It was a good match. She's really smart and she learns fast."

"Must be the name," he commented.

She didn't bother suppressing the grin that came to her lips. "Must be."

"C'mon," he urged. "Let's hit the pavement. I want to reinterview a couple of the neurosurgeon's former

patients. Since there haven't been any more *slayings,*
I'm thinking that maybe the idea that one murder was
planned and the others done as a cover-up might not be
that far-fetched."

Jaren was on her feet before he finished his statement.

They're coming!

Sweating profusely, he bolted upright in bed. His heart
was pounding so hard, it almost exploded out of his chest.

That was Derek's voice, calling to him. Warning him.
Derek always knew where the danger was.

There were lights everywhere, but still his eyes
darted around, searching the corners of his vast bedroom. Safe, he wanted to be safe.

When was he ever going to be safe?

Despite all the crosses he had hung about the room
and the large gold one he wore around his neck—a gift
from his protector, "To keep you safe when I can't," he'd
told him—he was still afraid.

Afraid because he'd heard the warning. Derek's
warning that they were regrouping.

And coming for him.

Unless he got them first.

Hands shaking, he threw off the covers and got out of
bed. He was fully clothed. He never undressed anymore.
Not since the Protector had been taken from him. He had
to be ready to flee into the night if it came to that.

He knew he had to destroy the next one. The one that
was out there, waiting for him. After the last, he'd
thought, hoped, *prayed* that he was finally safe.

But he wasn't, he thought, angry tears gathering in his eyes. He was never going to be safe. Not until every one of them was dead.

Such a monumental task, and he was only one lone warrior. But it had to be done. He knew the consequences if it wasn't.

For a second, he closed his eyes, praying. Seeking strength in his holy battle against the undead. The words the Protector had taught came back to him. They, and the cross he wore—he told himself, his fingers curling around it now—would keep him safe. And someway, somehow, he was going to kill them all. And only then would he have everlasting peace.

He went to arm himself.

Chapter 11

It was another long, tiring, fruitless day.

Kyle and Jaren had reinterviewed several people but their efforts yielded no more information. For the most part, they all had the same thing to say about the slain neurosurgeon. Dr. Barrett was an excellent surgeon, with few equals, but no one had wanted to share even an elevator ride with him. He had made no attempt to hide his God complex.

"I don't see wanting to kill someone because he was cold and detached," Jaren commented as they walked away from their last interview—Dr. James Wiley, an orthopedic surgeon Dr. Barrett had treated a year ago. Dr. Wiley had made time for them during his weekly golf game.

"And yet, someone killed him," Kyle countered as they walked to his vehicle.

"Maybe Dr. Barrett was one of the camouflage murders," she suggested. "If we're working with that theory," she added, glancing toward Kyle.

"For lack of anything better." Fantastic as it seemed, he kept coming back to the vampire-slayer theory. *Her* initial theory. Kyle felt he might need a vacation. "I don't know about you, but my brain is beginning to hurt."

"I'm getting a headache," she admitted. "How many more of the doctor's patients do you want to interview?"

Jaren tried not to be obvious about glancing at her watch, but it was past their regular shift. Again.

"There's only one left on the list, but he'll keep until tomorrow." He felt in need of rejuvenation. "Want to get a drink?"

The suggestion caught her by surprise.

"I'd love to," she told him honestly. Most of the detectives gathered at a local bar, which she'd found to be rather pleasant as well as atmospheric. However, thanks to Kyle, she wasn't her own person anymore. "But I've got someone waiting for me at home."

"Oh."

She saw him withdrawing and realized that he'd misunderstood.

"A certain four-footed furry creature who needs her dinner," she explained, then heard herself suggesting, "We could have a drink at my place. I've got some wine in the refrigerator."

He knew that he should say thanks, but no thanks. Knew that what he needed right now was the noise of a familiar crowd where he could unwind and then go home for perhaps a semi-decent night's sleep.

Even so, Kyle caught himself nodding. "You talked me into it."

The drive to her apartment wasn't far.

Kyle parked within the parking structure, in one of the free spaces near Jaren's assigned space, then followed her to her door.

The second she unlocked it and turned the knob to open the door, a caramel-colored ball of fluff came charging out, launching herself at what she obviously took to be her liberator. Because he was standing to the right of Jaren, Kyle turned out to be the recipient of his namesake's wild enthusiasm.

Kyle picked up the dog and immediately found himself on the receiving end of a madly working pink tongue.

"Hold it, hold it," he laughed, drawing the dog back in order to get a better look at it, and to bring a halt to the impromptu face washing. "She's grown," he said to Jaren.

"They have a habit of doing that," Jaren agreed with a laugh, locking the door behind them.

Very carefully, she removed her service revolver with its holster, placing it next to the microwave oven on the counter.

Kyle put the dog back on the floor and followed suit, depositing his hardware beside hers. With that done, he glanced out toward the living room. The last time he'd been here, the room was filled with towering boxes.

"Looks a lot bigger this way," he commented.

She'd broken down the last of the empty boxes and thrown them in the recycle bin just this past weekend. She smiled now.

"Yeah, I know. Gives Kyle a lot of room to run around. I'd leave the balcony open for her but she's such a friendly dog, she'd probably make a dive down at the first person she sees."

Opening the refrigerator, Jaren reached in and took out the white wine. The bottle, Kyle noted, hadn't been opened yet.

"Saving it for a special occasion?" he asked.

He also took note of the fact that the refrigerator was bare aside from a carton of orange juice.

"Just for my first guest," she answered. "I thought the occasion might be worth celebrating." She glanced at the bottle and noticed the date on it. "2007 was a very good year," she commented, tongue in cheek.

"If you say so." Kyle shrugged. "One year's more or less like another to me."

He didn't elaborate that 2007 was the year his mother had fallen ill. And a little more than a year before the bottom had fallen out of his world when he and his siblings had been told that they'd been fathered by Brian Cavanaugh's older brother, Mike.

After getting the corkscrew, Jaren sank it into the cork and brought the wings down in order to raise it out of the bottle. Meanwhile Kyle, she noticed, had picked up the puppy's small rubber ball and was rolling it to her. The Labrador was overjoyed as she chased after the red object and brought it back to his feet.

Jaren grinned as she took in the game. "You know, you're not nearly the hard-ass you like to pretend you are."

Kyle let the puppy keep the ball and chew on it. He rose to his feet and crossed back to Jaren in the kitchen. "Just ask my brother and sister, they'll tell you otherwise."

She'd always wished that her parents had had more children. She spent a good deal of her childhood yearning for a sibling, someone to share secrets with.

Jaren emptied a can of dog food into the puppy's bowl. She'd barely finished before the Lab came flying over and began eating. With a pleased laugh, she reached into the cabinet directly over the microwave, took out two glasses and set them on the counter.

"What's it like to have two people around who look almost exactly like you?" she asked.

He watched as the puppy polished off her evening meal. "Never gave it much thought. I just see them as individuals." He and his brother hadn't even indulged in the common adolescent prank of switching places. Their voices alone would have given them away. Ethan was far more outgoing than he was, and more soft-spoken. "We've got more differences than similarities," he told her.

Jaren poured two glasses of wine, handed him his and then walked with hers into the living room. She brought along the bottle in case Kyle wanted a refill. One was usually her limit.

Setting the bottle down on the coffee table, she took a seat on the sofa. He sat down next to her. Fed now, the puppy decided that their feet were fair game and curled up happily between them, occasionally raising her head to flick her tongue over Kyle's shoe as a sign of affection.

"Which one's the oldest?" Jaren asked.

"We're triplets," he reminded her.

"I know that, but there's always one that's the oldest. The three of you didn't make your debut at exactly the same time."

"I am," he finally said. Absently, he scratched the puppy's head. The Labrador had shifted over closer toward him. It was clear that she thought of him as the leader of the pack.

"I thought so," Jaren declared. "So, taking charge comes naturally to you."

He didn't like taking charge, just getting things done. His own way. "I'd rather do things alone," he informed her.

"But you don't. You take charge. If a leader's called for, you're it." She saw him frown. He didn't like credit, she concluded. "Nothing to be ashamed of."

"I'm not ashamed," Kyle countered, then took a long sip from his glass. "You're putting me in a niche and I'd rather not be pigeonholed."

She smiled as she took her first sip of wine. "Spoils the mystery?"

He laughed dryly. "There're enough mysteries around right now without that."

Jaren took a breath. Was it her, or had it suddenly gotten warmer? She realized that she was watching his lips as he spoke, letting her mind drift. Maybe the wine was a bad idea, at least for her.

She set the glass down on the table and cleared her throat. "Are you hungry? I can order some pizza," she offered.

He thought of the empty refrigerator. "Was that what you were going to have?" She nodded. "Not exactly a balanced dinner."

"Bread, meat, tomatoes, cheese," she recited the components of her favorite pizza. "Sounds pretty balanced to me." Rising to her feet, she crossed to the kitchen phone and began to dial the number of the local pizza parlor.

Kyle followed her, leaving the glass of wine standing next to hers. "You don't cook, do you?"

She paused for a minute. "Only if I'm looking to come down with food poisoning. Now," she resumed dialing, "what's your pleasure?" The line was busy. She broke the connection and began to dial again.

Kyle wasn't sure just what prompted him to do what he did next. Maybe it was reacting to her question. Maybe it was being alone with her like this and feeling the chemistry crackle between them without the usual distractions of work. And maybe it was the wine and the fact that he hadn't eaten anything in close to eight hours, and then it had only been half a sandwich.

For whatever reason, Kyle took the receiver from her hand and hung it up.

Her mouth turned to pure cotton. Jaren raised her eyes to his. "You want something else besides pizza?" she guessed, the words coming out in almost slow motion. This wasn't what she thought it was, she silent insisted.

Get a grip. The man just changed his mind about pizza, that's all.

Taking a breath, Jaren was about to rattle off the names of several other take-out places in the area she'd become familiar with in the last few weeks, but the words never rose to her lips.

Which was just as well because her lips suddenly had something else to deal with. The press of his against them.

Her heart slammed against her chest and she found herself falling into the kiss and the moment. He tasted like no wine she'd ever sampled.

His mouth slanted over hers over and over again, weakening her just a little more with each pass, dissolving her strength and melting her inner core. Struggling to remain grounded, she entwined her arms around his neck, rising up on her toes so that her body could press against his in all the important contact points.

A hunger raced through her, surprising her. She couldn't remember the last time she'd wanted a man to hold her, to kiss her. To make her forget everything else.

She kissed him harder, not wanting to disappear into oblivion without leaving her mark. He responded by tightening his hold on her. She felt a fire ignite in her veins.

This was only going to end one way.

But just as the thought came to her, she could have sworn that music filled the air.

No, not music, ring tones.

Her phone was ringing.

Oh no, not now. Jaren wanted to ignore it. With all her heart she wanted to pretend it wasn't ringing, but then she heard another ring tone. Kyle's phone was ringing, too.

The dissonance broke into the moment. A feeling of bereavement, framed in relief, overtook her. This would have been a mistake, she told herself. A glorious, mind-numbing mistake. With reluctance, she pulled back.

"The phones are ringing," Jaren told him needlessly, trying to catch her breath.

She wasn't the only one.

Breathing hard, wondering what the hell had come over him, Kyle nodded and took a step back. He dragged his hand through his dark hair, as if that would somehow restore his thinking process to normal—or as normal as could be expected. Swallowing an unintelligible oath, he pulled out his phone.

Rosetti, he saw, was doing the same with hers. They answered, announcing their names, at almost the exact same time.

"O'Brien."

"Rosetti."

By the way her face paled, Kyle surmised that she was getting the same message that he was. The moment they'd shared was gone as if it had never existed, blown away in the wake of the information they were receiving.

He later remembered thinking that this couldn't be happening. Except that it was. It had.

"When?" he demanded gruffly.

A shaken Riley was on the other end of the line,

calling to tell him that the vampire slayer had struck again. Telling him the slayer's latest victim. Kyle could tell it was all she could do to keep from breaking down. He felt sick to his stomach himself.

"The M.E. hasn't gotten here yet," she was saying. "I called you as soon as I—as we—found the body." He thought he heard a suppressed sob. "Holloway is on the other line, calling Jaren."

"Get a hold of yourself, Riley. Where are you?" he asked gruffly.

It took her a second to remember the names of the streets and get her bearings. When she did, Riley rattled the address off to him.

Kyle didn't bother telling her he'd be right there before he snapped his phone shut. That was a given.

He looked at Jaren who'd already gotten off her cell. She looked even paler than before. He thought of telling her to stay put, but that would have been playing favorites. Most likely, she'd just resent him for it.

"You okay?" His voice was harsh as he grappled with the situation himself.

Feeling like someone in a surreal nightmare, Jaren nodded, then added in a haunted voice, "I've been better." Pivoting on her heel, she crossed to the counter and picked up her weapon. She strapped it on quickly.

Maybe Holloway had made a mistake, she thought desperately. Maybe, but even as she tried to advance the desperate notion, she knew she was wrong. There was no mistake.

"Let's go," she cried, hurrying out the door before Kyle.

* * *

With sirens blaring, flying through all the lights, they lost no time getting to the back alley where the slayer's latest victim lay. Jaren approached the body on legs that grew progressively more rubbery.

Detective Diego Sanchez, his dark hair slicked back, wearing the black all-weather coat he favored, died with a surprised look on his face. A copy of *The Vampire Diaries* lay on the ground several feet away from him.

There was a stake through his heart.

Kyle crouched down beside the body. He looked at the book. It was facedown on the pavement, its spine broken and flat. Was that what did it? Had the book attracted his killer? Or was it the way Sanchez liked to dress? Kyle struggled against feeling sick.

He rose to his feet. "What's he doing with this book?" he demanded. The question was addressed to anyone who could give him an answer.

Holloway sighed heavily. He and Sanchez had been partnered for the last six years. For the purposes of the investigation, Kyle had assigned each of them to one of the other detectives on the task force, to give them the benefit of their experience.

"He said he wanted to know what all the fuss was about. Thought it might help him to figure out the inner workings of his girlfriend's mind," Holloway finally said, standing over the body and shaking his head. "Damn it, who's going to tell his mother?"

"I'll do it," Kyle said, his voice low, barely a rumble.

Holloway looked at him. "I didn't mean for you—"

Kyle cut him off. "My task force, my job," he said with finality. Forcing himself to focus on the crime, he scanned the area. None of this made any sense. Why Sanchez?

"Anyone know what he was doing tonight?"

Riley cleared her throat. Sanchez had been assigned to her. "He told me he was playing a hunch," she volunteered.

Kyle turned to look at the woman who, thanks to his mother's deathbed revelation, had become part of his family. "Which was?"

Riley shook her head. "He wouldn't tell me. He said—" Her voice cracked and she began again. "He said that if it didn't pan out, he didn't want to be left with egg on his face. I told him I'd go with him, but he said there was no point in both of us chasing this down." Riley pressed her lips together as if trying to force down the tears. "I should have gone with him."

Unable to witness her guilt a second longer, Jaren came up to her and tried to put her arms around the woman. Riley shook her off, then caved.

"You had no way of knowing what was going to happen," Jaren told her.

There was anguish in Riley's eyes as she said, "That's exactly why I should have gone."

"Don't waste time beating yourself up," Kyle told her. "We've got a killer to catch. Riley, I want you to find out all the calls Sanchez made on his cell phone in the last twenty-four hours. Maybe we can figure out where he was going tonight."

Riley nodded. "On it."

"Holloway, go with her," he ordered, and then looked at the three detectives in the alley. "From now on, I don't want anyone going off on their own."

"We can work faster if we split up," Holloway argued.

"No one is going alone," Kyle repeated with feeling. "Do I make myself clear?"

"Clear," Riley agreed, her voice hardly above a tortured whisper.

"He wasn't killed here," Jaren realized, just as the M.E. arrived. When the others turned to her, she explained. "There's no pool of blood. He was killed somewhere else and then brought here."

Why? Kyle wondered. Had the crime scene been too close to the slayer's home? "I still want a canvas of the area. See if anyone saw or heard something. A truck, a van, a car pulling into the alley and then leaving." Even as he said it, he knew it was too much to hope for.

"Tire marks do?" Holloway asked.

Kyle felt his pulse jump. "Fresh?" he asked, hurrying over to where Holloway stood.

Jaren had already joined the other detective and squatted down to examine the markings. "Looks to be," she answered.

"Have CSI run down the make and model," Kyle instructed. He could see the team members entering the alley. "Maybe our vampire slayer made his first mistake."

"His first mistake," Riley said grimly, "was killing one of our own."

No one argued that point.

Chapter 12

"I'm going with you," Jaren informed Kyle as she hurried to catch up to him outside of the alley.

Kyle shook his head. "I'm on my way to see Sanchez's mother."

Of all the things that a police officer did, Kyle thought, informing a parent or spouse of their loved one's death had to be among the worst. Even he wasn't immune to it, despite the fact that he did his best to distance himself from the people he worked with.

Jaren lengthened her stride to keep pace with him. "I know."

Kyle stopped abruptly. "Thanks, but I don't need someone to hold my hand. I've done this more times than I care to remember."

"Everyone needs someone to hold their hand once in a while," Jaren told him. No matter how aloof he pretended to be, she knew Sanchez's murder had gotten to him just like it had to the rest of them. Having to tell the man's mother the detective had been slain was going to be hard enough with support. She didn't want him doing it alone. "I'm coming with you so you might as well get used to it. Besides, Mrs. Sanchez might want a woman there."

He didn't want to waste time arguing, especially since he had a feeling that he was not about to win. Rosetti seemed the type to argue the ears off a brass monkey. And maybe she was right. Maybe having a woman there might give Sanchez's mother some measure of comfort, although if it were him, there would simply be no way to glean comfort from this kind of a situation.

Kyle resumed walking to his vehicle. They were parked one behind the other. "If you're going to come, let's go."

They drove separately, just as they had from her apartment. She hadn't thought to ask him for Mrs. Sanchez's address, so perforce, she had to follow closely behind him when all she wanted was to open up the engine and go fast. The tension she was experiencing reached critical mass.

The porch light was on at the Sanchez residence but the lights inside were off. Kyle seemed to hesitate, not wanting to wake the woman up to news like this. But in the end, he finally pressed the doorbell.

Several minutes went by before a light went on inside the house and they heard the lock being flipped open. Jaren heard Kyle take in a breath as the door opened.

Inez Sanchez was a short woman whose full-figured frame testified to her love of food. At sixty-three, her face was unlined and only a few gray strands had found their way into her midnight black hair.

Her dark eyes were still sleepy as she recognized the young man at her door. She smiled a sleepy greeting.

"Diego isn't home yet," she told him.

"I know," Kyle replied.

The two words erased the woman's smile. Horror took its place as her eyes widened.

"Oh no, no. Please, no."

Kyle forced the words out. "Mrs. Sanchez, I'm so very sorry to have to tell you this, but—"

"No. *Es la mentira.* No. He is coming home. Diego is coming home. He is just late," she insisted, looking from her son's friend to the young woman who had come with him. Her eyes begged them to tell her she wasn't wrong.

"He isn't late," Kyle said, raising his voice above her cries. "He's dead."

Mrs. Sanchez's eyes were wild as she heard the words that brought the end of hope in her life. Her knees buckled, refusing to hold her up. Kyle caught her, but it was Jaren who moved in, Jaren who put her arms around the woman and held her close. Mrs. Sanchez struggled, trying to shrug her off. Jaren refused to let her, holding on tightly until the detective's mother finally dissolved into a pool of tears.

In her misery, Inez Sanchez completely reverted to her native tongue. Kyle was surprised when he heard Jaren answer her.

Jaren said every soothing thing she could think of and then fervently swore to the woman that they would get the man who killed her son. She sealed her promise by taking an oath on her father's grave.

It was the latter vow that finally got through to the grieving mother and stilled her louder sobs.

At a loss, feeling as if he was in the way, Kyle quietly slipped out of the small, single-story stucco house.

Jaren was aware of his leaving, but her attention was focused on Inez.

She remained with Mrs. Sanchez another twenty minutes, until, utterly exhausted, the woman fell into a fitful sleep on the sofa. Taking out one of her newly printed cards, Jaren wrote a note on the back, urging the woman to call her anytime if she needed to talk. Time of day or night didn't matter.

She left the card propped up against the base of the lamp on the end table. With an aching heart, she tiptoed outside and quietly pulled the door shut behind her. She made sure she heard the lock click into place.

When she turned around, Jaren bit back a scream. Her nerves were closer to the surface than she thought.

"You didn't go home," she said needlessly. When he slipped out, she was certain Kyle had taken the opportunity to go home himself.

"I said we were supposed to do things in pairs, remember? I'm not about to have you out on the streets at this hour. Especially in this neighborhood. It's not safe." He nodded toward the house behind her. "She going to be all right?"

Jaren shook her head. "Not for a good long while," she guessed. "But she cried herself into exhaustion and fell asleep. I left her on the sofa. Sleep's the best thing for her right now. Is there anyone we can call for her?"

"Not that I know of." He led the way back to the cars parked at the curb. "Get in your car," he instructed. "I'll follow you home."

"Then what, I'll follow you to your place to make sure you got in safely?"

Kyle frowned at her. Why did everything have to turn into a debate? "I'm a man."

"So was Sanchez," she reminded him grimly. "Seems to me that this maniac only goes after men."

"So far," Kyle pointed out.

She stifled a shiver. O'Brien might be right, but she hoped not. There was already enough panic about this killer without bringing the female population into it.

Jaren couldn't remember ever feeling this restless, this unsettled. She wouldn't be able to sleep tonight. Not given the way she felt.

"There's no point in going back to my apartment," she told him. "I won't sleep. I'm too keyed up."

She was about to say that she might as well go to the precinct and see if she could get any work done, when she heard him say, "I'll come with you. We can talk until you wind down."

He'd surprised her again. Just when she thought she had him pegged. "Okay," she agreed, although she had her doubts that she would be able to unwind. She felt like a cherry bomb about to go off.

* * *

"I didn't know you spoke Spanish," Kyle commented as they walked to her door.

"I can get by," she said modestly. "My best friend in elementary school was Mexican. I liked hanging around her house after school." She smiled as a few memories came back to her. Jaren put her key in the lock and opened her door. "Her mother made the greatest meals."

"What about your mother?" He waited for her to enter, then followed her inside.

Jaren turned on the light switch beside the door. The light came on in her kitchen. Sprawled out on the kitchen floor, the puppy raised her head to see who was intruding into her home. Recognizing them, the Labrador came bounding over, greeting both as if they'd all been separated for months rather than hours.

"My mother tended toward getting takeout and frozen dinners," Jaren remembered. She picked up the puppy and gave her a hug.

"I guess the apple didn't fall far from the tree," Kyle speculated.

"The apple had better things to do than to experiment in the kitchen," she informed him. Between taking care of her father, keeping house for him and going to school, she had little time to be a teenager, much less a chef with a learning curve. "One day when I was twelve, my mother decided she could do better." She tried to sound flippant, but even so, the memory hurt. "I came home from school and found a note from her on the kitchen table, telling me she was sorry but she was dying by inches living her life. She asked me to take care of my father, saying I'd probably do a better job than she did."

He waited for her to continue. When she didn't, he asked, "And that was it?"

The note was the last communication she had with her mother. "That was it."

He found himself feeling sorry for the child she had been. That was a hell of a burden to place on a twelve-year-old's shoulders. "What did your father do when he found out?"

She did what she could to distance herself from the memory. As much as she loved her father, she was keenly aware of his shortcomings.

"Went out and bought another bottle of vodka." There was a bittersweet smile on her lips. Thoughts of her father always evoked a feeling of affection and protectiveness, mingled with guilt because she was so disappointed that he didn't try harder to get away from his demons. The demons that eventually took him away from her. "That was pretty much my father's solution to everything. Vodka. Black Russians were his favorite." And then, because she knew how that sounded, she quickly added, "He really tried to be a good father, but he just wasn't strong enough."

Her words came back to her. Jaren looked at Kyle, just a bit stunned. "How did we wind up talking about my father?"

"Doesn't matter." He watched her for a long moment. "You were right."

The compliment came out of nowhere. In order to savor it, she needed to know its origins. "About?"

"About coming with me to break the news to Mrs. Sanchez. I wouldn't have been able to handle her without you. Thanks," he concluded.

"Can't cook but knows how to comfort people on the receiving end of bad news," she declared, lowering her voice to sound as if she was narrating her good points. And then she smiled. "We all have our skills."

Again, he looked at her for a long moment, but this time, he caught himself experiencing the same pull he had before the awful call about Sanchez's murder had come through.

What was there about this woman that pulled him in like that? That tangled up his ordinarily straight thought process?

"Some," he said, combing his fingers through her hair, "have more than others."

Jaren felt her heart race again. Even harder than the first time. The same wave of warmth overtook her. But this time, she didn't even bother trying to avoid it. This time, she wanted to race to it. She *needed* the contact. Needed to feel human again.

This wasn't about forming an attachment or nurturing a relationship, she told herself. It was just teeth-jarring, unrelenting physical attraction. She didn't want to think for a space of time. More than anything, she just wanted to wipe away the image of Sanchez in the alley. Wanted to wipe out the sound of Mrs. Sanchez's sobs that still rang in her ears.

She took the plunge. Someone had to go first and she couldn't count on him. He was probably more grounded.

"Make love with me, O'Brien," she whispered as she laced her arms around his neck. "Nobody has to know. Just make me stop thinking."

Kyle knew he should disengage himself from her. Knew that he should say something about being her superior on this case and that they had a professional relationship to maintain. They were coworkers and these kinds of things—even if it was only a onetime thing— rarely worked out. He wasn't in the market for a relationship, and a one-night stand with a fellow detective just wasn't a good idea.

But for the life of him, he couldn't voice a single protest, couldn't put a single thought into words. He was only aware of the overwhelming desire pulsing within him.

He wanted her.

Wanted to make love with her until they were both mindless and cleansed.

Kyle struggled to verbalize a protest for both their own good, but he lost the battle before it ever began.

Jaren sealed her lips to his and suddenly, there was nothing else but her and the passion roaring through his veins like a runaway freight train.

The moment her lips touched his, Kyle found himself lost in a sea of passion. Passion of a magnitude that took his breath away. Never would he have even entertained the thought that he was capable of feeling something like this.

He gave himself up to it.

Clothes went flying as they stumbled from the kitchen to the living room, desperate for the feel of skin, for the hot sizzle of flesh on flesh.

Maybe her bedroom was the ultimate goal, but if so, they didn't get there in time.

Their bodies were naked before they were halfway there.

Over and over Kyle brought his mouth to hers as his hands familiarized themselves with all the inviting contours of her supple, firm body. He could feel himself reacting to the way she raked her hands over him. Everything within Kyle hummed with anticipation.

He wouldn't have been able to say who wanted this more, if he did or if it was she. In the end, he supposed it turned out to be a draw.

They both won.

Sinking to the floor, they were oblivious to the yipping of the puppy that kept excitedly circling them. The Labrador undoubtedly thought this was some sort of new game.

But if this was a game, it carried incredibly high stakes. His very soul depended on this, on losing himself within the sweet fire that she had created within his veins. Capturing both her wrists in his hand, Kyle raised them above her head as he pleasured her, pleasured himself savaging her mouth.

When he could feel her heart hammering against his, he allowed his mouth to roam, to take a swift detour along her throat, her breasts, her quivering abdomen.

And with each pass of his lips, his teeth, his tongue, he could feel Jaren twisting and turning beneath him, eagerly absorbing every nuance, every second of sweet agony he created for her.

Her very movement against his body both fed the hunger and made it more intense within him.

Breaking free of his hold, Jaren grabbed hold of his shoulders and urgently tugged on them, finally succeeding in pulling him back up to her until they were face-to-face with one another.

He saw his destiny in her eyes. It would have scared the hell out of him had he been thinking clearly.

But he wasn't.

He was feeling and that made for a world of difference.

An urgency drummed through every fiber of his being as he drove himself into her. Filling her and nullifying a void within himself.

At least for the moment.

The frantic rhythm of hips against hips increased until they reached the final peak. He groaned as the exploding sensation momentarily stole him away from everything else.

Kyle tightened his arms around her, as if to hold the feeling close for just a second longer. But even so, it was vanishing.

Moving off Jaren, he rolled onto his back, one arm tucked beneath his head. He was surprised to discover that his other arm was curved around her.

What the hell did that mean?

He was too drained to try to figure it out. Too drained

even to reclaim his arm. He let it remain until his breathing became regular again.

With effort, he recalled her last words to him. "Well, did it make you stop thinking?" he asked her in a low, hoarse whisper.

Jaren didn't answer. She *couldn't* answer. Her breathing was completely erratic. If she spoke right now, she'd squeak.

God, what had happened here? She knew she'd been the one to start this, to actually ask for it, but she certainly hadn't expected this degree of passion, this degree of *anything* to erupt within her. Granted, she hadn't been with many men, but nothing like this had *ever* happened to her before.

Pressing her lips together, Jaren took a breath, desperate to make light of a situation that was anything but light. She instinctively knew, without being told, that to do anything else—to attach any importance to what had just happened, to even allude to the possibility that this was the start of something rather than solely a onetime thing—would scare the hell out of Kyle.

It certainly did out of her.

She took another breath, hoping her voice wouldn't crack. "I can't even remember my name, rank and serial number," she quipped.

"Funny," he told her, turning his head slightly to look at her, "I can."

He felt her breasts brush against him as she turned her body to his. Her expression was serious. "I meant what I said."

His mind was a complete blank. Not a usual state for him. What was it that she had said? Had he even heard her? "About?"

"About no one needing to know about what happened here. I just—" She stumbled, searching for the right words. "—just wanted to forget."

"Hypnosis would have been less exhausting," he told her so matter-of-factly, for a moment, Jaren thought he was serious. And then she saw a glimmer of amusement in his eyes. Why that ushered in relief was something she wasn't able to explain.

"You have a sense of humor." Now there was something she wouldn't have accused him of harboring.

He laughed shortly. There was a time, he recalled, when he was quick to laugh. Before he discovered that life wasn't funny, it was a challenge. "Don't let it get around."

She smiled, running her fingers along the outline of his biceps. He was doing it again, she thought, reaching out to something inside of her. She wondered if he knew. Probably not. If he knew, he'd stop. He struck her as a man who didn't like complications.

"Your secret's safe with me," she promised. To bring the point home, she crossed her heart with her finger.

Moving her hand, he pressed a kiss to her breast. "As long as we're keeping secrets," he said softly, turning his body toward hers.

She could feel the fire starting again. Could feel the desire taking hold again. Suddenly, she wanted to lose herself in him just one more time.

"Yes?"

He didn't answer her. At least, not verbally. Instead, he began to make love with her again. Except far more languidly this time.

He was certain that he had missed areas the first time around because they had gone at it with such a furor. But a woman like Jaren deserved to be made love with slowly, underscoring every movement. And he had no idea what possessed him, but he fully intended to be the one who did it.

Chapter 13

Jaren woke up several minutes before her alarm, the smell of coffee teasing its way into her consciousness.

More specifically, the smell of coffee, bacon and toast.

Staring at the ceiling, her mind trying to focus, Jaren thought she was dreaming. And then she remembered Kyle and last night and was certain that she was still asleep.

But the aroma persisted, so she finally sat up. And realized that she was naked. She slapped down the buzzer as it began to ring. Maybe last night hadn't been a dream after all.

Getting up, Jaren quickly threw on a pair of shorts and a T-shirt, then went to the kitchen to investigate the source of the aroma.

She found Kyle standing by the stove with his name-sake sitting up at his feet. The latter was leaving drool marks on the floor, hoping for a taste of what smelled so temptingly good.

Kyle glanced over his shoulder. "You're up."

Her mouth curved. Now here was a sight she never imagined in her kitchen. "You do magic."

Kyle tried to place her comment in context. "If you're referring to last night, you were pretty inspiring yourself."

She felt a blush rushing over her fair skin, turning it a soft shade of warm. "I meant breakfast. You're cooking."

He looked back at the frying pan on the stove. "Oh, yeah."

Her head still jumbled, she tried to make her statement understood. "All I had in the refrigerator was wine and orange juice. You make eggs, toast and bacon appear?"

He laughed, finally understanding her confusion. She probably thought if he was going to go out for break-fast, he would return with a paper bag with a fast-food logo embossed on its side. "I went to the grocery store. You sleep pretty soundly."

"I had one hell of a workout last night."

There was a hint of a smile on his lips as Kyle peered at her over his shoulder again. "Yeah, come to think of it, me, too."

For a second, the only sound in the room was the siz-zle of the bacon. Jaren tightened her lips. "Is this going to be the awkward part?"

Silence had never bothered him. At times, it was a

welcomed companion, a place to seek shelter. "Not unless you want it to be."

Hunger got the better of her. She could see why the Labrador was drooling. "What I want is to sample what you've just made."

Kyle turned off the heat and moved both frying pans to cool burners. "That's what it's here for," he told her.

Two empty plates sat on the counter and he divided the contents of both frying pans. A second later, toast joined each serving.

Jaren carried the plates to the table while he brought up the rear, a cup of coffee in each hand. Without realizing it, he watched the soft sway of her hips as she walked, appreciation filtering through him.

She didn't wait for him, but started eating as he took his seat opposite her. "This is good," Jaren pronounced with feeling.

He shrugged off her compliment. "Kind of hard to spoil scrambled eggs." Breaking off a piece of bacon, Kyle held it out to the eager puppy. It disappeared in a heartbeat. She licked his fingers several times over to get every last bit of flavor off them.

"Not so hard, trust me," she countered, and then smiled. "It seems that you've got more than one hidden talent."

He raised his eyes to hers and smiled himself, not saying anything. Some things were better left without a comment.

Not wanting to let on that last night had shaken up his world as much as it had, Kyle moved the conversation toward the case while they ate. He was now convinced that they were dealing with a psychopath and that the vampire angle was the one to follow.

"After all," he said, draining his coffee cup, "Son of Sam swore he was getting his instructions from his dog. There's no reason to doubt that our killer went off the deep end and now thinks he's getting his orders from some *higher power* telling him to kill *vampires*."

She wasn't so sure she went along with the second half of his theory. "And that higher power is identifying the vampires for him?"

He fed a little of his toast to the dog. Jaren pretended not to notice, but the fact that he did warmed her heart even more. "Sounds good to me," Kyle said.

"By higher power, you mean the voices he might be hearing in his head?"

After he finished eatomg, he wiped his mouth with the napkin. "That's what I mean."

She followed his line of reasoning. "So, you think it's just random."

Kyle nodded. "Easier that way. And," he reminded her, "they did have the book in common."

"They had more than that in common," she countered. "They had the killer. There has to be some kind of connection between the neurosurgeon and the CEO that were killed." She hurried to explain her reasoning. "The killer had to physically see those books in their offices. He didn't plant them like a calling card. They were what set him off." She'd bet a year's salary on it. "Which consequently means he knew the men. He knew them well enough to get admitted into their offices."

"And Sanchez?" Kyle asked. "How do you factor in his murder?"

The mention of the detective vividly brought back his mother's anguish. Jaren did what she could to shut it out. Remembering would do no one any good right now. "The killer must have interacted with Sanchez."

Kyle followed her reasoning to its logical conclusion. "Which means that, technically, we've met the killer. Or at least Sanchez did. He's got to be one of the people who was interviewed."

"That's what I think." Finishing her breakfast, she retired her fork and took one last sip of her coffee. "What about the Count?"

That was the least complicated of the murders. "Wrong place at the wrong time," Kyle guessed. "Maybe the Count just crossed the killer's path. Or maybe the killer knew him, too. Hard to say but you're right, the murders weren't done at random."

"Nice to be in agreement," she commented. Rising, Jaren brought both plates over to the sink. "You're the guest so you can have the shower first."

He placed the two coffee cups next to the stacked dishes in the sink. "There's a drought on," he reminded her.

Nothing new there, she thought. California had been tottering on the brink of a drought for years now. The governor had just made it official. Turning around to look at Kyle, she wasn't sure just where he was going with this.

"I suppose we can both walk through a car wash but that might cause too much of a commotion."

Kyle fought back the urge to fold his arms around her. He had no idea just what was going on. Displays of affection were not what he was about, yet something had definitely happened last night—something that changed him.

"I was thinking more along the lines of showering together." He watched as the smile bloomed on Jaren's face.

"Showering together," she repeated. When he nodded, she laughed. "You are a constant source of surprise to me, O'Brien."

"Yeah, me, too," he confessed.

Without another word, she linked her fingers with his and led him to the bathroom.

When they arrived at the precinct an hour later, the lieutenant told Kyle that Brian Cavanaugh wanted everyone to gather together in the conference room.

As the various detectives and officers filed in the mood was somber. The usual banter and jokes were conspicuously absent. It hadn't taken long for word to spread and Sanchez's murder was on everyone's mind.

When the room was full, Brian went to the front beside the bulletin board and began.

"As you all know, Detective Diego Sanchez was murdered last night, the latest victim of the so-called vampire slayer." He scanned the sea of faces, some mourning, some angry. None were indifferent. The killer had hit them where they lived. "I don't have to tell you that this case has now taken priority over everything else. I am authorizing extra hours, extra manpower.

Whatever we need, we get in order to bring this psychopath in. Alive, if possible," he stressed. "Nobody is going off the reservation on this. I want no loose cannons, do I make myself clear?"

Muttered affirmative responses came from around the room.

Brian addressed each and every one. "There'll be no vacations, no time off until this case is solved and Detective Sanchez's killer is brought to justice."

Kyle raised his hand. When Brian nodded, he asked, "What about Sanchez's funeral? Does anyone know about the arrangements?"

"Not yet," Brian told him. "I'm going to go see Mrs. Sanchez as soon I finish here. There'll be a notice posted with all the information when I find out." He took a breath. Since he'd taken on the mantle of chief of detectives, not a single detective had died while on duty. This had hit him as hard as it had any of them. "According to my information, Sanchez's mother is a widow and he was her only child. I'm sure that all of you will find some time to stop by her home and pay your respects. The woman is going to need an awful lot of emotional support. Okay," he announced, "now let's go get that bastard."

As the others began to file out, Brian turned toward his stepdaughter. "Walk with me, Riley," he urged, leaving the conference room.

Startled by the sound of his voice, Riley turned to face him. "Sure, Chief. You want to talk to me?"

Brian nodded. Married to his former partner, Lila McIntyre, for less than six months, he was still trying to work out the logistics of taking on four stepchildren in addition to his own four grown children.

Part of this involved trying to arrive at what to be called by Lila's children, children he'd watched grow up into fine adults as well as law-enforcement agents. He might be their chief of detectives, but first and foremost, he was their stepfather and he intended to be more of a father than their real one had been. For the most part, he'd unofficially held the role for years now.

Walking out into the hall with Riley, he took her aside and, concerned, asked, "Are you all right?"

"Sure."

The assurance came out much too quickly, like an automatic response when someone asked a stranger about their health. "According to what I heard, you were the one who discovered Sanchez's body and called the others."

He watched as Riley unconsciously clenched her hands at her sides. As if steeling herself off from the memory. "Yes, I was."

His manner was completely sympathetic. "That had to be hard on you."

Riley raised her chin defensively. "I've seen dead bodies before, Chief."

He saw through her. "But you never shared a police vehicle with one of them. Never went out to lunch with one of them," he pointed out. "What I'm saying, Riley, is if you need some time off—"

She looked at him in surprise. "I thought you said that nobody's to take any time off until this guy's behind bars."

"That was a pep talk for the team," he clarified. "And for the most part, I meant it. But I'm not about to drive any of my people to the point that they snap. That includes you."

"That's favoritism," she protested.

"No," he contradicted, "that's just being a good leader. I'm not concerned because you're my stepdaughter, I'm concerned because you're one of my detectives, and I'm not about to sacrifice you or any of the other detectives to solve this case. We can do that without incurring any more casualties," he said pointedly. "Now, if you need—"

Riley shook her head. "I appreciate what you're trying to do, but what I need right now is to have that lowlife sitting in a jail cell, contemplating getting a needle in his arm."

Brian suppressed a sigh. Riley was just as stubborn as her mother. "If you're sure…"

"I'm sure." She forced a smile to her lips. "But thanks for asking—Dad."

Being addressed that way obviously pleased him. Brian smiled at his wife's younger daughter. "Okay, the first sign of *battle fatigue* and I'm pulling you out. Understood?"

"Understood," she answered solemnly. A little of her smile reached her eyes as she said, "I always told Mom you were a good guy. Now, if you'll excuse me, I've got work to do."

Brian nodded. He had to get going himself. He'd promised Lila that he would stop by to pick her up. She insisted on going with him to pay their respects to Sanchez's mother.

Parting with Riley, he walked toward the elevators. Even with his wife at his side, he knew this was going to be difficult.

There were days that he liked being chief of detectives less than others.

The funeral was held in the morning three days later. The sky was properly overcast, threatening a cloudburst that never materialized. Every detective and police officer from the Aurora Police Department turned out for the ceremony. This was only the third time in twenty-eight years that a police officer had died in the line of duty. Sanchez's murder left its imprint on each and every one of them.

In the church, Brian and his wife were on one side of Mrs. Sanchez, and Andrew and his wife, Rose, sat on her other, silently offering their support. There was no shortage of people to eulogize the fallen detective. By the time the ceremony was over, there wasn't a dry eye or an uncommitted heart left in the entire church.

The solemnity accompanied them all as they returned to the precinct and their duties.

The phones had been ringing off the hook and there was no shortage of *tips* to follow up on. True to his word, Brian had provided extra man power in order to track them all down.

But they were no closer to cracking the case than they had been three days ago.

* * *

That afternoon, though he loathed to do it, Kyle had to temporarily put his part in the investigation on hold. A case he'd worked on over a year ago had finally reached the trial stage and he was due in court to give his testimony.

Before he left, he stopped at Jaren's desk. "I want you to stay here and go over the testimonies we've gotten in. See if you can find inconsistencies."

Busy work, she thought. He was giving her busy work. He couldn't possibly want her to stay at her desk, reading through reams of reports.

"Wouldn't it be better if I just talked to these people again? People tend to slip up when they talk."

"Only if you get someone to go with you," he cautioned. "I was serious about nobody going off alone. We're too much of a target. The killer knows us, we don't know him."

Everyone around her was out on the field. They'd lost no time right after the funeral.

"How about if I dress up like Rebecca of Sunnybrook Farm? No mistaking me for a threatening vampire then."

Kyle frowned at her. "I'm not taking a chance on losing any more people. Just stay put," were his parting words to her.

Inside, she fumed, but she nodded. "Can I go to the bathroom by myself?" she called out as he crossed to the door.

"No."

She muttered under her breath as she went back to the

stacks of notes she'd taken. Wading through the combined names of interviewees and reviewing their connections to the first two victims, she found no overlaps.

The only name that was even remotely connected to both victims turned out to be a dead man. Not only that, but Jackson Massey had died before either one of the victims had.

Still, since it was the *only* name connected to both victims, Jaren decided to do a little more digging into the man's past. Part of her felt as if she was spinning her wheels but then, most police work was just that, working blindly, hoping for a breakthrough against all odds.

Availing herself of various newspaper archives that were stored on the Internet, she discovered that the late billionaire was a dynamic man who made his mark in the world early in life. He'd earned his first billion before he turned twenty-five and was regarded as a golden boy by his contemporaries.

But despite his incredible good fortune and keen business acumen, his life was not without its tragedies. The young wife he adored died when her appendix ruptured while they were vacationing in a remote part of Africa. She died while being transported by helicopter to the closest hospital. That was scarcely a year after Massey's twin sons were born.

As she continued reading, she found that the twins became the focal point of a statewide search when they were kidnapped at the age of four. Though the FBI had been called in, Massey himself actually rescued Finley, the only surviving twin. His brother, Derek, had accidentally been killed just a few hours before Jackson and his hired mercenaries had stormed the kidnapper's hiding place.

They'd talked to Finley, she recalled while going over the list of the neurosurgeon's patients. This was what had been nagging at her that first time. She remembered reading about this!

Questions began forming in her head.

Jaren managed to unearth some rather choppy footage that had appeared on national news stations right after the rescue. Jackson emerging from a run-down, abandoned warehouse in San Francisco, holding his son in his arms. Finley had his face buried in his father's chest, frightened by all the attention.

When one zealous reporter shoved a microphone at the boy and asked if his captor had hurt him, Jaren thought she heard Finley utter a single, muffled word. "Monsters."

Curious, she searched for more details on the rescue.

Most of what she discovered was repetitive but eventually, she found something more. It was an interview with Finley conducted on the fifteenth anniversary of his rescue. In it, he freely praised his father, once again calling Jackson his hero. She remembered that was what he'd said when grieving over his father's death. Finley went on to describe how, at four, he'd thought his kidnapper was a demon, a vampire who had killed his twin and that his father had slain him.

The word *slain* jumped out at her.

Jackson Massey had, in fact, told the police that he had been forced to shoot the man holding his son captive. The kidnapper never regained consciousness and had died before the ambulance arrived. None of the men who had been hired by Massey to help find his son contradicted his story.

Jaren felt a rush of adrenaline as she reread the article. The words *vampire* and *slain* stood out in huge neon lights.

Chapter 14

Jaren struggled not to get too excited.

This had to be it.

But even as she thought this, she told herself that stumbling across the article was almost too good to be true. However, every so often, things *did* fall into place, Jaren thought, and miracles *did* happen.

She looked at the article again, skimming it from beginning to end. Finley Massey *did* have a connection to both the neurosurgeon and the CEO, the vampire slayer's first two victims. All right, the connection was an indirect one through his father, Jackson, but even so, it was legitimate.

And Sanchez had talked to him at least once.

She needed to talk to Finley Massey face-to-face again.

During the first interview, when she and O'Brien were going down the list of the neurosurgeon's patients, she remembered that the young man had struck her as unstable. But then, she cut him a little slack because his father had just passed away. She vividly remembered what it was like for her those first few weeks after her father was gone. She had difficulty finding her place in life until she could finally redefine herself in new terms. If you loved a parent—she suspected that whether he was a billionaire or a fragile human being—the feeling of emptiness and being abandoned was the same.

What if Finley actually *was* unbalanced? And more than just a little bit. What if Finley blamed the surgeon for his father's death and had gone to confront the man in his office? Maybe the shock of his father's passing had unhinged Massey and when he saw the copy of the vampire book on the doctor's desk, that had sent him over the edge.

She knew it sounded a little bit far-fetched but right now, there wasn't anything else to go with. All the tips that had been called in by an eager-to-help public had gone nowhere.

Looking around, Jaren realized that she was still the only one in the conference room. Everyone else was partnered up and out in the field.

As she reached for her oversize purse, Kyle's parting words replayed themselves in her head: "Nobody goes out alone."

Indecision rippled through her.

If she waited for someone to show up, she could

very well lose an opportunity. If Finley took off for some reason, or killed someone else, she would never forgive herself.

Damn it, she wasn't some naive, vulnerable college freshman, she was a police detective, skilled at defending the public as well as herself. She couldn't just sit here, twiddling her thumbs until someone showed up to hold her hand on this detail.

Torn, Jaren glanced toward the doorway. She wasn't about to go in search of another detective and ask him or her to accompany her on an interview like some second grader who needed a partner in order to take the hall pass and go to the bathroom.

But if she went on her own, Kyle would be furious.

Since when did that matter?

Maybe Kyle was finished testifying. If he was, then he could meet her at the Massey estate.

Mentally crossing her fingers, Jaren pressed the keypad with the number to his cell phone. The second the connection was made, it immediately went to voice mail. She frowned, listening to the recording. This could only mean one thing. His phone was off.

Most likely, he was still in the courthouse since all cells were required to be turned off.

Frustrated, she exhaled slowly. And then she had an idea. She decided to cover her tail and leave Kyle a message just in case he did get out early and came back to the precinct. If he saw that she was gone, she knew he'd assume the worst and this time, he'd be right. But if she left him a message, then she was in the clear. Sort of.

"O'Brien, I think I just might have found us a lead. No, scratch that, I think I've solved the case. Finley Massey and his twin brother were kidnapped when they were four years old. His brother didn't survive the ordeal. The kidnapper accidentally killed him. When Finley was rescued—FYI, by his father and a band of mercenaries Massey'd hired—the four-year-old said that monsters, specifically *vampires*," she emphasized, "had killed his brother. Little footnote, the twins were kidnapped on Halloween while making their trick-or-treat rounds with their nanny. Could be that the kidnapper was disguised as Count Dracula. Gives you chills, doesn't it?" she asked. God knows, it did her. "I know this isn't going to exactly thrill you, but I'm going to go to the estate to talk to Massey again."

Anticipating what O'Brien would say to this piece of information, she added in a slightly lower, more seductive voice, "I'm a big girl—as I think you've already figured out." The next moment, O'Brien's voice mail cut her off. She'd exceeded her time limit.

So be it, Jaren thought, flipping her phone closed and tucking it back into her pocket.

Please let it be Finley, she thought as she double-checked the address to the Massey estate. Grabbing her purse, she left.

Jaren was out of the room, and halfway down the hall on her way to the elevator when she suddenly stopped and retraced her steps. Going to her desk, she opened the bottom drawer and took out the copy of *The Vampire Diaries.* She'd never bothered to take it home. Questioning Finley Massey might not get her anywhere, but if he saw the book in her possession, that just might trigger something in his head. At least, she fervently hoped so.

Kathy Hubert, the housekeeper who opened the door, instantly recognized her from the previous two visits to the estate. It was obvious that the woman wasn't happy to see her. According to what she had read, Kathy was a long-time employee of the Massey family.

This time, the housekeeper didn't even stand on ceremony or pretend to be polite. "Why can't you leave the boy alone?" she asked. She remained standing in the doorway and blocking any access into the mansion like a short, squat avenging angel.

"The *boy*," Jaren reminded her politely, "is over thirty. And I've got more questions for him. There's been another murder," she added, certain that the woman already knew that. There was no way to avoid the broadcasts unless you didn't watch TV. The all-news stations talked about nothing else.

"There've been lots of murders in this city," the housekeeper retorted stubbornly. She crossed her arms before her ample bosom. "And none of them have anything to do with Mr. Finley." Her complexion reddened with anger. "If Mr. Jackson was still alive—"

"None of this might be happening," Jaren speculated, but for a far different reason. "Now can I see Mr. Massey please, or do I have to arrest you for obstructing justice?"

The housekeeper's brown eyes narrowed and she snorted in disgust. "This way, please."

Kathy Hubert turned on her short, sensible squat heel and led the way to the entertainment room. The double doors were closed. She glared at Jaren, then knocked lightly. There was no response. Since the woman seemed reluctant, Jaren reached over and knocked on the door herself, harder this time.

The housekeeper gave her a dirty look. A second later, someone inside the room mumbled, "Come in."

The housekeeper turned the knob and opened only one of the doors. It was a mini movie theater, Jaren thought. There were several rows of seats—seven, she counted, with six seats across each row. They sloped down to the *movie screen* which appeared to be some sixty or so inches wide. The ultimate entertainment center. Also good for viewing movies without risking going out.

She had a feeling that Finley had been encouraged to remain on the estate whenever possible.

"I'm sorry, Mr. Finley," the housekeeper apologized, "but Officer Rosetti insisted on seeing you."

"Detective Rosetti," Jaren corrected. The woman merely gave her a condescending look but didn't bother to apologize.

"That's all right, Kathy." Finley, sitting in the first row, rose from his seat. He waved toward the screen. "I was just reminiscing."

Jaren saw what had to be a very old video playing on the screen. Two little boys, carbon copies of one another, were playing in their own private carnival. A handsome man was with them, laughing as he chased after one, then the other. The man bore a strong resemblance to Finley, except that he appeared to be buff and vital, while Finley was fragile and delicate.

Finley aimed his remote control at the screen and it went to black. The lights within the room remained on low as he crossed to her. The housekeeper left, closing the door behind her.

The smile Finley flashed at her might as well have been drawn on for all the feeling behind it. "So, what brings you back, Detective?"

Was it her imagination, or was his voice deeper, more confident than it had been the last time they talked? Jaren cautioned herself not to read into his actions yet.

"There's been another murder, Mr. Massey," she told him. "Same as the others. A stake driven through the heart."

Their gazes locked for a long moment. His eyes looked dead, as if there was nothing beyond the pupils. Eyes were supposed to be the windows to the soul, weren't they? She stifled a shiver that suddenly materialized.

"Why come to me?" he asked her.

Very deliberately, Jaren placed her purse down on the seat closest to her. "I thought that since you were up on vampires, you might have a theory about why these killings were happening."

"Up on vampires?" he echoed. He watched her very carefully now. She was right, she could feel it in her bones. Something about being in the same space as a cold-blooded killer, a stillness in the air, that got to her.

Maybe she should have waited for someone to come with her. "What makes you say that?"

"I read an article about you," she told him, keeping her tone neutral, as if they were just having a conversation. "You and your twin brother were kidnapped as children."

She saw his eyes darken, as if she'd just made a misstep. "I don't want to talk about it."

She pressed on. "In the article I read, you said that vampires kidnapped you. That a vampire was responsible for killing your brother."

Moving away from her, he walked to the front of the theater. "I said I didn't want to talk about it," he insisted, his voice getting higher.

Jaren followed him.

He was unraveling, she thought, nervous excitement telegraphing through her. Just like that. The strain of being on his guard, of being without his father—alone against his enemies—was getting to him, she could almost feel it.

"What are they like?" she asked.

His expression grew almost wild as he cried, "Who?"

"Vampires," she answered matter-of-factly. "Do they look like you and me?"

"I don't know what you're talking about." He covered his ears not to hear any more questions, desperate to get away from her. "I—" Finley stopped, his eyes widening in horror as he saw the book that she was taking out of her purse.

"They don't really look like this, do they?" Jaren pointed to the drawing on the back of the dust jacket. The publisher had a cover artist draw several blood-thirsty-looking creatures, all gathered around a victim, about to feast on him.

Seeing the cover, Finley breathed harder. A look that was close to demonic entered his eyes. It was as if Massey wasn't himself anymore.

For the first time, fear wove through her.

"They won't stop, Derek," Finley wailed, turning to address someone who wasn't in the room. He hardly seemed aware of her at all. "When are they going to stop?" he sobbed.

"Derek," she repeated. He turned full of fury in her direction. She almost had him, she thought. She just needed to have him confess to killing one of the victims, and everything else would fall into place from there. "That was your brother's name, wasn't it? What happened to Derek? Did they kill him, Finley? Did the vampire kill your brother?"

"No," he cried. "No, they didn't kill him. Derek's right here. He fooled them. He came back to me. To protect me now that Dad's gone. Derek protects me," he cried. "Derek protects me. Derek—"

And then, right before her eyes, Finley squared his shoulders and raised his chin. His expression changed, becoming more confident. More in control. When he spoke, his voice was deep.

"Right here, kid. I'm right here. You don't have to be afraid." His eyes shifted to her face. "I'll take care of this one, too, just like I did the others," he promised. "She's not going to hurt you!" he shouted, lunging at her.

Stunned at the transformation she'd just witnessed,

Jaren barely managed to jump back, out of Finley's reach. There was no room for her to turn and draw her weapon. Needing to put some distance between them so she could take charge of the situation, Jaren tried to dart up the small aisle, but Finley, assuming his dead brother's persona, was too fast for her.

Too fast and surprisingly, too strong.

Grabbing her by the legs, he brought her down. Caught off guard, Jaren hit her head against one of the armrests. Hard.

For a moment, a darkness encroached on her, sucking away the light. Threatening to swallow her up. Jaren struggled to keep it at bay, knowing that if she passed out, that would be the end of it. Finley, acting as Derek, would kill her.

"I'm not a vampire, Derek," she cried, struggling to stay conscious. "I'm human. It's all just your imagination."

He didn't seem to hear her. As she struggled to get up, he pinned her down with his weight, straddling her waist. Massey looked around for something to hit her with so that he could finish his work.

"That's what they all said," he jeered. "They said that Finley was crazy because he told them I wasn't dead. Well, he's not crazy and neither am I. And I know what they are. They killed my father and now they want to kill me," he shouted into her face. His eyes glowed as he accused, "You want to kill me."

He was too strong for her. She couldn't knock him off. The more she struggled, the harder he pressed down on her, his knees crushing her ribs.

"No, I don't. I just want to get you help. Your father would want to get you help."

"Don't you talk about him!" he shouted, furious. "Don't you *dare* talk about him, you vampire whore."

"I'm not a vampire," she shouted back. And then she remembered the keepsake she always wore around her neck. "Look, vampires are afraid of crosses. Would I have a cross around my neck if I were a vampire?"

He jerked her closer, holding on to her hair to keep her captive. She could all but feel it ripping out of her head. Disgust filled his voice as he dropped her head with a push. She hit the back of it against the floor. Jaren felt her teeth jar. "You don't have a cross," he shouted back.

"It must have come off in the struggle. But think back," she pleaded. "When I came in, I was wearing one. My dad gave it to me to keep me safe. He was like your dad. Your dad just wanted you to be safe."

Moving his weight farther up so that it centered on her rib cage, Massey doubled up his fists and began pummeling her. The blows made her dizzy.

"Shut up," he screamed, incensed. "Shut up about my father!"

Desperate, her head starting to spin again, Jaren screamed, hoping that the housekeeper was still somewhere close by and would come running in. The woman was protective of him but she couldn't be a party to anything like murder—could she?

No one came. She felt her lip swelling, felt blood entering her mouth.

"The room's soundproof," she heard Massey laugh just before he landed another blow. Pain went shooting through her jaw. "Scream all you want. It won't do you any good."

The next jarring blow made her ears ring. There was pain everywhere, seductive pain that urged her to slip into the shelter of unconsciousness. She fought against it, but she didn't know how much longer she could hold on.

In the distance, above the ringing in her head, she thought she heard a noise.

An explosion.

The next moment, she felt a heavy weight fall on her, almost smothering her. Her lungs felt as if they were going to burst as she struggled to suck in air. For a second, desperation filled her as it felt like a losing battle.

And then the weight was gone.

Someone called her name. The next moment, strong arms lifted her from the floor. The darkness that threatened to absorb her faded, giving way to light that came streaming into the room.

Pain seared along her ribs, preventing her from taking in a full breath.

When she opened her eyes—not realizing that they had been closed—she saw Kyle bending over her.

Was she dead?

Hallucinating?

Was this what it felt like to drift out of your body for the last time?

With almost superhuman effort, she forced out his name. "Kyle?"

"Idiot!" he cried with relief.

It was Kyle all right. "I'm not dead," she concluded, barely speaking above a whisper.

There were more people in the room. She could hear different voices threading into one another, but she couldn't make sense of any of it. The only one she was really aware of was Kyle.

Kyle, holding her in his arms.

She was safe. Relief wove through her.

"What the hell is wrong with you?" Kyle demanded, his voice breaking. "Do you realize what could have happened to you if I hadn't listened to my voice mail?"

She struggled to draw enough air into her lungs to be able to say, "You've got the same rotten bedside manner as Barrett did."

He didn't know whether to shake her or hug her. "And you have the sense of a flea."

She looked at him, a trace of a smile curving her lips. Or at least, she tried to smile. Whether or not she succeeded, she couldn't tell.

"I have enough sense to leave you a voice message," she reminded him. "Finley Massey is insane. He thought he was his dead brother, Derek, and that vampires were after him. He was trying to kill them all in order to protect *Finley.*"

Kyle glanced toward the inert body on the floor. Riley was slipping handcuffs on the unconscious man.

"He won't be killing vampires anytime soon," he promised her.

For a moment, all he wanted to do was hold Jaren close to him, to feel her chest rising and falling against his own. Silently, he offered up a prayer of thanksgiving that he had managed to get here when he had, and not ten minutes later.

It was the first time Kyle remembered praying in a very long time.

Chapter 15

"I don't need to go to the hospital."

Jaren used what felt like the last of her available energy to voice her adamant protest. It fell on deaf ears.

Instead of halting the transport, Kyle merely stood to the side as the paramedics loaded the gurney she was on into the back of one of the two ambulances.

The other took a wounded, unconscious Finley Massey to another hospital.

Kyle gave no indication that he even heard her. It was only once she was inside the ambulance and he had climbed in beside her, that he could examine her.

His eyes, she thought vaguely, looked angry.

"No arguments," he ordered. "Massey used your face for a punching bag."

He had no doubts that the deranged man had done it in order to knock her unconscious so that she could offer no resistance when he drove the stake into her chest.

The very thought made his blood run cold.

"We need to find out if he caused any brain damage— more than you already have," he amended, barely controlling the fear-fueled anger that boiled within him.

Her chest was killing her, but she managed to insist, "I'm fine."

The last thing she remembered before the world suddenly faded to black was Kyle looking at her and saying, "The hell you are, Rosetti. Rosetti? Jaren?"

In the distance, Jaren thought that she heard him urgently calling her name over and over again, but she was too far away to answer.

Kyle hated waiting. For that reason, he avoided surveillance work whenever he could.

But he found himself waiting now.

Waiting while the hospital technicians ran MRIs and lab tests on Jaren. Waiting and restlessly leaning against pastel-colored walls, moving from one to another like a man who didn't belong anywhere.

Waiting to be informed that Jaren was going to be all right despite her stupid stunt. Waiting as he became acutely aware of a feeling gripping him that he had never experienced before.

Concern wasn't anything new for him. He'd been concerned as he became aware of his mother's situation:

a single mother in failing health with three children to raise and care for. He'd always been protective of her and of his brother and sister even though he wasn't the oldest except for a technicality.

It was just the way things were, just the way he was built.

But this time around, something went beyond the concern. There had been a real, bottomless fear that Jaren was in real danger. That she could die before he reached her.

And that if she did, he would never be the same again.

The minute he'd gotten out of court, something—intuition maybe—had made him check his voice mail. As soon as he heard Jaren's voice, he could feel his gut tightening into a knot. He knew before he even listened to the whole message that she was going to go off on her own and do something stupid.

Something dangerous.

Like a man possessed, he'd lost no time tearing out of the courthouse parking lot, steering the vehicle with one hand while hitting numbers on his cell phone's keypad with the other. He pulled a team together for backup before he actually had a reason to believe it was necessary.

Because he *knew.*

Deep down in his gut, he knew Jaren was in trouble. Knew she was right about her hunch that Massey was the killer. And as sure as night followed day, he knew that she was going to be the man's next victim unless he got to her in time.

Driving like a madman, he'd broken out in a cold sweat as he shakily searched his mind for the prayers his mother had taught him as a little boy.

And even now, standing in this antiseptic hospital, the silence of the night echoing back at him, he was far from convinced that the worst was over. Jaren had been pretty badly beaten.

What if—?

His breathing grew short. He couldn't let himself go there. Not yet.

"Knew I'd find you here."

Lost in thought, he shook himself free as he looked up. Kyle saw Riley approaching him. She wasn't alone. Less than a step behind her were Greer and Ethan. Kyle struggled to pull himself together.

And then, as if someone had thrown open the main hospital doors, Brian and Andrew came in just several steps in front of what looked like an avalanche of Cavanaughs. Every last one of them and their spouses had come to lend their moral support.

Andrew reached him first. "How is she, son?" he asked.

Kyle shook his head. It took a second before he said, "They haven't told me yet." Even as the words came out, his throat felt as if it was closing.

"She's a tough girl," Brian told him with an unshakable certainty. "She'll pull through." He smiled at the younger man. "Nice work, by the way, catching Massey."

The praise meant nothing to him. There was a hollowness inside that he didn't know how to get around or what to do with. "Rosetti was the one who solved the case."

Brian merely nodded. He slipped a comforting arm around Kyle's shoulders.

Kyle's first instinct was to shrug the arm off. But he didn't follow through. Instead, he realized that he was actually drawing comfort from the simple gesture.

Maybe this, he told himself silently, was what being part of an extended family was all about. Having someone there who actually cared about what he was going through.

That realization was followed by another. He rather liked having the support. That instead of sucking away his independence, being part of a greater whole actually made him feel stronger.

"I brought food," Andrew announced as Callie, Teri, Rayne and Clay, four of his five children, came in, hefting coolers between them.

"Of course you did," Brian said with a laugh, shaking his head.

"Hey, you have a long vigil ahead of you, it doesn't hurt to have a full stomach," Andrew pointed out.

No one argued. They were all too busy clustering around the coolers, helping themselves to the covered containers that were inside.

Like Andrew said, there was a long vigil ahead of them.

She'd drifted in and out of consciousness several times. Each time, she was acutely aware that there was someone sitting by her bed. But she'd fade away again before she could focus or discover who it was.

Finally, struggling to hold on to consciousness, Jaren forced her eyes open and looked, half expecting that her imagination had conjured up the figure in the chair and there was no one there. After all, who did she know here who felt close enough to her to put in that kind of time, waiting for her to come around?

But when she focused her eyes, the figure didn't fade away. Instead, he took on features.

Kyle.

Looking at her and frowning.

Nothing unusual there.

She wanted to laugh, but couldn't. Her throat felt like rawhide. Had they shoved a tube down it at some point to help her breathe? No, wait, that maniac, Finley, had tried to choke her.

Massey.

Her head began to throb as her memory of the last events returned. But at least she was alive, she thought. And that was something.

A big something.

Kyle was still frowning. And not saying anything. She took in a deep breath, then another, trying to get to the point where she could talk.

It wasn't as easy as she would have liked. But she stubbornly persisted until she heard her voice weakly emerge.

"You're mad at me, aren't you?" she finally managed to ask, breaking the silence. Her voice sounded as if it belonged to a ninety-three-year-old chronic smoker, she thought disparagingly. But at least she could talk.

"Yeah."

The single word hung in the air. Kyle didn't trust himself to say anything else. He'd been here all night, after assuring everyone else that they should go home and that he'd call if there was any change.

Andrew had been the last to go after making him promise that if he needed anything, anything at all, he wouldn't hesitate to call. It was the only way the patriarch could be persuaded to leave the hospital.

Jaren sucked in another long breath. Her lungs ached and it felt as if there was a lead weight on her rib cage. She looked down, knowing that she wouldn't see anything. But it was going to take a while before the image of Massey, straddling her, would leave her in peace.

"But everything turned out all right," she finally said.

"Yeah, but it damn well might not have," Kyle retorted, his hold on stoicism abruptly shattering. His anger almost exploded and only the most extreme control on his part kept it under wraps. "What the hell were you thinking?" he demanded. "You were supposed to wait for me—or at the very least, not go running off like that on your own!"

In hindsight, she knew Kyle was right. But that didn't give him the right to talk down to her. She couldn't stand being treated like anything but the independent, capable woman she felt she was. "I'm not a child, Kyle."

"Then why the hell did you act like one?" he shot back.

Anger gave her strength.

"I was afraid Massey would take off and there wasn't anyone around in the conference room," she answered defensively.

"Did you even *try* to get in contact with anyone?" he demanded heatedly.

Her eyes narrowed and flashed. "I called you," she reminded him.

And thank God for that, he thought. "Besides me," he growled.

"No." She breathed out. Even worked up, she could feel her strength ebbing again. "What are you so angry about? We got him."

Was she serious? Didn't she realize what had almost happened? "I'm angry because if I hadn't gotten there in time, he could have killed you."

Kyle would have probably been happier that way, she thought angrily. "Then we wouldn't be having this argument."

"We wouldn't be having *anything*," Kyle shot back. He struggled to lower his voice, but wasn't too successful at it. "Damn it, Rosetti, do I have to spell it out for you?"

O'Brien had completely lost her. "Spell what out for me?"

As he spoke, he could feel his heart all but twisting in his chest. "That I couldn't have stood it if something had happened to you."

She shrugged, or tried to. "Don't worry. The Chief of Ds wouldn't have blamed you for losing two people in your group."

He stared at her as if she'd started babbling nonsense. "The hell with blame. The hell with all of it. Can't you understand what I'm saying?"

Her head aching—not to mention that the painkiller was wearing off—Jaren was more lost than ever. "Obviously not."

"I'm in love with you, Rosetti," Kyle all but spat out. It was hard to say which of them was more surprised to hear him utter the words. "I don't know why, but I am. And if anything happened to you—if you let your bullheadedness get you killed—I—"

Words failed him. Kyle threw up his hands in order to keep from sweeping Jaren into his arms and just holding her to him. He knew she was in far too much pain for him to do that.

"I don't know what I would have done," he admitted in a lower voice.

She stared at him, numb. Numb and dumbstruck. Of all the things she'd expected Kyle to say, to vent, that didn't even come close to being one of them.

He loved her?

Since when?

How the hell had that come out? Kyle silently upbraided himself, horrified by what he'd just blurted out without preamble. Since when couldn't he keep his own counsel?

Damn it, he shouldn't have said anything. His feelings were his own business, not anyone else's. Not even hers.

He had absolutely no idea what she felt for him—if anything—and he refused to look or sound like some kind of lovesick fool.

Kyle abruptly rose to his feet. His chair began to fall backward, but he grabbed it in time to keep it from toppling to the floor.

Emotionless, he stared passed her head. "I told the chief I'd call him when you regained consciousness. I'll see you around."

And with that, he left. Before she could say anything.

Kyle heard the doorbell ring just as he was about to sit down to eat the dinner he'd thrown together. The last couple of weeks, he'd been living off the so-called leftovers that Andrew had pressed on him after the former chief of police had swung by "just to talk."

For a second, Kyle thought of ignoring the doorbell, then decided that it would just be simpler to answer it. In the last two weeks, various members of the Cavanaugh family—his family, he silently corrected—had stopped by after hours, seemingly to shoot the breeze.

It was, he knew, their way of showing concern, and even though he acted like he was perfectly happy by himself, he was growing more and more open to their company.

It helped him cope with the emptiness that kept widening within him.

Getting up from the table, he went to the door. He

opened it, but the token greeting on his lips faded to silence. It wasn't one of the Cavanaughs on his doorstep. Or either one of his siblings. It was Jaren, looking a great deal better than she had the last time he'd seen her.

Still somewhat pale, the bruises that had disfigured her delicate face were a thing of the past now. She was as beautiful as ever.

More.

"You never came back to see me." Softly voiced, it was still an accusation.

Caught off guard, Kyle belatedly stepped back to let her enter. "I thought you'd be better off if I—"

How did he end this sentence? he silently wondered. His feelings were something he was going to have to come to terms with. He should have never burdened her with the revelation.

"If you took the coward's way out?" she supplied when his voice trailed off.

Kyle bristled at the portrayal. "I didn't want to make you feel that you were on the spot—that I expected you to answer. Or to return the feeling," he added firmly.

"You never gave me a chance to answer," she retorted heatedly. "It was hard for me to breathe, much less form a complete sentence quickly." Her eyes held his. "I can answer you now."

He remembered her little speech about their lovemaking not meaning anything. He didn't have to hear her formally tell him that she was flattered, but that she just didn't feel the same way about him that he did about her.

"Look, Rosetti—Jaren," he corrected himself, making it more personal. "You don't have to—"

"Shut up, O'Brien," she ordered. And then her expression softened just a little. "Let someone else talk for a second."

"Obviously, I don't have a choice in the matter," he commented, bracing himself. "Go ahead."

Doubling her fist, Jaren caught him by surprise for a second time in as many minutes when she punched him in the arm. He was even more surprised to discover that the blow stung. She was stronger than she looked.

"You big, dumb jerk."

"Nice start."

She gave no indication that she heard him. "You can't tell a woman you're in love with her and then just walk away."

He thought that telling her he hadn't intended on telling her that he loved her, that it had just come out, would only earn him another punch, so he refrained. "I didn't know there were rules."

"Of course there're rules," she cried. "And the rules say that you have to let the woman get a chance to answer you."

It was his own fault. He'd started this. "All right."

"I love you," she told him. "I don't want to, but there you have it. I do."

It took him a moment to recover. Something stirred inside of him. Something he didn't quite recognize at first. Happiness? Was that what this warm feeling in the pit of his stomach was? "Why don't you want to?"

She never thought that she would have to explain herself to a man. Didn't men have a natural phobia when it came to commitment?

"Because love makes you vulnerable. Love leaves you wide open to being abandoned. To being hurt, and I've had enough of that. I don't want to be hurt. Ever again," she said with feeling. And then she took a deep breath, her eyes hopeful. "Can you love me without hurting me, Kyle?" she asked in a softer voice.

He smiled at her. Maybe blurting out that he loved her hadn't been the stupidest thing he'd ever done. "That would be the plan."

"Then don't walk out on me again."

He took her into his arms. "I think I can manage that."

She could feel adrenaline beginning to rush through her veins, as if she'd just taken a dive off the high board and had scored a perfect ten.

"The doctor cleared me," she told him. "You can kiss me. For as long as you want to."

He smiled down at her as he framed her face with his hands. "Nice to know," he murmured as he began to bring his mouth down to hers.

For the third time, Jaren surprised him by placing her fingertips over his lips, stopping him. When he looked at her she said, "But first, tell me again."

He pretended not to understand. "Tell you what?"

"You know."

His mouth curved. Yeah, he knew. "I love you."

She raised herself up on her toes, bringing her mouth closer to his. Her eyes were shining as she told him, "Me, too," just before she kissed him.

And went on to completely lose herself in the safety of his arms. Where she knew she belonged from this day forward.

* * * * *

*Mills & Boon® Intrigue brings you
a sneak preview of …*

BJ Daniels' Montana Royalty

*Devlin Barrow wasn't like any cowboy
Rory Buchanan had ever ridden with. The European
stud brought status to her ranch – as well as a
trail of assassins and royal intrigue.*

*Don't miss this thrilling new story in the
WHITEHORSE, MONTANA mini-series available
next month from Mills & Boon® Intrigue.*

Montana Royalty
by
BJ Daniels

The narrow slit of light between the partially closed bedroom curtains drew him through the shadowed pines.

He moved stealthily, the moonless darkness heavy as a cloak. The moment he'd seen the light, realized it came from her bedroom window, the curtains not quite closed, he'd been helpless to stop himself.

He'd always liked watching people when they didn't know he was there. He saw things they didn't want seen. He knew their dirty secrets.

Their secrets became *his* dirty little secrets.

But this was different.

The woman behind the curtains was Rory Buchanan.

He began to sweat as he neared the window even though the fall night was cold here in the mountains. The narrow shaft of light from between the curtains spilled out onto the ground. Teasing glimpses of her lured him on.

As he grew closer, he stuck the wire cutters he carried into his jacket pocket. His heart beat so hard he could barely steal a breath as he slowly stepped toward the forbidden.

The window was the perfect height. He closed his left eye, his right eye focusing on the room, on the woman.

Inside the bedroom, Rory folded a pair of jeans into one of the dresser drawers and closed the drawer, turning back toward the bed and the T-shirt she'd left lying on it.

He didn't move, didn't breathe—didn't blink as she began to disrobe.

He couldn't have moved even at gunpoint as he watched her pull the band from her ponytail, letting her chestnut hair fall to her shoulders.

She sighed, rubbing her neck with both hands, eyes closed. Wide green eyes fringed in dark lashes. He watched breathlessly as she dropped her hands to unbutton her jeans and let them drop to the floor.

Next, the Western shirt. Like her other shirts and the jackets she wore, it was too large for her, hid her body.

Anticipation had him breathing too hard. He tried to rein it in, afraid she would hear him and look toward the window. It scared him what he might do if she suddenly closed the curtains then. Or worse, saw him.

One shirt button, then another and another and the shirt fell back, dropping over her shoulders to the floor at her feet. She reached down to retrieve both items of clothing and hang them on the hook by the door before turning back in his direction.

He sucked in a breath and held it to keep from crying out. Her breasts were full and practically spilling out of the pretty pink lacy bra. The way she dressed, no one could have known.

She slid one bra strap from her shoulder, then the other. He could hear her humming now, but didn't recognize the tune. She was totally distracted. He felt himself grow hard as stone as she unhooked the bra and her breasts were suddenly freed.

A moan escaped his throat. A low keening sound filled with lust and longing. He *wanted* her, had wanted her for years, would do anything to have her…

Instinctively, he took a step toward the back of the ranch house. Rory was alone. Her house miles from any others. Her door wouldn't be locked. No one locked their doors in this part of Montana.

The sound of a vehicle engine froze him to the spot. He dropped to the ground behind the shrubs at the corner of the house as headlights bobbed through the pines. The vehicle came into view, slowed and turned around in the yard. Someone lost?

He couldn't be caught here. He hesitated only a moment before he broke for the pines behind the house and ran through the woods to where he'd hidden his car.

As he slid behind the wheel, his adrenaline waned. He'd never done more than looked. Never even contemplated more than that.

But the others hadn't been Rory Buchanan.

If that pickup hadn't come down the road when it did…

The sick odor of fear and excitement filled the car. He rolled down his window, feeling weak and powerless and angry. Tonight, he could have had her—and on his terms. *But at what cost,* he thought as he reached for the key he'd left in the ignition of the patrol car, anxious to get back to Whitehorse.

He froze. The wire cutters. He didn't feel their weight in his jacket pocket. His hand flew to the opening only to find the pocket empty.

2 FREE BOOKS
AND A SURPRISE GIFT

We would like to take this opportunity to thank you for reading this Mills & Boon® book by offering you the chance to take TWO more specially selected books from the Intrigue series absolutely FREE! We're also making this offer to introduce you to the benefits of the Mills & Boon® Book Club™—

- **FREE home delivery**
- **FREE gifts and competitions**
- **FREE monthly Newsletter**
- **Exclusive Mills & Boon Book Club offers**
- **Books available before they're in the shops**

Accepting these FREE books and gift places you under no obligation to buy, you may cancel at any time, even after receiving your free books. Simply complete your details below and return the entire page to the address below. You don't even need a stamp!

YES Please send me 2 free Intrigue books and a surprise gift. I understand that unless you hear from me, I will receive 5 superb new stories every month, including two 2-in-1 books priced at £4.99 each and a single book priced at £3.19, postage and packing free. I am under no obligation to purchase any books and may cancel my subscription at any time. The free books and gift will be mine to keep in any case.

Ms/Mrs/Miss/Mr _____ Initials _____

Surname _____

Address _____

_____

_____ Postcode _____

E-mail _____

Send this whole page to: Mills & Boon Book Club, Free Book Offer, FREEPOST NAT 10298, Richmond, TW9 1BR